MW01104665

Republica

ALL SAME AS FAMILY IN A BIG 'OUSE

Edited by

George Papaellinas

Angus&Robertson
An imprint of HarperCollins*Publishers*

An Angus & Robertson publication
Angus & Robertson, an imprint of
HarperCollins *Publishers*
25 Ryde Road, Pymble, Sydney NSW 2073, Australia
31 View Road, Glenfield, Auckland 10, New Zealand
First published in Australia in 1994.

Copyright © in this selection HarperCollins *Publishers* 1994
Copyright © in individual works remains with their authors 1994

This book is copyright.
Apart from any fair dealing for the purposes of private study, research, criticism
or review, as permitted under the Copyright Act, no part may be reproduced
by any process without written permission. Inquiries should be addressed
to the publishers.

ISBN: 0 207 18406 2
ISSN: 1321–4918

Editor: George Papaellinas
Publisher: Angelo Loukakis
Managing Editor: Judith McGee
Artistic Director: Liz Seymour
Poetry Consultant: Robert Adamson
Printed in Australia by Griffin Paperbacks, Adelaide.
9 8 7 6 5 4 3 2 1
99 98 97 96 95 94

ACKNOWLEDGMENTS

The Editor thanks the English Department, University of Melbourne. This publication owes much to the generous material and creative support which the Editor has found there.

The Editor also thanks Catherine Murphy, Rosemary Creswell, Lyn Tranter, Amanda Lohrey, Peter Lyssiotis, Nicholas Jose, Sophie Gebhardt, Geoff Parish, Sharon Davis, Jenny Lee, Mabel Lee, Tony Haritos, Sue Spencer, Mick O'Regan, Lindy Woodward, Amanda Armstrong, Clare Forster, Maree Delofski, Simon Bayertz, Julie Hickson, Sasha Soldatow, Philip Mead and Zaineb Istrabadi, all of whom were so helpful towards the development of the first issue.

The essay 'Gods That Always Fail' was commissioned by the BBC as the sixth in their series of 1993 Reith Lectures by Edward W Said, 'Representations of the Intellectual'. These lectures were first broadcast on BBC radio 4 in 1993 and subsequently broadcast late that year on ABC Radio National. The essay is published with the permission of Professor Said and the BBC.

The lines of poetry quoted in Rebekah Sandell's story, 'Precious', are from 'Of Mere Being', a poem by Wallace Stevens. The poem was written in 1955 and is found in a collection of Wallace Steven's writings, *The Palm at the End of the Mind: selected poems and a play*, edited by Holly Stevens (Vintage Books, New York, 1972).

The contributions, 'I'm Going' by Dula Ngurruwutthun and 'What I See' by Galarrwuy Yunupingu first appeared in *Land Rights News*, the newspaper of the Northern and Central Land Councils in the Northern Territory. Galarrwuy Yunupingu's articles was first published after the High Court's *Mabo* decision of 3 June 1993. Dula Ngurruwutthun's story was told to his daughter, Nalwarri, and translated into English by Michael Christie. Thanks go to *Land Rights News*, its editor, Tony Haritos, Galarrwuy Yunupingu, Dula Ngurruwutthun, Nalwarri Ngurruwutthun and Michael Christie, for their permission to reprint these works.

For their help with his essay, 'Selling Yothu Yindi' (which was presented in an earlier form at the 'Confronting Racism' Conference at the University of Technology, Sydney), Adam Shoemaker wishes to thank Iraphne Childs, Alan James, Rob Moore and Sharyn Pearce, and he also acknowledges the assistance of Kaylene Walker and Judy Cho of the Australian Tourist Commission.

CONTENTS

CONTENTS

INTRODUCTION

By Angelo Loukakis

Welcome to *RePublica*, a biannual journal of contemporary writing. Angus & Robertson is very pleased and excited to be associated with what promises to be a most important initiative: the quality and substance of writings assembled for this first issue lead us to believe that there are great times and possibilities ahead for *RePublica*. My own view is that there is a need for a journal that aims to reconnect writing with our ways of life, with how we live and how we organise society.

It is hardly news by now that Australian society is original and derivative at the same time. The historical and cultural changes of the past decades have led to phenomena ('experiments' to some) on which we can speak with authority and knowledge. While some of these are of course only local effects of greater shifts occurring world wide, there is much around us to analyse and interpret. What are the relations between cultures in Australia, and between Australian cultures and elsewhere? What should they be? In looking at these and other questions, do our various cultural and artistic forms retain any investigative potency, or have they become terminally self-referential.

Which seems like a good place to offer some words of warning about what *RePublica* isn't and won't be. This journal is not the organ of any official, authorised movement, republican or otherwise. Rather, *RePublica* has been conceived as a journal of the kind of creative writing, thought, argument and artistic expression that is necessary *before* things can be formulated into policies and programs; it is also a journal, in its social and cultural orientations, in which various kinds of literary and visual creativity are ranged *against* expedient and provisional political expressions and their after-effects.

RePublica is not a forum for that tame something called 'issues'. Instead, we are aiming for a journal where every contribution, in whichever form or mode has a reason to be, a need to be. The latest tame form of 'belles lettres' has no place on these pages. It seems to

George Papaellinas, the journal's Editor, and me that much of what often passes a innovative today, or 'new' (now that post-modern is old), is writing that is seriously dated or sentimental. That which threatens expectations, be they artistic or political, belongs here. *RePublica* is a journal for those artists prepared to take risks.

George has drawn in under the umbrella of 'All same as family in a big 'ouse' a great deal of matter of contemporary significance. He has done so with the purpose of setting a fundamental frame of reference. The treatment of indigenous peoples and cultures, the relationship in a society such as ours (or in any society) between all cultures, be they 'ethnic' or class or gender defined, the relationship between nations, the very idea of 'nation', the forms of constitutional organisation a society takes, the political rights its citizens enjoy or do not enjoy—these are matters of discussion and debate, not only for Australians, but for all who wish to live in a civilised way.

As much as civilisation is a function of a democratic kind of public politics, it is also a matter of emotions. How we conduct our personal relationships, the things we do in the realms of feeling and attachment, these are among the crucial arts of civilisation too, and here we look to the best sort of fiction and poetry, the best sort of art, to show us the state of play. In this first issue, a number of splendid pieces explore the nature of attachment, endearment, affection, and sometimes the absence or destruction of those things.

I hope that these, and the other works to follow in coming issues of *RePublica*, will come to be seen as part of the *RePublica* 'story'—a story which we in turn would also like to think will be an episode or instalment in the greatest of civilisation narratives, the retelling of the world in the interests of human justice. For this to happen, enlightened readers as well as enlightened writers and artists have the most critical, in all senses of the word, parts to play. On my and the Editor's behalf, then, I would ask you to please make this contribution and to enjoy.

Gods That Always Fail

EDWARD W SAID

He was a brilliantly eloquent and charismatic Iranian intellectual to whom I was first introduced in the West sometime in 1978. A writer and teacher of considerable accomplishment and learning, he played a significant role in spreading knowledge of the Shah's unpopular rule and, later that same year, of the new figures who were soon to come to power in Teheran. He spoke respectfully of Imam Khomeini at the time, and was soon to become visibly associated with the relatively young men around Khomeini who were of course Muslim but assuredly not militant Islamists, men like Abol Hassan Bani Sadr and Sadek Ghotzbadeh.

A few weeks after the Islamic revolution of Iran had consolidated power inside the country, my acquaintance (who had gone back to Iran for the new government's installation) returned to the West as an ambassador to an important metropolitan centre. I recall attending and once or twice participating with him in panels on the Middle East after the Shah's fall. I saw him during the time of the very long hostage crisis, as it was called in America, and he regularly expressed anguish and even anger at the ruffians who had engineered the embassy takeover and the subsequent holding of fifty or so civilian hostages. The unmistakable impression I had of him was of a decent man who had committed himself to the new order, and had gone as far as defending it and serving it as a loyal emissary abroad. I knew him as an observant Muslim but by no means a fanatic. He was skilful at fending off scepticism and attacks on his government—this he did, I thought, with conviction and appropriate discrimination—but he left no one in doubt—certainly not me at any rate—that although he disagreed with some of his colleagues in the Iranian government, and that he saw things at this level as very much in flux, Imam Khomeini was, and ought to have been, *the* authority in Iran. He was such a loyalist that once when he came to Beirut he told me that he had refused to shake hands with a Palestinian leader (this was when the PLO and the Islamic Revolution were allies) because he 'had criticised the Imam'.

I think it must have been a few months before the hostages were released in early 1981 that he resigned his ambassadorial post and returned to Iran, this time as special assistant to President Bani Sadr. The antagonistic lines between president and imam, however, were already well drawn, and of course the president lost. Shortly after he was sacked or deposed by Khomeini, Bani Sadr went into exile and my friend did too, although he had a difficult time actually getting out of Iran. A year or so later he had become a vociferous public critic of Khomeini's Iran, attacking the government and man he had once served from the very same platforms in New York and London from which he had once defended them both. He had not lost his critical sense of the American role, however, and consistently spoke about United States imperialism: his earlier memories of the Shah's regime and American support for it were seared into his being.

I therefore felt an even greater sadness when, a few months after the Gulf War in 1991, I heard him speak about the war, this time as a defender of the American war against Iraq. Like a number of European Left intellectuals, he said that, in a conflict between imperialism and fascism, one should always pick imperialism. I was surprised that none of the formulators of this, in my opinion, unnecessarily attenuated pair of choices had grasped that it would have been quite possible and indeed desirable, on both intellectual and political grounds, to reject both fascism and imperialism.

In any event, this little story encapsulates one of the dilemmas facing a contemporary intellectual whose interest in the public sphere is not merely theoretical or academic, but also involves direct participation. How far should an intellectual go in getting involved? Should one join a party, serve an idea as it is embodied in actual political processes, personalities, jobs, and therefore become a *true believer*? Or, on the other hand, is there some more discrete—but no less serious and involved—way of joining up without suffering the pain of later betrayal and disillusionment? How far should one's loyalty to a cause take one in being consistently faithful to it? Can one retain independence of mind and at the same time *not* go through the agonies of public recantation and confession?

It is not completely coincidental that the story of my Iranian friend's pilgrimage back to Islamic theocracy and out of it is about a quasi-religious conversion, followed by what appeared to be a very dramatic reversal in belief, and a counter-conversion. For whether I saw him as an advocate of Islamic revolution and subsequently as an intellectual soldier in its ranks, or as an outspoken critic, someone who had left it in an almost shattered disgust, I never doubted my friend's sincerity nor did I lose my feelings of friendship for him. He was as fully convincing in the first as he was in the second role—passionate, fluid, blazingly effective as a debater.

I shouldn't pretend that I was a detached outsider throughout my friend's ordeal. He and I—a Palestinian nationalist during the seventies—made common cause against the ponderously interfering role played by the United States, which to our way of thinking propped up the Shah and placated and supported Israel unjustly and anachronistically. We saw both our peoples as victims of cruelly insensitive policies: suppression, dispossession, impoverishment. We were both exiles, of course, although I must confess that even then I had resigned myself to remaining one for the rest of my life. When my friend's team won, so to speak, I was jubilant, and not only because at last he could go home. Ever since the Arab defeat of 1967, the successful Iranian revolution—which was made by an improbable alliance of clergy and common people that had completely confounded even the most sophisticated Marxist Middle East experts—was the first major blow to Western hegemony in the region. Both of us saw it as a victory.

Yet I—as a perhaps stupidly stubborn secular intellectual—was never particularly taken with Khomeini himself, even before he revealed his darkly tyrannical and unyielding personality as supreme ruler. Not being a joiner or party member by nature, I had never formally enlisted in service. I had certainly become used to being peripheral, outside the circle of power, and, perhaps because I had no talent for a position inside the charmed circle, I rationalised the virtues of outsiderhood. I could never completely believe in the men and women—for that is what they were after all, *just* men and women— who commanded forces, led parties and countries, wielded basically unchallenged authority. Hero-worship, and even the notion of heroism itself, when applied to most political leaders, has always left me cold. As I watched my friend join, then abandon and then re-join sides, often with great ceremonies of bonding and rejection (such as giving up and then getting back his Western passport) I was strangely glad that being a Palestinian with American citizenship was likely to be my only fate, with no more attractive alternatives to cosy up to, for the rest of my life.

For fourteen years I served as an independent member of the Palestinian parliament-in-exile, the Palestine National Council, the total number of whose meetings, insofar as I attended them at all, amounted to about a week altogether. I stayed in the Council as an act of solidarity, even of defiance, because in the West I felt it was symbolically important to expose oneself as a Palestinian in that way, as someone who associated himself publicly with the struggle to resist Israeli policies and to win Palestinian self-determination. I refused all offers that were made to me to occupy official positions; I never joined any party or faction. When, during the third year of the Intifada I was disturbed by official Palestinian policies in the United States, I made my views widely known in Arabic forums. I never abandoned the struggle nor obviously did I join the Israeli or American side, refusing to collaborate with the powers that I still see as the chief authors of our people's woes. Similarly I never endorsed the policies of, or even accepted official invitations from, Arab states.

I am perfectly prepared to admit that these perhaps too protestant positions of mine are extensions of the essentially impossible and generally losing results of being Palestinian: we lack territorial sovereignty and have only tiny victories and little enough room to celebrate them in. Perhaps also they rationalise my unwillingness to go as far as many others have in committing myself completely to a cause or party, going all the way in conviction and engagement. I simply have not been able to do it, preferring to retain both the outsider and

REPUBLICA

sceptic's autonomy over the—to me—vaguely religious quality communicated by the convert's and true believer's enthusiasm. I found that this sense of critical detachment served me (how well I am still not completely certain) after the Israel–PLO deal was announced in August 1993. It seemed to me that the media-induced euphoria, to say nothing of official declarations of happiness and satisfaction, belied the grim actuality that the PLO leadership had simply surrendered to Israel. To say such things at the time put one in a small minority, but I felt, for intellectual and moral reasons, it had to be done. Yet the Iranian experiences I've recounted bear some direct comparison with other episodes of conversion and public recantation that dot the twentieth century intellectual experience, and it is those, both in the Western and Middle Eastern worlds, that I know best, that I'd like to consider here.

I do not want to equivocate or allow myself very much ambiguity at the outset: I am against conversion to and belief in a political god of any sort. I consider both as behaviour unfitting the intellectual. This does not mean that the intellectual should remain at the edge of the water, occasionally dipping a toe in, most of the time remaining dry. Everything I've written underlines the importance for the intellectual of passionate engagement, risk, exposure, commitment to principles, vulnerability in debating and being involved in worldly causes. For example, the difference that I see between a *professional* and *amateur* intellectual rests precisely on this, that the professional claims detachment on the basis of a profession and pretends to objectivity, whereas the amateur is moved neither by rewards nor by the fulfilment of an immediate career plan, but by a committed engagement with ideas and values in the public sphere. The intellectual, over time, naturally turns towards the political world, partly because, unlike the academy or the laboratory, that world is animated by considerations of power and interest writ large, that drive a whole society or a nation, that, as Marx so fatefully said, take the intellectual from relatively discrete questions of interpretation to much more significant ones of social change and transformation.

Every intellectual whose métier is articulating and representing specific views, ideas, ideologies, logically aspires to making them work in a society. The intellectual who claims only to write for him- or herself, or for the sake of pure learning or abstract science, is not to be and *must not* be believed. As the great twentieth century writer Jean Genet once said, 'the moment you publish essays in a society, you have entered political life; so if you want not to be political, do not write essays or speak out.'

The heart of the conversion phenomenon is joining up, not simply in alignment, but in service and, though one hates to use the word, collaboration. There has rarely been a more discrediting and unpleasant instance of this sort of thing in the West generally, and in the United States in particular, than during the Cold War, when legions of intellectuals joined what was considered to be the battle for the hearts and minds of people all over the world. An extremely famous book edited by Richard Crossman in 1949 that epitomised the strangely Manichean aspect of the intellectual Cold War, was entitled *The God That Failed*; the phrase and its explicitly religious cachet lived on well past anyone's actual memory of the book's contents, but those do deserve brief summary here.

Intended as a testimonial to the gullibility of prominent Western intellectuals—who included Ignazio Silone, André Gide, Arthur Koestler and Stephen Spender among others—*The God That Failed* allowed each of then to recount his experiences of the road to Moscow, the inevitable disenchantment that followed, the subsequent re-embrace of non-communist faith. Crossman concludes his introduction to the volume by saying in emphatic theological terms: 'The Devil once lived in Heaven, and those who have not met him are unlikely to recognise an angel when they see one.' This of course is not only politics but a morality play as well. The battle for the intellect has been transformed into a battle for the soul with implications for intellectual life that seem very baleful. That was certainly the case in the Soviet Union and its satellites, where show trials, mass purges and a gigantic penitentiary system exemplified the horrors of the ordeal on the other side of the Iron Curtain.

In the West, many of the former comrades were often required to do public penance, unseemly enough when it involved celebrities like the ones collected in *The God That Failed,* a great deal worse when—in the United States as an especially egregious instance—it induced mass hysteria. To someone like myself who came from the Middle East to the United States as a schoolboy in the 1950s when McCarthyism was in full force, it shaped a mystifyingly bloody-minded intelligentsia, to this day hung up on a wildly exaggerated internal and external menace. It was all a dispiritingly self-induced crisis, signifying the triumph of unthinking Manicheanism over rational as well as self-critical analysis.

Whole careers were built, not upon intellectual achievement but upon proving the evils of communism, or repentance, or informing on friends or colleagues, or collaborating once again with the enemies of former friends. Whole systems of discourse derived from anti-communism, from the supposed pragmatism of the end-of-ideology school to its short-lived inheritor in the past few years, the end-of-history school. Far from being a passive defence of freedom, organised anti-communism in the United States led aggressively to covert support by the CIA for otherwise unexceptionable groups such as The Congress for Cultural Freedom, which was involved, not only in the world-wide distribution of *The God That Failed*, but in subsidising magazines such as *Encounter* in the UK [and *Quadrant* in Australia: Ed]. The CIA was also behind the infiltration of labour unions, student organisations, churches and universities.

Obviously many of the successful things done in the name of anti-communism have been chronicled by its supporters as a movement. Other less admirable features are, first of all, the corruption of open intellectual discussion and a thriving cultural debate by means of a system of evangelical and finally irrational dos and don'ts (the progenitors of today's 'political correctness'), and second, certain forms of self-mutilation in public that go on to this day. Both these things have gone side by side with despicable habits of collecting rewards and privileges from one team, only for the same individual to switch sides, then collect rewards from a new patron.

I want to underline the particularly unpleasant aesthetics of conversion and recantation, how, for the individual involved, the public display of assent and subsequent apostasy produces a kind of narcissism and exhibitionism in the intellectual that has lost touch with the people and processes supposedly being served. Ideally, the intellectual represents emancipation and enlightenment, but never as abstractions or as bloodless and distant gods to be served. The intellectual's representations—what he or she represents and how those ideas are represented to an audience—are always tied to and ought to remain an organic part of an ongoing experience in society: of the poor, the disadvantaged, the voiceless, the unrepresented, the power-less. These are equally concrete and ongoing; they cannot survive being transfigured and then frozen into creeds, religious declarations, professional methods.

Such transfigurations sever the living connection between the intellectual and the movement or process of which he or she is a part. Moreover, there is the appalling danger of thinking of one's self, one's views, one's rectitudes, one's stated positions as all-important. To read over a *God That Failed* testimonial is for me a depressing thing. I want to ask: why, as an intellectual, did you believe in a god anyway? And besides, who gave you the right to imagine that your early belief and later disenchantment were so important? In and of itself, religious belief is to me both understandable and deeply personal. It is rather when a total dogmatic system in which one side is innocently good, the other irreducibly evil, is substituted for the process, the give and take of vital interchange, that the secular intellectual feels the unwelcome and inappropriate encroachment of one realm on another. Politics becomes religious enthusiasm—as it is the case today in former Yugoslavia—which results in ethnic cleansing, mass slaughter and unending conflict that are horrible to contemplate.

The irony is that very often the former convert and the new believer are equally intolerant, equally dogmatic and violent. In recent years, alas, the swing from extreme Left to extreme Right has resulted in a tedious industry that pretends to independence and enlightenment but, especially in the United States, has only mirrored the ascendancy of Reaganism and Thatcherism. The American branch of this particular brand of self-promotion has called itself 'Second Thoughts', the idea being that first thoughts during the heady decade of the sixties were both radical and wrong. In a matter of months during the late 1980s, Second Thoughts aspired to become a movement, alarmingly well-funded by right-wing Maecenases like the Bradley and Olin Foundations. The specific impresarios were David Horowitz and Peter Collier, from whose pens a stream of books, one rather like the other, flowed, most of them the revelations of former radicals who had seen the light and who had become, in the words of one of them, vigorously pro-American and anti-communist.

If sixties radicals, with their anti-Vietnam and anti-Amerikan (American was always spelt with a 'k') polemics, were assertive and self-dramatising in their beliefs, the Second Thoughters were equally loud and assertive. The only problem, of course, was that there was no communist world now, no empire of evil, although there seemed to be no limit to the self-bowdlerising and pious recitation of penitent formulas about the past that ensued. At bottom, though, it was the passage from one god to a new one that was really being celebrated. What had once been a movement based in part on enthusiastic idealism and dissatisfaction with the status quo, was simplified and refashioned retrospectively by the Second Thoughters as little more than what they called abasement before the enemies of America and a criminal blindness to communist brutality.

In the Arab world, the brave, if airy and sometimes destructive, pan-Arab nationalism of the Nasser period, which abated during the 1970s, has been replaced with a set of local and regional creeds, most of them administered harshly by unpopular, uninspired minority regimes. They are now threatened by a whole array of Arab movements. There has remained, however, a secular, cultural opposition in each Arab country; the most gifted writers, artists, political commentators, intellectuals, are generally a part of it, although they constitute a minority, many of whom have been hounded into silence or exile.

A more ominous phenomenon is the power and wealth of the oil-rich states. A lot of the sensational Western media attention paid to the Baathi regimes of Iraq and Syria has tended to overlook the quieter and insidious pressure to conform exerted by governments who have a lot of money to spend and who offer academics, writers and artists munificent patronage. This pressure was particularly in evidence during the Gulf crisis and war. Before the crisis, Arabism had been supported and defended uncritically by progressive intellectuals who believed themselves to be furthering the cause of Nasserism and the anti-imperialist, pro-independence impulse of the 1955 Bandung Conference which established the non-aligned movement. In the immediate aftermath of Iraq's occupation of Kuwait, a dramatic realignment of Arab intellectuals took place. It has been suggested that whole departments of the Egyptian publishing industry, along with many journalists, did an about-face. Former Arab nationalists suddenly began to sing the praises of Saudi Arabia and Kuwait—hated enemies of the past, new friends and patrons now.

Lucrative rewards were probably offered to cause the about-face to happen, but the Arab Second Thoughters suddenly also discovered their passionate feelings about Islam, as well as the singular virtues of one or another ruling Gulf dynasty. Only a scant year or two before, many of them (including Gulf regimes who subsidised Saddam Hussein) sponsored paeans and festivals to Iraq as it fought off Arabism's ancient foes, 'the Persians'. The language of those earlier days was uncritical, bombastic, emotional and it reeked of hero-worship and quasi-religious effusion. When Saudi Arabia invited George Bush and his armies in, these voices were converted. This time they installed a formal, much reiterated rejection of Arab nationalism (which they turned into a crude pastiche), fed now by an uncritical support of the current rulers.

For Arab intellectuals, matters have been further complicated by the new prominence of the United States as the major outside force in the Middle East today. What had once been an automatic and unthinking anti-Americanism—dogmatic, cliche-ridden, ludicrously simple—changed into pro-Americanism by fiat. In many newspapers and magazines throughout the Arab world, but especially those well known to be receiving the ever-handy Gulf subsidy, criticism of the United States was dramatically scaled down, sometimes eliminated; this went along with the usual prohibitions against criticising one or another regime which was practically deified.

A very small handful of Arab intellectuals suddenly discovered a new role for themselves in Europe and the United States. They had once been militant Marxists, often Trotskyists, and supporters of the Palestinian movement. After the Iranian revolution, some had become Islamists. As the gods fled or were driven away, these intellectuals went mute, despite some calculated probing here and there as they searched for new gods to serve. One of them in particular, a man who had once been a loyal Trotskyist, later abandoned the Left and turned, as many others did, to the Gulf, where he made a handsome living in construction. He re-presented himself just before the Gulf crisis, and became an impassioned critic of one Arab regime in particular. He never wrote under his own name but, using a string of pseudonyms that protected his identity (and his interests), he flailed out indiscriminately and hysterically against Arab culture as a whole; he did this in such a way as to win him the attention of Western readers.

Now everyone knows that to try to say something in the mainstream Western media that is critical of United States policy or Israel is extremely difficult; conversely, to say things that are hostile to the Arabs as a people or a culture, or Islam as a religion, is laughably easy. For, in effect, there is a cultural war between spokespeople for the West and those of the Muslim and Arab world. In so inflamed a situation, the hardest thing to do as an intellectual is to be critical, to refuse to adopt a rhetorical style that is the verbal equivalent of carpet-bombing, and to focus instead on those issues, like United States support for unpopular client regimes.

Of course, on the other hand, there is a virtual certainty of getting an audience if, as an Arab intellectual, you passionately, even slavishly, support United States policy, you attack its critics and, if they happen to be Arabs, you invent evidence to show their villainy (if they are American, you confect stories and situations that prove their duplicity), you spin out stories concerning Arabs and Muslims that have the effect of defaming their tradition, defacing their history, accentuating their weaknesses, of which of course there are plenty. Above all, you attack the officially approved enemies—Saddam Hussein, Baathism, Arab nationalism, the Palestinian movement, Arab views of Israel. And of course this earns you the expected accolades: you are characterised as courageous, you are outspoken and passionate, and on and on. The new god of course, is the West. Arabs, you say, should try to be more like the West, should regard the West as a source and a reference point. Gone is the history of what the West actually did. Gone are the Gulf War's destructive results. We Arabs and Muslims are the sick ones; our problems are our own, totally self-inflicted.

A number of things stand out about this sort of performance. In the first place, there is no universalism here at all. Because you serve a god uncritically, all the devils are always on the other side: this was as true when you were a Trotskyist as it is now when you are a recanting former Trotskyist. You do not think of politics in terms of interrelationships or of common histories such as, for instance, the long and complicated dynamic that has bound the Arabs and Muslims to the West and vice versa. Real intellectual analysis forbids calling one side innocent, the other evil. Indeed the notion of a side is, where cultures are at issue, highly problematic, since most cultures aren't watertight little packages, all homogeneous and all either good or evil. But if your eye is on your patron, you cannot think as an intellectual, but only as a disciple or acolyte. In the back of your mind there is the thought that you must please and not displease.

In the second place, your own history of service to previous masters is trampled on or demonised, of course, but it doesn't provoke in you the slightest self-doubt, doesn't stimulate in you much desire to question the premise of loudly serving a god, then lurching impulsively to do the same for a new god. Far from it: as you had careened from one god to another in the past, you continue to do the same thing in the present, a bit more cynically it is true, but in the end it has the same effect.

By contrast, the true intellectual is a secular being. However much intellectuals pretend that their representations are of higher things or ultimate values, morality begins with their activity in this secular world of ours—where it takes place, whose interests it serves, how it jibes with a consistent and universalist ethic, how it discriminates between power and justice, what it reveals of one's choices and priorities. Those gods that always fail demand from the intellectual in the end a kind of absolute certainty and a total, seamless view of reality that recognises only disciples or enemies.

What strikes me as much more interesting is how to keep a space in the mind open for doubt and for the play of an alert, sceptical irony (preferably, also self-irony). Yes, you have convictions and you make judgments, but they are arrived at by work, and by a sense of association with others, other intellectuals, a grass-roots movement, a continuing history, a set of lived lives. As for abstractions or orthodoxies, the trouble with them is that they are patrons who need placating and stroking all the time. The morality and principles of an intellectual should not constitute a sort of sealed gearbox that drives thought and action in one direction, and is powered by an engine with only one fuel source. The intellectual has to walk around, has to have the space in which to stand and talk back to authority, since unquestioning subservience to authority in today's world is one of the greatest threats to an active, and moral, intellectual life.

It is difficult to face that threat on one's own, and even more difficult to find a way to be consistent with your beliefs and at the same time remain free enough to grow, change your mind, discover new things, or rediscover what you had once put aside. The hardest aspect of being an intellectual is to represent what you profess through your work and interventions, without hardening into an institution, or a kind of automaton acting at the behest of a system or method. Anyone who has felt the exhilaration of being successful at that *and* also successful at keeping alert and solid will appreciate how rare the convergence is. But the only way of ever achieving it is to keep reminding yourself that as an intellectual you are the one who can choose between actively representing the truth to the best of your ability, or passively allowing a patron or an authority to direct you. For the secular intellectual, *those* gods always fail.

Giant Debbil Dingo

MUDROOROO

Ya know, we got tis story,
Bibbulmun story,
proper Nyungar story—
bout tis debbil dingo,
tis big dog.
Ya know, dreamtime story.
Lizard put an end to im ten.
But, ya know, e keeps on comin back,
all ta time comin back,
an e as ta be put down agen and agen.
Well, not so long ago now
e was livin ere. Just at tat place along road.
You know tat place. North Fremanta. Well sumtin like tat.
Big place too, big as dat prison ouse nearby.
E useta live tere. Is name, tey call im Bondee.
Disguise—ya know who e was, eh?
Tat fulla, Giant Debbil Dingo,
e come back agen.
Leave is paintin tere, ya know—
on ta side of tat big buildin.
Yuh can see tat big dog tere to tis day—biiiig dog.
But e gone now, Bondee. Only tat picture left.
Only is cry left—whinin on ta wind.
But, ya know, e still trying to come back.

E useta, useta, well, eat people. Lots of tem.
Come outa tat big ouse of is,
run down tere, grab im, take em back,
eat em, all gone. An e chew on ta bone,
chew em right down.
Is ouse fulla, fulla tat white bone dust—
an all aroun tat big dog picture, sandstones,
tat is shit,
all roun is ouse, is picture.
Ate all tem bone, come out of im like littul white pebbles.

E get fat tat dog, tat dingo.
Fatta e get, ungrier e get.
Eat an eat an tat dog still ungry—

e lucky fulla t'ough, tat one lucky,
for while, for some time, e veeeeery lucky.

Big fish, whale, e come long Fremanta beach.
Sittin tere, sun on is back, feeling good.
Feeling nice, warm now, not like bottom of sea,
an tat dog, tat Bondee, e look, see im tere,
e leap up, e jump, right down is mouf e go,
right down is troat.
Maybe didn't wanta do tat,
but tat ta way e go.

Start eat im from inside, guts, kidney, liver—
ave a sleep, begin on tat meat, eat it all up.
But bone e too big, too hard, an tat skin
e too hard too—
So tis Bondee fulla, e take bone,
rib bone, line em all up.
E take skin, stretch it right hout,
stretch it right hout, sun dry im.
E put that skin on line of rib bone.
E look—big boat now, big boat all ready for im.
Ready for tat yacht race.
Ya know tat yacht race?
An e call tat boat,
well, what e call it?
Yeah, Endeavour, cause e was—
well—just ear me out an ya'll see why.

Now tere tis littul fulla, is name Peta Pan—
E Horphan. You know, no mudda, fadda, sister, brudda.
But e live wit tese udder chilren, same as im.
Lot of kids, no mudda, no fadda, no brudda, no sista.
But live all along one anudda—same as family,
all same as family, in a big ouse.
You know where tat Waagyal, e useta live. Dalkeith.

So tat Bondee, e ungry agen,
belly growlin.
E come tat way,
sniffin, snufflin,
sniff, sniff, e smell em out.
E come running.

Peta Pan look hup, e see im.
E smart fulla, got this maban-power Tinkerbell,
make im real strong, magic man, tis Peta Pan.
E got ready for tat Giant Debbil Dingo.
Big fight now. Tis way, tat way,
steep bank tere before.
Get all flatten out from tat fight.
Peta Pan, e it im with gidja, spear.
It im with kylie, boomerang.
Take tat monument you see up tere,
take it up and it im with tat.
Down go Bondee, right on tose Crawley Baths,
can't see em now.
Bondee fall on em, you know.
E get back up, Peta Pan king it im,
down e go, urt ribber in is fall,
mess hup every ting, all mucked hup—
land not good tere afta.
Not good tat place hanymore.
People come tere, go silly in ta ead.
You know, fight an carry on.

Well, Peta Pan, e take up tommahawk.
Bondee bout to get up,
Peta Pan, e take tat tommahawk,
cut off is right and, cut it right off.
'Bondee finish now,' e tinks. 'No more.'
An cause tat land spoilt,
e go up in hair.
Take tat and,
up e go up with tose udder kids.
An e fly, fly, fly,
on an on an on.
Come to a place called Neferland.
Udder people, tey call it Maui.
Got mountain on fire on tat island too.
Big ole, at top of mountain, smoke comin out.
Like in our smokin ceremony to clean out place.
An Peta Pan, e settle tere,
e take tat and of Bondee,
e put in tat sacred mountain.
Bondee no can do arm now,
no writin cheques an tings.

Now Gub'ment fulla, is name Burke.
E come from Pope, im you know,
Tat fulla, e live in Rome.
E ear bout Bondee, sent im, tat fulla Burke:
'You look afta me mate, Bondee.'
So e come quick, pick im up, put im in ospital,
look at tat arm: 'No good, get you nudda one.'
So e look round, see, um, butcher shop.
Steel ooks angin tere for sheep an pig.
E take up steel ook, hey, new and
strong as steel, betta tan ole one, give im power.
But for one ting, ya know,
e can't write cheques with ook.

Now, cause of tat boat, cause of tat ook,
tey call im Capn Ook.
But e still same Giant Debbil Dingo.
Hit still im, ya know.
An e want is proper and back,
tat and secret of is power,
can't sign cheques with ook, eh?

Now, tis Pope—
e get gether with tat King of England,
an tem two fullas,
tey get together with tat fulla, Burke,
an e, well, e already with tat Bondee, tat Capn Ook.
Tey, you know, wanta use tat ship, tat boat,
want im go out in it, buy up hall ta world—
your land, my land, is land, er land—
buy um fulla's land all up,
get em cheap too, ya know,
use em gun an flag stead of money.

An tat Burke fulla, e go along with Bondee,
e change is name t'ough, e Sir Merchant Banker.
E keeps is money an when Bondee wants it,
e puts it down on paper.
Tricky one tat fulla, Burke.
But Bondee no catch on, too busy.
E want Peta Pan, want is and back.

So tey send Bondee out in tat boat.
Gib im some clof, sing im flag,
give im Burke too,

tell im: 'Take whole world, steal im, buy im.
Put tis flag up, tell em tose fullas,
tis country mine now, all mine.
If tey say no, show em tis gun.'

So Bondee, e say yes.
Get in tat boat leave Fremanta.
Come to tis place, Adelaide:
'Ah, nice place tis one.'
Put hup flag, tell em tose Nanga fullas: 'Tis mine now.'
Ten e ask tem: 'You know tat Peta Pan,
me want im tat fulla, talk to im.
E me mate, owe im a few beers, eh?'
But, ya know, e want is and back
ta sign tose cheques.
Got all is power in it.
If e don't get it, one day e finish—
bankrupt—no money anymore.

So e sail, e put up flag,
e say: 'Tis mine,' an an—
tat Merchant Banker, e writes it down
on tat piece of paper, e calls hit
keepin haccounts, keepin haccounts.
So e sail, e put up flag,
'Tis mine.' E goes on,
'Tis mine.'
Tem Koori places—
Gummingarri, Woorallajee, Yarburong.
Tem Murri places—
Terangeree, Talwalpin, Yarun.
All tem places.
Tat Papua-New Guinea—
Ao Tea Roa, Otaheite, Niue,
Nomuka, Tongatapu, Lifuka,
Eua, Huaheine, Borabora.
An tat Sir Merchant Banker,
e puts em all down on tat paper,
an Bondee, e can't, ya know.
Tat Peta Pan, e took is and.
An ya can't keep haccounts with a ook.

Well, e go on sailin, sailin on tat sea,
no land hanywhere, no country anywheres.
E look tis way, e look tat way, nuffin.

Ten e tell tat fulla, tat Sir Merchant Banker,
'Eh, get uppa tat mast, look for country.'
An tat Merchant Banker, e look up from paper.
All written down, you know, all on paper—
tis country to Pope, tis un to King George,
but cause e belong im too that England,
when e gives one to Pope, he gives two to English King.
An all time, tat Bondee, e too busy, busy worryin,
lookin for tat Peta Pan, an so e tells im:
'You get im up mast,' an Sir Merchant Banker,
E ides is paper an climb tat mast.
Right up e go, e like Possum.
Up tat mast e go, look—
e look tis way, e look tat way,
e look again. Mountain on fire over tere,
An e shout: 'Land ahoy.'
Tats what e say: 'Land ahoy!'
An down e come, an in tey sail,
Come on tat island, eat a sandwich.
Get on shore, put up flag, fire gun—
call it Sandwich Island.
Ten, tey fire gun agen,
an salute tat flag.

Peta Pan, e ear gun,
e look, e see em from Maui,
e come flyin to tat beach,
to tat place, tem fullas call Keala Kekua,
well, sumtin like tat.

Capn Ook, Bondee, e see tat Peta Pan,
e load up gun,
e fire one, two, tree.
E call tat fulla Merchant Banker to fire,
e fire four, five, six—
can't it im, too strong, too strong, tat Peta Pan.

E come down, get tat Capn Ook, fling im up,
up, up, up, land right in tat mountain fire.
Peta Pan, e pick up tat ship, chuck it afta im.
Ship go up, up, up, land on top of mountain.
Whoosh, up it go, all burn up,
skin dry, you know, all dry,
an hunderneaf ship, tat Capn Ook, e burn,
e gin cook. Nice smell come, roast dog smell.

End of Ook, e burn up in earth oven.
Tats when e got tis udder name,
Tey call im Capn Cook.
But all same Giant Debbil Dingo, ya know.

Peta Pan, e come to tat fire, tat oven,
e come an e see littul dog come out,
e call im. 'Eh, dog.'
E come an wag is tail.
Got mark like Ook on is back.
Tats Bondee, Ook or Cook.
Littul dog, e give im to Wendee.
She woman, tis Wendee,
she name tat cause she got tis red air.
She take tat dog an look after im.
Good woman tat one, kwobart,
woman power, tats why she make im pet.

Not end of story yet.

Littul bit more, just littul bit.
Peta Pan, Wendee an dog, e called Nanna.
Tat red-eaded woman call im tat,
call im Nanna, cause she get im,
get im look hafter ta chidren—
million to tis one, million to tat one.
Eh, no more money, no boyo hanymore,
no worries, no ands anymore,
e littul dog, e called Nanna,
Cause e look afta children real good.

An Peta Pan, e take ta flag, chucks it at sea.
It fly up, ang hover water like curtain.
No more Neferland to be seen, gone, finish—
no, it still tere. You know, idden black country.
All sand tere coloured black. You know, all black,
cause it black fulla country.
All time black fulla country.

An tat Sir Merchant Banker,
clefer fulla tat one, get inna littul boat,
Away e go, to Pope, to King, tey very happy.
Tey take all ta land, all our countries,
so we got nuffin left, all our countries gone.
No more Giant Debbil Dingo anymore.

No Capn Cook, no King of England hanymore.
Not Neferland t'ough. Peta Pan too tricky for tem.
Cause tat Peta Pan, e stay in dat Neferland.
Leavin us fullas, no good at all.
Just usun to set ting right.
Just us fullas to set tings right, you know.

So I finish ere now.
Tats ta story of Giant Debbil Dingo,
Bondee, Ook or Cook.
But watch hout, e might be back,
e dreamtime debbil, ya know.

Selling Yothu Yindi

ADAM SHOEMAKER

On 24 April 1993, in *The Weekend Australian*'s 'Weekend Review', the historian David Day described Australia as being 'a state in search of a nation'. He was writing about the republican debate in this country and he meant that the current (and future) republican movement and its popular groundswell were important harbingers of Australia's journey towards self-identification. Much of the debate's rhetoric is couched in terms of growth and inevitability, as if this next stage in our national character since 1901 must occur as surely as adulthood follows adolescence, in human terms. One word which surfaces so often in the debate is 'maturity'—which raises the question of what exactly an immature ninety-three year old looks like, even if it is a nation–state!

The same sort of schizophrenic rhetoric sees Australia being described simultaneously, for instance, as the 'world's most ancient continent' and as 'a young country'. Of course, both descriptions are correct, in a specific sense. While the pairing of archaeological and political images is unusual, it can also be relevant. Different stages of age and experience are continuously invoked in discussions about Australian culture—Australia is a country which is at the same time ancient and modern. This double image of Australia—our fundamental ambivalence in our understanding of exactly who we are supposed to be—is reflected in other descriptions of ourselves as well—as either urban and rural, as Asian and European, as theoretically egalitarian and yet actually unequal in many respects. This ambivalence is no more pronounced than in the relationship between White Australia and Aboriginal Australia.

Even the growing appreciation of Aboriginality by contemporary White Australia is qualified by uncertainty. There is still very much an obverse side to the White Australian prism of admiration; the gaze is frequently judgmental, discriminatory and racist. Aboriginality is lauded at the same time as it is exploited; while it is being praised in some quarters, it is being rejected in others. This ambivalence comes into the clearest focus when Australia is attempting to market itself, especially in such image-sensitive industries as rock music and tourism.

One of the most popular series of domestic advertisements sponsored by the Northern Territory Tourist Commission (NTTC) features the Melbourne comedian Daryl Somers alliterating as energetically as possible the slogan: 'You'll never never know if you never never go, see the Never-never now.'

I wonder what exactly is it that tourists will see when they travel to Australia's Top End? Does it bear any resemblance to the glib, punning picture that Somers gives the television viewer? More to the point, what *Aboriginal* image of the Northern Territory is being conveyed to overseas visitors—especially those from Japan—by advertising campaigns of the NTTC and the Australian Tourist Commission (ATC)?

Yothu Yindi, the most successful Black Australian rock band, is currently being marketed enthusiastically in Japan by the ATC in order to attract tourists from that country. Exactly what is the relationship between Yothu Yindi—a band which was described by Senator Bob Collins, in *The Canberra Times* in January last year, as being one of the Territory's 'best exports'—and tourism? And why is the selling of Yothu Yindi in this way significant. What Yothu Yindi (via the ATC) represents to the Japanese is as proximate to the Red Centre as Peter Pan's Neverland is to the Never-never. It can truly be said that visitors will never never know, even if they *do* go—because the images of Aboriginality they are being sold are dubious and misleading. They exist mainly in the minds of politicians, tourism promoters and record-label executives.

Even more, the case of Mandawuy Yunupingu as lead singer of Yothu Yindi is a classic example of Aboriginal talent being represented as the exception to what is a rule determined by intolerance and bigotry. The more Yunupingu comes to be praised as an individual, the more he becomes distanced in the public eye from his band, his family and his community, no matter how much he actually does deserve popular recognition as a major talent. He is being created as 'an individual success' or 'a model of Aboriginal achievement'. And Yothu Yindi and Yunupingu are being merged into a singular, inseparable entity by political, media and entertainment promoters— how many other members of the band can the average rock fan name? Can one imagine Yothu Yindi *without* Yunupingu? Mandawuy has been made into more than just a lead singer; he has become the very personification of the rock group.

Can it be counter-productive to have a widely recognised image of intelligent, talented Aboriginal leadership in the person of Yunupingu, especially when the media is already so saturated with pejorative stereotypes of Aboriginal people? Surely this is not just tokenism—is it not the invocation of positive role models, to which other Aboriginal people can then aspire? On one level, I do not argue with this at all; there is no doubt that Mandawuy Yunupingu can and does inspire many other Black Australians with his music, wisdom and philosophy of life. As Andrew McMillan put it, in a recent issue of *Juice*, 'He's a remarkable man, the first certified Black Australian pop star, a celebrated icon and role model for Aboriginal people, a blackfella from the bush who's been embraced by the whitefellas from the city. He's an intiated man, a keeper of sacred knowledge whose participation in ceremonial activity is integral to the cultural survival of the Yolngu people.'

This fascinating assessment underlines Mandawuy's prominence and high regard in the Yolngu community. However, it is very much worth noting that many earlier Black Australian achievements carry no *lasting* weight in non-Aboriginal Australia. Otherwise, the memory of Jimmy

Little, for one, could not be so easily forgotten by music critics who claim that Yunupingu is the first 'certified Black Australian pop star'.

But McMillan does prompt some crucial questions: how does the other 98.5 per cent of the Australian community, let alone the rest of the world, view Mandawuy Yunupingu? How is the lead singer of Yothu Yindi received in the non-Aboriginal mainstream? Is his position and his star status being abused for the sake of other, more dubious goals, despite his talent and ability? Is he, and, by extension, are the members of his band, being exploited in any way by governments, trade and tourism promoters or record labels? Is his anti-racist, pro-Aboriginal message not being warped by others into a sanctimonious commercial and public relations campaign which privileges non-Aboriginal people in a way which perversely has the potential to reinforce a racist ideology?

I should emphasise that this is not a criticism in any shape or form of the approach and accomplishments of Yothu Yindi; the critique here is directed towards 'their *representation* and *representing agencies*...to recognise the white hegemonic discourses which have created their cultural identity and thus the context of reception' as Philip Hayward put it in his 1993 article 'Safe and Exotic and Somewhere Else: Yothu Yindi, "Treaty" and the mediation of Aboriginality', in January's *Perfect Beat*. The media (including popular music magazines as well as newspapers, radio and television), the music industry in all its guises, and international advertising, especially in the realm of tourism, are all crucial vehicles for the transmission of such 'discourses' as Hayward describes.

But, to return to the question of leadership, why is it risky for individual Aborigines to be characterised as pioneers in various fields? Does not someone have to break down the door of resistance in order to allow others to enter? Again, the answer to both these questions lies in the domain of representation. In this context, what Mandawuy Yunupingu actually does is often less significant than the mass media version of his achievements. And 'achievements' is beyond doubt the operative word.

As Marcia Langton has argued with perception, the fixation of non-Aboriginal people on single or inaugural Aboriginal achievements itself underscores the presence of a racist ideological blanket. As she puts it in her publication for the Australian Film Commission of last year, *Well, I Heard it on the Radio and I Saw it on the Television*, 'There is an annoying tendency in the expression of the Australian paternalistic relationship with Aborigines: the first Aborigine to graduate, to play cricket, to box, and even to make a film.'

But there is more to it even than this. Langton also demonstrates how some Black Australians accept this same societal construction of success, with serious consequences. In her words, 'But why do whites and blacks get so worked up about the "first Aborigine to..."? It is a kind of declaration of having achieved some kind of equity, as if there were really something to celebrate in finally having overcome all the racism and other obstacles which Aborigines face in gathering the resources to do anything. Indeed, it is actually a denial of the racism against Aborigines. It is a way of saying that we are too backward to do it, not that we are denied the means to do it.'

This non-Aboriginal obsession with Black Australian ground breakers, in whatever field, is more than just a whitewash of paternalism. It is certainly a product of a racist ideology, but it works as a catalyst for one as well. If a Black Australian succeeds according to non-Aboriginal standards, he or she becomes an overnight hero; if he or she fails to measure up to these 'foreign' criteria, he or she is banished into silence by the majority. Most importantly, neither option gives any sort of genuine, collective respect to Aboriginal people as human beings. The racist milieu does not change in the least; in fact, the success of one Aborigine is often invoked to legitimise the status quo, for if someone like Mandawuy Yunupingu can do it, why cannot every other Black Australian?

For those who argue that this fixation upon mainstream achievements is the relic of a bygone era, consider the recent popular reaction to those such as the author of *My Place*, Sally Morgan, the 'first' Aborigine to write a 'best-seller'; to Pat O'Shane, the 'first' Aboriginal magistrate. It is undeniable that Australian society is obsessed with such historical moments, exactly because they are measurable, positive, familiar and reassuring. They all implicitly suggest that, at its core, Australian culture is open and welcoming and that Aboriginal people can assimilate successfully if they so choose.

The very fact that such a list of achievements can be produced with relative ease and that most Australians would be familiar with many of *these* names, supports this contention. One might ask whether all Aboriginal 'firsts' are recorded in the same way in Australian popular culture—for example, can Australians name the first Aborigine to die in police custody? The first Aboriginal guerilla leader? Can Australians name the first Aboriginal woman to be raped by a European on this continent? No. These names are lost in time—not individualised—because they bring shame to the memory and because there are so many Aboriginal people who fall into these categories. But until these names are accepted alongside the others, the limited and essentially racist nature of the naming enterprise will remain.

And Black Australian history is full of examples of the double-sided trap of achievement. The 1940s saw the emergence of Albert Namatjira, the first Aboriginal artist to paint figurative watercolour works. He was hailed as a genius, garlanded with praise—and then gaoled and destroyed for the alleged 'crime' of 'supplying liquor to natives' (who were members of his own extended family, to whom he owed kinship obligations). In 1965, Oodgeroo (then known as Kath Walker) became the first published Aboriginal writer of verse; she was an overnight success and became the highest-selling Australian poet in the 1960s and 1970s—but, at the same time, she was panned mercilessly by European critics, such as Andrew Taylor in the Winter issue of *Australian Book Review* in 1967, who claimed that what she was producing was not 'poetry in any true sense'. More recently, in the 1980s, Charles Perkins, who was the first male Aborigine to gain a university degree and the first Black Australian to head a federal government department, was hounded out of office for alleged misappropriation of funds—charges which (after extended investigation) were found to be totally groundless. The mainstream is often eventually far more unforgiving towards those Aboriginal people who do achieve prominence within it than towards other Australians: a classic symptom of systemic racism.

Here we see 'the curse of the first' being played out, because the mainstream places such heavy burdens upon those Aborigines who are deemed to have 'made it' in European terms. Overnight, such individuals become spokespeople and they are invited to represent Australia (and not just Black Australia) at overseas conferences, festivals and performances. But their capacity for dissent is severely circumscribed—and they often come to be hounded by the media for particular pronouncements. Some, like Oodgeroo, fought this process by returning awards and imperial honours in protest; and she is among those Aboriginal 'achievers' who altered their names in order to refuse non-Aboriginal categorisations. Others, like Pat O'Shane, have courageously set about to reform the agenda of Australian society despite the critics—in her case, in her legal and judicial profession. Still others, like Mandawuy Yunupingu, have worked with community elders precisely to devise strategies to offset these forces.

Can they succeed? Is it possible for any Black Australian to 'Aboriginalise' major White institutions or industries? Finally, do national awards help or hinder this process?

The reaction to Mandawuy Yunupingu's nomination as 'Australian of the Year' in January 1993 is one of the clearest cases of White Australia's ambivalence to Aboriginality.

The award immediately became a divisive social and political issue when the Sydney radio announcer, Alan Jones, criticised it as being tokenistic and retrograde. He alleged, in *The Australian* newspaper of 28 January last year, that Yunupingu would never have won had 1993 not been the United Nations' International Year of World Indigenous People. Some have vilified Jones as a solitary, ignorant racist; however, sadly, many Australian citizens share his point of view, judging by the public reaction to his broadcast.

An award of this sort is fraught with difficulties, precisely because the entire matter is transformed into a media circus. And the pattern of damning Aborigines as either western heroes or indigenous villains emerges here with disconcerting clarity. It is worth noting that every press article which covered Yunupingu's award as Australian of the Year did so in a similar fashion. In each case, Mandawuy's achievements were described in a way which Marcia Langton would recognise immediately. For instance, DD McNicoll wrote in *The Australian*, the day before Alan Jones levelled his allegations, that 'Mr Yunupingu had made achievements far beyond his artistic field, being the first Arnhem Land Aborigine to graduate with a university degree in education and the first Aborigine to become a headmaster.' This passage, like so many others, emphasises the fact that Yunupingu has succeeded in European terms. This is a classic case of a double-edged perception of Aboriginality: of individual Black Australians being good enough to make it in the mainstream at the same time that Aboriginal people as a whole are ignored and despised by many in the community.

And there is also a sense of propitiation here. Awards imply approbation—acceptance on a formal level. But the same man who was the 1993 Australian of the Year was, only eight months before his award, barred from service at the Catani Bar, a Melbourne nightspot, on the basis of his skin colour. This was denied by the management, who claimed that Yunupingu was denied service because he was not dressed properly. But Yunupingu describes himself in the June 1992 issue of *Rolling Stone* as being clad in 'clean jeans, Doc Martens and a shirt...bought in London for twenty-five quid.' It is significant that of all the column centimetres which have been devoted to Yunupingu and to Yothu Yindi, this *Rolling Stone* article is the only published one of which I am aware that is written by Mandawuy himself. It is hardly surprising that this involves by far the most direct presentation of Yunupingu's political convictions:

> Every day in every town in this country, Aboriginal people
> come up against discrimination that is based purely on the
> colour of our skin...Racism is something that we are all
> subjected to...We need to find a solution to this problem that is
> affecting every one of us...Australia practised cultural genocide
> to a large degree and wanted Aboriginal people to be like the
> Balanda [White Australians]...Racism is an every-day
> experience for Aboriginal people. Many of my countrymen
> don't have the kind of capacity that I have had in terms of
> exposure at a national level where the media took an interest in
> my case. Every day Yolngu people are experiencing that,
> whether it be in the Northern Territory or New South Wales,
> Western Australia, Queensland, wherever.

Even if, at the time, Yunupingu reacted more in sorrow than in anger, the clear message was one of *exclusion*, both racially and culturally. Can it be said in all honesty that the symbol of *inclusion* which his 1993 award represented was not, in part, an attempt to balance the *public* scales: to show the world that Australia is not as racist a country as it is often made out to be overseas? No sooner had Yunupingu been given his award than the Minister for Aboriginal and Torres Strait Islander Affairs, Robert Tickner, issued a statement quoted by Margaret Easterbrook in *The Age* on 27 January 1993, which certainly gave the impression that he at least was aware that a larger agenda was being served:

> The selection of Mr Yunupingu as Australian of the Year will focus the minds of non-indigenous Australians on the importance of the International Year and the need to address Aboriginal aspirations as being central to the process of reconciliation.

He then added, tellingly, that 'it would also speak volumes to people *throughout the world* (my emphasis) about Australia's dedication to change' and concluded, in a way which further illustrated an awareness of Yunupingu's international diplomatic potential that, 'Mr Yunupingu is widely regarded as an outstanding ambassador for Aboriginal people and their achievements and *for Australia as a whole*' (my emphasis).

This same uncritically positive tone pervaded all the press coverage of the Australian of the Year ceremony. One of the most frequently quoted lines from Yunupingu was the the reassuring homily—'I'm proud to be an Australian, because this is the best country in the world'—a phrase which would gladden even the most ardent racist's heart. The fact is, however, that this statement was taken very much out of context; the entire text of Yunupingu's speech was quoted only in Chips Mackinolty's unedited article in *The Age* of 27 January. The effect is dramatically different:

> I feel as if I'm Yolngu first, it comes from my heart. Australian is just a label put on to what has happened in the past. But I'll always be Yolngu. I'm proud to be coming from Gukula dhawurruwurru rilmitja. That's my Australia before the land we now know as Australia came into being. Australia is just 200 years old. What I believe is we were a nation before another nation took over, that's what adds strength to what I believe in.

The point is that I admire and respect Yothu Yindi's creative and political work, but I also believe that the band's image was exploited in various ways in the International Year of World Indigenous People. Australia gains immensely every time a Yothu Yindi video is played overseas; in fact, it is arguable that Australia gains more than the band itself gains. This takes nothing away from the talent or stance of the performers, nor from the fact that they have worked hard to get where they are today. What it does say is that there are bigger forces and issues at work—and one of these is the fact that the animus in the community against Aborigines is papered over by representations of Yothu Yindi's popularity and of Yunupingu's personal magnetism.

But if the media has played, at best, an ambiguous role, what has been the reaction of the Australian music industry to the Yothu Yindi phenomenon? Does the band's chart success mean that the trade is becoming more open to, and supportive of, indigenous musical artists? The extent to which the members of Yothu Yindi are singled out in Brent Hampstead's November *Time Off* article, 'Freedom Says the Tribal Voice', as the 'undisputed heavy-weight champions of indigenous pop' or, as the group's manager described them in *The Sydney Morning Herald* in October 1992, as 'the flagship for Aboriginal Australia', does propose problems of representation.

Yothu Yindi are being created as *the* Aboriginal musicians, *the* representatives of 'indigenous pop', a subset of the commercial genre of 'world music'. What does this mean to people? How is Yothu Yindi actually being presented and described? Just what is being sold? The November issue of *Rolling Stone* carries an article by Michael Dwyer which straitjackets the band. The blurb for the article reads, 'When Yothu Yindi performed in London, previewing tracks from their new album *Freedom*, the Brits experienced Vegas-style showmanship laced with a few political reminders.'

Las Vegas? It's a long way from Arnhem Land. And it would be obvious to any Yothu Yindi concert goer that such a North American motif is as misplaced as a description of Midnight Oil as a jazz ensemble would be. This reductionist and dismissive rockspeak continues in the article, which is entitled 'The Velvet Revolution'. Says Dwyer: 'While the huge multicultural entourage makes a political statement simply by existing, backstage they're filling in time like any other group of musicians.'

What did the author expect the band members to be doing backstage or in their hotel rooms? Toasting witchetty grubs? In a final snipe at this 'surprising revelation of humanity', he states: 'Scratch a cultural envoy and you'll find just another band from the Northern Territory. Maybe this is only rock & roll, after all.'

What exactly does he mean? He seems to have become entangled in expectations and prejudices of his own devising. But there *is* little doubt that the Australian music industry has not experienced any major institutional or attidudinal change post-Yothu Yindi. It seems fair to concur with Lesley Sly, the author of *The Power and the Passion* (a recently released guide to the industry), that, 'despite its glamorous image, the Australian music business remained an appallingly sexist industry that excluded women from positions of power and promoted sexist and racist stereotypes...(and that) Aboriginal people played no part in the industry's power structure at all, despite the growing popularity of acts such as Yothu Yindi.'

The conclusion is not that Mandawuy Yunupingu and the other band members are somehow unwittingly being duped into playing parts they would otherwise reject; instead, the point is that the racist matrix is so ingrained in western society that it takes more than one Aboriginal rock group—no matter how talented and committed—to effect serious change.

Nor is Yothu Yindi betraying its cultural roots by garnering success; quite the contrary. As Black Australian musician Kev Carmody put it in his interview with Rob Johnson, published in *Perfect Beat* in January 1993, the band's success has 'put black music back on the musical agenda in this country...If you look at Yothu Yindi and their land and their country which is very very significant in black culture, that is their reality there. They're not selling out their way of doing it. They're doing it their way, you know?'

Even so, there is little point in fetishising Yothu Yindi into a musical (or social) revolution, just as there is no reason to transform them into an exotic representation of Aboriginality.

Unfortunately, this seems to be exactly what has occurred in the area of Australian tourism advertising over the past two years. Take, for example, the most recent campaign which was coproduced by Qantas and the ATC in Japan. For three weeks in February 1993, an intensive 7.5-million-dollar promotional campaign which featured Yothu Yindi was mounted in that country. Following the theme 'Wonder Continent Australia', fifteen-second and thirty-second television ads were screened 805 times on thirty-two television stations as well as in eighty-two cinemas over that period of time. These figures were referred to in the ATC's *Market Report* in December 1993. According to ATC research, 89 per cent of Japanese homes were reached in the target areas, and the television spots were seen an average 7.2 times by each household. Compared with the average mass campaign, this is a phenomenal level of market penetration.

In addition to the above, colour advertisements appeared in twenty-eight magazines and ten newspapers nationally, 'while 596 railway-station billboards were used in five major markets over a two-week period.' And the results? The campaign was one of the most successful ever run in Japan: there were 50 000 responses, 70 per cent of which requested holiday packages; the number of inbound Japanese tourists to Australia rose 8 per cent over the past financial year (from 602 500 to 651 600), despite the severe Japanese recession. This is obviously a huge amount of business, but what does it mean?

According to Fiona Carruthers, writing in *The Australian* newspaper of 30 April 1993, in an article entitled 'Aboriginal Rock Brings Japanese Tourists Back', 'the sound of didgeridoos has come to the Japanese airwaves, sparking a fascination with Aboriginal culture that is rapidly turning into a multi-million-dollar boost for tourism. The Japanese made a record number of enquiries about travel in Australia after the screening of the commercials. More than 15 000 calls resulted, with 8000 Japanese requesting regular information about holidays to Australia.'

This front-page article is both fascinating and revealing as regards the 'value' of Aboriginal culture to non-Aborigines. First, even if one is restricted solely to a discussion of economics, this trend shows beyond doubt that Aboriginal people are major contributors to one of the fastest-growing sectors of the Australian economy: tourism and leisure. The oft-repeated claim that Black Australians contribute 'nothing' to the country's economic well-being is totally false. And this is nothing new: Aboriginal art has been one of the signal successes of the Australian export art community for the past twenty years, with works worth millions of dollars having been purchased by overseas buyers. Yet Aboriginal people are still popularly characterised as net debtors in the Australian economy, and many commentators still describe the first Australians as effectively being wards of the state.

Returning to the 'Japanese situation', it is clear that the ATC, at least, is extraordinarily sensitive to any marketing strategy which will give Australia a more 'mature' image. Remember that word. As the ATC's Public Affairs Manager, Bill Gray, has explained, the Yothu Yindi campaign was introduced in Japan 'after research indicated that they were curious about Aboriginal culture.' But there is more to it than this. The unprecedented success of this strategy is directly linked to the dualistic perception of Australia mentioned at the outset: that it is a land which is somehow simultaneously ancient and modern. For example, the ATC's regional director in Japan, Mr Tony Virili, observed in *Aboriginal Rock*, that 'there is a spirituality about the Aborigines that is very striking to the Japanese...Until recently, people here thought Australia had a history of 200 years. Now they hear Yunupingu on prime-time radio talking about things that happened 40 000 years ago—the history, music and beliefs of an ancient culture—and of modern issues like the environment. Yothu Yindi represent ecological awareness and a kind of consciousness about important issues that more people here are also voicing.'

The Aboriginal ability to integrate the ancient and the contemporary, the spiritual and the practical, is laudable in itself. The whole world can begin to appreciate the depth and wisdom of Black Australian culture. But the questions remain: to what use is this knowledge being put? Who is benefiting? And what is the underlying ideology of the images?

The reaction to previous ATC campaigns—especially the most famous Paul Hogan 'shrimp on the barbie' series of advertisements— shows that what is symbolic locally may be taken literally overseas, or may even become reduced to the damaging level of exotica. Many Americans to this day believe that Crocodile Dundee is a real type of human being in Australia, an archetype, rather than an exaggerated and satirical larrikin figure.

It does seem that the major aim is to encourage the Japanese to book holidays, plane flights and hotels (with a marginal possibility of compact-disc sales as a spin-off for the band).

Carruthers's article, referred to above, quotes the case of an elderly couple from Osaka, who, immediately after seeing the commercials, 'promptly paid extra to have their Australian east-coast itinerary expanded to include a few days at Ayers Rock, which they associated with Aborigines.' And this association is hardly accidental when one looks at the content of the campaign posters.

The design components are fascinating, if disturbing. A Japanese woman, young, attractive and expensively dressed, is smiling as she contemplates the beauty of Uluru and 'Wonder Continent Australia', as the Japanese Kanji script can be most closely translated. The message is clearly: put yourself in this picture—Japanese high fashion meets exotic primitivism and monolithic beauty.

But is there any real *respect* for Black Australian culture being promoted here? The Japanese female is the dominant figure in the foreground, somehow floating ethereally in front of 'Ayers Rock'— and note that it is explicitly *not* named Uluru, although that has been the correct title for the rock since the federal transfer of custody to the traditional owners of the Anangu tribe in October 1985. Then, figured on top of the rock but clearly not *on* it (according to the warped scale of the poster image) are members of the Kumara Dance Troupe, all adorned with ceremonial body paint. Interestingly, the Kumara dancers are based on the Gold Coast and have no formal relationship with Uluru or the Anangu people of the area. Most important, the performers are in the background, static and overshadowed by the Japanese figure and by the rock itself.

In other words, all knowledge of Aboriginal culture is reduced to the form of a souvenir; the desired result is only an economic one, the encouragement of a buyers's decision to invest in a trip.

But what would the elderly Japanese couple hope to find when they arrived in Alice Springs? Would they expect to see an allegedly 'primitive' Aboriginal person on the streets, bedecked with feathers and playing the yidaki? Would they hope to have their pictures taken standing next to an apparently 'authentic' Aborigine, as so many tourists have their photographs taken standing beside a Bobbie when visiting London or a Mountie when touring Ottawa? And where would such a photo be taken? On top of Uluru, as the poster weirdly suggests?

Some might argue that these remarks are all irrelevant. What the campaign is trying to do is elicit an emotional response, to heighten curiosity about Australia. And, of course, it is working exceptionally well—at least in the short term. The problem is that the campaign sets up false expectations. It is simply not the case that 'cultural tourists' will gain a guaranteed access to Aboriginal people of the type they hope or imagine. And as Helen Ross, writing in *Australian Psychologist* (1991, Vol 26, No 3) has noted, 'Cultural tourism creates a demand for face-to-face encounters which are seldom relished by Aborigines, particularly when their small communities (about 150 people in Uluru National Park, 250 in Kakadu) are overwhelmed by over 200 000 tourists per year.'

In other words, hundreds of thousands of dollars might have been spent to discover that throngs of Japanese visitors are eager to interact with Aboriginal people, but has anyone undertaken research to find out if Black Australians wish to interact with the Japanese in such numbers? As numerous commentators have observed, Aboriginal communities are particularly concerned about the way in which their culture is being portrayed. And sold. Whether it is in tourist brochures or in the spiels of bus drivers, Aborigines, according to Helen Ross, are often presented in a 'sensational, outdated, unrealistic and unfavourable light.' Many tourism officials rhapsodise about Black Australians for their own purposes.

Importantly, research is also indicating a growing level of dissatisfaction on the part of foreign visitors to the Northern Territory over the fact that 'traditional' Aboriginal culture has not been presented to them to their satisfaction; that access to Black Australia and cultural tourism is restricted. In fact, unless Aboriginal people become far more directly involved in the planning, organisation and control of tourism, especially in the Northern Territory, this overseas marketing will backfire in a serious way. A 1992 report (*A Study of Cultural Tourism in Australia* (AGPS) by Peter Brokenshaw and Hans Guldberg) found that, while over fifty Aboriginal people were employed as guides in national parks, employment of Aborigines 'by the private sector in hotels, tourist operations [and] tourist transport...[was] negligible.'

Again, racism is found to be systemic. Traditional Aboriginal *culture* writ large is important enough to figure in the vast majority of tourist advertisements, but the Aboriginal *people* themselves?

All of this imagery of Aboriginality is presented as if it is owned by the Australian government, and yet one might ask what kind of respect for Black Australians is being reflected? The ultimate racist bind is that, as Ross notes, 'Aboriginal people are offended, and sometimes blamed for not living up to the images constructed of them. This failure may ultimately disadvantage Aboriginal people in other ways, by under-mining sympathy for national Aboriginal aspirations such as land rights and development finance.'

So, who does benefit from such a tourism campaign in Japan? On one level, Yothu Yindi does, because of increased exposure and record sales. On every level, the ATC does, as does the Australian economy. But do Aborigines *as a whole* benefit? Or have they become just another Australian icon, beside 'Ayers Rock', the koala and the Sydney Opera House? The ATC's construction of 'Australia' carries both benefits and risks, and, needless to say, the risks are not being borne by the tourist promoters, certainly not as much as they are by the Aboriginal people themselves. But the benefits are flowing almost entirely to a tourism industry which has remarkably little direct Aboriginal involvement.

And have the members of Yothu Yindi been consulted about this campaign? Have they seen the final product? Have they been paid for their involvement?

The answers to these questions are central to any debate over the appropriation of Black Australian culture for other ends. As the band's manager, Alan James, commented in a personal letter dated 3 December 1993, the 'ATC exercise' was 'one of the few usages where Yothu Yindi has derived any commercial or marketing advantage.' However, he added—tellingly—that 'our feelings are that overall the usage of the Yothu Yindi phenomena has been of more value to tourism in Australia than it has been to the band.'

So, in addition to representing Aboriginal success, Mandawuy Yunupingu and his band signify *Australian* success, even if they do not fully share in the latter.

Even in the realm of Foreign Affairs and Trade, Yothu Yindi's diplomatic potential has not gone unnoticed. Portions of an official Foreign Affairs report on the band's tour to Papua Niugini early in 1990 are reproduced in a remarkable article published in *Simply Living*'s March issue of that year. Entitled 'Where Ancient Voices Meet', it quotes the Foreign Affairs report as claiming that 'the tour achieved a great deal for Aboriginal Australia, for the Australian government, for the High Commission and, equally as important, for Papua Niugini's bilateral relationship with Australia.'

Here, an Aboriginal band has become an effective arm of federal government foreign policy! This must be some sort of apotheosis for performers in the rock music world—this is certainly far in excess of any brief given to other Australian musicians on overseas tours, even those which are funded by the taxpayer!

And now, set aside all this, we have the mythologising of Mandawuy Yunupingu—he is not only a school principal, not only a musician and Aboriginal leader, he is also rendered as a spokesperson, a diplomat and an advisor in the non-Aboriginal world. This process is accentuated by his selection as Australian of the Year; and he was the first of seven Aborigines to deliver the 1993 Boyer Lectures on ABC Radio National.

Mandawuy's response to the mainstreaming debate has been to cleverly redefine the terms of reference. As he said to Samantha Brown, who was interviewing him for *The Weekend Australian* of 27–28 May in 1989, 'When we came back to Arnhem Land, we came back to our mainstream, don't you see? You have to understand, this is *our* mainstream. Sure, we might have "made it" into what you call the mainstream in *your* culture, but we have our own mainstream and our own structures...we have a mainstream that we talk about, but ours is literal. For us, the mainstream is a literal stream, a stream that carries knowledge. We have streams—knowledge—and they all carry knowledge.'

In addition to his other abilities, Yunupingu has a very poetic appreciation of Aboriginal culture: a Yolngu philosophy of balance which informs all of his work. And this sense of balance and reciprocity is central to the image of the interracial project he is trying to accomplish. As he continues the metaphor, 'Now there are knowledge structures about salt water and there are knowledge structures surrounding fresh water. And there is a point where the two streams meet, the fresh water and the salt water, and where the two meet is brackish water. But that water is drinkable. And where the two waters meet is the place where the two knowledge structures meet...Through our music we are trying to suggest ways and means to build our relationship together in Australia. That will come when we both respect and come to understand each other's knowledge structures and knowledge streams.'

A fascinating philosophy, and one which is as relevant to the republican debate as it is to issues of Aboriginality, ethnicity and gender.

But, despite the appeal—indeed, the necessity—of this political and philosophical programme, I think that even Mandawuy might admit that the conditions for this reciprocity do not yet exist in Australia. This does not lessen the value of aiming towards that state with the energy and commitment he marshals through Yothu Yindi. But if the two streams he refers to are of vastly different sizes—a trickle and a torrent—and if they are conceptualised as being in damaging competition, the metaphor simply does not work. If those from the large, dominant watercourse try to swamp Yothu Yindi with a combination of commercialism, adulation and patronising racism, even the most resilient talent runs the risk of drowning.

As another poet and philosopher of Aboriginality, Oodgeroo, once warned ('Assimilation—No!' in *My People*):

> Pour your pitcher of wine into the wide river,
> And where is your wine? There is only the river.

Nowhere to Go

ARCHIE ROACH

We've been here
for about nine years
And we have watched our children grow
Happy New Year
No resolutions here
Now they have nowhere to go
No they have nowhere to go

A school could be more
than just a corridor
A place where science meets their Dreaming
But they locked the door
What do we need a school for?
We can drown in a bigger stream
We can drown in a bigger stream

Now our children roam the streets
And they let their feelings show
Remember me when they throw away the key
Cos I had nowhere to go

Lies and threats and discrimination
Yeah, we all know the situation
Government says that it's inflation
But it's just another kind of assimilation

How can we be
The best that we can be
When all the doors have closed
And you don't want to see
What's to become of me
Cos this is not the life I chose
No, this is not the life I chose

Now our children roam the streets
And they're moving kind of slow
Remember me
When they throw away the key
Cos I had nowhere to go

Northlands Secondary College, which was 'owned' by Melbourne's Koori Community, was amongst the state schools shut down by the Kennett government in 1992, soon after it was elected to power. Many Koori students, Archie Roach's two sons amongst them, chose to attend a place where they could feel their cultural values were respected at the same time as they were receiving an education. Most of Northland's Koori students are now attending no other classes. The only part of the old school being used is the old hall which is rented occasionally by the government for use as a bingo parlour.

Raki

B WONGAR

They call me Gara. Darky.

Anyway, the night before they took me to gaol my village mother turned up to see us. We didn't notice her come into our shack but as she sat down by our bed her spindle hitting against the floor sounded in the dark. It seemed she was making thread from hemp like she often used to on a long winter's night back in Milinkovo.

That was about a whole life ago—back then she used to use a piece of wick dipped in animal fat which cast a faint light, not so much for her to see the thread, but light enough to enable her to move about without bumping against the walls. But now she whispered loud enough for me to hear her: 'That dreadful war is on again—you are safer without the light.'

Lowering her whisper even further, she explained to me that it would be cold in gaol—by the time they came for me she hoped to have something ready to be worn.

The moon rose and silhouetted the trunk of an old gum tree against our window. It brought some light inside by which you could see Mother's *kudela* and the ball of hemp fastened on top. I could see her fingers pulling fibres out of the ball and spinning it fast into thread.

'I should make you a new linen shirt.'

Would I like it to be dyed in bark of black birch or in onion peel, she asked. But the colour should not matter, she added then—it is often dark in gaol and people can seldom see what it is they're wearing.

Someone yelped behind me on the bed—I thought it might be Angelina. She was only two years old and often dreamed of chasing wallaby or possum out in the bush. I wanted to tell Mother that the young dingoess was my older sister, reborn with four legs and a furry coat, and that she always slept like that behind my back and often kicked me through the night.

'She grew up that way.'

Mother seemed pleased to know that Angelina had been reborn. She kept quiet for a while as she rolled a newly made length of cord around her spindle. She sighed. And she began to speak of the war which had broken out again in our old country. A village next to ours had been burned down: 'Only blackened chimneys still stand.'

She must have felt that I was going to ask where the villagers were going to shelter during the winter.

'Slain people need homes no longer,' she said. 'They all huddle in a large pit.'

Mother stopped spinning for a while, to remove a shiver she'd felt under her fingers in the hemp. She hoped there would be enough thread to weave a bag as well as the shirt, so that she could pack inside some warm damper bread and a ball of feta cheese: 'It'll last you for days in the gaol.'

One of the dingoes snored; that must have been Father. I explained to Mother that Father had gone grey—his whiskers and eyebrows had both turned white. But he was still the pack leader and wary of humans: 'One needs only to point a finger at him and he will snatch at it, even before he growls.'

Mother reminded me that Father had lived through two big wars and that he'd returned home from one of them with eighteen bullet holes in his uniform. But luck does not last forever.

I told her that ever since Father had been reborn as a dingo I had groomed him every day, for he shed his hair often. Mother thought that his hair felt fine. That she was going to mix it with the hemp: 'It'll make fine cords.' She'd found a whole bag of the fur—I'd kept it, whenever I brushed Father, to make a pillow.

Mother told me that people do not use a pillow when in gaol, not in our old country. She moved closer to the bed for a look. In the bottom corner rested two of my brothers, almost grown-up dingoes, but they still hugged together like pups. Mother gently stroked the whiskers of each of them. Then her fingers moved through the hair behind their ears.

One of the young dingoes used to have epileptic fits—it happened rarely, but when the fit would strike him, then my furry brother would lean on me and whimper. There is little one can do but stroke his whiskers and hold him until he feels better again. I was about to tell her that several months ago he was caught in a trap and he'd had to chew one of his front legs off so he could break loose from the metal jaws. Mother thought that dingoes were hardly any different from people. She remembered a child from our village who had lost a limb during the war and lived with epileptic fits for the rest of his life. She sighed again. The new war now was just as ugly as the last one, she explained—a whole group of young men had been found beheaded and mutilated in our village, unable to be recognised, even by their own mothers. She must have sensed that I was going to ask who had beheaded them, because she told me that the man who raided our village during the Second World War was around again: 'He now wears different clothes and a white helmet.'

I wanted to remind her that the raiding of our village had happened a whole life ago and that the SS officer who headed that raid would be too old to wear a uniform any longer. But she said, 'Men like him hang around forever.' Only a handful of people from our village had survived during the last war: 'Lucky you were among them.'

Mother went back to making the threads; for a while only the sound of her spindle could be heard as it occasionally jabbed the ground. On the bed behind me rested the old dingoess, fast asleep. I thought to tell Mother that the old dingoess was actually her—born again. The dingoess was growing old and toothless but only a few years earlier she had given birth to a large litter as a good mother would. So life could go on in time of war. Mother looked at the dingoess on the bed. Then she began to talk about the village. Someone had died there lately, she said, from bubonic plague. I tried to tell Mother that the woman had more likely died from AIDS for I remembered hearing earlier that UN soldiers had inundated our old country, smuggling arms and infesting local women. Mother agreed that the country was swarming with soldiers in blue helmets; they drive about in Red Cross vans, loaded with arms instead of sick and wounded; they stir villagers to fight one another. Mother repeated however that the woman may have died from bubonic plague. 'It could wipe out all of us,' she sighed again. The officer, she explained, who raids our village now had been telling people it was much safer to be put into camps than to stay behind and die from the plague. I thought that the officer in the blue helmet she was talking about must be Kurt Waldheim, from before. I told her that some years ago that same man had become the head of the United Nations. He, like the men who put him there, had often spoken of 'peace' and 'human endeavour'. I felt glad my dingoes were humans no longer and were outside his concern.

Mother wanted to know if dingoes in Australia were rounded up the way people are in our old country. I explained that the dingoes had been condemned ever since the white man had arrived here. For the whites never believed that dingoes could be your dead relatives, reborn. Dingoes had been hunted and trapped, I explained, for centuries— some are brave enough to chew their own limbs off to break away from the trap—others are left to howl for days until they die.

We all kept quiet for a while. Mother sighed again but spoke no word. I felt she was going to ask what would happen to my dingoes when they take me to gaol. 'Dingoes will hold on to the bush,' I tried to tell her. I tried to tell her that they have grown wise enough to live in packs and to stay away from people.

A possum rattled over the shack's tin roof but no dingo seemed to notice it. Mother felt a length of newly made cord and told me it was very strong. She thought that mixing dingo fur with hemp gave the threads extra strength. She expected that there would be enough of it to make a length of cord for me to hold up my trousers. She told me that she had heard of prisoners using cord from their trousers to tie around the bars of the gaol window to help themselves out. She did not say though how one goes out through the bars.

Kudela—plank-like device used by Serbian women to support the ball of hemp or wool during the spinning process
Raki—Yolngu word for rope

What I See

GALARRWUY YUNUPINGU

YUNUPINGU

Politicians come and go but Aboriginal law remains.

People seem shocked when I say things like that. But they are only shocked because these words do not fit in with white fella thinking, which is to get excited because some politician says something today—even though I know what he says will be changed or forgotten tomorrow.

I have stacked a lot of politics into my years, so that is why, when people talk about the situation at Gove, I can't believe that people cannot see the simple truth.

The truth is that Nabalco, a Swiss company, started up a mine on Yolngu land in the early sixties, with the permission of the federal government. They did this without *our* permission and without proper consultation. And even now there is still no agreement with us in place. The mine is on our land and we have no say. But we are fighting for an agreement.

The truth is that Nabalco are even now doing all they can to destroy the harmony of the Yolngu, so we don't get together in a united way. They make special promises to some people, they buy others second-hand Toyotas and give them second-hand mattresses. They are trying to split us up with plain old-fashioned divide-and-rule tactics—beads and trinkets stuff—straight out of the book. They are doing this so that they do not have to make an agreement with the Yolngu landowners, which we say is the only fair and proper thing to do.

Like I said, I have seen and heard a lot of things which make me realise the real reason why many words are spoken.

At Yirrkala, in the early sixties, I saw Harry Giese from Native Affairs stand on a forty-four-gallon drum for twenty minutes and tell us about this new mine and how it was going to be so good for us. That was our consultation.

I have seen, as a fifteen year old in 1963, my father present the bark petition to the government to try and explain our feelings against the mine. I have seen my father's humiliation when the petition, which was our last expression asking the government to leave us alone when all the words had failed, was ignored. I have seen, as a court interpreter, the most senior Yolngu people present ceremonial objects to the Supreme Court to show the power of our ownership over the land. I saw the suffering on my father's face in 1971, when Justice Blackburn ignored all this and said that we did not have a say over our land. That was the first 'Mabo' case.

I saw the bulldozers rip through our Gumatj country. Bauxite mining doesn't just mean digging a hole in the ground—that would be bad enough. It means bulldozing the land, many square kilometres, scraping off the surface. I watched my father as he stood in front of bulldozers to stop them clearing the sacred trees, and chase away bulldozer drivers with an axe. I watched him crying when our sacred waterhole, which was one of our dreamings and a source of our water, was bulldozed. I could see him suffering physically when this was happening, and he never forgave Nabalco for what they did.

Now this town of 3500 people has wrecked our homeland forever.

Later, as Chairman of the Northern Land Council for four terms, I have seen Prime Ministers and Aboriginal Affairs Ministers come and go. I have heard all the promises in the world, and then watched as most of them came to nothing. So when I say that white fella fashions come and go but Aboriginal law remains, people should see that this is true.

It amazes me that people cannot see some simple things.

And that's why I talk about Mabo, because Mabo is about looking back to the time before 1963 and before Nabalco, and even long before Captain Cook turned up. Mabo is about Aboriginal people having a say in what happens on our traditional land. It is about Australian people accepting that we Aboriginal people cannot be ignored any longer, that we are real, with real desires and real rights, and that we don't have to step aside for mining companies.

Mabo is saying what I always knew—that my father's fight was a good and just fight. After being powerless for so long, some people resent that we now have a voice and have to be treated with respect. Now, finally, a law is saying many of these things. That's what I see.

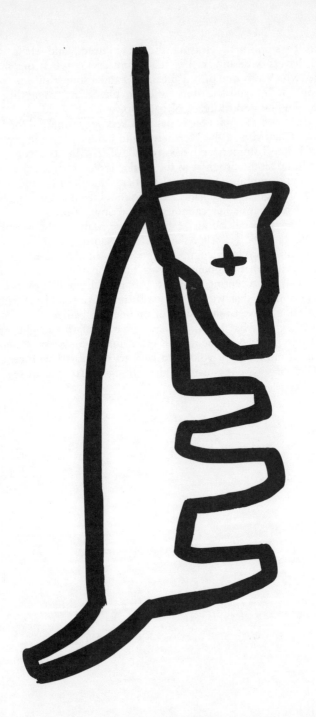

Raki

Rope

TONY HARITOS

I hitched a ride in a land cruiser with a ranger from Jabiru. He was stopping off for a beer at the Leaning Tree Hotel. We entered the cool and leaned on the bar and watched a pair of bikers and their girls playing pool on the verandah, silhouetted against the white light outside. The ranger didn't stop, but I stayed back. The beers were soaking in well and it was a fair while later when a flash of light illuminated the room. The bar door had opened and heads turned. I made out the outline of bandy legs. A small man with a snowy beard stepped in, his shorts sitting under a gut, and hanging below his knees. He was wearing a blue cap, the brim turned up. A younger, taller man with dark hair and a moustache followed stiffly behind. He was wearing a black shirt.

'Hey, Uncle,' I called.

The older man looked at me blankly, blinking to adjust to the darkness inside.

'Alex...,' he waved.

'You made it okay.'

We shook hands.

'Alexis, this is Bill...Bill, my nephew, Alexis.'

'Pleased to meet you,' Bill growled. We shook hands. Firmly.

'Three green cans, please, Jan, when you're ready.'

'No, no,' Bill cut in, 'I'll have a bundy and coke.'

'I was goin' to say, Bill, you're a big bundy man from way back.'

'Sure am,' Bill beamed. He reached down and unbuckled his belt. A pistol, a big magnum or something. The belt was home-made from buffalo hide, with a rough holster. He placed it on the bar and glanced about the room.

'Look, Jan,' he said in that grave tone, leaning forward confidingly. 'Can you put this under the bar again? Just in case. I'll get it from you when we leave.'

'Sure, Bill.'

She smiled at him and then sideways at us. Stratos winked at me and shook his head.

✦

Going back, my relationship with Stratos would have been like anyone else's with their uncle, I suppose, except for the trips. He'd had a twenty-metre cargo boat then, the Milikapati, which he'd bought from the Methodist missions. At the time of my first trip, he had a contract to supply them with stores and aviation fuel. The night we set sail, I went down to the boat which was moored fully loaded by the wharf. The boat was in darkness. I climbed aboard and waited.

The Milikapati sat high and white in the water. She was a good looking boat. She had a cabin and wheelhouse near the stern; forward of that was the cargo hatch, a mast and the fo'c'sle. The mast supported a boom crane which was used to haul out the cargo at the missions. There were forty-four-gallon drums covering the deck.

At last, a taxi pulled up. The passenger door opened and Stratos nearly fell out. He swung aboard and went below and started the Gardiner engine. I sat in the bow, amongst the coils of hemp rope and anchor chain and all the sounds and the smells of a timber ship at sea, and I watched the lights of Darwin disappear and the emptiness engulf us.

◆

Stratos cooked beautiful meals—mackerel cutlets, deep fried, or namas, the fresh raw mackerel flesh soaked in onion, vinegar, soy and chilli for an hour or so; or curries from the 'killers', the buffaloes they'd shot on a trip and hacked up and thrown in the freezer; or his favourite, chicken with soy and ginger and garlic. He'd lovingly ladel the sauce over the chicken steaming in a pot on the old gas burner, and he'd turn with a wink or a smile that suggested his offering was yours.

◆

We unloaded at two missions. I went ashore and wandered about the run-down houses and debris, staring at black kids who stared at me. Young girls smiled and giggled. I kicked a football on the bare oval with the boys, joining in with not much said. Along the gravel streets, men and women sat about in frontyards in the shade beside smoky fires and stared. Stripped houses stood empty behind them, their timber doors and window frames gone, up in smoke. Coconut palms and mango trees stood here and there. There were a few rusted cars lying about.

◆

Later, a year before the 1974 cyclone, Stratos was working out on the Ashmore reef, south of Timor, contracting for an oil company. The company was surveying, dropping charges off the stern, reading the thickness of the earth's crust and gauging the possibility of oil or gas. Stratos worked a grid pattern inside the lagoon while the oil men dropped charges. The explosions astern sent columns of water skyward and a wrenching shudder through the timber hull. Everything lay afloat across the surface the next day, even the tough old gropers. The slaughter, he said, was complete.

A few months later the Milikapati fell apart in a cyclone off the north coast of Arnhem Land, its timbers groaning, the already-loosened caulking coming free. The vessel was kept afloat by the cargo of empty forty-fours in its belly. Stratos and his crew abandoned ship and were picked up by a navy frigate a day later. And the beautiful, white Milikapati drifted onto a lonely beach and quietly fell apart.

Stratos surely must have grieved, just as my father had wept when he lost his boat in a storm years ago. I remember the wet, windy dawn when we'd scrambled down the gully. We stood side by side, watching as the boat was hurled onto the rocks, the timbers smashed to splinters. People weep for timber boats.

And then came Cyclone Tracy, and Stratos's family lost their home. A fortnight after Tracy, I left to start a later-abandoned tertiary course in Adelaide. I returned and found Stratos sitting about, smoking cigarettes and drinking coffee, staring out over the harbour, or getting drunk in the Workers' Club, swapping tales of grandeur with his old cronies. He told me he'd die soon if he didn't get back to work. Maybe that's when I came to really feel an affinity with him.

This was the time of the Vietnamese and dozens of their wooden refugee boats lay rotting about the mud flats around Darwin. Stratos hauled one off the mud, paid the owners the few thousand dollars they wanted for it, dropped in a freezer and an engine, and was back in business and debt, a fisherman again. But he didn't have a licence; he'd relinquished his after the cyclone, and with the government cutting back he couldn't renew it. At the Workers' one day, he ran into Bill, newly arrived from the South and wanting to make it big in the Territory. Bill had a licence and now he had a good fisherman.

A crew was easy to find. The Workers' was always full of seamen on temporary, or more likely permanent, shore leave.

I remember some of the names and their stories over the years. Snowy Rattrey, who ran the Koepanger to Timor for sandalwood and who, during the slaughter in Indonesia in 1965, shipped Chinese to Hong Kong. Eddie Ah Matt and Billy Lew Fatt, both part-Aboriginals who crewed with Stratos at various times. Manny Macrides, the gnarled little Greek pirate who, they say, after Tracy, had already stripped half the wrecks in Darwin harbour by the time the sun come up. Insurance Job Jimmy from Broome, another part-Aboriginal. Jimmy had a million good stories. Once, he was sinking his boat for insurance in deep, clear water out over the Timor Gap. His crew were standing off in the dinghy, about a hundred yards away. He told them not to come near the boat in case they were dragged down by the suction, and then he opened the seacock. The boat began to settle and the crew were idling off, and Jimmy was about to leap over and swim for it when he looked down. The clear water was full of sharks.

'Hey!' he called. 'Come and pick me up!'

'No way, Jimmy. You reckoned suction.'

'Come on. Pick me up. There's big mob sharks down here!'

'Nah. You reckon suction. It'll suck us under.'

Jimmy raced inside and grabbed a rifle and aimed it at them.

'Fuck the suction!'

Who else was there? Hydraulic, who lifted everything in sight. I'd heard of him taking people into Norman Ross Discounts, and inviting them to point out the air conditioner or washing machine they wanted. And Temptation. Her name was Rose, Stratos had told me, but they called her Temptation. He didn't elaborate. Kinjo Yamamoto, whose fellow crewmen were axed to death by Yolngu in the Gulf of Carpentaria in the forties after some 'trouble involving women', and who was walked hundreds of miles to safety by another Yolngu. Barramundi George, who saved Lily Pok Pal when she jumped off the wharf one night, fifty years ago. He used to row a sixteen-foot clinker-built dory across the harbour to go fishing. That must have been an eight-mile round trip. He's long gone now, but she's still alive. When she'd come into our family store, old Mrs Pok Pal would ask my grandmother, 'Mijjij Mijiji (Mrs Megiste), you gottum chooky chooky?' Jimmy Yuen, the wharfie, who my father said was the only drunken Chinaman he ever knew. He introduced my parents to Asian cooking, inviting them over to his house and telling jokes while he cooked on his wok. He'd been on the wharf when the Japanese bombed Darwin in '42. He was thrown into the sea by a blast. A rescue boat came by.

'He's a bloody Jap, throw him back in,' a rescuer said when Jimmy grasped the side.

'I'm no bloody Jap!' Jimmy called in that thick Australian accent of his. 'I'm a bloody Aussie!'

The Workers' was pre-cyclone headquarters and they'd all gather round swapping stories, the parasites clinging to the mate just in off a boat, a pocketful of money and some relaxing to do.

'Hey Stratos, got a tenner?' someone would ask.

'Tenner? Here's twenty! Beers all 'round!'

And after one too many beers he'd inform them again, once and for all, who was the best skipper on the coast. And Rory, who'd been lost at sea with Stratos once for a week in a twelve-foot dinghy when the bowpost on the Capricornia split open outside King George Sound back in '65—he was now running barges up to Irian Jaya—old Rory knew.

'My friends, it is indeed a fact that Strat knows every reef on the coast,' he'd say, slapping Stratos on the back. 'He's hit them all, that's why!'

'I am just a humble seaman,' Stratos would add.

And then Stratos would shout a few cartons of beer down on the boat, so that when the bodies spreadeagled on the deck surfaced in the morning to the deep thump of the Gardiner, Stratos would already have cooked breakfast, the Milikapati would already be out of sight of Darwin, and they'd be the paid-up crew for the trip. Time and tide wait for no man, Stratos always said.

'Ime enas trellos cavalyeros...I am a crazy cavalier,' he'd sing to the old couple who ran the little Greek cafe on the corner, where he'd order dinner. And he'd grab the woman and dance a Greek step between the tables and sing a traditional song about some smuggler who'd swim ashore and lop off the heads of a few Turks.

◆

Late afternoon. Slivers of golden light were shooting into the pub. Laughter echoing. The crack of a ball.

'Old Sugarbag...'

Stratos had started off on another story.

'...He was a Tiwi, see. He worked with us for a while. Great storyteller, old Sugarbag. When I was on the tiller, he'd sit up at night and talk. Sometimes we'd fish over on Melville Island, in Tiwi country, which was his tribal area. For allamoonga. That's Tiwi for barra. Anyway, we'd be walking waist-deep through the creek with barra slung over our shoulders, or up to our necks setting a net, any time of night, and he'd never be frightened. The crocodile was his dreaming see, and the crocs wouldn't harm him. But then over on the mainland you couldn't get him near the water, no way in the world. He reckoned the crocs on the mainland were real bad bastards. He was shit scared. And don't try and tell him any different, don't tell him it didn't make sense. He wouldn't have listened.'

Stratos shook his head. He took a sip of the beer.

'Anyway. One night at the tiller, Sugarbag said, "Hey, Strat, what your dreaming?"

'I said, "I got no dreaming, Sugarbag. White people don't have dreaming."

'"Mmmm, that no good," he said. "Everyone should have dreaming."

'Well, Alex, just then a star fell out of the sky and I said, "Hey Sugarbag, that my dreaming. That shooting star my dreaming."

'And every time I saw a shooting star on that trip, I made a prediction, and you know what, Alex? They were all bloody spot on.'

Stratos laughed.

'And what do you reckon?' I asked.

'Don't know,' he shrugged. 'It's their myth, I suppose, just like we've got ours.'

'Hey, Alex,' Stratos went on, 'I tell you, I wish I'd had a tape recorder then. I could have had the best stories from that old bloke. You know how he got his name, eh? From sugarbag honey, wild bush honey. Beautiful stuff too. He'd clamber up a tree with a tomahawk— and he was even pretty old when I knew him—and cut this bush honey out of it. No problem.'

It was dark outside. A comfortable room, this, and Stratos, the First

Sea Lord, after saluting his companions, was off to the toilet. Bill was sitting back on his stool at the end of the bar, away from us, gravely looking about. I called to him to join in but he nodded no. I wanted to chat.

The bar door opened. It was Patrick FitzPatrick. When I was a kid watching the footy from under the raintrees at Gardens Oval, Patrick FitzPatrick was the best footballer I ever saw. Slightly built, not tall, he was the magical one who made the others look like they were standing still. He'd climb on their shoulders, pull down screamers, weave past their pathetic gropes and kick goals on whatever foot he chose.

He was a Buffalo, a team of part-Aborigines of every mix—wogs, chinks, spics and spans—a sort of outcasts team and the best in town. They'd walk onto the oval, scratching, farting, even puking, which would annoy the hell out of the silvertails, and still they'd win. The Buffalo supporters—and they'd all once played for the team and they were like a family—would roar, throwing beer cans in the air, pounding their eskies, slapping each other on the back and shaking the tears from their eyes. Frail old men, stars themselves back when the meat workers on Bullocky Point first formed the Buffaloes, sat with their wives and mates, watching the youngsters and grandsons come through the ranks.

Then the talent scouts came and made the offer to go to Melbourne. It was big news in Darwin then.

'Go down south, Patrick, and show them mob a thing or two!'

'Patrick'll tear them apart,' the talk was.

'But he's too small. As soon as Patrick starts showing them, they'll fix him...And it's too cold down there. Brass monkey weather, with no mates, no old Buffaloes. It's gonna be lonely down there!'

'And they'll call him a boong!'

Then I heard something about a knee injury and don't know what happened after that. But here he was with a beer gut, a slight limp and a mess of shaggy hair, walking into the pub.

'Hey, Country!' Stratos called to him.

Patrick smiled and walked over. Bill nodded.

'So, you going to stay with us?' Stratos asked, pulling up a stool.

'Country, have a beer!'

'Nah. You know me. I go horrors. One can's too many and a month on the piss isn't enough.'

Patrick and Bill had left the pub an hour earlier, taking the other dinghy. Then just as we walked out the door of the pub, each with a carton of beer on a shoulder, the cops turned up. They knew Stratos and offered us a lift, saving us the long walk to the landing.

We jumped into the back of the paddywagon with our gear. They

55 ROPE

REPUBLICA

locked us in, slamming the doors shut. The wagon rattled down the dark dirt road. I lay on my back with my head on my sleeping bag, looking out at the stars. I saw the Southern Cross framed in the mesh.

'Hey. Better not let 'em see the nets in the dinghy,' Stratos muttered in the dark.

A still mist was rising from the glassy river. The dinghy was cold and damp with dew. I clambered over the springy monofilament nets back to the outboard. Stratos slid the dinghy to the edge of the bank. I squeezed the fuel bulb as Stratos huddled in the front, rolling a cigarette.

The mist, lying soft and low near the surface of the water, parted as we idled through these upper reaches of the river. Up here, the water was fresh, the edges thick with lily pads. I picked up speed.

This dinghy, this creek, this moonlit night, was Stratos. Shivering, I pulled two jumpers from my bag and threw one to him.

Later, I idled into the top side of a gutter by the side and nudged the mud, revving the motor, running the dinghy up a little, sticking fast. I reached inside the outer mangrove branches and grasped a thick, main stem. I'd tie the corkline to the base of the stem and leave the leadline free. A bowline? Yes. Must do this correctly. Megistes did these things right.

◆

At five, Stratos rose and boiled the billy.

'Mozzies. What mozzies?' He laughed at my complaints. 'Slept like a baby...You have to get used to it.'

'Obviously.'

He lit a cigarette and sipped on his first strong black coffee of the day.

'Ah, this is the life,' he smirked with a hint of overkill.

Stratos wandered over toward the dinghy resting now halfway down the steep mud bank to the river. He untied the taut rope from the tree. The dinghy didn't budge. He cursed and absently flicked the rope.

Suddenly the suction broke and the dinghy began sliding. The rope was whizzing through his hands as he tried to slow it down. The mud dried on the rope was rising like smoke from his hands. 'Oh,' he called quietly. 'Oh.'

I leapt to my feet and rushed towards him. The dinghy was still sliding and picking up speed. The short rope came to an end and Stratos gripped it tight. The dinghy began to take him with it. Heels dug in, he skidded over the bank and flew off the edge. He disappeared from view.

I rushed and looked over the lip. Stratos was just a torso and head, the rest of him was buried in mud. The dinghy was sitting quietly in the water and he was still hanging onto the rope.

With all the respect I could muster, I tried not to but couldn't. I laughed. Loudly.

Stratos squinted up at me with a look of hurt pride. Then he smiled and laughed himself.

'You know, Alex,' he said, shaking his head slowly, wringing the mud from his hands. 'A bloke'd be a fuckin' mug to do this for a living.'

We were both laughing.

The river surface steamed, swirling in parts with the last rush out of the tide. Patterns along the bank took shape before the dawn. Clumps became mangroves, distant rounded shadows became hills. A flash off the water as the sun first pierced earth's skin. The pale shroud was lifting slowly.

We'd pulled the three nets and had a good haul. Some threadfin and catfish but mostly barramundi. My hands were slashed from freeing the gilled fish with a screwdriver, but I felt contented as we rounded another bend and saw the Nanhai.

The Nanhai was a typical Vietnamese fishing boat, heavy-timbered and narrow, with a square stern and straight sides. A basic box cabin stood near the stern, the freezer forward. A few forty-fours sat on top of the cabin. Rusted fastenings streaked the sides.

Bill was asleep, up front, it turned out. Patrick was out in the other dinghy, up the island hunting turtle eggs.

Mary stepped out of the cabin. She was in her early forties maybe and she'd seen better days. There were a few bruises on her arms and one on her neck.

'Hey, Strat,' she called.

I climbed up and looked inside the cabin. It was small. A grubby double mattress leaned against one wall next to two old rifles. Potatoes and onions hung in bags from nails in the roof. Boxes and tins of rolling tobacco, matches, cartridges in a plastic bag, thin battered cowboy novels and stained Mills and Boon romances lay scattered on a shelf. In one corner on a bench was a rusty gas ring surrounded by a circle of old oil and food droppings, which was some work of art. Also chipped plates and greasy mugs, blackened pots, tins of coffee and powdered milk, jars of sugar and rice and spaghetti. And four plates of steaming breakfast. I don't think a meal ever looked or smelt so good.

Later, I couldn't wait to get the filleting finished, because then I could sleep. You sharpen your thin-bladed knife on a spittle-covered stone to get the edge just right, testing it along a finger. You delicately slice down the edge of the top fin of the fish, the cut just right. Bad filleting means less fillet and less money, so you get it right. What's left is a bare backbone with a sad, untouched, shapely head and tail. The spent carcass is hurled overboard. And the fillets are then packed into meshed plastic trays to freeze, and the frozen blocks go into cardboard cartons. About fourteen kilos a tray, Stratos reckoned. Six trays we'd caught—a good night's work.

◆

The Nanhai had turned with the tide, which was strengthening fast. The nylon line was creaking under the strain. Stratos squinted and rose. He walked to the bow.

'Can you give us a hand with the anchor rope, Alex,' he called. 'Want to let out some slack.'

Stratos began untying the knot off the main bollard.

'Now,' he said, 'We'll just ease the line out forty feet, then retie it. Okay?'

'Right.'

Stratos slipped the last hitch off the top of the bollard. We both took the strain, letting the rope slide through our hands. It was hard to hold.

'This boat's a heavy bastard,' he muttered.

The rope slid. Then stopped. From below in the locker the coil wouldn't budge. A tangle had caught.

'Shit.' Stratos shook his head. 'I'll have to go down and free it. No slack to do another turn either. Reckon you can hold it?'

'I'll try.'

He let go and scrambled down into the locker. He picked at the tangle. The rope slipped a fraction. I tightened my grip. The rope slipped. Then held. It slipped again. I couldn't hold it.

'It's going!'

'Just a sec.'

I held. It slipped.

'Shit! Hold it!' Stratos yelled.

I looked down. The knot had tightened on his hand and he was being pulled out of the locker. His hand was being crushed. The rope was sliding and he was being dragged up nearer my hands and the bollard. If I didn't let go my hands would be mashed on the bollard. If I couldn't hold it his hands would be.

'Hold it!' he yelled.

I strained one last time and held it a moment, and he freed himself. He leaped up and whipped another turn around the bollard.

I inspected his hand. It was burnt and he'd lost some skin.

'Christ, that hurt,' he groaned, shaking his fist.

'Sorry mate.'

'Wasn't your fault. I should have checked the rope was free. You know, in this game you can't rest up a second or you're gone.'

I held up my hands; they were shaking. My legs felt weak.

'Let's have a beer,' Stratos said. 'We've earned it.'

He pulled two cans from the freezer. We opened them and sat down.

'Whathappen'?' Mary called sleepily from the mattress inside.

'Nothin',' Stratos answered.

'Ropes just aren't your dreaming, are they?' I said.

'They'll hang me yet.'

Later, we were silently watching an eagle gliding overhead, and Stratos asked me, rising.

'Another beer?'

'Paris a city?'

We sat and drank cold beer and soon Stratos was in a story-telling mood. He told of his great-great-something grandfather on his mother's side. Manuel the Turk they'd called him, because of his willingness to kill them. He was from Spetsas and fought the Turks before and following the uprising in 1821. After they won freedom Manuel went to Athens. Then when the Greeks introduced a foreign monarch he protested fiercely—peasant mentality, he'd claimed—and he was imprisoned and due to be executed. But he escaped through the sewers of Athens, picked up his sweetheart in Hydra and sailed east to Kastellorizo, the last island in Greece, the last point of Europe. Before the fighting he had been a shipwright by trade and a smuggler by choice, and in Kastellorizo he became a trader between Marseilles and Odessa in the Black Sea. Then things went bad and he returned to smuggling.

The sun was going down as Stratos told the story, and he was glowing. Maybe he was happy to be sitting on the edge of a reef with the sun going down over the open sea and with a beer in his hand.

'How're your hands?' Patrick asked, holding his pale palms up before the firelight.

'Sore,' I said, 'but a good sore.'

'Coffee?'

Patrick filled the billy and placed it on the edge of the fire. Water spilled over, sizzling in the flames.

'What was that story you were going to tell?' I asked.

Patrick stared into the blaze. He reached over and poked about.

'Well, I had a message from Leaning Tree. From cousin Johnny at the Land Council in Katherine. So I rang him up.

'"I think we found your mother," Johnny said. "She's down FitzPatrick Creek, near Bounty River...She lives there."

'This old woman reckoned to Johnny that my father was a policeman down that way. Sergeant Thomas Patrick. That's how I had a white name. But he'd gone away and never come back, then I came along.

'She reckoned to Johnny, a few years later, the welfare mob came up one day when she was off getting food at the river. When she came back I was gone. Poor fucking bitch, eh?'

Patrick heaved, throwing a stick into the fire we had.

'So, when I got the call from Johnny, I had to go and see this old woman and find out. But I was really nervous. Where do I come into it now? Is she my mother anyway? Does she even speak English? God, is she a dirty old gin with straggly hair like I've seen 'em in the beer garden at the Parap pub. My mother? I don't know a black woman, not really, not one who's lived in the scrub all her life. We never wanted to be black when I was in Darwin. At school we used to put shit on them, put them down. We used to call the blacks "boongs" and "coons". We half-castes'd try and be white. At the pubs we'd even bash the blacks. I guess we all got sucked in.

'Johnny said he'd bring her up to Katherine, but I said no—I wanted to go down to FitzPatrick Creek, to the camp.

'And it was really dirty, with only a bit of water, still in shacks and humpies and with hessian and stuff just like I remembered, or how I imagined it. Dust everywhere, empty tins of bully beef, beer cans, bottles. The camp was excited. They all must have known that I was coming. People came running up and crowded around the Toyota. Then they took me to this woman, this old woman, and she was like I thought she'd be. Old and with grey hair and shiny blackfella skin and big wide blackfella nose. She was dressed up a bit, in a nice new cotton dress, and her hair was brushed up. We just stood there and looked at each other, with everyone standing around watching. Kids were giggling.

'Then she started crying and wailing. "My boy, my child," and some Aboriginal language. She knew. They all knew. And we hugged each other. And the camp broke up too. Women were wailing, old men were carrying on. But I felt a bit strange. I didn't feel anything much for her, not really. I didn't feel that, you know, like "Oh, my long-lost mother, my people," or anything. She was a black woman. I dunno.

'Well, Johnny took us back to Katherine, and now she's gonna live there for a while. We stayed together for a week. We're kinda friends. I believe she's my mother, and since I've been back here it's sinking in more...'

'What are you going to do now?' I asked.

'Dunno, dunno...' he said.

I wandered up to the bow and stretched out on the sleeping bag, using the coiled anchor rope for a pillow. I dreamed. When I opened my eyes, Stratos and Patrick were looking down at me.

'Dreaming?' Stratos smiled. 'We were just letting out more slack on the rope.'

'I'm here,' I muttered, still half asleep. It was near dark now and cooler, but I was wet with perspiration. I leaped out of the hot, damp sleeping bag. I stripped and threw the bucket overboard; pulled it in and poured the water over my head. It was crisp now with the sun gone and the sea breeze billowing in. I heard a shout.

'Don' Bill, don't!' Mary cried down in the cabin. 'Leave me alone you mongrel dog! You don't fuckin' own me.'

I heard the dull thud.

'You filthy slut!' Bill yelled. 'I'll teach you! I see you near Patrick again, I'll kill you, you black bitch!'

'Bill! Don't touch her again,' I heard Patrick call.

'You keep out of this.'

'I'm telling you. Just don't touch Mary again, okay? Punch her again and you'll go!'

'Yeah, see this gun?!'

'Bill, don't!' Mary yelled.

There was a dull thud of fists and I rushed down the deck. Everyone was screaming and swearing, Mary was bleeding from the mouth and Bill and Patrick were rolling near the edge, almost falling into the strong current. Patrick had Bill pinned to the deck and was laying into him. Stratos was hovering on the edge.

'Take the gun!' Patrick yelled and Bill twisted again. They were on the edge, Patrick's head right over the side, his back arched under Bill's savage weight. Bill gripped him by the throat. I grabbed at their legs to try and pull them back in. Stratos was pulling at them as well and suddenly he got caught up. They rolled over on top of him, crushing him there against a bollard, and he grunted dully as if he'd been winded. The three of them rolled again and went over the edge, into the dark swift tide.

Mary screamed and all I could see were splashes as they drifted quickly astern. I jumped aboard the dinghy tied alongside. Mary whimpered, 'hurry, hurry.' But they were already gone.

'Grab the spotlight!' I called, clamping the alligator clips onto the battery terminal, squeezing the fuel bulb with the other. The light burst into life, pointing up at the sky. I pulled at the starter rope. Nothing. Come on. I pumped the fuel again and pushed in the choke. Nothing. Again. The motor screamed and I spun the dinghy in a wide, fast arc. Mary was hanging on with one hand and guiding the powerful beam with the other. I headed straight astern from the boat, skimming along high on the plane. I throttled back. They should be around here. Mary was moving the beam in slow, broad sweeps.

'There's someone!' she called, pointing the beam, and a dark head bobbed. One arm rose, waving at us. It was Bill. Where's Stratos? Patrick? I turned and headed straight at Bill. Even from this distance I could see some fear in his eyes.

'Reckon we're gonna run you down, Bill?' I turned away a fraction and throttled back at the last moment and slammed the outboard into reverse. The outboard leg leapt up, the prop screaming. Bill threw a drenched arm over the side.

'Come on, get in!' I yelled, tugging at the arm. I grabbed his belt and pulled the big frame over. The dinghy tilted, and Bill lay heaving on the nets.

'There!' Mary called, and I spotted something along the beam. I twisted the throttle and the bow lifted. I saw him. I idled in close, and could just make out the outstretched arms, hanging over a low mangrove branch. Then I saw his head just above the water. His hair was hanging over his eyes. It was Patrick. He waved. 'Hey, where ya been?'

'Where is the old bastard! See anything?' I called to Mary. 'He must be out there.' I spun out and around, over again but nothing. Further up? I idled along, the current taking us along a few knots as well.

'What's that,' Mary called. Red eyes glowed, and I could see the gap between the eyes. A big bastard.

Was he dead? Had the old fella finally gone feeding the crocs?

'Look,' Mary called. No, that was a log, racing and tumbling a little.

It was when we were back and I'd cut the motor and we were gliding in that he appeared out of the cabin, framed in the light.

'Billy's boiled,' came his voice. Mary sobbed and covered her face with her hands.

'You fucking old bastard,' Patrick groaned and threw him our rope.

'When we went over,' Stratos said, 'I was kicking around and I felt a rope. Someone left the stern rope on the dinghy out. I just hung on till I got the strength to pull myself in. I yelled but no one heard. Then you pissed off in the other dinghy. And we had no ammo left so I couldn't fire a shot.'

'Jesus,' Mary said, 'we thought you were croc bait, eh?'

'Not me. Not yet.'

'That rope *must* be your dreaming,' I said.

'Must be.'

Australia Day, 1994

AMANDA LOHREY

LOHREY

The twenty-fifth of January and the morning of my daughter's dress rehearsal for the official New South Wales Australia Day ceremony at Darling Harbour. It's another hot and humid day in an unrelenting Sydney summer. Often on a school holiday like this, I would begin to think about taking her to the pool, but on this particular morning my daughter is in full uniform, sitting on the kitchen step trying on her new black boots. And I realise that while I have signed the consent form for her to participate in the ceremony I am only vaguely aware of why she and her classmates will be there. Something to do with flags, I recall.

'What are you actually doing in the Australia Day parade?' I ask.

'We're flag bearers,' she says, intent on lacing up her imitation Doc Martens.

'What kind of flag?' It may seem a silly question but in these ceremonies children get to wave all kinds of flags.

'I'm carrying the white flag,' she says.

The white flag? Which one is this?

'There isn't much white in the Australian flag, is there?' I say, thinking aloud. 'Only the stars of the Southern Cross and a few white stripes in the Union Jack.'

'No, no,' she replies, frowning with mild impatience. 'You know, the *white flag*. Not the Aboriginal flag, not the Torres Strait Islander flag, the white flag.'

'You mean the Australian flag? The one with the Union Jack in the corner?'

'Yeah, that one.' She sighs again, as if pained at having to spell out the obvious. 'Have you seen my blue headband?' And she stands, pleased with her new boots, and wanders off to the living room to search for her headband, leaving me to sit at the kitchen table and ponder the 'obvious' or, more precisely, the gap between what is obvious to me and what is obvious to a ten year old growing up in the inner city of Sydney in 1994.

THE INTERREGNUM

This is a narrative about what I am going to call the interregnum, that is, that period in the nineties when we move from being the old Commonwealth of Australia, presided over by the Crown, to the new republic of Australia, presided over by God knows whom; when we rewrite our constitution and rethink the symbols of our nationhood, including the flag. We may even decide on a new day of national celebration that doesn't focus primarily on colonisation.

When could the interregnum be said to have begun? Some would argue for 1972–1975, the era in which the Whitlam government changed the national anthem from 'God Save the Queen' to 'Advance

Australia Fair', retitled the Crown as the Queen of Australia and took a number of other relatively unobtrusive steps like removing the crown insignia from post boxes. I would be inclined to argue for this as a pre-interregnum phase: for me the interregnum proper begins early in 1993, on the day that Paul Keating made his electrifying speech in the House of Representatives on Britain's responsibility for the fall of Singapore and its abandoning of Australia. Another definitive moment in the interregnum is Keating's speech on Aboriginal issues at Redfern Park, later in the same year, and the signal it gave of an intention and a political will that was to culminate in the Mabo legislation. And there is more to come. Australians are supposed not to be passionate about their nationalism but I don't believe this to be the case. A significant number of them are very passionate about it, as the current debates about the monarchy and republicanism reveal. What Australians are not, on the whole, is psychotic about it.

THE FLAG BEARERS

For the New South Wales Australia Day ceremony, the flag bearers are to be drawn from three public schools—Lansvale East and Liverpool, from the outer metropolitan area, and Darlington, from the inner city. Darlington Public School, which my daughter attends, is a medium-sized government school (circa 200 children) that stands at the intersection of Abercrombie and Golden Grove Streets and occupies a small space of territory between Newtown and Redfern. One of the few modern schools in the inner city (opened in 1975), it has the predictable multicultural blend of students, one third of whom are Koori, though not all of these are drawn from nearby Redfern.

Everywhere in the building (red is the dominant colour), there are signs of Koori culture; large art displays on the wall, some of them drawn by Koori artist Neil Thorne (who is also a full-time teacher at the school) as well as smaller signs such as the labels on the toilet doors: 'janagan/BOYS' and 'dubaygir/GIRLS' (a smaller sign beneath each says 'Bandjalung Lingo'). There's a Community Room for the local Koori community run by Koori Education Officer, Norma Sides. The school has its own Aboriginal dance troupe and music group and there are three didgeridoo players in the amazingly eclectic school band; but other cultures are regularly featured in school ceremonies. Not surprisingly, the overall emphasis is on cultural diversity.

Five years ago, Darlington was in decline. Its numbers were down to around fifty students, almost all Koori. The school was perceived by white parents in the area as a problem and they avoided it. Then in 1989, when the small (sixty children) Blackfriars Infant School in Chippendale was threatened with closure, the staff, aware of an almost empty school up the road, negotiated with the Education Department for an amalgamation of the two schools, and the Blackfriars staff and kids moved in. To quote former Blackfriars and now Darlington Principal—Colleen Hayward: 'It was Captain Cook's invasion all over again.'

The new teachers joined with those of the old who chose to stay on in their commitment to a quality education for Koori children, and that included, and includes, the fostering of Koori tradition and values. There are two Koori teachers in the school, one under the Aboriginal Early Language Development Program, and one teacher recruited in the ordinary way who happens to be Koori. In five years the school has become one of the most highly regarded in the inner city, by white and Koori parents alike.

A few weeks before Christmas, a longer than usual circular was sent home to the parents by the Principal. The Education Department Performing Arts Unit, which is often co-opted into the management of public rituals in New South Wales, had invited Darlington and the two other schools to participate in the Australia Day ceremony at Darling Harbour. There were to be several official events around the city on the twenty-sixth, including the re-enactment of Governor Phillip's landing, but the Darling Harbour ceremony, set for late in the afternoon and presided over by Prince Charles, was to be the climax of the day.

This invitation presented Colleen Hayward with a dilemma. Many of the students and parents in her school would have no truck with an Australia Day celebrated on 26 January which commemorated a white invasion of Aboriginal lands and the destruction of so many Aboriginal people and their traditional way of life. Nor were there only the local Koori parents to consider. There was a wide spectrum of opinion, oppositional and not so oppositional. Several of the non-Koori parents planned to travel out to La Perouse on the twenty-sixth to join with Aboriginal people from all over New South Wales in commemorating Invasion Day. Others objected to what they regarded as chauvinistic flag-waving ceremonies of any kind—'mindless nationalism'; some had no objection to nationalist celebrations as such but objected to the monarchist element in the form of Prince Charles; others were 'ecstatic' at the opportunity for their children to participate. And there were parents, like me, who were in two minds; it seemed an interesting opportunity for a child to think about many of the current debates about what it means to be Australian, in a dramatic and experiential way.

In the end, Colleen Hayward decided that, handled right, participating could be a valuable educational experience. This was a time of flux, of changing attitudes. Nothing was set in concrete, and the ceremony was there, after all, to be debated: a site of contradiction that might be more productive to engage with than to ignore. Or as Colleen put it: 'I'm going to get into trouble if I do something and I'm going to get into trouble if I don't do something and I'd always rather get into trouble for doing something.'

And so a somewhat long-winded circular was sent out expressing reservations about the ceremony and an appreciation of those Koori parents who preferred to boycott it, while at the same time setting out the educational reasons for participating. And the parents of three Koori children agreed to be in. On Monday, 24 January, twenty-one children assembled outside the school and waited for the bus to Lansvale East Public School where the first flag-waving rehearsal would be held.

After the first rehearsal, Colleen Hayward spent a sleepless night. The children were not to wear school uniform (which featured the school's Koori motifs), as at first thought. Instead they were to be given special Australia Day T-shirts (dark blue with green and gold wattle on the pocket) and each child was to carry an Australian flag. 'I lay awake thinking that whatever I did would be wrong, but some things would have to be renegotiated. I remembered Jack Beetson from Tranby College (Tranby College is an Aboriginal educational institute in Glebe) and the course he ran on Aboriginal issues for Sydney University's Continuing Education. The one thing that came through in that course was this: if you are somewhere and don't object to racism, then you are part of it. Clearly it was going to be my job to inject the Aboriginal element into whatever it was we were about to do at Darling Harbour.'

THE DRESS REHEARSAL

On Tuesday the twenty-fifth, the children are conveyed to Darling Harbour where the dress rehearsal, complete with military bands and speechmakers, is to be held. Here the pomp and pageantry are already underway and the children begin to get excited, although the more impressed the children become the less the teachers are. The tenor of the event is to be much more militaristic than they had expected. In the morning, the children are lined up in formation and told that they are marching behind the Heritage Band. An officer in the band steps forward and asks the children if they know what the Heritage Band is. No, they chorus.

'Well, he says, this band represents the first people to set foot on Australian soil.' At this point the teachers gulp and look at one another. He did say 'the first people', didn't he? And not 'the first white people'? The children look at him blankly for a moment until their attention is distracted by one of the nearby militia producing a bayonet, and then it's on with the parade, the flag bearers sandwiched between the Heritage Band and some mounted police in the costume of colonial troopers. Ahead of them march several phalanxes of the armed forces and the New South Wales police. 'I'm surprised at how militaristic it all is,' says one of the parents attending the rehearsal, 'and how *British*. I thought that sort of thing was all in the past.'

The combined schools contingent is to be made up of a group of forty children in the front, wearing the national costumes of their countries of origin and representing the ethnic diversity of contemporary Australia. These children are from Lansvale East and Liverpool Public Schools where particular ethnic communities are represented in larger number than at Darlington. Behind the national costumes march another forty children wearing Australia Day T-shirts and carrying Australian flags. Among these are the Darlington children who don their harnesses for the first time and stand very still, almost to attention, while the tall flags are inserted into their canvas sockets. As this process is taking place one of the non-Koori children asks: 'Where's the Aboriginal flag?'

It was a good question, says Colleen Hayward. Leaving her Vice-Principal Pam Hubbard in charge, she approaches the Education Department representative on the organising committee and raises the question of the Aboriginal flag. The Department officer agrees that it should be represented and agrees to put the case to the ceremony's Protocol people. After a long discussion with the Protocol people, approval is finally granted and two additional flags are brought to the rehearsal site—the Aboriginal flag and the Torres Strait Islander flag. Meanwhile Colleen makes a mental note to stop off at Black Books at Tranby on the way home and buy three T-shirts bearing the Aboriginal flag for Darlington's three Koori children to wear.

Rehearsal day is a day for thinking on your feet.

When in the afternoon the extra flags arrive there is a further issue to be resolved, namely, the question of their placement. How to display them without their being swamped by the forty Australian flags? The first row of schoolchildren is to be made up of three *ethnic* children in national costume and one *ordinary Australian* child (the organiser's words). They can't add a Koori child carrying a Koori flag onto this row without throwing out the symmetry of the marching formation, made up of rows of four, and they can't move one of the ethnic children back from the front row without offending both the ethnic group (and the school) that the child represents. As luck would have it, Darlington has miscalculated on numbers and turned up with twenty-one children instead of twenty. This means one left over from the formation of rows of four. Colleen Hayward points to her smallest Koori child. 'Look,' she says, 'Lauren is extremely small. Why not let her carry the Aboriginal flag and march alone in front. Because she's so small she won't obscure the others in the front row and everyone will be happy.'

The organisers agree. Thus it is that the Aboriginal flag gets to lead the flag-waving contingent into the arena.

Late in the afternoon of that day, the children line up for their final walk-through. As they are marshalling in front of the Exhibition Hall and the Aboriginal flag takes its place at the front, a parent of one of the ethnic children approaches Colleen Hayward. 'Why are you having this (Aboriginal) flag?' she asks. 'You should all march under the Australian flag. We are all Australians here. We should be one under the Australian flag. I and my family came from Chile but we are Australians now and we carry the Australian flag.'

'Yes,' says Colleen, accustomed over the years to instant debate in a number of forums. 'But it's different for you. You chose to come here. Aboriginal people didn't choose to be invaded. They were forced under the sovereignty of the British crown. The Australian flag means something quite different to them, especially with the Union Jack in the corner.' At this point, the children are summoned to enter the arena and the woman withdraws, still murmuring her dissent.

Finally, at around 8.30 pm, after a long hot, tiring day, the dress rehearsal straggles to a halt and is dismissed. The children line up for the buses that await them at the back of the Exhibition Centre where they are instructed to return the following day, at 4 pm sharp, to Darling Harbour.

THE SITE

Darling Harbour is Sydney's number one site of public spectacle. Any student of what art critic Peter Fuller called the 'shared symbolic order' of our culture need look no further than downtown Ultimo for a spatial emblem of the hectic eclecticism of a style that might best be described as post-modern Sydney carnivalesque. But like many new or emergent spaces, Darling Harbour presently promises more than it delivers. For one thing, it cannot deliver depth-time, that is, rich and resonant memory, because it is too new; it has no symbolically inscribed History (as opposed to the lesser [h]istory of mere origins). Here is the post-modern city in its newest and showiest detail, a chaos of surfaces that 'quote' at random from elements of the social; objects plonked down, here, there, anywhere (as if the planners had blindfolded themselves and used a series of pins), without a rationalising structure or narrative.

From the very beginning Darling Harbour was a political project, in both the narrowest and the broadest sense: it was Sydney's major project for the 1988 Bicentennial and Australia's biggest (a fifty-four-hectare site), the country's most ambitious and imaginative urban-renewal scheme. Its show-piece and the building that defines its skyline is Philip Cox's Exhibition Centre, five staggered halls on a podium with a vast roof of white corrugated steel from which rises a fretwork of great white spires, masts and cables, clearly intended to suggest the rigging of old sailing ships. This graceful quotation from colonial history—stylised, light, white and pristine—is the definitive image of how a post-modern culture might assimilate and project its past: free-floating, sanitised and without burden.

Darling Harbour is as close as you'll come in the Australian urban landscape to the post-modern notion of collage city. There is no beginning (because there is no narrative), only approaches: Chinese gardens with traditional stone lions, ornamental pagodas and gold carp ponds; a children's playground with swings and slides shaped like comic-book castles and coloured in bright pastels; an authentic, fully restored carousel with gold-tasselled horses and heady wurlizter organ; a bronze sculpture of sheep jumping over a fence rail into the sheep dip; a modernist water sculpture with Zen influences, a spiral inlaid into the ground so that children remove their shoes and tread gingerly all the way down to the centre; a modest rectangular harbour where ferries ply their languid trade; a tinsel fun park with dodgem cars and ferris wheels; tennis and basketball courts with bronzed adolescents in chic new NBA gear; a smart coffee shop concealing a state-of-the-art gym; the Aquarium; the National Maritime Museum with historic ships moored outside, including a huge rusting hulk as counterpoint to the brash white cruisers berthed further along; the high white tracery of the shopping arcades and food hall (American burgers, Japanese tempura) designed like a modern day Crystal Palace; the new Novotel hotel for Japanese tourists, a flattened out and elongated Mayan temple built from meccano, outlined against the night sky in a bold squiggle of neon. And around all this, the futuristic, pale blue monorail, while overhead the Ultimo freeway cuts the sky in half, its grey concrete sweep diminishing the effect of the avenue of tall palms. Behind this pleasure park, this Antipodean Xanadu, is the fire-gutted shell of the old wool stores, the tarted up exterior of the Powerhouse which was once a power station and is now a museum, and the stolid Victorian freemasonry of the Goldsboro Mort building, soon to be turned into luxury apartments. Everything here is reminiscent of or has the potential to become something else.

Darling Harbour is not Hyde Park. Nor is it the Domain. It has supplanted both as Sydney's main forum for public congregation. No Grecian temple of high art here, no French designed neo-classicist fountain, no neo-fascist war memorial, no Sunday afternoon spruikers or banner-waving rallies. And Darling Harbour is most definitely not Harry Seidler's Australia Square. Darling Harbour is the defeat of modernism, the defeat of repressed desire and repressed history, the defeat of uniformity and the search for a meta-language or a meta-narrative that would tell one story and one story only.

Its critics argue that on this site history goes from being repressed to being trivialised or carnivalised; to being broken up into random elements of free-floating spectacle, rather like the exhibits in the foyer of the Powerhouse Museum where a seventeenth-century steam engine from the English Industrial Revolution is displayed alongside a nineteenth-century French clock, without much explanation of either. In Darling Harbour, different stories, or fragments of narrative, jostle for attention in a layout so chaotic, so insouciant, that the visitor might feel equally at home, or not at home, with any of them.

Amidst all this, the most domesticated, the most vernacular space must surely ·be that modest spread of green turf situated opposite the Exhibition Centre and known as Tumbalong Park. Bordered by a low stage and makeshift grandstands, Tumbalong Park resembles nothing so much as the sports oval of a country town, one of the hundreds of small ovals—dry, featureless, empty—dotted across Australia. Somewhere in this playground of spectacle and consumerism is a site where even the National Party can feel at home. Modest in scale, unpretentious in character, Tumbalong Park is to be the site of the Official New South Wales Australia Day ceremony. I could almost say that, amid the stylised elements of spectacle that surround it, Tumbalong Park appears incongruous; but so eclectic a melange is the whole of Darling Harbour that for one element to look truly incongruous would be impossible. The site is so full of contradiction that in the end the outcome must surely be the annihilation of the *effects* of contradiction.

Anything goes.

And what, I ask myself, does this mean? What are the politics of this? Is contradiction being celebrated here? Or simply cancelled? If modernism denies contradiction, then what does post-modernism do? Celebrate it? Or trivialise it out of all reckoning?

AUSTRALIA DAY

The morning of the twenty-sixth. Another hot and humid day. We draw the curtains in a vain attempt to keep the house cool. In the early part of the day, I keep my daughter home to rest. With muted excitement, she consents to playing indoors and spends the morning washing her hair and preparing her 'costume'. After lunch, she sits in the dim little front parlour of my 1870 cottage (built on what was once the estate of Governor Bligh) and watches a Madonna movie about women in baseball called *A League of Their Own*.

At three o'clock, I pack an afternoon tea into her schoolbag. She is too excited to eat now but we have no way of knowing when she will get to eat dinner and I don't want her fainting from hunger. My memory of state occasions held in the hot sun is that one child always faints, and one soldier in the guard of honour. We climb into the car and drive through Ultimo to the massive parking station beside Chinatown, at the eastern end of Darling Harbour. From there we join the throng on the concrete walkways to the vast white Exhibition Centre where most of the Darlington children are already gathered within the air-conditioned coolness of one of the halls. Colleen Hayward is there, having spent the early part of the day at La Perouse where some of her other Koori children are commemorating Invasion Day. Behind her a squadron of khaki-uniformed soldiers are noisily rehearsing their drill, their barked commands echoing up into the high white spaces of the roof. Several police, in full dress uniform, stroll self-consciously across the glossy floor of the hall.

I kiss my daughter goodbye, tell her to have fun and I walk, reluctantly, out into the stifling heat. As I push against the heavy glass doors, I hear one of the Darlington children say to a nearby adult: 'Guess what! We're marching in front of the Prince's jeep!'

Because, of course, HRH Prince Charles, Prince of Wales and son and heir to the Queen of Australia, is to be the special guest at the upcoming ceremony. Charles has arrived only two days before as part of his brief ten-day tour to restore his domestically tarnished image as a less than devoted husband and a somewhat eccentric heir to the British throne. His trip has been 'realistically' planned as low-key and low security and until today, he has been met with a friendly but luke-warm reception. It is to be characteristic of this day and its rituals that there is some ambiguity as to the Prince's status as a participant in the ceremony. Is he to appear as a special guest, that is, as an outsider, or is he here to preside over something that is his, that is, as a symbolic stand-in for the Queen of Australia? The fact that few people in the rapidly massing crowd could vouch for either with absolute certainty is one of the signs that we have entered into the interregnum.

THE CEREMONY

A lot of things will go bang during the Australia Day ceremony, including the now infamous starting pistol of David Kang.

One of the timeless and enduring images we have of politicians is of clusters of men wearing dark suits on a hot day. And here they are, a solemn knot of them on the dais, with their smaller and more festively adorned wives. So dark and so uniform are the suits that from a distance it is difficult to distinguish the politicians from the security men. Only the Prince wears a suit in a lighter shade, and he sits in the middle of the front row with none of the ponderous Victorian heaviness of the Premier or the sharp contemporary stylishness of the Mayor, both of whom look, in their own way, completely at home. No, the Prince sits and gazes at the proceedings with a slightly distracted air, and the unmistakeable detachment of the observer.

As always at Darling Harbour, there are many Asian and Arab faces. Like me, some of them are sitting on the grass of Tumbalong Park. On my right is a family of Japanese tourists, two parents, son and daughter, who accept with smiles the Australian flags that are being handed out among the crowd by officials. On my left is an Anglo family whose young son gets excited when the ceremony's co-compere, Stan Grant, takes his place at the microphone on the dais. 'Look Mum,' he points, 'there's the guy from Real Life.'

The first item in the official ceremony is announced as 'The Dance of the Icons', to be presented by Hammondville Primary School. Forty or so children, dressed in extravagantly designed costumes, frolic about the dais as waratahs, sprigs of wattle, jars of Vegemite, Minties and Fosters beer cans. The centrepiece of this is a young swagman, a boy who appears, from where I am sitting at the back, to have a dark skin. Could he be Koori? (Maybe this is an ironic gesture by a tongue-in-cheek schoolteacher, well up on the latest research that indicates that the hero from *The Man from Snowy River* was in all likelihood an Aboriginal stockman.) The crowd offers up its languid applause and as the Icons run at full pelt from the ground, the choir starts up with that dated dirge, 'Song of Australia'. This is one of several tepid renditions of mediocre songs (without which no state occasion would be complete) and it is followed by the recitation of a poem. Is it the Catholic character of Premier Fahey that decides this particular item— a 'Prayer for the Nation' read by Father Paul O'shea? Father O'shea wears a dark lounge suit and red tie and speaks the words of his colleague, Father Hugh Murray, who is ill and unable to attend. As poetry it's basic ('where many lives weave a wondrous strand') but occasionally trenchant: 'to restore justice after the greed and ignorance of our forebears.' Sorry, what was that? *Greed and ignorance?* Is he talking about those same forebears who read the proclamation of George III in Botany Bay (re-enacted in costume early this morning), who founded, among other things, the Heritage Band? Trust a Catholic to say something irreverent; they have become respectable over the years, but sometimes they can't help themselves.

FIRE (I)

It had to come, I suppose: 'A Salute to our Fire Fighters'. Premier Fahey takes centre stage, looking as always like a headmaster about to deliver a warning homily. Everyone falls silent. For the crowd this promises to be the most galvanising event of the programme (it has no way of knowing what David Kang has in store for everyone). Fahey says a few words of opaque circularity ('we are building upon the Australian spirit which makes us what we are...') and then stands silent while a blaring melange of recorded highlights from the commercial news coverage of the recent fires bursts forth from loudspeakers and echoes across the ground. It's not easy, in the carnivalesque collage of Darling Harbour, to evoke the ground of catastrophe, of burning bush, and the 'highlights' are discordant and jarring rather than evocative and moving. A procession of bright red and yellow fire trucks trundles onto the grass arena and the crowd stands (mostly) and claps along to the band's rendition of 'Click Go the Shears', 'Tie Me Kangeroo Down Sport' and 'The Road to Gundagai'. When eventually the crowd settles down after its one spontaneous outburst of feeling for the day, the New South Wales Commissioner for Bushfire Services, Phil Koperberg, a man built like a brooding cube, makes a moving speech free of conventional pieties, with a distinct quality of the heart. When he is twice chivvied by an official who thinks he has gone on too long, he makes a sardonic, almost bitter joke about not letting the heroism of his men and women get in the way of the official programme.

CITIZENS

But enough of real life. On with the ceremony.

By far the most stylish element of the entire programme is the citizenship ceremony conducted by the Lord Mayor, Frank Sartor. Remember when citizens were 'naturalised'? A naturalisation ceremony might be conceivable in the Sydney Town Hall but surely it's unthinkable at Darling Harbour where nothing is natural and everything is a stylised parody of something else. Not that there is anything natural about the Town Hall, but it does belong to a culture that constructed itself as 'natural' while Darling Harbour belongs to the culture of the simulacra, the flagrantly artificial.

Sartor, whom I haven't seen in public before, brings a distinctive style to his officiating which is difficult to label and which I'm going to call, simply, Australian contemporary. It is laid-back but considered, authoritative but not patriarchal, serious yet somehow insouciant, with a sharp edge of brevity and intelligence that contrasts with the self-regarding sanctimony of Fahey. Sartor manages to get the tone just right. Three women and three men (all cosmetically selected, all young and presentable) are called up to receive their certificates. Each is accompanied by a flag bearer bearing his or her flag of origin. From memory, there are two from the United Kingdom, one each from Russia, South Africa and Korea and, forgive me, but I forget the sixth. As they descend from the dais and begin their walk back to the Reserved grandstand, Sartor concludes the presentation with the words: 'Ladies and gentlemen, you've just seen the making of six new Australians.' This sounds much more impressive than it looks in print, partly because he omits that dreary word, 'citizen', but chiefly because of the tone. Perhaps because Sartor's own parents were immigrants, it does not sound condescending; no hint of *noblesse oblige,* indeed the reverse, a slight undertone of challenge.

And still the Prince hasn't spoken. An interminably dreary choral rendition of 'I Still Call Australia Home' follows the citizenship ceremony, and then, finally, it is announced that HRH will present the school prizes. Charles stands and begins to walk towards the microphone, to languid applause.

THE PRINCE

Prince Charles is different from other members of the royal family. And it's not just because he's more, or at least *as,* interested in urban design and the environment as he is in horses and dogs. No, it's something else; it's that wherever he goes and whatever he does, he exudes that most un-Windsor like characteristic, a sense of almost melancholy irony. This sense of irony creates around him a permanent aura of uncertainty which seems perfectly apt for a post-modern prince. Take the nervous mannerisms. Can anyone recall having seen the Queen display a nervous mannerism? She is the most composed public figure I have ever observed, almost inhumanly so; a perfect icon of the Anglo-centric fifties.

After he is introduced, the Prince stands, and walks slowly to the front of the dais. At that moment, I hear a gunshot. At least I think it's a gunshot but then, considering for a moment, I decide that, no, it has a more familiar sound (I'm not accustomed to guns), like a firecracker. I look at the Prince. His head turned slightly, he looks inquiringly across the dais and nervously adjusts the cuff link on his left wrist. Just then, three more 'shots' ring out in rapid succession. The crowd gasps and people in front of me leap to their feet obscuring my view. My husband and I stand up, hearing the sound of a tremendous crack on the dais, and I see a pile of dark-suited bodies wrestling on the stage. Looking at this absurd, writhing tableau, my pulse quickens and I feel slightly sick. A woman behind me collapses onto the ground. 'Oh, my God!' she gasps, 'they've shot the Prince!'

The rest of us just stand there, staring into the heat haze of the afternoon.

But no one is dead, or even wounded. A tall, grey-haired security man shields the bemused-looking Prince with his body, the security man looking anxiously over his shoulder to see if the assailant, who seconds before had run up the steps and hurled himself across the stage, has been contained. Co-compere, Penny Cook, addresses the crowd in the ringing tones of a schoolmistress and asks them to sit down and settle down. 'Don't be alarmed, children,' she adds, 'everything is okay. The situation is under control.'

The security police march a young man dressed all in white away behind the Police Band and out of sight. And it's as if he had never appeared. On the dais, the men in dark suits re-compose themselves, adjusting their jackets, straightening their ties, patting their ruffled hair and taking their seats again. Order is restored. The Prince is still standing to one side of the stage. The Governor rises and introduces him a second time, as a 'very courageous and brave man' and the applause this time is a good deal louder than before. The Prince has become transformed, momentarily at least, into an underdog, he-who-almost-might-have-been-assassinated on Australia Day.

He begins his walk towards the microphone and then hesitates. There is a long pause of silence, of uncertainty. Is the Prince in shock? A dark-suited official approaches, mutters something discreet into his ear and the Prince steps up and begins to speak into the microphone. There is nothing in his demeanour to suggest that he is shaken, except for a few unnaturally elongated vowels in his first sentence; a kind of defensive, ironic drawl. 'Oh, well,' he begins, 'it seems I have to make a speech. I thought I was going to get away with just making the presentations but it seems I have to say something.' Oh well, he seems to be saying, just wheel me on and I'll do whatever you like. I know the game's nearly over.

FEU DE JOIE

And now, after that false climax, the *planned* coup de grace. The original procession of armed forces and schoolchildren that had escorted the Prince onto the ground and then marched off again now marches back. I crane my neck in the hope of seeing my daughter (the only reason I am here) but she is obscured. So is the Aboriginal flag. The armed forces line up on the grass arena and the children line up in front of the dais. The various chiefs of staff and Police Commissioner walk slowly and solemnly down to the centre of the arena to take the official salute. High above the dais on a special platform built for the occasion and in front of a giant Australian flag, twenty-one servicemen raise their rifles and fire off a twenty-one-gun salute. At this, many of the children, lined up in front of the dais, jump with alarm. The final gesture, then, is to be one in which national identity is to be equated definitively with territoriality and its symbolic armed defence. Believe it or not, this jarring display of arms is listed in the official programme as 'Feu de Joie'. *Joie* indeed! After the unplanned intrusion of that other gun, albeit 'only' the starting pistol of David Kang, this strident display of arms, this piece of military theatre is less than thrilling. It doesn't say *pageantry*. What it says, all too bluntly, is *guns*. With cannon it might somehow have been different. They're ornamental now, almost quaint, and they give off a fine booming rumble that resembles nothing so much as thunder and can produce the same momentary elation as a storm. But the sound of a rifle is a mean, whining high-pitched *crack;* the sound of the sniper. And the effect is of a sour aftertaste.

Better the vapid songs, the empty speeches, the children dressed up as cans of Fosters lager; better all of that, interminably, than one minute of this. To me, the decision to make this the final climactic gesture of 'celebration' says everything about the Liberal imagination in Australian politics at the current time.

And as if we haven't heard enough bangs for one afternoon, there are several more loud retorts as firecrackers explode in the air, releasing tiny parachutes from which hang suspended small Australian flags. But by this time a hot wind has sprung up and these are soon blown away. What's left is smoke; smoke from the guns, and the firecrackers, wafting across the arena.

DID THE PRINCE DUCK?

Back in the cool interior of the Exhibition Hall, we congregate alongside some of the other Darlington parents, waiting to collect our children. Two of the fathers who had been involved in shepherding the flag bearers tell of how peremptorily they had been dealt with by the security men, and there are tales of how, backstage, even Kate Ceberano's mother had been pushed up against a wall and searched until she could establish her identity. 'They got everyone but the right bloke,' says one of the fathers. We all agree that there had been an uncommonly long pause between the pistol shots and the assailant's headlong run at the stage, plenty of time for him to have been intercepted. 'Look at those security guys,' says one of the fathers, 'they've all got grey hair. They're past it. The older ones might have the experience but they need a few twenty year olds with quick reactions.'

'What about Charles?' someone calls. 'How did he react? Did he duck?' No, I say, he hadn't ducked, he'd kept his dignity. He'd looked momentarily disconcerted, and then, oddly uncaring. That detachment again.

'I was standing in the line as he walked off the field,' says one of the mothers, 'and I found myself clapping him. And I'm a republican! I hope none of my friends see me on national television.'

'What did the children think of the Prince?' I ask Colleen Hayward, who by this time has joined us.

'They liked him,' she says. 'On his way out he stopped and lifted one of the kids' Australian flags out of its holster and said: "Are these things heavy?"'

At this point my daughter runs up beside us, flushed and elated and dressed in her Australia day T-shirt that is too big and reaches down to her knees.

'And you know what?' adds Colleen. 'You know that mother who objected yesterday to the Aboriginal flag? Well, just before the parade started this afternoon she came up to me and said: "I've been thinking about what you said yesterday and I think you're right."'

She turns to her son. 'Come on, I'm exhausted. Pam (her Vice-Principal) and I feel like we've been doing Aboriginal Studies for three days.'

FIRE (II)

There remains only one thing to do, which is to work our way through the thickening crowd and climb the long elevator of the shopping arcade so that we can stand out on the white tracery of the balconies, overlooking the water and the city skyline, and wait for dark and the firework display. When it comes it is just as you might expect, unannounced and completely chaotic, without any semblance of pattern or design.

From two flat barges moored on the water, a series of fireworks explode, one after the other, cascading in showers of coloured sparks. High on the terrace, we're crammed in among hundreds of other bodies. My daughter stands on the rim of a giant terracotta pot, her hands resting on her father's shoulders. All along Darling Harbour the crowd is packed to a standstill, craning their necks up at the purple laser beam emanating from Sydney Tower and raking the sky at random intervals. From the tops of five of the city skyscrapers, ranged around the harbour, cones of fireworks fizz up into the sky in intermittent jets of pink and yellow and blue. Out on the water, on two floating platforms rigged up with canvas canopies, musicians and singers play and sing, their images projected onto a giant screen beside the funfair park. But the acoustics are terrible, their amplification is lost and they can barely be heard against the din of the fireworks.

And then, on the far side of the wharf, a giant crane is activated and begins, slowly, to draw from the deep water a huge Australian flag. With the high slippery sheen of wetness, it emerges from the black water of the dock until at last it waves in the tepid breeze beneath the exploding showers of light.

'Look,' says my husband, laughing, 'it's torn.' And sure enough, the bottom of this monstrosity has caught on something beneath the water so that the lower half of the Southern Cross has emerged into the raking spotlight, ragged and dripping and incomplete.

At that moment the last shower of sparks subsides. The fireworks are spent. My husband lifts my daughter down from the rim of the potted palm. 'Australia Day, finito,' he says.

THE LATE NEWS

Not quite, as it happens.

When we arrive home, my daughter resists going to bed. 'I had the best time,' she says. And I envy her, remembering an age when I could enjoy any kind of party in an uncritical way—before, that is, politics entered the scene. But finally, overcome by fatigue, she gives in and after she has gone upstairs I sit with my husband and watch the late news. Who was this man who might have shot the Prince of Wales? The news replays the incident in an uninspired and unworried slow-motion, and to everyone's surprise the starting pistol man in no way resembles the images of the urban terrorist or the psychopathic crazy. Is it another sign of the interregnum that the not-quite-assassin is not some joker republican but a young Chinese student protesting about the continuing incarceration of Cambodian boat people locked in detention centres in Sydney's Villawood and Western Australia's Port Hedland?

The incident is written up in tabloid outrage as 'Australia Day shame—All the horror in pictures', as well as the more sanguine, 'Charles the Lucky'. 'Defenceless but calm amid the chaos, Charles waits for order to be restored.'

David Kang, in his early twenties, is described as 'an Australian arts student of Korean descent from the exclusive Sydney suburb of Hunters Hill.' Kung is said to have posted over 500 letters appealing for help for the Cambodian refugees, many of them to heads of state. One of these letters had been to Prince Charles, asking him to visit Villawood while in Australia. It emerges that Kang also wrote to ABC broadcaster, Andrew Olle. 'I have come to realise representing the boat people is the most *un*popular thing to do...*UNPOPULAR!* Nobody cares, nobody gives a damn. Please understand me, I have become too tired and exhausted.' Olle eventually manages to contact Kang's sister, Caroline: 'The fact that the boat people are forgotten, he just thought...if he didn't do anything, if he just got on with life and forgot about it, then he was doing the same thing as those who were doing nothing,' she told Olle.

It is only after reading this that I remember that my daughter's partner in the the official New South Wales ceremony, marching in the Australia Day procession, carrying the Australian flag, had been a girl from Lansvale East School called Sid. Sid was from Cambodia.

THE MORNING AFTER

On the Saturday morning after Australia Day I sleep in. When I get up and wander out into the kitchen my daughter is sitting at the table with her art set spread out above her drawing paper.

'What are you doing?'

'I'm designing a new flag.'

This isn't so surprising to me, as the previous year her class had been given the design of a new flag as one of its assignments. At that time, perhaps because she had been learning some Yothu Yindi songs for the school band, she had favoured Mandawuy Yunipingu's simple transformation in which the Union Jack is removed from the current Australian flag and the Aboriginal flag replaces it in the top left-hand corner. Today, however, she is drawing a series of flags for a display on the fridge, including, at this moment, a very accurate Union Jack. 'I quite like the Union Jack,' she says, deftly etching in a series of red strokes. 'You know, just as a design. Not for Australia.'

'What's *your* choice?' I ask.

'This one.' She shuffles through various bits of paper and produces a drawing in which the blue and white Southern Cross occupies the right half of the flag. The left side is divided into two blocks of green and gold. Drawn squarely in the middle is a large brown Kangaroo.

'I like this one,' she says. And with that she pushes back her chair and strides over to attach her drawing to the front of the fridge.

'Do you like it?' she asks.

'I like the overall design,' I say, tactfully, 'but I'm not crazy about the kangaroo.'

'I am,' she says. 'It tells you that it's Australia.'

Yes, but does it have to be a kangaroo? I've never liked animal iconography. On this occasion, however, it seems pointless to argue. There will be other flags, other designs on that fridge before long. This is the interregnum.

CODA: THE INTELLECTUALS

14 February 1994—How to be Australia

The Dixson Room of the Mitchell Library of New South Wales is a gloomy space, a long way in feeling from the bright white spaces of Darling Harbour. The two great windows are hung with heavy magenta silk blinds which are kept permanently drawn so that the room is always used in artificial light. There's a huge oak bookcase filled with ancient leather-bound volumes, gold embossed. Sombre oil paintings decorate the walls, among them Sir Joseph Banks, and Henry Goulburn (Undersecretary for War and Colonies) and next to them a landscape, *Sydney from Bell Point*, in which a cluster of dark figures occupies the middle ground of an open field.

There are sixty people gathered here for one of the series of seminars that are the culmination of Professor Donald Horne's 'Ideas for Australia' project. This one, listed as a Round Table Discussion, is entitled 'How can we celebrate Australia?' The Chair is Philip Adams, writer and broadcaster. Other participants are Professor Sol Encel, political scientist; Dr Elizabeth Kwan, Research School, Social Science, ANU; Joanna Kalowski, anti-discrimination conciliator; Dr Helen Irving, School of Social Science, University of Technology, Sydney; Dr Chris Cunneen, Australian Dictionary of Biography, ANU; and Associate Professor Peter Spearritt, Director, National Centre for Australian Studies, Monash University. All are seated at dark wooden tables, while above their heads hangs a large silk flag, a new design featuring the Southern Cross.

Among the audience there is a heavy sprinkling of the faithful Library Society women...and hardly anyone under fifty. I read my programme and discover that the panel seated at the head of the room have just come from an Intellectual Breakfast. This was held at 8 am in the library coffee shop, aptly named The Glasshouse (almost too apt really and if I were writing fiction I would not dare to call it this). So what is an Intellectual Breakfast? Intellectuals benedict? Compôte of research fellows? There's something innately absurd about the title and this is a bad sign, bad because it betokens a worrying lack in the organisers of this programme of any sense of the ridiculous—an essential quality, you would think, in those preparing for the task of devising Australia's new symbolic order.

Donald Horne stands and begins by addressing us diffidently as 'Fellow Citizens'. This sets the tone of the forum: we are among polite suburban Jacobins. What are the things that can hold Australians together, he asks, announcing that he and the others taking part are looking to formulate a 'civic minimum', a kind of minimalist glue. After a few more remarks which are hard to hear (bad acoustics), Horne sits with the audience and hands command of the proceeedings over to Chair, Philip Adams. Adams gives an opening address that is his usual style of tongue-in-cheek deconstructive. He is here to argue for an irreverent democracy, a post-modernist, good-humoured democracy. The best image for Australia is not the big rock that splits under pressure, but a large bucket of gravel. As for a new national flag, he favours the Dickie's tea towel, or better still, no flag at all. Australia could be identified by an absence. ('Whenever anyone around the world saw an empty flagpole they'd think of us.') He then announces that this seminar is to take the form of an imaginary exercise, a simulation. We are to imagine that this is the year 2001, and the panel a committee which has two weeks to 'sort out the celebrations'.

First question: What is to be our national day?

Helen Irving begins the discussion. She thinks we should celebrate several days instead of one and suggests making some acknowledgment of 9 May, the day the first federal parliament was opened in 1901. Someone else suggests 10 May, commemorating the day in 1962 when the national vote was given to Aborigines. Why not Wattle Day, comes the suggestion. It is, after all, the beginning of spring. Someone else on the panel, I don't remember who, has by this stage developed reservations about both 9 and 10 May—too close to Mother's Day (8 May). It makes no sense, after all, to have all our celebrations at once. At this point contributions are invited from the floor.

A member of the audience stands: Why not make United Nations Day our day of national celebration? That way we could recognise 'the true equity of all cultures'. This prompts an interjection from the floor: Why not 1 July, the beginning of the fiscal year?

Things are getting out of hand. Tongue-in-cheekiness can only take you so far. We must hurry along, says Adams, the clock's ticking over and we still haven't come up with answers for 2001.

Sol Encel asks the question: Why all this focus on federation? Why not commemorate Henry Parkes's speech in Tenterfield or the Constitution Convention at Corowa (30 July)? I'm not quite sure why but somehow the subject of Mother's Day comes up yet again. This surprising and touching preoccupation seems to periodically swell and subside as the discussion moves from panel to floor and back to panel again. Jo Kalowski says that on balance she favors 1 January, but really she thinks we need more spontaneous eruptions and demonstrations— like the quickly organised parade for the firefighters—rather than officially staged, fixed-in-the-calendar days. (Adams: Do we need a regular catastrophe to ensure these occur?)

This is all a bit too much Sydney for Peter Spearritt who intervenes to put the Melbourne view. He agrees with Helen Irving that we need not one national day but a number of days. What we can't afford, he says, is a repeat of the 1988 experience where 'all the celebrations centred on Sydney and most of the money got spent in the one spot.' Let's have lots of submissions, he says, for money from different groups around the country who can each hold their own day—Tenterfield Day, Dubbo Day, and so on.

Floor (1): You could have different days for various regions.

Floor (2): The English don't have a national day at all.

Chorus: Yes, they do, what about St George's Day?

Floor (3): What about 26 January? That was the day selected by the Emancipists and children of convicts to 'celebrate our land, boys and girls, our land.'

Is it Chris Cunneen who at this stage suggests 22 September, the morning Ewart Smith was awakened by a magpie which gave him the idea of defeating the Australia Card? To commemorate this 'extraordinary democratic triumph' over the state would be to have a national day that was about argument and protest *against* government (unlike other national days that celebrated the state).

Sol Encel: In that case, what about the Eureka Stockade?

This produces a long pause. Nobody knows the date.

Adams: November the Eleventh? A day of National Recalcitrance?

Floor (1): Too close to Christmas.

Floor (2): Why not all of February? Any day in February is a nothing day.

This almost nihilist suggestion seems to function as a signal to Adams to call a halt. We'll have a referendum, he says. Hands up for (and he calls out the options). The winner is 1 January.

Now, says Adams, our panel has to choose a flag.

Following up her suggestion that we have several days of celebration, Helen Irving suggests we also have several flags. She points out that in 1901 on the day of federation no one was sure what flag to fly, so they flew several.

And the next round of debate begins. A strong feeling emerges for the Southern Cross, in some form or other. It was the flag of the Anti-Transportation Movement and has been associated with various other democractic movements: it would therefore be a good flag to teach in schools. Sol Encel wants to put the map of Australia on the flag (Spearritt: an actual map or a logo of it?).

Floor: There's a question of dignity here. If 1 January is the national day there will be too many people sleeping off hangovers.

At this point a discussion on flag etiquette follows, the point of which eludes me, but then by this time my concentration is on the wane. Perhaps I lack the stamina for this sort of thing.

Floor: Let's have the lyrebird.

Adams: Too hard to find, and too fussy in outline. Too hard to reproduce.

Panel member: Let's avoid any form of cross, it's too Christian.

Adams: Lots of nations use things in the sky—the crescent, the sun—what about the rainbow to signify multiculturalism?

Professor Henry Reynolds (historian) from the floor: Don't look up, look down. I like the Northern territory flag with its red earth. Most of Australia is red earth.

Floor (interjection): No, it's not.

Peter Spearritt: I think we should adopt the Aboriginal flag.

Adams: I don't think that would get past a referendum in Queensland.

And so it goes on, from Uluru to various sprigs of wattle, until a referendum is taken in favour of the Southern Cross.

And there is much more to come—national song, national honours, citizenship ceremonies—but I am flagging. It's like listening to talk-back radio: fun at first but then wearying. There is another hour of this to go before a break, so I gather together my programme and the various pamphlets and position papers given out at the door and slip off to the CBD for a coffee.

In John Ubaldi's new coffee shop, Euro, just down the road from the library but a world away from the Dixson Room, I take up a table among the young property analysts and investment brokers who read their reports over short blacks and iced water. I spread the 'Ideas for Australia' material out on the table. I am, as usual, in two minds about what I have just heard. There's something about the panel format that seems to guarantee a degree of intellectual laziness, not to mention political gaucherie. On the other hand, there was something in the forum's good-natured silliness that was reassuring. No ugly symptoms, no nationalist psychosis, no latent hysteria. Everyone at the forum had more or less enjoyed themselves and there was a marked element of civilised playfulness. This of course had much to do with the limited character of the audience. There was no Tony Abbott with his 'muscular Christianity' (one of the kindest of euphemisms), no Bronwyn Bishop and her diehard troops from the land of the Crown and the Orange Lodge.

And the tone of the printed material was in keeping with this; 'dry and unremarkable', an editorial in *The Australian* later judged it. Reading the pamphlet *What is a Citizen?*, I thought it a bit like listening to Mr Chips: on the one hand amiably ponderous ('Our own word, *citizen*, comes down to us indirectly from the Romans: their word was *civis*. To be a *civis Romanus*, a Roman citizen, was a cause for pride at a time when Rome ruled virtually all the known world'), on the other quippy and light-weight with a certain carelessness about language ('How can we celebrate [civic identity] in a way that would *ring true*?'; 'Could the top awards in Australia be *lifted in scope*?'), as well as an apparent blindness to the resonance, ironic or otherwise, of its own metaphors ('How can we *hold together* ?').

Sitting in the Euro, and thinking back to the events of Australia Day, it seems to me that when the time comes for the big all-in stoush between the proponents of change and the forces of reaction, the ground troops like Colleen Hayward will be well under way, but the intellectuals might have to try a little harder. Certainly they will need to come up with arguments more intellectually robust and emotionally compelling than those aired in today's seminar, especially if they are to demonstrate that significant change has already taken place to the point where we can neither go backwards nor stand still. And that people like Bishop and Abbott are not the beacons of a new populism—more like the last gasp of Empire.

With this thought, I leave the Euro and walk on down Bent Street into Bond Street where the usual small crowd is gathered outside the black granite edifice of the Australian Stock Exchange. I join them for a moment to stare at the giant electronic scoreboard that can be read through the plate-glass window.

Today the board is advertising its free weekly Lunchtime Lecture Programme in the Stock Exchange Theatre. A talk by Ian Huntley (of

Huntley's newsletters) is being offered—'Developing Your Portfolio—Investing Verses (sic) Speculating'. The lights blink. The board goes blank for a moment. The numbers come up. *Gold 2346.7 All Mining 1027.8 All Resources 1297.0 All Industrials 3295.6 All Ordinaries 2012.9.*

And it's business as usual.

The Australian Crawl

ROBERT ADAMSON

I watched your body fluttering across
the pool, your hands little buckets
chucking water on the flames. The bushfire
was background music as the kids

sploshed about in the wading area.
All this time and we believed our bodies
meant something, life at least.
Birthdays shivered up our spines

sparks in the pallid undergrowth of hair
greying and uncurling. In this dream
our first picnic sails along
on a blanket just above the flames.

The women wearing gingham frocks
making it seems so very sad, Uncle John
juggling his belly on a tricycle.
The bacon rind on the sliced bread

a wizened hieroglyph meaning nothing,
the cucumber circles sitting on the sockets
of your mother's eyes. Back at home
on the shelf conch shells

sitting next to books become
little inkwells of nasty beliefs.
The silver we never used dancing
on the table like soft silver tadpoles

sequential meanings drift into meltdown.
The pale headed rosella a smudge
on the bathroom mirror, the whole house
full of an awful music chuffing

and percussing into your head—
a rat a tat and an Australian
Threadfin Salmon came down South
while you were fishing hookless in the sky.

A picture becomes three-dimensional,
it's Tassie the cat, fleas scooting down
his tail into the fishtank, outside cockatoos
flurry, inside a Wettex shivers in the sink.

Rock Carving with Kevin Gilbert

ROBERT ADAMSON

The fish outlined on the rock
is the shape of a mulloway.
We are moving here
under a fine yellow rain

pouring from the spear wound
in its side. A lyre-bird dances above
trembling the morning silk air.

We fish with two swamp harriers,
sweet whistling killers like us, who cut
fish throats and clasp up

bunches of silver-nerves—
calling under stars convicts
hacked in cliff face.

We crush oysters with rocks
and throw them as berley into the tide
we call our Milky Way,

after a while stingrays
come on the bite, and one after
another, brown-winged,

hump-backed, yellow-bellied
bullray, fights to its death—
but we cut some free to watch slide

over carvings of themselves,
back into the drink, as the rock mulloway
moves its shallowing groves.

Secrets

BRIAN CASTRO

(Semi-darkness. Railway waiting-room/bar. Beam of red light on a bar counter. Print of Magritte's Time Transfixed on the wall behind the bar. A panama hat on the counter. Empty glass. Half-full whiskey bottle. Actor, who appears to be in his late thirties or forties, is dressed in a white, slightly dirty, linen suit, tie loosened, sitting on a bar stool beside a table. He is unshaven and wears wire-rimmed spectacles. There is a white handkerchief in his top pocket which he takes out from time to time to mop his brow. In another pocket is a can of spray deodorant. A saxophone on a stand next to him. Doctor's bag on the table, opened to reveal little shelves of bottles, syringes etc. A stethoscope entwined around the handle. A phial and a hypodermic in clear view. The scene is in three movements: red, blue and yellow. There is a slight pause between each.

Takes out his white handkerchief. Gestures to the audience.)

D o you know anything about loneliness? (Mops his brow.) 'You don't know what loneliness is, boy,' my father told me once at the gun club. He squeezed off two shots and then stepped back onto my spectacles, crushing them. I was blind for two weeks. But it was then that I heard my mother's sighing...amplified. Heard the prostitutes upstairs. The murmur of the streets. The hiss of the iron as she pressed his cold suit, the same one the Vinnie's people came to get when he died in Australia twenty years later.

Then once on the phone I heard him say to a woman who asked for him in a soft voice: *Do you know anything about loneliness?*

(Puts hanky back in his top pocket.)

(Red lights turn up.)

That was when I knew my father and I shared no secrets.

(Pause. Smiles. Beckons with his hands to the audience to move in closer.)

Come in. Come in. Make yourself at home. Meet the family.

(Suddenly frowning.)

'The family, they fuck you up.' Freud. Or was it Nietzsche? Well, that's the translation anyway, by Philip Larkin, the English poet who, like me, was into jazz and porn. Blues and blue movies. Phonography. That's the technical name.

(Plays a few lascivious bars on the saxophone. Puts it back on its stand.)

Schoolgirls like to hear that, when they come in here for abortions. Puts them at ease. Before the pain. The needle. The payoff. The penalty for love. Of course, whenever I fall in love now, I think constantly of death...even when showered with kisses from those I'd saved from it. A masterful practitioner.

(Holds out his hands.)

Steadiest hands in the business.

(Pause. Takes out handkerchief. Wipes his glasses.)

So much for love.

I first heard the word 'fuck' when I was seven. The English word. I liked it immediately. It had the sound of a cork being pulled from a bottle.

(Demonstrates in mime, making a popping sound with his lips.)

F-f-f-f-fuck!

Every Saturday we used to have steak. It was gristly and I tried to swallow without chewing. When I choked, Father uncorked the bottle and poured me more wine. 'Fuck!' I once yelled across the table...in pure happiness...and then ducked, waiting for his fist, but he burst out laughing instead. *Fuck* became a pleasant word. (Sighs.) Those were temperate times.

But the family never intended anything pleasant. Nobody pointed out the evening light, the pall of the city, the mystique of the Orient in the long day's waning. I used to mark each day off and worry about how I'd get through the next.

(Straightens up and tightens his tie.)

Well, I'm still here.

(Lights dim. Red hues.)

Listen.

(Sound of a steam train, approaching.)

It crosses the bridge over Prince Edward Road, Kowloon, Hong Kong. It used to come from China; once a day, every day of the week.

My father told me of the turmoil 'over there'; 'across the border'. Fascinated by the border, fascinated by the train, by the beast which came once a day, every day of the week, I imagined the train bursting into our lounge room. Years later I saw a painting by Magritte. It was the same train, coming out of the hearth. It was...(indicating the print on the wall)...'the train of History'. Uncontrollable. Coming from the outside into our lounge rooms. And it was always louder on Sundays, puffing across the border.

My mother washed her hair on Sundays. She wrapped a towel around it and cried very softly, reminding me that Magritte's mother drowned in a river, her nightgown wrapped around her head.

The train came across the border on Sundays. And my heart began to beat faster. But history no longer promised anything. It turned around just past our place and it went back.

(Sound of train receding into distance.)

One day, for an excursion, we walked to the border. I looked out over the barbed wire. The land was essentially the same. But the people...I was told...the people weren't free. I looked at them. They seemed happier than my family. Happier than me.

(Lights bright red. Train can be heard very faintly.)

(Sings softly.) Chattanooga Choo Choo, won't you choo choo me home...a ditty from eternity. God, I wish I had amnesia! Head full of tunes and no vision.

On the way back from the border I stuck things I found on the railway line; a Zam-Buck tin, a broken clog. The next day, playing beside the line near Embankment Road, I saw the train stopped. It was chugging, breathing silently. I ran, thinking I'd caused a derailment. Ran and ran past wagon after wagon and found no way across. It was too long. So I climbed aboard a car whose doors were opened and when my eyes were accustomed to the darkness, saw that it was loaded with coffins. Terrified, I slipped out the other side moments before the whole line creaked and moved and bellowed forth.

Six days later, on the day after the Queen's birthday, when the Centurion tanks had rumbled past, each with its British officer like a statue in the turret, the disturbances began.

(Lights turn up.)

Excuse me. A whiskey? Yes? No?

(Pours himself a glass.)

Why don't you remove your cape?

(Looks at his glass.)

An ancient practice this, gleaned from all those meetings on Tuesday nights when men in Sam Browne belts and revolvers on lanyards appeared around my father. He was the Chief Inspector. There was the wife beater, the drunk, the jazzman, the boxer who wore furry slippers...all aspects of my father. He was the light-heavyweight with tattoos on his forearms flipping peanuts into his mouth, then filing a shotgun cartridge with a penknife, shooting the beads into the ashtray. When they left I poured the remains of their whiskeys into a tumbler and drank it in bed and in the morning the Nationalist flags had come out, blossoming like flowers from balconies, while I gathered buckshot from the sheets and listened for the train which no longer came.

(Winces. Holds his stomach.)

There it goes again. That pain. For centuries, pain and disease were codified and classified and all that did was to add to the confusion. Death made all knowledge impotent. Then Bichat, the famous anatomist, said: 'Cut up a few corpses. Bring the darkness to light.'

(Lights up bright. He looks up.)

That was the Enlightenment. It was a greater invention than the bulb. Ah! (Waxing ecstatically.) That light was the flame of the individual! It broke rules. It pulled the cork on repression and superstition. Prior to that, death was the only way out.

(Slumping.)

But even the Enlightenment stalled before the family of man.

Well, I defied my father. Broke the code. Brought the darkness to light.

Aaaargh! That ulcer's relentless. It's worked its way into the soul. Nights I used to lie awake contemplating suicide. Actually, my first attempt was at the age of eight. I jumped from the roof of the school, two storeys high, and landed on a soft lawn. The English principal was sitting sozzled with gin on the balcony above the crest which said: 'Good Hope'. He must have noticed a shadow flit across the bamboo blinds. He was a kind man who took an interest in birds. Nobody else saw me thumping down, making a hole in the lawn. I limped off to class, feeling I could do anything then, it didn't matter. Resolved to try it again one day, until I started to hear distant gunshots and we were told we had to wait for our mothers to pick us up. From that day on, school was closed indefinitely.

(Holds his stomach.)

Arrgh! A gentle tug at first. Then the pain. Hooked like a fish! Just to remind me, I know, that things are wrong inside. Bichat. You know Bichat. Marie-François-Xavier. French anatomist. Founded the science of histology. 1771–1802. Had a short life. Discovered twenty-one kinds of tissues made up the human organs. Let me name them:

(Says the following very slowly.)

despair

despair

despair.

Need I go on? Do we fall ill and then die as a result? No, said Bichat. It's because we may die that we fall ill. We are dying at every moment. The inevitability always within us. Not subject to fate at all. We are, in fact, constructed from despair. (Pause.) How I hold this dear to me! A friend, this pain. There is no other philosophy so friendly...this internal disharmony which breaks up the body, the family, the unity of nations. (Grimacing.) Rejoice! It breaches tyranny!

(Pause. Recovers.)

To breathe; to sleep. A gentle stirring in the loins to ward off boredom...and then...revolution!

(Long pause.)

(Lights change to blue.)

My mother was one of those capable women...you would have seen that. She ran a private hotel. You know the kind: shabby but quaint. There were two lifts with calliper gates which lumbered up and down...past drunks and fallen women.

My mother swept the lobby and turfed out anyone who required doctors or disinfectant. She was respected. You know the kind: bespectacled, beseeching, Baptist. Quite in contrast to the fury of which she was capable. You wouldn't have thought she kept a baseball bat under her pillow, an American Slugger dented on one side where she'd hit the water pipe and flooded three floors. See, my father crept up on her one night dressed as Santa Claus and pretended he was a burglar. He tore off his beard, yelling, 'It's me!' She took another swing then. On New Year's Eve Father and I lobbed firecrackers through the upper windows of double-decker buses. At midnight, he lit a Roman candle under her bed and the hotel caught fire.

Freud said the practical joke was a mark of aggression.

Father spent a lot of time on jokes. He shoved potatoes into car exhausts and once jumped overboard from a ferry to save a drowning man. It was in the papers. Only thing is the drowning man was his friend and they'd planned the whole thing together. He did these things quite often. Then he'd put on his uniform and go out on patrol, my mother reminding him to wear his tin hat because the rioters threw bricks. I think he wore white gloves but I could be mistaken. Memory, you see, refuses to be hypocritical; and therein lies madness. I do the same now...wear plastic gloves for sanity...sanitary...reasons.

One day...I think it was an overcast day in December...close to Christmas, although I don't know why I think that...perhaps it's the smell of pines...

(Takes spray can out of his pocket, opens his jacket and sprays under his arms. Sniffs deeply.)

Ah!

(Blue lights intensify.)

Memories flooding in. Chestnuts raining down. Bing Crosby filling the air waves. The family in a good mood.

One day in December, I found my father's revolver at the bottom of the drawer where he kept the Mentholatum for his piles and the Vicks for his sinuses, each bottle placed strategically so he could use them in the night. I switched the bottles first, and then fondled the gun, a heavy Webley which I could just hold up, two fingers on the trigger. The hammer clicked back and forth. I put on his gas mask, the black rubber coated with powder, and the helmet which he never wore. I saw myself in the mirror. Death was staring back.

He returned that night, his beret matted with hair and blood, carrying a Greener shotgun. He removed the shells while my mother tenderly stitched him up. There was some concern on my part, blood being thicker than water, although I thought that was a terrible disadvantage. If we were jellyfish we could form and reform without recourse to blood. I felt amorphous. I stayed up half the night watching troops in the street exacting the curfew. (Demonstrating.) Pointed the Webley at them from the window.

(Blue lights dimmed.)

In the afternoons my mother slept, listening to the radio, to the hourly reports on trouble spots, to the news from China; slept to the rumble of armoured cars cruising between posts, barbed wire coiled from banyan tree to banyan tree; slept to the stamp of Ghurkha boots in the lobby, to the orgasmic frenzy and operatic Chinese unleashed by the girls upstairs.

For recreation, Father dragged me to the Catholic Club to meet interesting young women. They wore tiny crucifixes around their necks and asked me in Portuguese if I would marry them just to see me blush. Look at me. Such sensitivity. To other languages; other motives. Everyone practised upon me what they would like to say to him.

(Picks up saxophone and plays a few bars of 'Blue Moon'.)

Other people's songs.

I loaded the Webley with five brass cartridges. Left the breech empty for safety and hid the gun behind the cistern.

(Lights: turned up a little more.)

Another whiskey and I'll sing you another song.

(Pours out a glass.)

My parents separated when I was eleven. I'd known it for a while, when Father didn't come home any longer. He began to decompose, in the same way that Bichat conceptualised decomposition as positive and natural. It was at this point that I felt an immense eroticism. I was free, and within the space of this freedom...(enthusiastically)...*love* made an entrance.

(Blue lights up full.)

There she was. Maria Jungfrau. She lived in the opposite apartment. She had blonde hair and her father was head of Volkswagen Hong Kong. He'd been a Panzer commander during the war, so it must have been a bit of a come-down tooling around in a Beetle. Well, I couldn't have asked for anything more. My father was crazy about blondes too. Blondes were archetypes. His Alsatian was called Wagner. When he arrived in Australia he went crazy. He used to sit in trains going gaga over blondes, getting to know all of Sydney on the one ticket. He once said to me that if you understood a healthy blonde you've got the measure of Western civilisation.

I tried hard with the daughter of the Panzerführer. I bought her lots of Cokes and blow-waved my hair and told her how I hated Annette Funicello, who was just about the most pinned-up girl around. She thought that was nice. I was a nice guy for an eleven year old. I think I was in love with myself being in love. But it's always in moments like these, when one's dreaming of the most wonderful martyrdom, dying for an image—yes, I really believed Maria Jungfrau and I would dance to the great jukebox of love after I'd rescued her from a street full of rioters—yes, it's always in moments like these, when reality takes on a nasty hue and the gods of coincidence turn the screw; pull your wings out for sport.

My father came back. To get his saxophone. He was dressed as Santa Claus and said he was doing a charity function. My mother scoffed but said nothing. The last charity function he played, naked girls popped up out of cakes and distributed free bibles to hoteliers. It was for the blind and it raised a million dollars. Father said I should kiss his ring and say 'bem-vindo papai!', since I wouldn't be seeing him that often. Then he asked me where I'd put his revolver.

Listen.

(Sound of steam train, going fast.)

A hacking cough, deep in the hills. The erratic rhythms of the dying. Oh, would that this piteous heart mimic the living instead! See the smoke: black...and white...a kind of mobile crematorium.

My mother died happily. At least she died without pain, which is something you could say for dying, that pain is brief and death is long...which is a great comfort to those who don't believe in art. She died in Sydney, clutching a sheaf of fifty-dollar bills I'd just given her. Deaf and almost blind, she smelled the new crisp notes and expired. Later I had to pry them from her hand. From beneath the leering eyes of the undertaker. My father arrived soon after, by ship, ruddy with whiskey, wearing black and white shoes and sporting a Fedora. He refused the chauffeured limousine I had waiting on the dock and asked to walk a little with me. He said he was a very lucky man. Yes, I answered. 'Bem-vindo papai.' I didn't kiss the ring he wasn't wearing, and looked across the pearling waters to the Opera House, glowing like the inside of an oyster shell I'd seen on someone's plate.

Ah! Listen! A steam train. What? Yes, I know there are no more steam trains. I'm glad. I hate them. I'm not an afficionado. No, not me. Gimme a whiskey.

(Pours out a glass.)

One for the road. On Stonecutter's Island, a thousand old women dressed in black broke rocks for paving. Each day, one or two would die. We found bodies in the water when we went fishing. My father, then a sub-inspector, filled out a thousand reports, sitting at his deathly typewriter, humming, whistling, practising the evening's night clubbing.

(Drinks.)

Yes, that was one for the road they built. A highway to hell.

(Pause. Bright blue lights.)

Well, my father came back for his saxophone, but he remembered something else.

'Where's my revolver?' he yelled, dragging me to the balcony.

(Twists his head sideways and upwards.)

Here you are: his fingers twisting your ear, head turned resolutely up. Here you are: grabbing at the parapet and far out across the rooftops, over the washing and the awnings and the wells and the dry burnt rust of hillside shanties, you see the smoke of the train from China. Here you are: listening for it when your head is thrust the other way (jerks his head violently down), and you see the wet courtyard below, (spreading out his arms as though he was about to dive)...and the canvas awning onto which all the upper tenants threw their refuse, you count the chickens jerking back and forth between the water trough and vegetable scraps. Here you are: watching the callipered lift settle onto the ground-floor landing, watching Miss Chan in her split skirt (arms still outstretched, twisting his hips), weaving out into the street waving to the trishaw coolies (fluttering his fingers), who are struggling up the hill with knotted muscles and a lounge room on their backs. Here you are: crying out in pain and the hawker thinks you want a twist of ginger and he's ready to throw it up if you drop a coin. Here you are: the back of your head stinging with slaps and when you look up (looking up), tears in your eyes...you see Maria Jungfrau on her balcony, her haughty face impassive, sweeping her blonde hair back and walking inside.

(Hands on his heart.)

Oh, Miserere nobis!

(Pause.)

She never spoke to me again.

My father never found his revolver.

(Long pause.)

(Lights change to bright yellow.)

After that, my mother saved up enough to send me to Australia. To boarding school. Good training for gaol. At university I studied medicine and discovered sport. Like anaesthetic, sport was a great antidote to sensitivity. I played rugby and performed passable surgery...I was quick, you see, could read the game (using his hands as though passing a rugby ball), whip out the bladder and have everything sewn up fifteen minutes before full-time. I established a happy practice.

Then, as I've said, my father arrived and proclaimed himself a lucky man. I think it was then that I had a sort of breakdown.

(Pause.)

The family never left you alone.

My father's health was fairly shaky. I mean, you can imagine. All those decades of night-clubbing with cigarette smoke heavy in the air. Drink flowing from dusk till dawn. Constant attrition of the spirit.

(Yellow lights very dim.)

There it goes.

(Sound of steam train slowing.)

The train of history is terminal. It ends with each death, each body in its final deterioration. Yes, don't fool yourself that somehow there's a future. Just like the train of history, the train of the family is *going nowhere*, except perhaps into mechanical reproduction, readying for war...for *the birth of a nation*. Yea, I could have been a speech writer, a pamphleteer, a talk-back host...a mid-wife for misanthropy...a politician! (Sighs.) But I was always too negative.

(Air-raid sirens. Takes a sip of whiskey. Holds up the glass.)

(Yellow lights turned up.)

It was my twelfth birthday. I can remember it clearly, flowing out of an amber time, like the light in this glass. My father was working the tables in the casino when he spotted me carrying the note for him in a sealed green envelope. He tore it open with his teeth while placing a chip on the line. It was in my mother's handwriting. It said: 'Today is your son's birthday. You should visit him.' I know what it said because I wrote it. He threw it into an ashtray. Then he won and lost and won again.

Three hours later he cashed in his chips, took me to the gun club and taught me to shoot clays. It was important to squeeze and not pull at the trigger, he told me. He was happy. He took the gun from me and squeezed off two shots and the plates shattered in mid-flight. That's when he stepped on my glasses and said that I would see him later, at home.

That, I suppose, had been the most important day of my life. Not just the most important day up to that point in my life, but the most important day for the whole of my life. Because it was on that day that I decided to get as far away from my family, any family, as I could, forever. I decided quite single-mindedly to gather the resources to live completely alone; to live as reclusively as possible, far from a world which was always trying to get on, to improve, to progress...(his voice gradually rising to a crescendo)...a world which made the family a stronghold of the basest instincts; a world geared to infantilism, greed, self-righteousness, sentimentality and breakfast cereals; a world, in short, which forced a permanent and aching smile on my lips...the logical end of which was...murder.

(Pause.)

I became the country's number one. I terminated life at both ends of the spectrum. Those who couldn't be helped begged me to finish them off. The dying are many. Think of them, waiting for dusk or nightfall so they could speak to themselves. I've seen it often. The essence of dying is the ability to speak well to yourself at dusk...about the forming and re-forming of oblivion; the rising and falling of curtains; the sun; eyelids.

You know, it's hard to die of heartbreak, but there was some money to be made in it...anyway, abortions and euthanasia were better performed by someone who understood suicide.

(Pause. His voice drops. He speaks more slowly.)

No. Reclusion was the answer for me. I knew it on the day of my twelfth birthday, and again, many years later, at the height of my medical career, I gave myself up to it. I became a stonewall fanatic. Within me, I carried my own Iron Curtain.

In an unused theatre, you can imagine...stainless-steel tables, instruments beneath powerful lamps, scalpels labelled from one to ten,

REPUBLICA

a saw or two...I tried to amputate my own hand.

(Looks at his empty glass. Lights turned down.)

I know what you're thinking. The hand of a murderer. No. It was on account of a higher purpose. You see, if I were disabled, reclusion would be mine. But at the last moment...at the last moment it began to rain. There was a sort of skylight in the theatre, a dome in glass, a turret which allowed in natural light, although natural light was useless in an operation, and I was looking up at the droplets and then at the lightning, and then, because of some electrical short-circuit, the generators were turned on, and I found myself looking straight at a nurse who had come in to check the theatre. It was part of her rounds (smiling lewdly), a regularity which I had once enjoyed, but now overlooked...particularly as I'd administered a block and my fingers were all but useless.

Anyway, the germ of reclusion had already settled in my heart on my twelfth birthday. Father came to our hotel at a late hour and unpacked an enormous electric train set. Despite the time, Mother was pleased. We stayed up, all three, to assemble it. There were one or two mild shocks from the transformer, but otherwise everybody was light-hearted and excited. I noticed a wagon the locomotive pulled; one with sliding doors. Overcome with dizziness, I sent my train to China and back throughout the night. Then, way past my bedtime, I stacked the train set beneath the hearth. My father opened a bottle of whiskey and my mother retreated to the lobby and did the accounts, as she always did, ticking off a set of figures from two enormous ledgers behind the desk. Django Reinhardt was playing on the radio: soft, tingling, gipsy notes full of catgut and whimsy. Father fell asleep on the lounge.

(Takes out the hanky and mops his brow.)

I got up out of bed...it must've been around three in the morning. Mother's door was locked. Father was still asleep and the radio buzzed and crackled. I went to the bathroom. I retrieved the revolver from behind the cistern. A slimy layer of rust coated the grip, but otherwise it seemed in perfect order when I pulled back the hammer. I tiptoed softly to where Father was sleeping. There was a faint glow of light coming from the corridor. I pointed the barrel of the Webley at my father's head, went up closer, placed both index fingers on the trigger and squeezed it in the same way as I had always been taught.

(Long pause. Pours some whiskey. Takes a sip.)

There was a loud click, but nothing happened. I half expected the bullet to explode later, like a firecracker with a lit fuse. My father snorted and shifted. Suddenly the door opened and my mother came into the room. She took the gun from my hand and took it to the balcony. Then she calmly dropped it down onto the canvas awning below. I heard it thump. Maybe it was the sound of my heart. It's been beating like that, in my ear, all these years since.

I often wonder why it misfired. It could have been wet and rusted. It could have been the empty chamber I had left, out of caution, out of practice, out of good gun management, out of a family code that you always left an empty chamber. The cylinder, like a roulette wheel, must've come full circle. As my father said, when he arrived in Australia twenty years later, he was a lucky man.

(Pause.)

I could have told him about it then. And *that* would probably have killed him. Telling him that would have finished him, right there across from the Opera House, instead of the stroke which exploded in his brain while he was blowing on this saxophone.

(Blows a few bars of 'My Blue Heaven'.)

But my father and I had never shared any secrets.

(Pause. Lights bright.)

Well here I am, waiting for another train. Waiting to cross the border. It is dusk (points) and there's a conference over there.

(Shakes his head.)

There's nothing worse than waiting. (Indicating a wall.) The dying light paints one wall of this room with blood.

(Gestures towards the audience in puzzlement.)

All these familiar faces. And all this waiting. Well, whistle whistle...my story's over.

(Holds up the hypodermic. Sound of an approaching steam train, slowing.)

Cheers.

(All lights go out as slowing train gets louder and louder. It screeches to a halt. Then all sounds stop abruptly.)

Twenty Thousand Ks from the Warzone

GLENDA SLUGA

I was 20 000 ks from the warzone, but I could not keep my distance.

My parents were born in what is now called Slovenia. They grew up there and they went hungry there. In another time, before another war, they were taught in Italian schools, their fathers fought in Austrian armies there. And so, my parents lived out a dream of assimilating in Australia. I am a historian now. Born in Melbourne, working in Sydney. I have been spoon-fed multiculturalism. But even back then I knew that I was growing up in a society which espouses tolerance so it can absolve its guilt about its own discriminations.

I had to make the war over there my war as well. It's a war, after all, between my convictions and uncertainties. But I have to be careful how I tread, because in places like this, the ground can shift along with the borders.

SARAJEVO, DECEMBER 1990

Christmas holed up in the hills of Sarajevo. Sarajevo is an ex-winter Olympic site but monstrous, empty hotels are lining the alpine road now. They have no hot water, so I end up in a more welcoming youth hostel in the middle of a snowy field.

The rustic timber cottage houses only me and the concierge—a shy, young Sarajevan who feeds me and shares with me the bloody drama of the Romanian revolution, screened live on local TV. Only next door, Romania's communism, its desperation, still seem worlds away from the slower, quieter political frustrations of Yugoslavia. The only fears we express to each other are for Kosovo. Kosovo is an autonomous province within the borders of the Serbian state. And we regret the plight of the Albanians there who have been harassed, imprisoned and killed for nearly a decade now by the Yugoslav military acting on behalf of the Serbian communist government. Even the most prominent intellectuals of a once dissident community have come out now to declare that Kosovo Albanians are a threat to the Serbian race. So, the Albanians have little option but to pursue a policy of passive resistance.

Do I need to point out that the question of the concierge's identity never arises? We both assume that he is simply a Bosnian and that we are in Yugoslavia.

LONDON, JUNE 1991

When war does break out in ex-Yugoslavia in June 1991, it is not in the deepest south of the South Slav lands, in Kosovo. It breaks out in the more heavily industrialised, more economically successful Slovenia, which lies along the northern border of a disintegrating Yugoslavia. The Yugoslav People's Army is unabashedly turning its guns and tanks against its own people—the population of Slovenia, newly and nervously declared independent by its right-wing Christian democratic government, with its ex-communist President. When war does break out, I am not wandering the cobbled lanes of downtown Ljubljana. Instead I am in London and it's the BBC putting me in the picture. Revolution by television once again.

I am feeling a déjà-vu. Is it because I am here in London, because I am an Australian, or is it because I feel so close to Slovenia?

I participate in demonstrations against the use of armed forces to solve the question of Yugoslavia's political future. Behind barricades provided by the local police, we hold up our placards and taunt 'TANKS OUT'. The days of our opposition accumulate. So do our numbers and the flags we represent. In the space of a week, national flags have become the emblems of opposition to Yugoslav military policy. The flag of independent Slovenia, the tricolour, featuring the three-peaked mountain top, is joined by the Croatian flag with its more conventionally serious shield-shaped emblem. This second flag has been introduced by members of London's Croatian communities. Their hope is to defend a tentatively sovereign Croatia from what is still only the threat of military attack.

In Trafalgar Square, our demonstration is harassed by young, aggressively muscular men who thrust black flags bearing the Cetnik skull and crossbone. These are Serbian nationalists. Supporting them, and perhaps more frightening, are little old ladies who tout blurred photocopied images of decapitated bodies from the Second World War. The captions assert that these were Serbian victims of Croatian brutality. Pro-Croatian speakers take the opportunity to provoke the Cetniks. They attack not the Federal Army, not the Belgrade politicians, not the Cetnik revivalists, but all Serbians, all of whom, the pro-Croatians claim, have a historical mission to annihilate the Croatian race.

The few Kosovo Albanians there are stirring for a fight with the Cetniks, but they go largely ignored by the organisers. The Slovenes and Croats are having to deal with the call to remember, as if they had absent-mindedly forgotten, that their own historical mission is one of national statehood.

Calls to violence are being countered by calls for opposition to violence; but these calls for an opposition to violence are increasingly being tangled with invocations of national, rather than human, rights. Principles and outrage are both being registered, but only as a consequence of exclusive, group-centred identities—a political war, for independent nationhood, is being wrapped and rewrapped in a rhetorical mantle of ethnic hatred and paranoia. Soon there will be only the layers of labelling, counted in days of suffering and anger, over piles of mutilated corpses.

MELBOURNE, OCTOBER 1993

The first refugee from the war whom I come to know is sitting next to me in a Vietnamese restaurant in Richmond. He is a young electronics technician from Banja Luka, a large town in Bosnia. I want him to see how multicultural his new country is, or could be. Until now we have avoided discussion of his experience of the war. Suddenly he has things he wants to tell me. He talks about betrayal, disillusion, about the hell that is other people. He points across the table, across the unfamiliar plate of Vietnamese noodles that he has barely touched, at my friends. He asks me how long I've known them. He asks me to imagine them, after twenty-five years of knowing them, after I have come to feel that this is my family, to imagine them pointing a gun at my head one day, calling me a Croat, and then proceeding to destroy my life.

You have become a Croat, they have made you a Croat, and now they are not your friends, not your family, they are Serbians. Bosnia, he says, and stops...was a...ummm...a multicultural place?

But now he never wants to go back. He could not trust anyone. It is a place filled with hate.

He is no longer just V. He is not even a Bosnian any longer. He is a Croat. Once he used to call his language Yugoslav, or Serbo-Croatian. Now he cannot call it that; or even just Croatian or Serbian, not even Bosnian, without adding something else as well, all of the rest. So he just calls it the language that he speaks. V could have a Croatian passport, but he has refused. It would remind him, he says, of the difference the war has made.

The pro-Croatians here are organised defensively; the pro-Serbians are the enemy of the Croatian nation and so they would understand him only as one of theirs. And mimicking the war 20 000 ks away, the pro-Bosnians too have ended up splitting their allegiances. V sends me a copy of a Melbourne Bosnia-Hercegovinian newspaper, the *Bosnian Mirror*—but it's the last edition. Rumour has it that it was forced to close by a local pro-Muslim group who objected to its policy of eschewing partisanship. Fragmenting fragments.

And I have to ask myself where I belong, what is my place, amongst communities whose labyrinthine jealousies and allegiances seem more confusing to me here than the factionalisms of the warzone. Maybe, I'm thinking to myself, Australian multiculturalism might be like that. Maybe it too won't let him forget that he has to choose an *identity*—like choosing from among the available dishes in one of those restaurants where the menu never changes.

SYDNEY, NOVEMBER 1993

The conflagration is already history—the kind that makes you uncomfortable because its has no neat ending. The meanings of the war have shifted daily, just as the alliances have. It's a war where the main protagonists proclaim their identities and ambitions to be *natural*. And yet their competing objectives and their consequent legitimations are continually being reinvented.

The war, which some defended in the name of a socialist Yugoslavia against a traitorous, capitalist and chauvinist Slovenia, has become the war of Serbian survival against Croatian fascism. It has then become the war of Christian survival against Muslim fanaticism. And through each transformation, the key actors remain the same, with an ever-swelling chorus of volunteers, recruits and victims.

The more contemporary accounts from the warzone I read, the more I am exposed to the historicising rhetoric of the protagonists and commentators, and the more I shy away from *historical* explanations. I am convinced this war is not the upshot of ethnic hatred, nor did it stew away for hundreds of years. It was not brought to overboil by post-communism. It is an opportunistic war, for megalomaniacs and the desperate. It is a testosterone-fed war for young men brought up on diets of western Rambo and Schwarzenegger.

As a historian, I want to salvage an unanachronistic *before*—a sense of transition, a multiculturalism that preserves the otherness of different pasts at the same time as the communalism of political presents. I want to understand. And sure, while there are warring factions, there are also those who stand in opposition to the principle of ethno-territorialism, who do believe in many kinds of difference, as well as the right to be the same. I want to believe in them.

Later in November, I am reading the words of Slavenka Drakulic, writing in her autobiographical account of the war (*Balkan Express*, Hutchinson, London, 1993).

> Along with millions of other Croats, I was pinned to the wall of nationhood—not only by outside pressure from Serbia and the federal army but by national homogenisation within Croatia itself. That is what the war is doing to us, reducing us to one dimension—the Nation. The trouble with this nationhood, however, is that whereas before I was defined by my education, my job, my ideas, my character—and yes, my nationality too— now I feel stripped of all that. I am nobody because I am not a person any more. I am one of 4.5 million Croats. What has happened is that something people cherished as a part of their cultural identity—an alternative to the all-embracing communism, a means to survive—has become their political identity and turned into something like an ill-fitting shirt. You

may feel the sleeves are too short, the collar too tight. You might not like the colour, and the cloth might itch. But there is no escape; there is nothing else to wear. One doesn't have to succumb voluntarily to this ideology of the nation—one is sucked into it.

Sydney, on a sweaty November Saturday. A group calling themselves the Bosnian Inter-Committee Council have organised a rally to 'Stop Genocide in Bosnia/Save Multiculturalism in Bosnia' and I have agreed to speak. Those, within ex-Yugoslavia and without, who wish to avoid or denigrate the rationale of *pure* ethnicities and *natural* hatreds, have allied themselves to a vision of the Bosnia-Hercegovina of *before*—a multicultural society.

I meet a local Bosnian. He is telling me despondently in broken English that his family lived near Tuzla and he is concerned because he has not heard from them for over a year. The rally begins. An articulate and charismatic young woman dressed in the garb of folklore laments the absence of members of the Croatian community who would have joined them once upon a time. The territorial ambitions of the Zagreb government against the Sarajevo government have had local repercussions. This demonstration has been most obviously organised by the local Bosnian Muslim community. They are currently the desperate ones, the outcasts. Is multiculturalism only the plaint of victims then?

Two members of the New South Wales parliament make speeches supporting a multicultural Bosnia and rejecting territorial acquisitions through violence—this is, of course, Mabo speaking, I decide. But in giving their speeches, they are not offering the simple solution that is being demanded by the most vocal and intimidating members of the audience—more weapons—and the implicit rejection of armed intervention is greeted with jeers.

It's the turn of my man from Tuzla. He has found a different voice and also a new past. He speaks not of a disappeared Tuzla family, but of a mother and father who have been raped and killed, a brother who has been genitally mutilated and a sister who has been raped and massacred. Yes, such occurrences have become tragically commonplace in the war. But so has their use as a rhetorical weapon. This man then, in a fair approximation of the communist-speak of the seventies, starts to exorcise his paranoias by naming 'Masonic-Zionist' propaganda and 'British geo-imperial policies' as the real problem.

I have accepted an invitation to speak here. I am standing here because the demonstration's organiser had spoken at a colloquium I had organised a few months earlier. That event was an attempt at a constructive discussion of the war and the issues at stake—who was fighting whom and why? And I wanted to do this on a university campus because Australian universities were already being involved in this war. Each organised local community was busy raising funds for the establishment of local academic positions to help legitimise the existence of each community's new-fangled nation. The Serbians and Croatians had so far been the most successful; the Slovenes were hurrying to catch up.

I imagined my colloquium addressing the *political* dimensions of so-called ethnic self–identification—but the academics spoke instead, in what they determined to be 'apolitical' intellectual spaces. My Bosnian Muslim guest was an outsider to this kind of setting—he chose to speak along *historical* lines. He spoke about 400 years of multicultural history, and this was his rejoinder to the disruptive claims of Serbian and Croatian nationalisms.

The audience was made up of interested bystanders and involved community members too. But there were also some intimidating, macho students who had come to proclaim their Greekness and to insist on Macedonia's Greekness as well. A journalist—whose newspaper had once aimed to represent the plurality of Yugoslavian languages and experiences—began to berate my guest's 'multicultural' message, claiming it only bore 'gifts of veils for Bosnia's women'. History was mobilised against other histories, stereotypes abounded, discussion lapsed into the ridiculous, and my Bosnian (now Muslim) friend became the favoured target. I began to think it might be impossible in multicultural Australia to have any useful understanding of a multicultural Bosnia, or to resist the conceptual shifts that the war for territory was legitimising.

Now, at the 'Stop Genocide in Bosnia/Save Multiculturalism in Bosnia' rally, I am beginning to think that this request for me to speak here might well be my guest's revenge. I am worried by the success of the speech of the man from Tuzla. And I am dazed, anyway, by the flu. I ascend the podium and gesture dramatically at the list I have brought with me, of grass-roots welfare organisations from the many regions of ex-Yugoslavia. These all advocate human rights and an end to war. I praise the position of groups associated with Helsinki Forum, and I suggest that the Australian government should recognise and support these multi-ethnic groups as alternatives to the representatives of chauvinistic governments in the ex-Yugoslav republics. A young man with his head shielded by a paper mask begins to jeer. Others join in. And I begin to feel vulnerable. Even naïve. Perhaps there *is* just too much hate. And to witness such hatred, it's just too much for me.

I read. This is what Indijana Hidovic Harper says in her 'Personal Reactions of a Bosnian Woman to the War in Bosnia' (Feminist Review (1993) No 45).

> Born fifteen years after the war ended, I belong to the second generation of the post-war Bosnian Muslims, for whom our Muslim identity was a quaint aspect of family heritage,

something to marvel at, rather than be immersed in. Islam as a religion became our past rather than present or future. I identified myself as Muslim by nationality, which meant I had no ties to either Serbia or Croatia, but saw my social and cultural identity as a part of an ethnically mixed Bosnian tapestry, from which I drew all my cultural and emotional experiences, and to which I belonged together with all other non-Muslim Bosnians.

Bosnia, ethnically mixed, culturally integrated and interdependent, was a source from which I emerged into the wide spaces of the outside world and my own inner adult being. To identify myself only with the Muslims in Bosnia would have seemed an act of betrayal, not just of my own land, but my very identity. Nothing in my life, in any of my experiences, was solely Muslim. Being a Bosnian, I used to say to my European friends, was like being one of the three kinds of meat and a dozen kinds of vegetables that made up the Bosnian pot, the only Bosnian dish ever to make it into the Western cookery books. To me, it was a poignant parable about what Bosnia and being a Bosnian was about and how I came to claim a part in the European identity.

London, Melbourne, Sydney have nothing, and everything, to do with Yugoslavia. This war is undermining the language of pluralism and multiculturalism at the same time as it is reminding us of the worlds we might lose or have already lost.

The word in the smaller, quieter Australian Slovene community (to which I do—and do not—belong) is *do not speak out*. Alliances keep shifting. Just stay friendly, ignore politics, and keep your mouth shut. A censored sort of multiculturalism. And maybe they are right.

I spoke publically against the war, against territorial ambitions, I spoke rejecting essentialist ethnic interpretations, and within days I am being sent a set of pamphlets anonymously from Canberra. The cover note menacingly announces 'Greetings!'. At first I'm not sure which group has sent me the material, but it smells of an all too familiar type of sneering hatred. Alongside an article describing the murder of hundreds of thousands of Serbians during the Second World War in the Nazi puppet state of Croatia, are the familiar blurred photos of decapitated bodies and trunkless heads—not unlike those proffered by the little old ladies in London. These leaflets also feature the portrait of the Ustasha's 'criminal leader Ante Pavelic' (responsible for the Serbian 'holocaust'), which is said in the leaflets to be prominent these days in Australia, in Croatian clubs, Croatian homes and at soccer games.

I recall the Ante Pavelic Memorial Hall in the inner suburbs of Melbourne, funded by a folklore and an official multiculturalism that is ignorant of the politics of ethnicity in Europe. That recollection is overlaid with other thoughts just as discomforting—demonstrators in the streets of Australian cities wearing the hats of Cetnik guerrillas; influential political representatives of Australian Greek communities who will not speak out against the chauvinism of Greece's national policies; pro-Macedonian newspapers that appeal to what once seemed obsolete nationalist sentiments. Local once-Yugoslav organisations are raising money for clothing and food for refugees, for their *side*, and if some of it goes astray and buys guns instead, then what can they do? A friend tells me his young Croatian neighbour has gone to fight for the Croatian state in Bosnia. Why do young men living in Australia head for a warzone, to defend a country many of them know only from the tales told by their parents? They are *returning* to fight for a cause which has stolen the past from V, a Croat according to the new order. And if there are only 'sides' and none are without sin, does that make them equally guilty?

I continue to read. This is what Maja Korac tells me, in her article 'Serbian Nationalism: Nationalism of My Own People' (*Feminist Review* (1993), No 45).

> How can one be objective in confronting abstract nationalism without facing the nationalism of one's own people? Moreover, in the case of former Yugoslavia, to be a Serb means to face the burden of the greatest responsibility for what has happened within the country.
>
> To be a Serb, to live in Serbia nowadays, and not to be nationally obsessed, means to be accused of betraying your nation, and labelled as a 'bad' Serb. Distinctions between 'bad' and 'good' Serbs have become very important to our national mythology which is a warrior mythology, extrapolated from Serbian history, overburdened as it is with liberation wars. Through their history, Serbs have been brave soldiers, fighters for their national liberation and the liberation of their 'brother' nations of South-Slavs. They have been glorified as 'honest' and 'fearless' soldiers, constantly at war, suffering terrible losses, regarding themselves as the greatest victims of the 'violent cauldron' of Balkan history. Always, at some point, they come to feel 'betrayed' by their 'brother' nations during or after these wars...There are numerous horrifying and sad stories, collected by women volunteer groups in Belgrade, of women who scarcely recognise their men when they return from the front. They act differently, they talk differently, they walk around in full uniform, they even sleep with their Kalashnikovs. And they are completely psychologically destroyed. They, in turn, then destroy the lives of their partners, wives and families...We live in a sick society. Nationalism is a horrible disease.

MELBOURNE, DECEMBER 1993

I'm sitting in the Jugoslavija, waiting, 20 000 ks from the warzone. Is there more than one war going on here? Are my Australian Bosnians, Serbians, Croatians, Muslims fighting a different war? Well, multicultural Australia sends you to the restaurant table for answers.

Here, in the inner streets of Melbourne, there is still a Jugoslavija, alongside The Vardar and The Macedonian, where once you came seeking ethnically and religiously unspecific Balkan food. Platters of unethnicised *cepvacice*, *raznice* and *pleskavica*—a plurality of difference shaped from the same mince.

I can't remember if anything has changed. My eye has trouble distinguishing meaningful signs.

Early this century, before she'd heard of the Holocaust or Hiroshima, the English Dame Rebecca West reflected that violence was all that she ever knew of the Balkans. Will the Balkans ever just be a place with no impinging *before* of all-engulfing violence and hatred? Is the Jugoslavija still just another restaurant?

The Jugoslavija has its Karajorge schnitzel—a gesture of some sort to the father of nineteenth-century Serbian nationalism. Does that make it a nationalist restaurant? Do we resist the urge to label it Serb, just as the real Jugoslavija is now indistinguishable from Serbian nationalist ambitions in the eyes of those who are that nationalism's victims? The two Macedonian restaurants tantalise me further with their own menu improvisations: a Napoleon special, and the fruit salad that is internationally served under the name 'Macedoine' is now called an Alexander the Great. Both men have infamous reputations, to say the least: Napoleon as an egotistical imperialist and as liberator of Illyrian nationalisms; Alexander as slayer of thousands and also as the contested hero of both Greek and Macedonian nationalisms.

It was in defence of Alexander's Greekness, that the Greek government recently imprisoned a young student for a year. The student had been hawking pamphlets which proclaimed Alexander, dead now for two thousand years, a murderer.

National histories are being used at this very moment to resuscitate the empire-building Napoleons and Alexanders of the world as objects of veneration. I ask a particularly vocal pro-Greek student at my university why he, born and living in Sydney, is so concerned about a Macedonian threat to Greece. He answers ingeniously that his mission is to save *future* generations of Greeks who might be threatened by a more powerful Macedonia. Are historicised visions of ethnic hatred now to be imposed not only on the past and present, but on the future as well?

Discussions of multiculturalism in Australia have too often been limited to the dimensions of restaurant ethnicity, with no one looking closely enough at the menus. How are we to read them? Are the

REPUBLICA

specials with human names on the menus of Melbourne objects of the pre-war or post-war imagination of ethnic communities? Or both? Are the various communities' menus being offered as threats to each other, or are they being exhibited because people simply have human rights to a cultural identity (even if few of them are willing to acknowledge these as invented, in common with all cultural identities)?

This war asks us to read those menus in only one way—as legitimations of the conflicts of interest represented by the co-existence of otherwise irreconcilable groups.

Those Greeks who are actively members of an Australian Greek community protest in the name of an issue which the Greek government overseas has opportunistically portrayed as a national threat—a Mediterranean Yellow Peril. The Slav-Macedonian community replies with images of Alexander, protesting its own right to ethnic existence (recognised in Australia, but refused in the colder climes of northern Greece), but they do not bother to defend the equally threatened rights of an Albanian minority in Macedonia.

For all their being victimised, they have more in common with the organised Greek community than they realise—their mutual mistrust and active dislike of Albanians. Albanians, the 'lowest of the low' in the pre-war Balkan ethnic hierarchy, come after Gypsies, but before Bosnians.

Yes, there is always racism, always mistrust, always betrayal. But they are only as much a way of life as their opposites are. And I try not to forget. This war offers up stories of heroism which cannot be nationally defined.

I read a report from the United States Information Service. 'Additional atrocities documented in former Yugoslavia, Fourth United States report to United Nations' (5760):

At about 7.00 am, on May 9 or 10, military units wearing the insignias of Serbian Cetniks and the Yugoslav army entered the area (near Sarajevo airport) and ordered all its residents out of the cellars in which they had taken refuge. Once outside, Serbs were told to stand in one place and Muslims in another.
One Serb, a fifty-year-old man known as 'Ljubo', refused to be separated from his Muslim neighbours, with whom he apparently had lived peacefully for many years. His refusal to be separated from his neighbours enraged the Serbian soldiers. They dragged him to the ground, and five or six of them beat him until he was dead.

Salman Rushdie, before he ever became a victim of Fatwah, reminded us that there are no hiding places, not for academics, not even for conscientious members of ethnic communities (Anglo or otherwise), no matter how urgent their sense of victimisation.

What is the distance between Australia and ex-Yugoslavia? It can still be measured in opportunities for living and those for dying. And I cannot keep *my* distance. Just as some in the warzone have taken responsibilty for making an 'instinctive' multiculturalism, we are all responsible for making the history of this war, even 20 000 ks from the warzone.

That is how I would have liked to end this essay—with a neat ending for my fragmented history.

But M sends me a fax from Ljubljana that turns my face red. She tells me not to believe the fairytales about multiculturalism that writers like Drakulic are fabricating—they just pander to the desire of outsiders who would rather hear fairytales than the truth, she writes. And that the writings of Drakulic and others only manifest the ambitions of American literary schools that have trained them to be successful Easterners in the West, that they only fulfil the West's expectations of what the East might be like. And I remember that *multicultural* may have been a word I handed over to V, to describe his own place. I may have even offered encouraging sounds as he began to pronounce it for himself, I don't know. And I need to remind myself that yes, the valuing of difference may offer a language which can arm aggressors, but surely it also offers one to those defending peace.

Black Bit, White Bit

IAN ANDERSON

When people ask me what field of post-graduate study I work in, I sometimes lie. I mumble something about doing social sciences or sociology. I don't always like to admit what I do. But my unwillingness to confess is not so much due to what *I* do, because I know that for many years, deep down, I have had a fascination for hidden secrets and, therefore, for anthropology. It's because of what some anthropologists have done.

When I was younger, my mother gave me a copy of Elkin's *The Australian Aborigines* as a gift (or maybe I was being punished). I spent many frustrated hours trying to comprehend the kinship systems of northern and central Australia. To my shame, pharmacology and pathology came to be more understandable systems of abstract knowledge. It was this experience which promoted in me a deep sense of the impossibility of ever being able to better understand my own Aboriginal heritage—I couldn't hear the voices of any of the people I knew (or know) in those texts through which I was attempting to stumble. Nowadays, I am not so naïve. To my relief, my own cultural experience has been confirmed, perhaps even despite anthropology.

I am a child of the post-referendum era. I have grown up in an era in which I can assert my Aboriginality *and* claim the rights of citizenship. So it's true, there are many aspects of my life which I and my generation are beginning to take for granted, such as participation in higher education or access to a broad range of community services, which were not available for those who grew up during the assimilation era. This colonial period, which stretched from the late 1930s until the late 1960s, has had a powerful influence in shaping the contemporary Koori community. But we, the younger generation, do share the Aboriginal experience of this time, through the passing on of experience and stories. Being little more than a generation old, this historical link is still an immediate one. In reading the ethnographies of this era, I expected to encounter a part of my history. On the contrary, even though I could often sense the muffled voices of an older generation, the experience of reading these works was, at times, like being only a voyeur on my own history.

A substantial critique of anthropology as a discipline has emerged since the 1960s. Ever since this moment, the discipline has been in a state of crisis. Anthropologists have found it increasingly difficult to locate the traditional target of the anthropological gaze: non-western peoples who could be construed as untouched by western civilisation. And indeed, one key source of this critique has come from anthropology's traditional subjects. Consider, for example, the Native American Vine Deloria, who in 1973 wrote *Custer Died For Your Sins*, a satirical appraisal of the relationship between anthropologists and Native Americans. 'Into each life,' he wrote, 'some rain must fall.

Some people have bad horoscopes; others take tips on the stock market. McNamara created the TFX and the Edsel. American politics has George Wallace. But Indians have been cursed above all other people in history. Indians have anthropologists.'

Deloria's parody of the regular summer pilgrimage of the anthropologists into Indian communities reflects an experience common to many indigenous communities throughout the world. The ironic dimension of his caricatured representation of anthropologists is somehow muted, however, by the resonance of anthropological representations of Native Americans which sentenced them to the imaginary twilight zone of the distant, exotic and backward past.

The work of Edward Said, who formally works in the arena of comparative literature, has been influential to those interested in criticising the traditional cultural gaze. In my case, I wish to develop a contemporary critique of traditional ethnographic representation of Aboriginal people. At the core of anthropological discourses are 'two words', as Said suggests in his 1989 article, 'Representing the Colonized: Anthropology's Interlocutors': 'difference' and 'otherness', which have by now acquired 'talismanic properties'. The 'other' has been increasingly appropriated as a concept, even as a word, in a manner analogous to imperialist expansion. In Orientalism, Said situated the production of Orientalist discourse within the colonial power relations which bound the west with the east. The colonised were represented within a discursive regime which not only misrepresented their reality but actually produced their 'truth'. The colonised became no longer just 'different'; they became the 'other', defined by their 'otherness' in relation to the coloniser's sense of reality. What is striking about all colonial representations of colonised people is that these are infiltrated by the representer's world, and yet by a sleight of the textual hand, these representations become only about 'difference'.

I am concentrating on the representations of Aboriginal people in the ethnographies of the assimilation era, especially in south-east Australia. This inevitably takes us into the world of what the post– Second World War ethnographers of this era labelled 'mixed-blood' or 'part-blood' or 'half-caste' Aboriginal communities. Although I find such names deeply offensive, especially when applied to me, I have to refer to them constantly, for in themselves they evoke the very issues I wish to examine. This construction of Aboriginality, the 'hybrid' or 'ambiguous' Aborigine, must be properly understood as a product of assimilation colonialism.

On the early frontier, the invader culture constructed the invaded as their 'other'. The Aboriginal stereotypes which emerged in popular representations, such as the Jacky Jacky, have their roots in an invading culture which pushed its frontier further and further, towards the

Australian interior. The displacement of the invaded, and their entrapment within colonial society, resulted in the invaders imagining Aboriginal people only as the bewildered remnants of the stone age. As such, the invading culture was able to construct its own identity as the masters of nature and the torch bearers of civilisation. These Aboriginal people were sentenced to a colonial reality—an authenticity—based on notions of Aboriginal life as primitive and uncivilised.

The constitutional arrangement of 1901 defined a nation of white Australian citizens which excluded Aboriginal people (amongst others). Entry into the new Commonwealth was, for Aborigines, contingent on them discarding the remnants of their tradition and embracing the customs and practices of the invading culture. The anthropologist AP Elkin argued in 1959, at a conference on New South Wales Aborigines, that Aboriginal preparation for citizenship must include lessons in hygiene, cleanliness, and the value of money and property. The construct, the 'authentic' or 'traditional' Aborigine, remained a key figure in the imagination of White Australia. Oppositional by definition (and not just different), Aboriginality continued to be excluded from the Australian community. To be an Australian citizen, for a person of Aboriginal heritage, meant nothing less than becoming a white Australian with a black skin.

During the first half of this century, Aboriginal life in Australia was dominated by two forms of social relations: segregation and assimilation colonialism. They are often spoken of as if they are distinct and unrelated colonial practices. In the early federation period, protectionism (with its segregationist overtones) was practised in all states; Aboriginal people were said to be dying out as a result of contact and so were gathered into reserves and 'protected' from further abuses. This policy of 'smoothing the dying pillow' was replaced eventually by a more assimilationist approach, especially since Aborigines did not just die out. Advocates of assimilation tended to try and construct a radical historical juncture between these colonial periods, but they failed to recognise that the practices of assimilation and segregation operate dualistically—the practice of one *necessarily* presumed the existence of the other; only the emphasis shifts.

In practice, the policy of assimilation presumed the continuing exclusion of groups of Aboriginal people who were seen as less able to be assimilated than others. The difference between who could be included and who should be excluded from citizenship was highly contested. Disputes about which Aboriginal peoples were suitable for assimilation were common; there were disputes about even who, in legislative terms, was an Aborigine. What did remain central to the tensions throughout this Commonwealth era, despite a shift in policy towards a promotion of assimilation (migration, amongst other challenges, was causing a rethink of strategies to do with definitions and maintenance of Australian identity), was the dichotomy of invader and invaded. Certainly until the 1967 referendum removed the constitutional barriers to Aboriginal citizenship and resolved all ambiguities around this issue, the invaded continued to remain on the other side of the frontier. In this regard, assimilation colonialism is no different to segregationism; they are just flip sides of the same coin.

What was new in the representations of the post-war assimilationist decades was the increasing attention given to a new categories of Aborigine: the 'mixed blood', 'urban' or 'non-traditional'. The 'hybrid' Aborigine mediated the relation between the key oppositional category of Aborigine and non-Aborigine. The 'hybrid' Aborigine was constructed as ambiguous (bit of black, bit of white). This ambiguity is well captured by the historian Plomley, when he declared in 1977 that, 'structurally, physiologically and psychologically, hybrids are some mixture of their parents. In social terms, [these people] belong to neither race (and are shunned by both), and lacking a racial background they have no history.' There is no clearer statement of the social location of the 'hybrid' Aborigine in the mind of the coloniser—belonging nowhere, having no history, the 'hybrid' Aborigine exists in what Elkin termed, 'a cultural hiatus'. In this infamous description, Plomley was referring to my families. I read this as a teenager, and it is difficult to describe the feelings this statement evoked. It was something like grieving; but a grieving over a tremendous loss which is in itself then denied as being yours.

Plomley also exemplifies the tendency of this analytical tradition to conflate race and culture. Even though they are distinct processes, ideas of biological and cultural assimilation often tend to be merged and so can obscure each other. Within such schemes 'half-castes' are simply seen to assimilate better than 'full-bloods'.

Given anthropology's traditional pursuit of the 'real' Aborigine, it is perhaps not surprising that the discipline had a troubled interest in people who were 'non-traditional'. The ambiguity of the 'bit of black, bit of white' people is fundamental to (and enhanced by) the ethnographies of the period. It is sometimes difficult to divine motives. But from the 1940s on, anthropological interest bloomed with respect to this 'depressed segment of Australian society' (as Marie Reay described it in her 1988 Foreword to *Being Black: Aboriginal Culture in 'Settled' Australia*, a collection of ethnographic writings). Apparently, such communities lacked the exotic charm of other ethnographic targets. In south-east Australia, the communities studied included the Bundjalung mob of north-coast New South Wales, communities in Moree, Walgett, and western New South Wales and the Melbourne Aboriginal community. The anthropologists did not venture further south to Tasmania, where I was born.

These ethnographies were self-consciously described as 'sociocultural'—they were interested in cultural and social constructs of difference. But the social anthropology of this period often overlaid an older analysis, based on race, straight out of the discourse of physical anthropology, with a new form of essentialism: that of culture. Cultural essentialism now defined the 'authentic' Aborigines by their cultural forms, as surely as biological essentialism had once fixed them by their racial characteristics. In other words, now you could pick a real Aborigine by his or her 'authentic' or 'traditional' cultural practice. Legendary anthropologists, such as Radcliffe-Brown and Elkin, were the myth makers of definitions driven by kinship structures, section systems and the totems of the 'traditional' Aborigines. As south-eastern groups of Aboriginal people were situated between the 'authentic' cultural realms of black and white, it is not surprising that the work of the 'mixed-blood' ethnographers oscillated between representing a lack of distinctive Aboriginal culture to demonstrations of its presence.

But the invasion of older concepts of race continue to be apparent. Fink, for example, comments that 'the only way in which coloured people can hope to attain status within the non-coloured group is by trying to breed out the coloured element through marriage or liaisons with white or lighter coloured individuals. For it is only by ridding themselves of their [A]boriginal features that they can escape the stigma of the caste barrier.'

Many of the titles of studies from this period themselves refer to a strong awareness that the communities under study were of mixed genetic admixture. For example: *A Half-Caste Aboriginal community in North-western New South Wales* was presented by Reay in 1945; *Class and Status in a Mixed Blood Community (Moree, N.S.W.)* was presented by Reay and Sitlington in 1948; 1957 gave us *The Caste Barrier – An Obstacle to the Assimilation of Part-Aborigines in North-West New South Wales* by Fink; Beckett wrote *Marginal Men: A Study of Two Half Caste Aborigines* in 1958; and *Economic Absorption without Assimilation? The Case of some Melbourne Part-Aboriginal Families* was presented by Barwick in 1962.

Notions of social difference due to culture or social structures and (older) notions of race were simply collapsed together, and then projected as the basis for Aboriginal disadvantage—this clearly suggests that disadvantage could be eased if Aborigines just changed their skin colour. This logic of race evokes the reductionist notions of an evolutionist anthropology. And there is little attempt in these ethnographies to analyse miscegenation as a process of colonisation. I still remember being told by some Koori community elders that they had believed, at that time, that 'marrying out' was indeed the only hope for their children and grandchildren—an understandable response to oppressive times. But for these ethnographers, miscegenation is only a metaphor. In their writings, cultural hybridity is a feature of communities which they first perceived as biologically mongrel.

'White bit, black bit' ethnography began with the work of Reay on the Walgett community in New South Wales (1945). Her account of this Aboriginal community is divided into two, almost autonomous, sections. The first, which begins with the heading 'Contact with the White Community', outlines the attitudes of white people to Aborigines and their associates, and has sections on Aboriginal 'Labour and Liquor' and Aboriginal 'Offences Against the Law'. Prejudice, rural labour, the law and booze are seen as dominating the white side of these Aborigines' world. The reader is then taken into the black side, via an account of the Namoi Riverbank camp, which describes the tribal origins of its residents, *their* gambling and diet. This section, with its description of kinship structure, marriage rules and traditional bush cures, is directly commensurate with any work inspired by Radcliffe-Brown or Elkin—except, of course, for the prevailing motif of decay and loss. With the disintegration of Aboriginal tradition, the trajectory of social change was implied to be 'naturally' towards the white side. This strategy, devoid of any historical or social context, is perhaps even more obvious in some other projects, notably those of Fink, and Reay and Sitlington, and to a lesser extent Calley, where Aboriginal life is represented only as a combination of opposing fragments, some black, some white.

It's not until later that this form of essentialist representation is undermined. What was unique in the work of Beckett, and also in Barwick's work, is the location of Aboriginal experience within a colonial history. In placing Aboriginal people within the context of colonial history, the relentless and inevitable movement of Aboriginal into the non-Aboriginal cultural realm, suggested by earlier studies, is perhaps less certain. However, notions of what is essentially black and essentially white still penetrate the later work of Barwick and Beckett. For example, Beckett, in 1964, in an essay which challenged the legal restrictions on Aboriginal access to alcohol, contended that, 'like dress, popular music, and games, (alcohol) is one of the features of the invading civilisation which are easy to appreciate and to adopt, and its exhilarating effects provide a novel diversion at a time when traditional satisfactions are either discredited or rendered impracticable. But since native people are neither physically nor culturally accustomed to its use, the consequences may be extreme.' Alcohol is constructed only as a morally dangerous product of civilisation on an unprepared (primitive) people. Such a proposition of naïveté rests both on the empirically incorrect assumption that pre-colonial Aboriginal communities did not use analogous mind-altering substances and the possibility that naïveté was sustainable through 176 years of colonial history. As a cultural trait, alcohol use is constructed as white.

Similarly, Barwick contended in 1964 that 'certain characteristics of the Victorian part-[A]boriginal population are not specifically [A]boriginal, but are common to other migrant workers such a Caribbean plantation workers, Canadian lumbermen, and Californian farm labourers.' For Barwick, even though the economic position of Aboriginal people had developed throughout the colonial history of Victoria, work patterns such as these did not belong to Aborigines. Several generations of Aboriginal rural workers whose lives were patterned by these seasonal movements are constructed only as role players in an alien global economic field. Yet the labour was Aboriginal. How is it that a group of people can participate in a work process such as this, over a number of generations, and not be able to claim such practices as a specific feature of their lives? Like other ethnographic ventures of this era, Barwick mobilises reified constructs of Aboriginal and non-Aboriginal culture in describing Aboriginal life practice in this way.

As I say, in the ethnographies of the assimilation era, Aboriginal social change is charted as occurring on a continuum of black to white, with a number of intermediate positions. In their 1948 ethnography, Reay and Sitlington analyse class and status in the Moree Aboriginal community, not through the more usual economic criteria, but on the 'basis of hygiene and home making, the main criteria of class in this community.' Not surprisingly, the 'upper class mixed-bloods' (more white bit than black bit) displayed domestic and personal habits more commensurate with the white people of Moree. In situating this group of Aboriginal people as Moree's black upper class, the value presumptions about the required direction of social change are explicit. 'Flash' blacks (my term) are better—it is presumed that no one desires to be downwardly mobile—because they are like white people.

The continuum of social change is charted in cultural terms, as I've suggested, but also in biological terms (as well as in a temporal dimension and in terms of spatial movement). An assimilated Aboriginal future was to be realised, it seems, by the movement across a number of dichotomised barriers: black culture into white culture; out of tradition into white history; from the camp into town; swapping a black skin for a white one. The natural direction of change was presumed (out of 'other' into 'self'). What remained to be demonstrated was the extent to which this had, or could have, occurred.

The 'mixed-blood' community, the 'not quite others', actually constituted 'an anomaly, if not a danger', as Beckett reflected in 1988. The most fundamental threat to the symbolic legitimacy of White Australia was, in fact, presented by those impure forms of Aboriginality which blurred the distinction between black and white.

The threat of cultural throw-backs continued to subvert the maintenance of an Australian nation, whose history was imperial, and whose culture and race were white. And so the removal of the black bits from the lives of Aboriginal people has been systematically practised by White Australia, symbolically as well as literally.

This conceptualisation of Aboriginality—as something straight-forwardly replaceable, culturally as well as biologically—not only protected the moral and aesthetic purity of white nationhood, it also protected state-legitimated institutions from any assertions of inequity of access. The question of civic rights is impossible to resolve to the satisfaction of claimants if they are ambiguously situated as citizens. The 'authentic' Aborigine is always outside of the institutional forms of modernity; but the 'ambiguous' Aborigine is only partially and, therefore, more dangerously so.

Reay, in 1945, contended that 'there is an invariable preference for their own traditional remedies. The [A]borigines are unwilling to enter hospital, even in the case of serious illness. They cling to their belief in their own remedies until the patient is dying; then, if these are unavailing, they consult the white doctor.' These Aboriginal people were aware of the functions and activities of hospitals, but apparently they were held back by their black side. There is no solution other than acculturation. No mention is made by Reay of any need by these services to respond to specific Aboriginal claims for service, or to demographic or economic or other systemic barriers to access. Poor access to services is merely a consequence of a residual tribal logic.

Anthropology is the study of human beings. As people, we have one life experience. Hopefully, I am stating the obvious, yet assimi-lationist ethnographic practices suggest otherwise. The experience of 'non-traditional' Aboriginal communities is represented as fragmented, as standing only between two worlds. What is lost is any sense of the humanity of these Aboriginal people. As human beings we need to eat, to experience emotion, to find relief for distress. How we are propelled through life is shaped by our sense of a changing world, by our symbolic life and by an experience of being able to mobilise resources. Yet in the ethnographic context, this widespread and contemporary Aboriginal experience is portrayed only as a titanic struggle between the opposing black and white bits.

As I am an Aborigine, I inhabit an Aboriginal body, and not a combination of features which may or may not cancel each other. Whatever language I speak, I speak an Aboriginal language, because a lot of Aboriginal people I know speak like me. How I speak, act and how I look, are outcomes of a colonial history, and not a particular combination of traits from either side of the frontier. I agree with Deloria, that representations which describe indigenous peoples (or any other peoples) as caught 'between two worlds' become 'conceptual prisons'. In the transforming experiences through which Aboriginal people grow, those qualities which constitute our identities are constantly reforming as we engage and re-engage our world. This is one experience which coheres us, despite all ambiguities and contradictions. It is with one experience that we encounter institutions such as the health and legal systems. Inequities arise, not because we are retarded by the black bits, but because the system we relate ourselves to either fails to orient itself towards our total needs, or else has created barriers which discriminate against access.

The era of assimilation colonialism has had tragic consequences for significant numbers of Aboriginal people. In responding to this, we must not only meet our therapeutic and rehabilitative needs, we also need to develop strategies which undermine those forms of representation which deny our ability to develop identities which are both coherent and sustaining.

The
Embarrassment
of the Kangaroo

NICHOLAS JOSE

TAIPEI, 1994—THE LEAP OVER

I chew my first betelnut. It is eaten fresh from a packet that is kept in the refrigerator. You take two at once, cream-coloured balls, like hazelnuts, harnessed together with a strip of leaf, like a tiny bikini top. You pop the whole thing into your mouth and chew. The taste is musky and anaesthetic, and after gentle chewing you feel a rush of heat to the face. Your earlobes flush, your senses lift a little. The body is subdued: not unlike a controlled exercise in glue-sniffing, or a very mild popper that peaks quickly. In five minutes the betelnut is a mass of tasteless red fibre. You can remove it from your mouth and delicately swallow or you can spit a scarlet dart, if your aim is good. You follow with a mouthful of beer which tastes wonderfully sweet as your body expels its damps.

I am sitting in the New Phase Art Space in Tainan, old southern capital of Taiwan. In 1661 the people of the district besieged the occupying Dutch with ramparts of bamboo straw and left-over rice, and they drove them out. To this day, Tainan boasts the ruins of Fort Zeelandia. New Phase Art Space occupies a made-over commercial building from the 1960s, the days when Taiwan's now dragon economy was Newly Industrialising—almost as long ago, now, as the seventeenth century. Gallery space, book and craft stores, seminar rooms, cinematheque, dance hall and Tuscan restaurant are all included in this stylish private centre for contemporary culture run by artists and their backers. The enterprise is fuelled by a combination of boom-time money from the 1980s and the 'Taiwan consciousness' that has intensified since martial law was lifted in 1987.

The courtyard cafe abuts an old wall made of beautiful apricot-coloured bricks held together by meandering tree roots. 'It's at least ninety years old,' Joan Du, the manager, tells me. I could kiss her for her local pride. This is real history in a country that dates its calendar years from 1911. It's a refreshing change from mainland China where everything is a glorious 3000 years old and no one knows the actual age of anything.

The betelnut is another difference. It belongs to a different cultural tradition from that of the Chinese mainlanders who crossed to the island in 1949, a difference as profound as that between beer and wine cultures in Europe. In the south of Taiwan, *bingnya* is everywhere (I use the local Malay-derived Hoklo word for what has no name of its own in Mandarin). The artists sitting in the courtyard under the stars, exhausted by compulsive talk about the future of their place, chew it appreciatively as they sink into their tea leaves.

The bearded artist has a stoned glow in his eyes as he gives me a parting souvenir of betelnut. He waits for me to examine it. The logo on the green-and-gold packet turns out to be a kangaroo and her joey. It is Kangaroo brand betelnut. 'Good Friend', it says. Green is a

curative and refreshing colour, and gold is for the riches of sunlight—
the island of Formosa, once the greenest place in the world, is now the
place with the most gold. The drug and the colours too come from
the deepest roots of this shamanistic, hallucinatory *and* materialistic
culture. Australian colours as well, of course. The kangaroo and her
joey are speaking volumes to me. Marvelling at the piracy of images, I
vow to treasure the gift.

When I tell my Australian friends back in Taipei, they warn me
never again to eat betelnut. It's treated with chemicals to make it more
addictive. The chemicals give you gum cancer.

I'm in Taiwan for the opening of 'Identities: Art from Australia',
the first survey exhibition of contemporary Australian art to be seen
here. My involvement in the project had its whimsical beginning in
the air over the Snowy Mountains when my fellow passenger and I,
strangers, abandoned our studied silence to admire the sparkling snow
cover. We got talking. She was from the University of Wollongong and
she had a Taiwanese graduate student who had been agitating her
about taking some Aboriginal art to Taiwan. From there, it had been
two years to this opening at the Taipei Fine Arts Museum, as part of
Australia Now month.

Like everything else in Taiwan, the private artistic impulse achieves
its dynamism, for artists, dealers, critics and buyers alike, precisely
because it exists in a zone of resistance, not always comfortably
condoned by officialdom. 'Private' has become something of a dirty
word in my world these days, but I am using it here in its better sense,
as the unregulated source of new creative ideas.

Our Australian assumptions about the 'public' and 'private' largely
do not suit the situation in Taiwan, where bourgeois money is a more
radical agent of change than is state-sponsored culture. Arriving in
Taiwan, we, largely state-sponsored, find ourselves crossing the lines.
We are taken, for example, to a private Salon de Muse, where a dealer
shows us his 'Ten Future Master Pieces', among them a painting of
Botticelli's Three Graces belatedly reaching this once-paradisal island,
tired, sallow and sagging-fleshed as they sink to the ocean floor
beneath the weight of industrial devastation and cultural garbage.

The trick here is to tap these private energies. The Australian
exhibition, curated by Deborah Hart, does so by boldly representing a
whole number of different and contending Australias. The charged
question for us—how can art discover a society's consciousness—is
compelling to the Taiwanese arts community too, which is seeking a
local *Taiwan* identity, removed from Chinese tradition at the same time
as it is removed from (Western) internationalism. It becomes a problem
when the Taiwan partners in the project, wishing to market the
uniqueness they find in the Australian works, somewhat inevitably
suggest that the exhibition should be promoted with the image of the

kangaroo. Despite its major Aboriginal and environmental components, the exhibition features no kangaroos.

More than 100 000 Taiwanese tourists visited Australia in 1993, an annual increase of 76 per cent. The trip could not be complete for any of them, it seems, without their seeing a kangaroo on native soil. So, what more natural way of attracting Taiwanese audiences to an Australian art show?

But the problem is that the kangaroo is no longer kosher, not as far as we're concerned nowadays. Our official effort overseas is going into the promotion of an image of Australia as hi-tech, innovative and pluralist. No more kangaroos. The kangaroo, therefore, has been kept off the cover of the catalogue. Its bouncy form appears only in the Australia Council's logo. Another major sponsor, Australia–Asia Airlines, has its hands differently tied. Canberra prevents this Qantas subsidiary from using Qantas's Flying Kangaroo for fear of offending the People's Republic of China across the Straits. Australia–Asia Airlines is not supposed to be a 'national' carrier. So Australia–Asia Airlines uses Chinese-style streamers instead of kangaroos as the logo for its four mostly full direct flights a week between Australia and Taiwan—while Qantas does not fly to mainland China.

The exhibition is on the third floor of the enormous museum, and to help people find it the museum staff take matters into their own hands and lay a trail of kangaroos from the entrance, across the marble floor and up the stairs to the haunting images of Australia. It is a populist induction which is echoed in the contemporary Aboriginal dance performed by Ladu, from the group Sirocco, to lead the audience into the show. But artist George Gittoes sees this dance as a 'stand-off', an image of cultural divide. The art the Sultan likes best, observes Gittoes in a satirical drawing he pins to the wall, is his own reflection in the mirror. Other people's treasures don't mean a thing.

So maybe it's lucky to have a few playful symbolic marsupials around to jump across the gaps. Because it's true, if we're not prepared to be cute, others will do it for us.

I hear that Skippy the Boxing Kangaroo in the visiting Russian International Circus was the hit of this year's Chinese New Year holiday in Taipei.

The surprise success of Australia Now is the visit of Miss Australia—no, *two* Miss Australias, 1992 and 1993, a lofty brunette and a lofty blonde who have the taxi drivers of Taipei queuing around the block to be photographed with them. One on each arm, perhaps?

The laminated photographs will by now be adorning many a rear-vision mirror. These Miss Australias come with impeccable professional credentials. *Diana* magazine, Taiwan's *Vogue*, headlines its photostory on Miss Australia at Phillip Island: 'Which Would You Rather Have, the Beauty or the Penguin?' Work that one out.

With unemployment at a twelve-year low of 1.45 per cent, only the seriously unemployable become taxidrivers in Taipei—either betelnut-chewing young locals or drunken veterans who came across from the mainland with Chiang Kai-shek's army in 1949 and are ready for a rave in the crosstown traffic jam when they pick the Peking accent in my mongrel Chinese. One was only a teenage kid when he hopped onboard ship at Shanghai with a platoon of Nationalist soldiers, he tells me, leaving behind his family and friends. After a week the ship reached a place called Taiwan where he has since spent a lifetime's exile, as bootlicker to some officer whose mission to retake the Motherland was endlessly deferred. He has just been able to make his first trip back to the mainland. His sister waited for him at the provincial airport for five hours, with her limousine and driver. She's the Deputy Mayor of the provincial capital now. My taxi driver had backed the wrong horse for this particular lifetime.

He begins an obsessive litany about the unstoppable expansionism of China. 'Tibet used to be independent. It's returned to China. Hong Kong used to be British. It's returning to China. Mongolia used to be Soviet. It will return to China. Central Asia's returning to China. It used to be Soviet...Korea...Vietnam...' I guess his logic is that Taiwan will return one day too. The only place that will never 'return' in this way is Japan, he claims. When he finds out I am Australian, he asks if it can be true that we are letting the Japanese build independent cities on Australian soil over which we Australians have no sovereignty. He warns that it is only a matter of course before these Japanese cities demand their own representatives in the Australian parliament—the thin end of the wedge. He has seen the Japanese fight the Chinese in the area around Nanking where he grew up. It is hard to argue with him. It is hard to explain that Australians, unlike East Asians, are mostly not given to five-year plans or long-term paranoias.

We leave it that as long as Australia has 'good air' it will continue to be an object of desire. It's true. Southern Sky, the largest Buddhist temple in the southern hemisphere, is being built by the Taiwanese Pure Land sect on the freeway south of Wollongong, which translates as Five Dragon Harbour in Mandarin. It's clean and green and the *fengshui's* good.

Later, I run into friend Lisa in Taipei. She is there to source seductive packaging for the deer penises being produced in Goulburn for sale as aphrodisiacs to the Australian duty-free trade. I hear Barry Humphries's character Daryl Dalkeith, the embrace-Asia entrepreneur, gushing: 'I am thinking of bath gel, scented with West Australian wildflowers. We can put the dozers through the wildflower crop. We can pulp them up, get the juice out of them and bung it into the bath gel. They've never had it. They don't know they need it. You invent a market!'

Australia's international image is something our government would like to massage into better shape. But our image will probably never be much better than the substance that lies behind the image, and that substance is nothing more nor less than the agglomeration of all the different contacts that already exist between our community and other communities, often in crazy ways, ways which my experience tells me we are in no position to dictate or police, and which we would be foolish to resist or deny.

Maybe we can learn some useful tips, even truths, by looking into these unlikely crossover points between us and others and asking why. The spark only jumps when there is a build-up of charge on both sides. *Why* did 100 000 Taiwanese visit Australia last year? Was it just the low dollar? *Why* the kangaroo?

Different countries do not map neatly onto each other. Countries cannot 'mesh' thoroughly. The profoundest connections are unpredictable ones, and are often quite trivial at the outset. The translators, the mediators, the bridging people are our society's eyes and ears in this process, out in front, their antennae picking up the crackle in the air that means there is a message that *wants* to get across. It is a highly random, hit-and-miss business, in which misperception and fantasy play as important a part as accurate mutual apprehension. And the points of connection are not always flattering. In searching for the 'fit', it's necessary to recognise the points of non-connection too. And, since opposites can attract, the points of resistance, even of repulsion, may also reveal relationships, as between the twin halves of a duality. Are Taiwan and Australia two island extremes which are being drawn inexorably to their inverse reflection in each other, the one to breathe fresh air, the other for a spin in the scarlet karaoke palace of economic superpowerdom?

The dynamos of Asia elicit a knee-jerk horror from many Australians: corruption, crowding, cheap labour, exploitation, lack of humanity—a fouled nest, the flip side of Asia the Beautiful. Sometimes the horror is put to rest by the notion that Asians do, 'after all', live by different values. They have their convenient oriental spirituality which enables them to passively endure suffering and hardship, to put up with bad environments and low wages, and other restrictions on their human rights, in the name of some higher ideal. At other times, the moralistic response, the horror, barely conceals the Australian's fascinated envy of the oriental opportunity zone. In that lotus land, to be sleazy—to give or accept deal-sweeteners, to jelly the truth, to pander to your negotiating partner's personal interests and appetites— is, after all, only being polite. That's the way things have to be done, in a place where corruption is fabled and accountability evaporates in clouds of unknowing. How unlike our own highly regulated home, where a government minister can be brought down by a peccadillo in his own sandwich bar.

How to be? What to think? How to act? How to see and be seen? Whether horror or envy, moralism or blinkeredness, our perceptual connection with the various societies that make up Asia reveals an area of clumsiness or naïveté in how we relate. It is a problem which is aggravated by the fact that so many disparate activities are grouped under the heading of Australia's turning to Asia, all with our government's encouragement. It's a nice-sounding idea that needs rather a lot of qualification before it can really make sense.

For some people the issue boils down to whether we can only get involved with Asian countries if we actually turn a blind eye to what we don't like about them. Others respond, using that word beloved of diplomats, that a 'nuanced' approach is the best. It is easy to ridicule such an approach or see it degenerate into a craven double standard, but the reality is that there *are* cultural differences, just as there are also cultural similarities, and that we are working through complex sets of assumptions and expectations, and we don't even understand what these are, unless we are in there on the ground. But that does include knowing *what* we are, *who* we are, and *where* we come from. Only then can we use what we've got.

Stephen Fitzgerald, in his article 'Ethical Dimensions of Australia's Engagement with Asian Countries', develops the idea of Asia as a moral mirror or conscience for Australia. He notes how the decline in Australian business ethics in the 1980s coincided with Asia's emergence as a priority area for government and business, and observes that the unseemly haste of the 'institutional discovery of Asia' at that time made the proponents of the new relationship oblivious to pre-existing histories of connection or to any understanding that looked to longer-term, perhaps unpalatable, outcomes. Now, in the 1990s, our Academy of Social Sciences is looking for an 'ethical framework' for doing business with Asia. It is no doubt a worthy consciousness-raising project, but it does beg the question of whether we need *different* ethics for dealing with Asia and, if so, whether that's because their ethics are different or ours are inadequate.

Ethics is a big word. At one end of the scale, it can refer only to matters of custom and etiquette. When do you take your shoes off on entering a home? When do you allow the other person to pay for your drink? If the other person insists on paying for all the drinks, are you then under an obligation to return the favour in some other form? At the other end of the scale, ethics is, of course, a matter of moral choices, of good and evil; and in between are all those areas of passionate social concern—environmental issues, the situation of women, policy towards minority and indigenous peoples, the preservation of cultures and heritage, consumerism, and so on. I am no philosopher or sociologist, but I suspect that the ethical dimensions of the behaviour of any one of us may be complicated by unfamiliarity where Asia is involved, but are otherwise no less complicated than the morality of our lives generally. Externally imposed ethical frameworks don't have a good record of straightening the crooked timber of humanity, even when people do try to live up to them. It is hard to believe that there will be many subscribers to the ethical guidebook to Asia. Fitzgerald, being a veteran of many committees that have looked at issues of this kind, knows how often sensible, improving recommendations go unheeded. Being as interested in nurturing a process as in getting results, he opts for an open-ended ecumenical approach, rather than anything too evangelical. He suggests that Australians should be encouraged to work together with Asian societies to seek a new commonality of ethical consciousness that goes beyond the existing moral givens of any one society.

Although this too sounds good, it is hard to see how it would work in practice. We might exchange pieces of legislation, or family structures, or religious beliefs, or social support structures, but values are surely different. They are not swap cards. They are not tradable, unlike other commodities. They express what you are, even without your knowledge. And they do not belong to you exclusively. Someone else, in another place, can have the same values, whether supported by their society or in defiance of it. Australian or Asian, it is a matter of individual consciences, first and last.

But in the 1990s, values have become counters in political and economic manoeuvres. Ethical questions have gone beyond the question of individual conscience, as individual consciences have united to form interest groups to lobby governments, putting their ethical positions into the scales with other kinds of interest (hence, for instance, the unholy, but not unpragmatic, balancing acts we see China and the United States perform over trade and human rights issues). The Chinese argue that the United States has no right to meddle in their family affairs—and plenty of Americans would agree. The United States counters that these are issues of global concern—and plenty of Chinese would agree. And there are plenty of Chinese Americans and plenty of Chinese Australians in both camps. Ethical commitments slide into personal agendas or harden into platforms. And subtle abstractions are turned into cartoons so the international media can continue to tell an old story of Western cowboys and Eastern injuns.

It is ironic that, in the latest act, in the current telling of this story, the best of the West—justice, freedom, participation—has been turned by us into a club such as Fred Flintstone might have wielded, while one of the West's worst inventions—Asia the Other—has been adopted and is being exploited by the less than free regimes of the region themselves, as their rationale for operating by 'different' values, for not giving their own people what they want. When someone in power uses the phrase 'different cultural background' to excuse an unacceptable state of affairs, I bristle. It's like being told that you don't know what you're talking about. Usually when someone says that, you should know you're onto something.

Of course Australia must be its own country, independently forming an array of relationships with different Asian communities, in a whole host of ways, where it is possible to do so, from trade and defence to the arts and tourism, and these relationships must include mutual ethical questioning. Battering others about their ethics, and being battered in turn, becomes a mere Punch and Judy show, if we take our own self-exploration as a society for granted. But if we are committed to a spirited, open and confident sifting of *our* public and private moralities, as a distinctive part of our social life, then there is no reason why we should not expose that process to others.

The formulation of values and the creation of a good society should be one of the most exciting things about Australia, engaged in vocally and unapologetically. Too often the challenge stuns people into silence, where it should become something *expected* of us by oppressors and oppressed alike, something for which some people prize us and others respect us in a take-it-or-leave it way. We gain nothing by hiding this potential core of our Australianness for the sake of currying favour overseas, or avoiding embarrassment, or strutting through a round of regional *realpolitik* in exchange for a payoff that never comes. On the contrary, our regional adventures should catalyse and inform our definition of the kind of place we want *Australia* to be.

We can become victim of our own relaxed attitude to our own morality. We should not become ethically superior or rigid, and we should also be wary of others who seek to exploit our tentativeness (or is it tolerance?) about our own ethics by making us uncertain about how to behave towards *their* unethical behaviour. It is here that Australia's becoming part of Asia is most troublesome, where it seems to imply that we must abandon something of ourselves that we treasure, even if we're not very sure what it is. But this is a difficulty that can be turned into something positive. Unless we work to develop a clear realisation of what we are and what we stand for, our role in the region, ethically or otherwise, will never make sense. It is partly a question of self-image. It is also, fundamentally, a question of self-knowledge.

We can't just let go of our own values, however much of a nuisance they may be at times. What you believe and what you know are inseparable from what you are, the expression of a particular history, even as you are continuing to change all the time. Your values are what others see, even when you can't see them yourself. They're what others have to filter, like the good air. They're what others may want, or may like to imagine, like the kangaroo. Why be embarrassed? They may even be the best thing we've got. Only don't be surprised when they turn up and are put to unexpected uses in strange places.

PEKING, 1989—THE GAP

I had my own experience of kangaroo embarrassment.

With a reputation for being one of the most corrosive critics of the Chinese government, Liu returned to Peking from New York to take part in the protest movement. Skinny, with spiky hair and bad skin, he delivered outrageous remarks in a husky stammer. I liked him. He wrote that Chinese intellectuals must become citizens of the world before their minds can be free. To be able to see China in a larger context, away from the centre, as he could, was already a big step. He had developed a taste for XO cognac. In the days of Tiananmen Square we got through quite a few bottles together.

The reason he came to my place the first time was to use the guest bedroom. Like other fiery iconoclasts, he was irresistible to some women. He had a loyal wife at home, a lover in the Square, and a new girlfriend. When it was all over I found two pairs of female knickers and one pair of his in the abandoned flat. His were like a child's. He had very narrow hips. I also found his Florida T-shirt. Palm trees against an orange sky.

Since a foreigner's residence was relatively convenient, he used my place as a base. He made and received international phone calls there. He could come and go. Writers, journalists, photographers, students— not all Chinese—did the same, and it became a drifting party, with dark intelligence flying around in a cool counterpoint to what was happening a few blocks away. In the nearby Square, thousands of impassioned people were calling for the overthrow of the government. Parades of support passed my building. Ferocious rumours of every colour flew about. And, as the days went by, a running-down of momentum challenged my friend to take on a new role as activist. He placed an envelope in my desk for safekeeping. It contained, I believe, his Chinese passport and American visa, and US$2000 from supporters in New York. He would need those things to escape. He did not retrieve the envelope until the eve of the army crackdown. It was in the backpack he left behind in the Square, to be incinerated, crushed by the tanks, or taken in evidence against him. A visiting Australian theatre director nicknamed my place the Last Salon in Peking. From the seventh floor balcony you could see columns of smoke across to the west. Helicopters buzzed overhead. And when the tanks did occupy the intersection below, a barrel was aimed at the living-room window and an officer shouted through his megaphone that we would be shot if we took photos. So the party moved to the other end of the flat, until the fridge was bare.

Before all this, what used to happen below my window instead was a form of vocal exercise which the old men from the old low houses on the other side of the ring road practised at dawn. I would wake to their cries and look down at them lifting their legs to the perpendicular onto a bit of low wall. Old men in the smoky haze of a summer morning that dissolved my views of the Temple of Heaven in the distance.

But now I wasn't at home much of the time any more. I had my work and my own involvement in what was happening, which I had lived every day for nearly four years, in private as well as professionally; bonds formed, allegiances and decisions made. And now everything was accelerating. I was out and about a lot, aware of the gravity of events outside, and the danger of the comings and goings at my flat. I'd come home only to sleep and to read a few pages of my bedside books. One was a study of Shakespeare's *Troilus and Cressida*, about the mixed meanings in great historical moments. The other was the *Six Chapters of a Floating Life*, the exquisite, intimate Ch'ing dynasty classic.

There were persistent rumours growing that one part of the army would turn on those divisions responsible for the 3–4 June attack. Diplomatic missions were becoming preoccupied with deciding whether their people should stay or go. An unexplained shooting directed at the foreigners' residential compound tilted us towards a 'go'. It was my job now to find and inform the Australian students and teachers living in the vicinity of Peking. I was also worried about my Chinese friends, many of whom had reasons to fear a clamp down. It was a very confused situation, unfolding by the minute. As our convoy passed army trucks burning in the road, we saw sniper patrols carrying out raids. No one went out on the streets who didn't have to.

By 6 June there was no food left in my flat except for some Bega cheese in the deepfreeze. I won't go into the complexities and the emotions of the evacuation, save to say that eventually everyone was taken care of. One Chinese on the wanted list moved to the embassy where he sought asylum. But Liu was more of a problem. We made a plan that during the afternoon someone would collect him and his girlfriend and another friend from my flat and get them where they needed to go.

I was busy organising things until well after the curfew. After being out all day I had to go home one last time, a thirty-minute round-trip, to pack a suitcase. Leave everything else behind. Throw perishables down the chute. Bring notebooks. Address book. Anything that should not be found in case of a search. A few personal irreplaceables.

The usual lift attendants had been off for days. Now a spade-faced plain-clothes cop had replaced them. On reaching my flat I found the lights on and music playing. The three people who were supposed to have gone during the afternoon were still there, waiting for me to return.

The security man studied us as we came out of the lift. I was lugging my suitcase. Then he noted the telltale plates of my car, the only car, the only moving light, in all those vast dark boulevards. The petrified city of the future. I drove to where Liu's two friends had parked their bicycles and dropped them off. Then I drove on with my friend, who had become a Black Hand.

We stopped under the trees outside the embassy. The moment had come for him to choose whether to drive inside through the automatic gates with me, to diplomatic immunity (a form of extraterritoriality such as had existed in China's concession ports in the old days), or whether to cross the road instead, to his friend's home, where his girlfriend would be waiting. There he could consider. He had said he wanted to call on the world's forces of justice to intervene in China's fate. Or he could run for it into the Chinese hinterland.

What happened is we reached out and shook hands. Firmly and for a long time. He opened the car door. Then he was gone, wearing my jeans, which were loose on him, and my jacket.

In the embassy everyone was smoking, although it was supposed to be a smoke-free zone. People for the next day's evacuation flight were bedding down on the floor. There were a lot of things to be done, and the character of the players there showed up in the crisis, as if through glass: there were those who acted on a sure instinct of humanity, those who, at a loss for any guidance of the heart, fell back on form, and there were others who were learning to embrace the decisions that the situation demanded. It was around eleven o'clock when a phone call came through to my office from the girl. She and Liu had attempted to ride a bicycle to her house a few blocks away. At a certain intersection an unmarked van overtook them. Some men jumped out, dragged Liu into the van and drove off with him. The hysterical girl was ringing from a public phone. She didn't know what would happen to him after the arrest. He would be denounced. He would be tortured. He would be made to tell stories. She proposed to rush back to the embassy and jump over the compound wall.

Why had they done it? Why had Liu gone out with her on bicycle through those empty streets? Why hadn't they come with me? Was it to get fresh clothes? To make love? Was it the intellectual's intoxication with action? Did he want to proclaim his fearlessness or something? The jaws of a monster lying in wait in the darkness had snapped into place.

I lay on my back pressing the floorboards. The peculiar woolly grey of the Peking dawn came up before I slept, as it had done for centuries now, according to the ancient calendar, over the low roofs of the walled city, the sacred groves of the emperors' outlying tombs, the craggy mountain fastnesses of the aspirant and the disgraced, the yellow deserts beyond.

Should I have forced my friend inside the safety of the diplomatic compound for his own good? Should I have insisted?

He was a bright hope of China, one of few able to articulate what was needed to renovate this rotten place. Wasn't he? And now a person was gone forever, down those jaws. I even wondered if I hadn't failed the China that had given me so much.

The most one can hope, perhaps, is to help a few people. But which people? Chosen on what basis? Those on your own side, or those you must cross the road for? I owed him nothing except that I admired him. And the reason for that was his rasping character. I liked him because of the way his taste for XO cognac enhanced the hoarse stammering delivery of his outrageous remarks.

In the end, I had *allowed* him the choice of whether to come with me or go. Beyond a certain point I had not joined cause with him. I had not taken his life into my own hands. I had not presumed to know how he must act. His reckless caprice proved costly, and it continued to cause me pain and regret as well, whenever I thought of him.

He was an actor in a history that dictated its own merciless outcomes. I was only a bit player in that same history, at the point where it entered my life and where I was part of the connective tissue between China's epoch and our own subtler, wryer Australian history, in which quite different, democratic pulses can be heard. I was reluctant to let go of that gap that held me from identifying with a Chinese friend who identified himself with his own people. That was always the basis of our relationship—he had his history, I had mine. The gap wasn't such a large one, it turned out—simply the moment in an idling car when an individual decides. I grieved for the existence of that gap, lying there on the floor. I understood in those anxious hours that I come from another place, that I should go home and wait another day.

In the small hours of the night on which martial law had been formally declared, through loudspeakers and under searchlights in the Square, I had walked back under the willows beside the palace moat and away into the maze of alleyways that was the city. I was walking with a wandering Australian scholar of China who knows more about all this than I shall ever know, and we met two girls morosely going home.

'Our movement is defeated,' they cried out to us. 'Our movement is defeated.'

That's when I learned to read the dove-grey Peking dawn. It's no kangaroo fur. The light—it seemed so worn—was a blanket that smothers what might be, under the pretence of reinstating what is.

Amnesty, PEN International and other organisations made Liu's case a priority. He was vilified throughout China because, they said, he had sold his motherland. But he was adulated too, throughout the country. Australian friends smuggled him a jumper of top-quality wool, Made in Australia. Sick in prison, he had been allowed Chinese classics to read. When he appeared on television to tell a tailored version of his story, his face looked puffy, as if he had been beaten. Then, after two years, he was released. He has even visited Australia to give lectures, which he is forbidden to do in China. But his views no longer inspire. So he must wait another day too.

And I, having recognised the gap, continue compulsively to explore it, probing the places where lightning can jump across and scorch.

Professor Yang Xianyi, a great literary translator, never approved of Liu. He was a mad dog. He wanted to move too fast. When asked what is going on in China, or what he thinks of Australia—are we part of Asia?—Professor Yang has a mouthful of Scottish tea and smiles. 'I like your koala. He is sleepy. He hates to move. I like your kangaroo. Although she cannot fly, she can leap. She can go faster than one hundred miles per hour.'

In 1992, there was a Celebrate Australia week in Peking, featuring a preview of *Strictly Ballroom*, a grand barbecue, and the usual players—Foreign Affairs (Austrade), QANTAS, arts bodies etc.—taking their partners for another whirl round the floor. A feud broke out when it was suggested that the five-star China World Hotel, the host of the event, get a giant kangaroo suit to enliven the festivities in ways to which all Australians were expected to warm. The word came down the line—tacky tacky tacky. The fencekeepers of Australia's overseas image had decided that the Chinese people were too refined to be amused by a bouncing humanoid kangaroo. Or if they were amused, it might mean that they were laughing at us, not taking us as seriously as we deserve to be taken.

The costume is still available for hire.

A Few
More Minutes
with Monica Vitti

ANAMARIA BELIGAN

Ｉf there was ever an archetypal Sensitive-New-Age-Guy, that person would be me.

Sensitive because, beyond my cool exterior, beyond my beard and my crusty jeans, you wouldn't have to dig too far to discover the blushing flower of my fragile yet well-balanced inner self. New Age, because I'm so new despite my age: born a feudal relic of an anachronistic family of Moldavian landowners, I became a youth of the Stalinist–Leninist promised land; a gravedigger of putrid, irrevocably compromised capitalism; and then, without the support of any ideological rationale, I was metamorphosed into a traitor of my country, an Eastern refugee with no sense of direction, knocking on the door of imperialism-with-a-human-face. Now here I am, in the southernmost moment of my questionable existence, resting on the ruins of a post-industrial purgatorium, listening to Brunswick Street crystals and mourning the ozone above my head. Here I am, the irrefutable SNAG. With my ponytail, my Himalayan vest. My balsamic vinegar, my flute, my tai-chi in the morning, my mantras at dusk, my home-made wholemeal French sticks, my daily foccacia at Mario's, my short blacks at Cafe'Cuccina, my organic vegie patch and, especially, especially!...my gentle but ideologically firm, caring-and-sharing intimacy with Mina.

Her real name is Hermina Van der Walde. She's on the right side of twenty; I'm on the wrong side of thirty-five.

Hermina Van der Walde who understandably hates her name, which betrays the geographical antecedents of her C cups and her size-14 posterior that would have made any old Rubens see purple (this is my uncontrollable, beastly unconscious speaking again: don't take it into consideration, don't let it compromise my hard-won New Age identity!). Hermina Van der Walde, with her red, carnivorous gums, with her oversized canines which make you wonder which of her great grandmothers had been wandering on the wrong side of the Danube, into some Transylvanian nightmare of lust and fangs. Hermina Van der Walde, the Adelaide born, cosmically aware student of Human Bioethics with whom I collided, incidentally but fatally, on Collins Street, on a September Saturday twelve months ago, in the middle of a demonstration against the latest Americo-Japanese toxic cargo roaming our seas in search of a furtive nest. Well, Hermina known as Mina is the real godmother of my SNAG persona. Thanks to her, I finally belong in the scheme of things. I have a lifestyle of my own. A sociological, demographical and cultural niche.

I like almost everything about Mina, my sister, my godmother, my carnivorous friend. I cook our pasta, I recycle our garbage, I clean our beaches on Sundays. I die every morning when she leaves with her rucksack on her back, and I am resurrected every night when she comes home with a bunch of wildflowers or a bag of half-priced avocados or a new outfit fished from the depths of some improbable op shop. I love her red, untidy locks, her skin which rebels against any form of make-up. Her unmistakable scent of rainwater and wild strawberries. For her sake I could even become a Marxist–Leninist all over again, if it wasn't for...if it wasn't for...

If it wasn't for *what*? How can I let this cat out of my bag? How can I disclose this hideous skeleton hidden inside the darkest of my closets? How could I face myself, after articulating those dreadful thoughts that keep rising from the murky waters of my despicable unconscious?

The painful truth, the crude reality, the objectionable but ir-refutable fact is that I could be head over heels in love with Mina...if it wasn't for her determination not to shave her legs.

I accept and I admire her sound principles and I would never dare to question the rationale behind her strong commitment to hairy legs. But how can I help myself when, in the middle of her unpredictable, tempestuous embrace, the touch of the hairy surface of a leg is enough to kill my ardour, to neutralise the magic. I am left limp with embarrassment, not so much at my physical incompetence but at the laughable, sweetly pitiful reason behind it!

The reason behind it belongs to that realm of our existence over which principles are as impotent as my flesh under the spell of Hermina's hairy leg. The reason behind it is so remote and so uncontrollable that it has taken me twenty years to understand it. To despise it, but to secretly cherish it as well. The reason behind it is that collective dream of which I was only a modest recipient, that formidable frenzy, that ultimate fantasy, something which, translated into words, would sound like...like...*a few more minutes with Monica Vitti*.

As a bright but immature nineteen year old, living in a grim city of a communist country whose fantasy of building the workers' paradise had left its workers completely drained of fantasies, I was interested, like Hermina, in the survival of endangered species. And there were no creatures more endangered than our dreams. I flirted for a while with the psychiatric disciplines but unfortunately was kicked out of medical school after an attempted ESP experiment on a feline inhabitant of the school morgue. It was not the Rector's concern for the welfare of the cat in question (who had a good time anyway) which brought about my expulsion from university, but his anger at my sacrilegious inclinations towards things paranormal whose undeniable existence was casting a serious doubt on our creed concerning the absolute reign of matter over spirit. My ESP endeavours so abruptly aborted, I became a film student instead.

The cradle of my cinematic studies was a pale green aberration of crumbling bricks and decomposing mortar, a gangrene of a building which faltered under the burden of too many revolutionary changes and under the intense vibration of its occupants' uncontrollable dreams.

At some early stage in her dubious history (I say *her* because I think the building was essentially feminine, displaying a mixture of resigned pride and maternal magnanimity that transcended her external devastation), at some point in the short breath of time when my country, recently emancipated from its agrarian-feudal identity and before being swept by a hurricane of Bolshevism, had become engaged in a brief affair with the demons of capitalism, the building had served as a factory of some sort, a sweat-shop filled with pedal lathes and noisy clouds of metal splints. Their echoes still reverberated in the memories of those ageless survivors, the building's enormous and melancholic rats, whose sad eyes made me wonder if they weren't reincarnations of some fallen lamas from the East.

After the Second World War, which she unexplainably survived unscathed, after the victory of communism over capitalism, during the terror-filled late forties and early fifties, the building had become unlisted. This means that she stopped living objectively—in the registers and archives of the city—and started living subjectively, in the private nightmares of its citizens. These were being efficiently and randomly interrogated behind her thick, pale green walls by the vigilant *securitate*, those zealous batallions of secret police. Even under her new, unlisted identity, the building continued her services to production. Only this time, instead of the nuts and bolts which the capitalists had manufactured under her roof, the output emanating now from her walls and telephone lines was a production of a more sophisticated kind. An uninterrupted flux of induced declarations, denigrations, denunciations and renunciations, signed unconditionally by gullible prisoners dreaming of a passport to some improbable survival.

Of course, there were many accidental deaths during those years. So, in the same spirit of economic efficiency, the *securitate* dumped the unregistered corpses into a communal pit, which they had hastily set up one night, somewhere in the building's backyard. The pit's unlisted existence had by now taken a centre-stage position in the communal nightmare of the city but it was not allowed to be probed by any objective means. Thus, by blurring the boundary between reality and hallucination, the communists managed, skilfully and at a reasonably low cost, to turn a humble, flesh-bone-and-mortar pit into a sophisticated metaphor of terror and control: the metaphor of the ubiquitous communal grave which started right at your doorstep, ready and waiting for you to step in. Once again, as far as the perimeter of our building was concerned, the only ones, during those metaphor-infested fifties, who had access to the objective, palpable truth, were the perennial rats in their silent, serene wisdom.

But this was not the only secret with which the increasingly fat rodents had been entrusted by a providence with a clearly ratty sense of humour. There was something else they knew about the building. A few metres under the fresh layer of corpses and mortar from the late forties and early fifties, right under our building, her backyard and her surroundings, lay the much more decomposed, hardly recognisable remnants of yet another communal grave. This one had been set up two hundred and fifty years before, and had owed its existence, most probably, to the last wave of bubonic plague. It is not therefore by chance that the rats in question flourished physically and matured spiritually: they had always had plenty of food for their bodies as well as for their thoughts. The bubonic plague, I think, is a rather questionable hypothesis: only the providence and its rodent messengers know if the real cause behind that earlier communal pit was not some black-magic-induced, head-chopping orgy set up by some forgotten, psychopathic tyrant capable of selling his soul to the devil and his country to the Turks. And only the rats knew exactly how many other, more ancient communal graves had slowly effaced themselves under the burden of the more recent arrivals, rotting back into nothingness.

At some point in the late fifties, as my mother released me into the world in the hospital right across the road, the building whose destiny was to become so meaningfully entangled with mine also underwent a rebirth of sorts: she became registered again. She thus graduated back into the realm of objectivity. She received her final and fatal assignment, that of housing the country's fledgling film school, the young but robust talents who were to be initiated into the mysteries of the cinema in order to film the imminent and universal victory of communism and the final spasms of a capitalism receiving its deadly blow from the cosmic arbiter of history.

In her new, refurbished state, the building contained an enormous sound stage on the ground floor, a theatre on the first, and various sound and editing chambers on the crumbling second and third floors. Very soon though, it became clear that the sound stage could never successfully satisfy its purpose for the simple reason that the humid clouds of unexplainable noise emanating from the walls and from the basement at certain times of the day were blurring the professional silence of film sets and the professional cleanliness of camera lenses. Was this the building's own vaporous memory, condensing in the humid air and giving birth to some lost cry or whisper?

The basement of the building was permanently flooded by a compromised toilet that had collapsed under the strain of long decades of service. Sometimes it would regurgitate its waters into the front lobby, leaving the freshly installed bust of Lenin suspended lonely over the liquid surface, with ever wider shades of doubt growing on his pensive forehead.

Little by little, starting with the increasingly decrepit sound stage, whose desertion was accelerated by the students' quest for kitchen-sink naturalism, the aesthetic ideal of the times, the building became more and more underused. The students' interest in the premises became limited to the first-floor theatre where we watched the compulsory masterpieces of the Soviet cinema, the cardboard fantasies of Méliès or some pirated copy of a second-rate foreign film which our country did not have the hard currency to purchase. And, as far as the second- and third-floor cubicles were concerned, anyone who could raise enough money to bribe some State Television employee to allow them after-hours access to editing or sound facilities was happy to avoid any contact with their unhealthy air and prehistoric equipment.

During those years of decline, there were, apart from the loyal rats, only three occupants you would be sure to find in some corner of the building, at any hour of the day. They were the two projectionists who, by the end of each day, were so drunk that they could not even make it to the closest tram station, and Corriere, the head of the editing department, who was also spending his nights there, unofficially, of course, ever since his wife had kicked him out of their one-bedroom apartment.

Nobody knew exactly what Corriere had done in the past. The only fact known about him (and which accounted for his current position) was that he had been a classmate of the Rector. The students accepted him as yet another non-entity they had to put up with, and they didn't make any effort to hide their mild disdain. That explains why he was nicknamed Corriere. Because, one evening, in the middle of a class, when someone made a snide remark about the obscurity of his career, he stood up and yelled: 'You will find this hard to believe, but once upon a time I used to be a student like you, bright and smart, and with a promising career! There was even a paragraph written about a film of mine in the famous Italian newspaper, *Corriere della Serra!*'

As part of our editing studies, Corriere decided we were to spend the entire semester analysing sequences from important films. He would fit us into a cubicle on the third floor, load the antiquated editing console with whatever the projectionists on the first floor couldn't use any more, and the rest was 150 minutes of indescribable boredom.

Until that magic evening when, with a flicker in his eyes, Corriere loaded a certain reel of film which was to change the course of our existence.

This celluloid treasure, initially stolen by the two projectionists during an unofficial screening of Michelangelo Antonioni's *Avventura*, became Corriere's hot property after he had spent a whole night and three bottles of first-grade plum brandy convincing the duo from downstairs to leave it in his capable hands.

It contained precisely that part of the film where Monica Vitti, exhausted by a night of passion, wakes up to give her lover a goodbye kiss before he leaves the bedroom. Between the first movement of her lazy eyelids and the final kiss on her lover's lips, Monica Vitti tosses languidly between the sheets, lost in the delicious memory of the night that has just elapsed, smiling to herself as she uncovers the full splendour of her mystical legs, which she lifts nonchalantly up in the air, up in the air.

How could I forget those unearthly shapes! So transparent in their voluptuousness, that smooth, silken surface, reflecting the chiaroscuro of the bedroom? Its unspeakably sweet memories and the memories to come?

I am watching Hermina, as she frowns in her sleep. Even now, when her body, free from tension, breathes lazily in its indifference, I can tell her mind is still busy, still fighting for a serious cause. The furry, reddish growth, the mortal enemy of my carnal instincts, is right there in front of me. I clasp my Philips electric razor nervously in my right hand. Wishing I had the courage, the guts...

It goes without saying that from that fateful evening on, the rest of the editing classes became dedicated exclusively to the official study of Michelangelo Antonioni's mastery and to our unofficial re-encounters with Monica Vitti's legs. At the end of each class, Corriere would invariably say, 'You're free to leave, boys...I'll stay back a bit...I want to spend a few more minutes with my friend Michelangelo...'

'*A few more minutes with Monica Vitti*, that's what you want, old sleazebag!' we would answer back, whizzing down the steep stairs leading to Lenin's increasingly worried bust, as soon as Corriere had closed the door and couldn't hear our laughter.

It is perhaps useful to bear in mind that I was a virgin at the time.

I had turned twenty-one, I was rather well built, and women found me attractive, judging by the way some of them looked at me. The reason for my virginity was purely logistical: in the workers' paradise, there was no room for out-of-wedlock activities. The moral purity of the masses had to be protected at all cost. My parents had moved out of the capital, into some provincial town, and I was spending most of my holidays with them. But the mere thought of bringing a woman into their one-bedroom apartment was a tasteless aberration. In

Bucharest, where accommodation was definitely more crowded, my occasional girlfriends had to face similar problems. Using the public parks was absolutely out of the question. All of them were solidly staffed by vigilant guards who couldn't wait to set their hands on a couple of virginal victims and blackmail them with telling their parents or even reporting them to the People's Militia. The ransom could be five packets of Kent cigarettes or a full bottle of Johnny Walker—eight weeks of a student's allowance, on the black-market—enough to cure you of desire for the rest of your life!

Our communal school dormitory, housed in a former military barrack at the outskirts of the city, was the only feasible alternative. An efficient roster system had been set up and there was always a bottle of Havana Club around to make the old guardian turn a blind eye. But somehow I couldn't bring myself to perform what was expected of me, unless I was completely convinced about the privacy of the matter. Even those of my colleagues who were brave enough to conduct affairs in such a sordid environment had to do everything in a hurry within the strict constraints of the roster.

In other words...for various reasons...there wasn't a single creature of the masculine sex within that pale green building, within that prehistoric cradle of my cinematic years, who had not been moved right to the deepest core of his most intimate thoughts, by the ritual dance of Monica Vitti's luminous legs.

Those legs heralded a land of forbidden passion, of physical love indulging in its own sweet abandon, a land indifferent to the outside world, to the People's revolution, to the building of communism, to the final spasms of imperialism, to the triumph of the masses, indifferent to the workers' paradise with its chaste one-bedroom apartments, with its puritanical parks and bushes, with its vigilant patrols, with its dormitory guards drunk on voyeurism and Havana Club.

Our common temperature would rise with every jerk of the rattling editing console as it tirelessly endeavoured to replay *that* sequence. The rats of the building themselves started marvelling at this new, mysterious source of vibrations and heat. And I suspect now that the main reason why Lenin's brow had become so miserably sad in the last few months there, was that he was the only occupant of the building who was physically and ideologically excluded from the collective fantasy of *a few more minutes with Monica Vitti*.

That afternoon in March when the Rector's avuncular secretary announced to me that my father had died of a heart attack, I used all my limited resources in a desperate but resolute effort to get dead drunk. I emptied everything that I could remember or imagine, anything that contained something remotely alcoholic. I swallowed every drop of plum brandy hidden away in the locked suitcase under my bed. I finished our meagre, collective supply of Havana Club. I even started to force open my colleagues' suitcases, sucking whatever I could find. In most cases, just modest remnants of illegally home-made plum brandy, with one or two happy exceptions of strong, Transylvanian palinka. As my stubborn lucidity refused to give in, I began reluctantly to swallow the few bottles of medicinal alcohol and aftershave lotion that I could dig out. Slowly but steadily, my despair became more subdued, until it received its final blow from an unexpected, nauseating dosage of eau de cologne...

The next thing I knew it was night.

And the pale green walls that surrounded me in a kind of comforting, maternal embrace were vibrating, almost imperceptibly. There were unexplainable beams of light coming from the sound stage and familiar clouds of humid whispers were floating in the heavy air around me. I proceeded slowly towards the source of that mysterious light, taking great care not to step on the fat rats who had been aroused, like me, by an irresistible wave of curiosity.

I quietly penetrated through the unlocked gates of the sound stage and hid behind an old cardboard porch.

It was Corriere, a few metres away, yelling at the gaffer to subdue the crude projector lights. He was dressed in a stylish Italian suit and looked at least twenty years younger. The cardboard that surrounded him had been metamorphosed into a kind of warm, inviting bedroom whose limits were lost in a subtle, chiaroscuro uncertainty. He focused his attention on the king-size bed at the centre of the set. He ruffled the sheets with nervous fingers and directed the gaffer to increase the shades on the silky surface of an abandoned nightgown. He grabbed one of the pillows, sank his face into it, then picked up a gracious little bottle of *Vol de Nuit* from the side table and sprayed its contents on both pillows and in between the sheets. The magic vapour dissipated in the air. And we, the rats and me, the silent but intense audience behind the sets, desperately tried to catch at least a modest sniff of that languorous, velvet and gold scent.

And suddenly, Monica! Her unmistakable laughter. And the two projectionists burst right in! Their naked bodies entangled in miles of celluloid, two noisy, dead drunk satyrs running in all directions to catch the image of Monica Vitti that had somehow escaped from the theatre screen, that they must have been chasing hopelessly throughout the building. Monica's teasing, crystalline laughter was echoing relentlessly all around them! Driving them insane, in their fruitless, increasingly entangled pursuit. Sometimes the black and white projection of Monica's smile, of her fingers, of her shoulder, of her knee, would appear and disappear on the cardboard walls, or would pause for a moment on the projectionists' own chests, or backs, and add to their desperate confusion. They ended up chasing each other until they finally collapsed, interlocked, straight into the middle of the king-size bed. Enraged, Corriere grabbed them at once and threw them out of the set with solid kicks in their drunken butts, until they ended up, with a noisy splash, in the stinking waters under Lenin's faltering bust.

Back on the set, Corriere quickly fixed the mess, sprayed another whiff of *Vol de Nuit* into the air to kill the stench the two satyrs had left behind, and put finishing touches back to the chiaroscuro-bathed ambience. He sat down on the bed. And then he asked a cameraman who was perched on a dolly somewhere in the dark to come closer and closer, until he had nothing but Corriere's melancholic eyes in the frame. 'Framed!' whispered the cameraman, gliding into the light. I was unsettled to discover that the cameraman looked very much like me—he even smelled, like me, of an unspeakable mixture of Havana Club, plum brandy, eau de cologne and Transylvanian palinka.

'Roll the camera! Action!' commanded Corriere to the cameraman and to himself. For a few seconds, everything went silent except for the camera's grinding, monotonous noise. Then Corriere picked up a flute and started singing softly, letting a few tears roll down his freshly shaved cheeks. The cameraman glided back into the dark. The camera kept rolling, embracing the whole expanse of that chiaroscuro expectation. The darkness behind the set was dense and alive, bursting with muffled heartbeats.

And then, before we understood what was happening to us, a luminous blur appeared from nowhere, as if the stifling vapours of our expectation had condensed into a single, sublime vision. Slowly but clearly, the blur became the skin, the hair, the teeth, the lips, the shoulders, the fingers, the knees, the ankles, the toes of Monica Vitti. But this time they were the real thing! Not some black-and-white, edited illusion—the real, palpable and palpitating ensemble of pale, slightly freckled skin, and languidly messed hair, and small, voluptuous teeth, and full, whispering lips, and slender, transparent fingers, and delirious, indescribable scents, and smooth, aerial legs...

The carnal yet vaporous apparition wafted jocularly before our eyes. Then stopped for a few seconds on the king-size bed. She recognised the *Vol de Nuit* in the smell of the night, smiled, sniffed the pillows and pensively ran her fingers through Corriere's hair. Mesmerised, Corriere continued playing his flute, until she stopped him gently. She extracted the instrument from his paralysed lips, grabbing him softly by the hand.

She then started walking slowly from the set, leading Corriere into the staircase. We were following them in the darkness, blindly and faithfully, like pilgrims. We were climbing the stairs behind them—me, the cameraman, the gaffer, the two, wet satyrs back again from their drunken stupor, the pensive rats who looked increasingly more human, and all the other uncountable and uncertain creatures of that building, except, of course, for Lenin, left impotent on his pedestal. We were all embarked on a blissful ascent up the steep stairs of the crumbling building. Guided by that sweet hurricane, that maelstrom of divine sensations, as Monica Vitti, suave and freckled, kept leading us higher and higher and higher, up the stairs...

Finally, as our blood pressure was reaching an unbearable height, as the dizziness of our ascent became more lethal than any mix of Transylvanian palinka and aftershave lotion, as the staircase itself was on the point of collapsing under the weight of our frenetic pursuit, Monica stopped in front of Corriere's cubicle. She opened the door with a firm gesture and disappeared inside with a look in her eyes that he—and we—had no trouble understanding.

Corriere slammed the door behind him!

Our collective pulse became so intense that the building itself started to give in. Big cracks appeared in the walls, as imperceptible vibrations became stronger and stronger, more and more unisonous, until their combined power jolted every corner of the building, down to her basement, to her foundations, to her undisclosed graves, to her deepest memories, to her most forgotten visions.

As bricks started to fall, as windows started to shatter, as wires started to short-circuit, as pipes started to burst, as ceilings started to cave in, as the banister started to falter, as the floors started to glide from under our precarious feet...it became clear now to me that the pale green building who could stand so many revolutionary changes, who had put up with so much senseless history, with so much death, despair and torture, that building whose foundations extended straight into our unnumbered and innumerable communal pits and beyond them, straight into the heart of our deepest communal nightmares— well, that building was in no way equipped to resist our fatal, frantic, ecstatic and seismic encounter with Monica Vitti!

'Move your drunken arse or else you're going to croak right here and now!' yelled one of my colleagues, painfully trying to extract me from my sticky bed. The whole dormitory had been taken by hysteria. People were running in all directions, clinging to whatever was left of their possessions after my indiscreet search for alcoholic oblivion. The floor was rocking madly, the lights were out, the lamps were swinging and banging against the ceiling. Chunks of plaster and masonry were raining from all directions. Someone smashed a window and jumped out from the height of our third floor in a desperate attempt to escape this sudden, unexplainable inferno. I somehow ended up in a shower recess, pressed against other bodies who were shivering violently in the dark, too frightened to scream, praying for an end to the earth's sinister, ever increasing spasms.

'Forgive me, Jesus! Take me to your Kingdom! MARX SUCKS!' cried one student actor who had reached the end of hope. Even I, in my inebriated confusion, realised that the probability of our survival was becoming ever more unlikely. But what was bemusing me even more than the unexpected prospect of a slow death through mass asphyxiation under a mountain of debris and flesh, was the inescapable suspicion that the epicentre of the horrific earthquake which was shaking the entire city down to its strongest foundation stone—down to its sanest inhabitant—was located right there, in my dream about *a few more minutes with Monica Vitti.*

◆

This suspicion, however mellowed by the passing of the decades, still visits me sometimes as I lie in bed, during the small hours of the morning, when Hermina's troubled sleep succumbs to slumber. In moments like these, my heart becomes filled with a delicious poison of voluptuousness and guilt, and all I can think of is the nonchalant yet fatal dance of *those* legs.

If only I had the guts to use my double-action Philips electric razor! Hermina wouldn't even wake up. In her sleep, she will mistake its gentle tickle for my caress. Later, when she realises what I have done, I will explain.

But how could I explain? What is there to explain?

◆

A few hours later, when, thanks to the biting cold and my frozen underwear, I had regained a certain percentage of my lucidity, I found myself in a truck that was driving us through the rubble of the terror-stricken city to some unknown destination.

Through the truck's dirty windows I could catch glimpses of the general devastation, whenever the headlights of a vehicle pierced the heavy darkness reigning everywhere. The whole city was standing still. Holding its breath. Short-circuited in ill-omened obscurity, with open pipes and leaking sewers. Every now and then a beam of light would reveal the wreckage of a building, its balconies stacked one on top of the other, like a grotesque harmonica designed to accompany the earth's *danse macabre.* Or a mother or grandmother, silently lighting candles in front of a heap of debris. Or the claws of an excavator picking bizarre objects from the remnants of a block of flats: a bath tub, a toy, a human arm, a sheepskin coat, a kitchen sink, a hidden treasure of *Playboy* magazines. Or a park filled with frozen citizens in their pyjamas, too scared to make a move, too frightened to question the darkness.

Some of them who had been lucky enough to salvage anything had no choice but to exhibit their most precious belongings. Like that little old man in his grey nightgown, sitting on a prehistoric suitcase and holding a wedding dress and the single, gigantic leaf of a tropical indoor plant. Or that girl with Shirley Temple locks dressed in a boy's pyjamas and clutching a grandfather clock. Or that young woman in the purple negligee, holding four bottles of Havana Club and a meat grinder close to her breast. Or that middle-aged man with the worn-out hat who was carrying a demijohn of plum brandy and the icon of a golden Orthodox Madonna holding a morose baby Jesus in her arms.

Inside the truck, one of my colleagues who was anxiously manipulating his portable radio managed to catch a few words from Radio Free Europe before the short waves were jammed by the always alert *securitate*. Apparently, the earthquake had been the strongest in the region in over three hundred years and its tremors had been felt all the way to Vienna, Istanbul and even Leningrad.

Trying to redeem himself after that embarrassing outburst in the shower recess, the student actor embarked on an unstoppable spree of jokes. 'Do you know how the guys of Oltenia jerk off?' he exclaimed. 'They bury their pricks in the ground and...wait for an earthquake!'

The truck stopped with a jolt. We were unloaded at the site of what had once been the pale green building. We were handed picks and shovels and told to dig into the humid mountain of debris and search for survivors.

We dug all night, waiting for an excavator which never arrived. Ten hours later, we found Corriere's body. It had remained intact, except for a dark red, sticky wound on the left side of his head. He must have died quickly, hit by a falling brick. There was a serene, babyish smile on his face and his hands were clasped tightly around a roll of celluloid.

That was the last I saw of him and the pale green building. The next day, the whole area became forbidden to the public. The excavators finally arrived, and the deeper they dug the more consistent the rumours became. The city was swept by yet another cyclone of whispered, unconfirmed accounts concerning the existence of certain unlisted, communal graves, and everybody started to secretly panic about a possible new wave of bubonic plague.

How could I explain? What is there to explain?

The best I could hope for is that Hermina would send me to see a therapist.

But I already have, dear Mina! I have already seen a therapist, an analyst, a hypnotist, a herbalist, an acupuncturist. And they all agreed there is no cure!

No, my love, there is no cure.

Simply because I cannot, I will not, give up my vision of *a few more minutes with Monica Vitti*. This vision is the only certainty I have ever possessed. In the chaos of my shipwrecked existence, Monica's luminous legs have been the only permanence I could ever cling to. Without them, my life would be a pale green heap of rubble. A cut-off leaf. An empty demijohn. A grandfather clock with a frozen heart.

So, if you still care for me when you wake up, just accept my humble razor without scrutiny.

In the chiaroscuro of our bedroom, I am waiting for the first movement of Mina's eyelids.

Will I dare?

Snowdome

between Appin and Campbelltown, early

DEB WESTBURY

i
New housing estates for the poor—
spreading inflammation
on the soft emerald thighs
of the country—
by tricks of light and distance appear
a close neighbourly glow
of red roofs and harmony.

For now the spotted gums
meet limb to limb above the road
and make for us
a long green tunnel
pierced with light.

Here where it never snows
the tunnel fills with swirling flakes
that catch the light—
feathers on our windscreen,
feathers in the air.

I overtake the source,
a factory-truck of chickens
rushing between deliveries.
The remnants stare,
dead or bewildered, at the emptiness
of their cages and the blizzard.

ii
In the window of TV
and direct
from the latest third-world disaster
another cairn of bodies,
uniformly bloated,
cold and discoloured,
their legs and wings askew—

neighbours mothers friends
for the fire
for the ground.

iii
And we, driving straight
for the graveyard,
see nothing but the snow.

Bluey

GEOFF GOODFELLOW

All play & no work
help make Bluey a colourful
bloke
     & though he grew up in the
sixties with full employment
     'Clockwork Orange'
& pinball machines
     he never hung around
pinball parlours

i can't say the same about
front bars
     waterfront pubs
& other low-life dives
     & convictions record
those points

but Bluey is just an old-
fashioned Aussie bloke
     with old-fashioned Aussie
values

he likes real pubs with
real lino bar tops where
real blokes drink real beer

he like pubs where as close
as a copper gets to the bar
     is on a cruise through
the car park

he likes pubs where real blokes
make a real earn moving TVs
videos CDs lawn mowers
bits of jewellery
sheets of iron
     or stamps
     or double bed sheets
or whatever else can be pushed
or carried or lifted

he likes pubs where you can bet
on a sweaty old bloke with a thick
gold chain
    or a skinny young bloke with a
diamond ring to take your bet
    & let you in on the nod—
as soon as your form is known

so it surprised me to hear he was
still drinking in the same pub
    even though they'd decked it out
with electronic pinball machines

but it didn't really surprise me
when two weeks down the track
    he picked up the bar stool
he'd been propped on for years
& proved to the publican that
even though he'd been out of work
for a while
    he could still make real short
work of a pub pinball machine

it's fair to say too that there was
no shortage of bright sparks
in the bar to urge him on

he staggered away after the
flashing lights stopped
    but not before he moved back
to his beer & raised it saying
    'i've never liked those bloody
things'

he's barred of course
    but so was the pinball machine—
& unlike it
    Bluey's a moral to be still
ticking over.

The Violence of Work

GEOFF GOODFELLOW

i work in a factory
Monday to Friday
    punch on   punch off

i work a rotating roster
Monday to Friday
    punch on   punch off

i wear earmuffs & gloves
Monday to Friday
    punch on   punch off

i stamp on a press
Monday to Friday
    punch on   punch off

i still had my fingers last
Monday to Friday
    punch on   punch off

i make repetitive pieces
Monday to Friday
    punch on   punch off

i work on a tally
Monday to Friday
    punch on   punch off

i'm told to work faster
Monday to Friday
    punch on   punch off

i have smoko with Billy
Monday to Friday
    punch on   punch off

i play euchre at lunchtime
Monday to Friday
    punch on   punch off

i just do my best
Monday to Friday
    punch on   punch off

i'm paid the award for
Monday to Friday
    punch on   punch off

i don't complain to the boss
Monday to Friday
    punch on   punch off

but complain to my partner
Monday to Sunday
    want to punch on
         punch on.

What I Do

ANGELA LYNKUSHKA

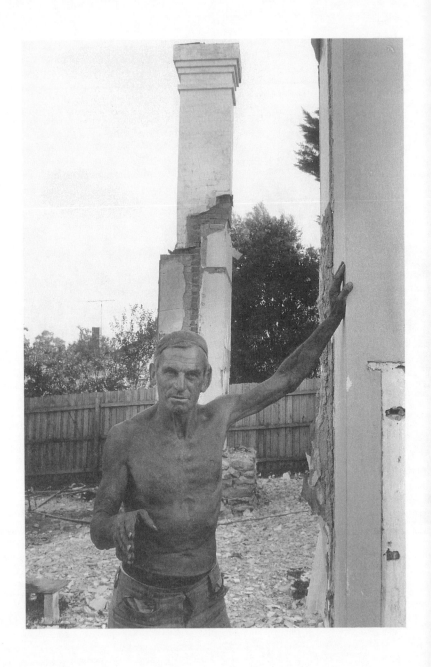

Bluey

Cutting It Fine

NOTES ON *THE PIANO*

CLAIRE CORBETT

PRELUDE — AUTUMN, 1992

Veronika rang me at work today and offered me the job of second assistant editor on *The Piano*. She knew I wanted it. The wages are low but every assistant editor on earth wants this job. I'm elated but anxious. I can't consciously remember all the skills I need. But the knowledge is in my hands. As soon as I touch the machines I will know what to do.

I often wondered why it took me so long to realise I wanted to crew on films rather than act in them. My father was a television director, and though I didn't grow up with him I spent a fair amount of time around film crews. They were all men, which may explain why I was so slow to figure out that women could be behind the camera too. As a child I sat in the control room of the television studio and watched as the cameramen on the daytime soap my father was directing amused themselves between takes by zooming in on the lead actress's breasts. I was confused by this because I didn't know how to imagine myself working on films in the future; I didn't want to become the actress whose breasts were played with by remote control nor could I see myself as one of the technicians doing this.

I liked being with crews when they were shooting on location. There we were, a self-contained world that operated by its own rules—irresistible for a child. In this sealed world of the location set, control and chaos battle constantly for the upper hand; the film production itself introduces dangerous elements such as mountain lions and then attempts to control the results.

My first paid jobs in film were as an extra, and the ultimate film extra experience was the month or two of night shooting for the Bartertown sequences in *Mad Max Three: Beyond Thunderdome*. Bartertown, built in the old government brick pits at Homebush, was a world unto itself. We extras arrived, some of us from our day jobs as cooks, waitresses, saleswomen at David Jones, bouncers, bodybuilders and deliverers of Fat-a-grams, as the sun was going down. We immediately got into our costumes. Our faces and hands were smeared with a vile brick dust and we milled about waiting for dinner. We sat on the ground, we played in the dirt, we didn't care about the state of our hair or clothes.

Every night there was an incident on the set. One night several extras were removed for shooting up in the car park. A couple of bikers had to be sacked for spraying the 'Fat-a-gram lady' with wardrobe blacking spray. We cooked hot bread on the set, flirted with bored and weary crew members, fell asleep hanging off the Thunderdome or crept into bales of hay scattered over the set. The assistant directors rounded us up constantly, like sheep dogs. I always loved the feeling that normal rules didn't apply to film crews on location.

My first leap forward into film crew work was being accepted to do the BA Communications (UTS). In the middle of my second year there, I was taken on as an assistant film editor on Jane Campion's first feature, *Sweetie*. My film apprenticeship took place in the cutting room. This calm, intimate world was very different to the controlled anarchy of the location set.

The period that followed was one of the best in my life. I was studying full-time at university and working full-time learning the craft of the cutting room on *Sweetie*. Jane Campion and Veronika Jenet, her editor, and the first assistant editor, Jane Cole, were the sweetest, funniest and wisest teachers, each in her own way, that anyone could have had. One night I stayed back synchronising film rushes alone until one or two in the morning. I wept with frustration as I pitted my newly acquired synchronising skills against the unslated rushes. When I came into the cutting room next morning a bouquet of exquisite white roses was sitting on my assistant editor's bench from Jane Campion.

As the cut entered its final phase, we lived fourteen-hour days in the cutting room. We ate all our meals there. At one point we worked fourteen days straight. I remember stretching out full-length on the cutting room floor, and feeling a motor, my engine of will, grind to a halt inside me. I wondered how I would get up again. On the last Sunday of the fourteen days, when we were almost delirious, our producer John Maynard came in and cut up a banquet of fresh melons and berries for us.

Jane Campion gave Jane Cole and me sequences of her film to cut under her direction. We knew Jane wouldn't let us go wrong. And Jane set me the task of writing my own versions of the opening voice-over. I have never met a creative person more pleased by the talents of those around her. It is the best quality a film director can have, but that doesn't mean it is common.

THE FINE CUT—MONTH ONE

My job begins in the first month of the fine cut in Sydney, after the film and its makers return from the shoot in New Zealand. The fine cut is the form of the film which the editor and director work towards, applying themselves again and again to the rough cut, the very long version of the film assembled by the picture editor from the daily footage.

At the end of the shoot, the whole rough cut is screened. In the Roxy, Film Australia's screening theatre carpeted in vivid purple, we see the two-and-a-half-hour rough cut, a film that will never be seen again by anyone. At this stage, the film is still called *The Piano Lesson*. We are emotionally exhausted but happy at the end of the screening.

And it will evolve as the weeks go by—I wouldn't give this up for the spurious excitement of a purely on-set job.

The Roxy Theatre is *icy*. We ask them to turn up the heat, but they don't seem to be able to do anything about it. After nearly three hours in there we are frozen, especially after watching the final underwater shots. Heidi, the first assistant editor, and I have to leap up at the end and carry the silver cans of film and sound back to her car. Each big film can holds about ten minutes worth of film. There are about thirty of them. Working as an assistant editor is the only time I develop biceps. 'You girls are so strong,' Veronika marvels when she sees the great stacks of them we carry.

When I come into the cutting room for the first time, I arrive before anyone else that day. I am nervous. I am joining a team already forged under the pressure of the location shoot. Sound editors have to deal with this feeling on every single picture because they always start so long after the shoot is over. It is the privilege of picture editors to start work on the first day of the shoot.

Pictures from the shoot in New Zealand line the walls of the cutting rooms: pictures of the actors in costume, pictures of the crew, a picture of Harvey Keitel in a dress. Jane Campion always has a 'dress day', at least once during her shoots. All cast and crew have to wear a dress. The men love it. The most macho of them change their dresses several times in a day. The women often find it more traumatic. Jane says she feels much closer to her male crew members once she's seen them in a dress.

At Spectrum there is always an unofficial hierarchy of films at any one time, based on the prestige of the project. *The Piano Lesson* is in the happy position of being at the apex, literally and figuratively. Our rooms are at the top of the building and have dormer windows that open out onto the rooftops. It reminds me of Paris except for the unmistakable winter gold of the Australian sun.

Here, there is an outer room at the top of the stairs. It is our domain, Heidi's and mine, the two assistants. Here we have our benches where we wind and rewind film, usually by hand, as we search for the exact pieces of film that Veronika and Jane want to look at next. A complete breakdown of the film by scene numbers and shot numbers is written on cards and tacked on the wall. Each card identifies the physical reel of film where the scene numbers can be found. This is how we keep track of the film. Here the reels and reels of film rushes are stored in square white pizza boxes on racks. There are over a hundred each, of sound and image, the image labelled in blue, the sound in red. We follow this convention rigidly.

While the film is in the editing stage, the sound and image are always kept separate. The 'synching up' of sound and image is one of the major skills assistant editors must possess. The sound and image are finally 'married' on the 'release print', the final version of the film released to cinemas; the soundtrack has been transferred onto a magnetic stripe on the print itself. But it is vital that sound and image be separate during the editing stage of the film, or no creative work with the soundtrack would be possible. For example, sound from a scene is often laid over the beginning of the next scene for a particular effect, such as providing a smooth transition or to increase a sense of foreboding. Sound editors work with the sound intensively and separately to the image, redoing lines of dialogue, adding sound effects and so on.

Here, in our outer room, we all eat together. Heidi and I make coffee, bring in breakfast and make elaborate lunches for the four of us. Two more rooms open off the outer room. One is a small office for Jane where she keeps a desk, a typewriter, books and ring binders filled with research and preparation for the film. A list of possible titles, other than 'The Piano Lesson', is stuck to the wall. We are urged to think of others. 'The Piano Lesson' is the name of a play and the copyright holders have advised they will sue if the film is released with that title.

The other room is the inner sanctum. This is the cutting room itself, where the sun is never allowed to shine, where the two massive Steenbecks whirr and roar as they wind reels of film backwards and forwards on their horizontal metal plates. The cutting room must be kept dark so that we can see the small image of the film on the Steenbeck's screen. Although this is where the picture is cut, the world of the cutting room is a world of sound. You can only see the images if you're actually sitting at the Steenbeck but you can hear bits of sound from the film all over the rooms, sometimes all over the building. Sometimes the sound from several different films floats up the stairs to us from other cutting rooms. Sound is such an emotional medium that I find my feelings suddenly prodded by bursts of music, snatches of dialogue played over and over at high volume, speeded up, slowed down, reversed. Peter Weir has said that there is nothing that can compensate for the emotional cost of making films you don't really care about, and the truth of this is very clear in post-production. To be subjected to the sounds and music of a film you disliked for months on end would be a refined form of torture. We are especially lucky to have Michael Nyman's music flowing through the cutting room for hours every day. Working to this is grand, and the most mundane work becomes uplifting.

Looking at the cutting rooms, it strikes me that there is hardly a machine or procedure carried out there that would not have been much the same a hundred years ago. Film is a nineteenth-century art. Unlike video, it is a physical and chemical medium, not an electronic one. A film camera is a simple mechanism that works along the same lines as a sewing machine or a machine gun and was invented at about the same time. These machines all work on the principle of grabbing a strip of perforated material (a sewing machine makes its own perforations), advancing it by a fixed amount, holding it, grabbing the next frame and so on. The perforations at the top and bottom of film are called sprocket holes and they enable the film to be wound back and forth onto a number of different machines.

The technology of the cutting room has traditionally been simple. Film is handled and stored on 1000- to 2000-foot reels so each machine in the cutting room must accommodate feed reels and takeup reels and be able to wind from one to the other. Handling these reels can be tricky. Film is glossy, slippery stuff, intolerant of moisture or grit. The assistant editor's nightmare is for the plastic core at the heart of a 2000-foot reel of film to suddenly slip out of a loosely wound reel. You are left with a mass of film and no way to unwind it except by hand. Sometimes you just have to cut your way through the mess.

There are other films sharing the building with us, and the technology they're using seems to be a sign that the traditional method of editing films is coming to an end. Veronika and Heidi and I are all concerned that the changes might be destructive to the craft of editing. It is easy to see, given the constant winding of large reels of film necessary to find particular shots, that film editing is a time-consuming process. The advance of computer technology promises to change that. Shots will be stored on computer and instantly called up by the editing program. The film will be essentially edited on video. Just because a film can be cut in a month, however, instead of three or four, does not mean that it ought to be. Once it is possible to edit a film in far less time than it now takes, the pressure on editors to do so will become irresistible. This could be disastrous because editing is not just a logical process. Editors and directors rely on time spent in the cutting room to give them a feel for their film. The often tedious time spent looking at sequences over and over and over again is necessary for directors and editors to make the intuitive leaps that pull form and meaning out of chaos. Editors and directors need time to think.

Heidi and I talk as we work, sorting and filing trim bins (on which the 'trims' of film, sorted by scene, shot and take, are suspended by their sprocket holes and hang safely and cleanly into linen bags), and working from lists of shots that Veronika has given us to find for her. We put the film away by running the reels through the gang synchronisers on our editing benches, to put the sound and image back in synch. Sometimes we sit with Jane at the second Steenbeck in the inner sanctum, and run through reels of film with her while Veronika cuts a sequence she and Jane have already discussed. We pull shots out of the rushes under Jane's direction.

We need a sound-mixing theatre in a few months, but another

director has booked everything in town for months ahead. He cannot possibly need *all* the facilities. We are exasperated with his selfishness and lack of professional confidence but we say nothing to him, though he is just down the hall. We know when the time comes that we'll get what we need.

We buy white grease pencil to write on the film, white cotton gloves to keep the film free of oil from our hands, squares of cotton velvet, a big bottle of fast-drying liquid Freon (to clean the film before screenings), and rolls of splicing tape for our splicers. Editors are particular about the quality of splicing tape they use. B ad tape is hard to peel off and leaves streaks of glue on the film. We wait for shipments of splicing tape from Japan.

THE FINE CUT—MONTH TWO

One of my favourite times in the cutting room is early in the morning before anyone else comes in. Heidi and I take turns to come early or to stay late. Early is 6.30 or 7 am, late is anywhere between 7 and 10 pm. It's the depth of winter, so the first thing I do every morning is turn all the heaters on. Veronika's Steenbeck is temperamental and needs to be warmed up for almost an hour before use. I turn it on and set all the plates spinning. The machine flashes 'Hello' in red LED letters. I turn my Prince tape up loud or sometimes the music Michael Nyman has already composed for the film and I bop around the cutting rooms as I clean the Steenbecks and get everything else ready for the day's work.

Our rooms are filled with flowers. Jan Chapman, our producer, sent us a magnificent bouquet of Australian wildflowers and a card after a particularly good screening. The card thanked us all for our work on 'this wild beauty of a film'. A gorgeous Maori carving of a woman with shell eyes, holding a boat with another figure at the prow, arrived from the Maori cast and crew this week from New Zealand. It was made for Jane and has now taken up residence in our assistants' outer room. We fill the boat with flowers and fruit.

The post-production schedule is tacked to the wall in the inner sanctum: there is a screening next week, there are so many weeks until Michael Nyman comes, so many weeks until the sound editors start, so many weeks until the end of the fine cut, so many weeks until the recording of the music, until the final sound mix. Michael Nyman has already booked the orchestra in Munich.

Heidi and I have talked to Benita who is assistant editor on the TV series, 'Police Rescue', downstairs. They are using the new computer programs for editing and Benita confirms, as we suspected, that it is much more exhausting to work from a computer or video screen than it is to cut and tape film with your hands. This is because cutting film is a more physical task. The body has a chance to move and you are not subject to the debilitating emanations from a video screen. The body is very much part of film making. Even in the fairly sedate world of the cutting room, assistant editors must be strong and have real stamina.

In spite of its recent origins, film making still preserves 'mediaeval' craft resonances, the frustrations and satisfactions of working in a *craft*, and some of the most highly skilled film technicians literally belong to craft guilds. Entry to the American Society of Cinematographers or the British Society of Editors cannot be begged, bought or commanded. It is by invitation from peers only, when they feel there is a body of work good enough to merit inclusion, that is, when you are a 'journeyman' no longer. Until recently, almost all technicians worked their way up from unskilled positions, relying on their mentors to teach them their trade. These apprenticeships were unofficial but essential, and the lore of film making was thus passed on and enriched.

The hierarchy within any given film is rigid—again, almost feudal. While the director and ultimately the producer (depending on contractual obligations) do have the final say on almost every aspect of a film, there is no single ladder of rank on which the rest of the film crew is lined up. A film consists of a *set* of hierarchies, each ruled by a head of department. These heads of department include the picture editor, the sound editor, the director of photography (DOP), the production designer and the composer. Each head of department has absolute power to hire personnel and run his or her department as he or she sees fit. Rank within a department is not transferable to another department. The DOP has no authority in the cutting room. A production designer, though much more senior, has no power over an assistant editor. The assistant editors belong to the editor and are for the use of the editor only. I have heard of problems between male editors and female assistants where some editors have become almost sexually proprietorial and jealous of their assistants, not even wanting them to work for other editors. Strictly speaking, even the director should not tell assistant editors what to do but, in practice, working so closely in the cutting rooms, we oblige each other. Sensitivity to the nuances of the hierarchy is never lost though. If Heidi and I ask Jane if we can go home early, she says, 'I'm not your boss!', and we ask Veronika instead.

Prerogatives of rank are jealously guarded from above and below. A director who so much as touches the camera on set commits a serious breach of propriety. A DOP would not dream of interfering with his or her camera assistants and would never touch any other technician's equipment unless specifically invited to do so. These examples are not equivalent to union rules which bar workers from tasks not in their job descriptions; they are courtesies extended by skilled professionals to other skilled professionals. Film technicians obey the demands of film hierarchy but insist on respect for their expertise. And this hierarchy applies only to *work*. Rank is not supposed to apply to any time spent not at work: during meals, at wrap parties or any other socialising.

And finally, most importantly, film making, like its older craft cousins, is not only *process*, it is *product*: you are making something. This is why artists are envied by bureaucrats in secure jobs with high salaries. Because, when all is said and done, few jobs in late-twentieth-century capitalism involve making anything. In classic Marxist terms, workers are alienated from the product; if most middle-class jobs can be said, that is, to result in a product at all. A great deal of lower echelon film work is tedious: difficult, repetitive and painstaking with much attendant anxiety. What matters though is that no matter how dull the process it is regularly transformed through screenings into meaning, into sound and images that have the power to enchant no matter how many times you see them. When the exhausting work has been forgotten, the film remains.

THE FINE CUT—MONTH THREE

Thanks to Veronika and Jane and ultimately Jan Chapman, my wages have been increased. They had been a source of embarrassment to all concerned. Many people would have done my job for nothing, for the sheer privilege of working on the film, but the envy of others doesn't pay the bills.

I have been offered work as first assistant editor on a documentary after *The Piano Lesson* finishes, but I have decided after talking to Jane and Veronika that this will be my last film as an assistant editor. It is the best experience a crew person could have and I want to leave it at that. Assistant editors aren't hired to be creative. We are hired for our mechanical skills and to create a pleasant working environment for the editor and director.

Working with Jane should be intimidating because she is so incredibly successful. It is inspiring. I've absorbed a lot from working around her, especially about the kind of risks you can take. I was especially impressed when she decided on the spur of the moment (or so it seemed to us in the cutting room) that she wanted a brief animation in the scene where Flora is describing her fantasy of the death of her father. Jane got Heidi to make a brief scratch animation, to give us a feel of how that might work. Scratch animations are the way we distract child visitors to our cutting rooms. We give them some clear film or black film leader and let them draw and scratch pictures on it. When they've done a long enough strip of film, we lace it onto the Steenbeck and let them see the results of their work.

This week is intense, as we get ready for the screening. Veronika doesn't think I am careful enough doublesplicing the work print for the screening (putting the tape on both sides of each cut so that the film won't come apart in the projector). I think it is the first time she has been cross with me since we've worked together. I am doublesplicing very quickly because we have so little time, but I accept her criticism and slow down. Veronika is quite correctly concerned about how the work print looks during a screening. Every hair, every streak and speck of dust is agony to her.

The rest of the week is a horror because of lack of sleep. Both Veronika and I are too wound up to sleep easily and by Friday I am operating on less than seven hours' sleep in two days. I fall asleep during the screening. The Roxy is freezing, again.

The more important it is that we sleep, the more our anxiety prevents us. I have to get up at 5 am and find that I am awake at 3 am. This can't go on. Jane staggers her hours a bit, comes in later, and sometimes spends whole days away from the cutting room when Veronika has enough work to go on with. She is drawn with fatigue. She has been working non-stop for well over a year. I get horribly sleepy in the afternoons and I can't concentrate. Jan Chapman gives us a good bottle of champagne after a screening but we can never find time to drink it. Jan must think we are ungrateful.

These final exhausting weeks of the cut are the real test. These are weeks composed of six or seven ten- to twelve-hour days, as Jane and Veronika struggle with their last chance to make the film perfect and ready to face the world. Whole scenes are taken out. A long sequence where Baines gets some schoolgirls to read Ada's message to him on the piano key is dropped. After the film is released reviewers will quibble over why Ada sent a written message to a man who can't read. This seems utterly irrelevant to us. There is no doubt Baines gets Ada's message just by receiving the piano key.

We have another screening. A scene is put back in. It is modified. Undone. Taken out again. Jan Chapman says, 'But that is one of my favourite scenes.' At some point in this process each one of us loses her sense of humour, though the loss is temporary. It is easy to see that, all other things being equal, film personnel are often hired on the basis of personality; there are lots of people in the lower ranks of the industry who have the technical skills. But the relationships in the cutting room—between the director and editor, between the editor and the first assistant and between the first assistant and the second assistant—*must* work. I don't know whether our intimacy is easier because we are all women, but it does seem that way.

Jane is grey with exhaustion. Veronika is drawn, and even Heidi is suffering intermittent losses of humour. On Monday, Veronika was in a foul mood; it was her eighth straight day of work and Jane didn't agree with her about the cutting of the underwater scene. Veronika couldn't hide her frustration over the loss of one shot Jane wanted out. I could see both points of view. The shot of Holly Hunter underwater, hair and clothes swirling, is stunningly beautiful. It also slows the scene down. Veronika is a disciplined and objective editor, totally supportive of the director's control over the project. She complies but she is unhappy. 'I'll get over it,' she says.

The cutting room is used to rehearse a few lines of voiceover. Veronika feels so stressed when she is forced to stop work for a few minutes that she paces back and forth in our outer room.

The screenings at the Roxy, icy though they are, are vital. The doctrine of frequent screenings of the cut on the big screen was taught to us by producer John Maynard on *Sweetie*. He knew it was essential to see the film on the cinema screen to know whether the cut is working or not. As Veronika explained it to us, the eye physically takes longer to roam over an image on a big screen than it does to look at an image on a Steenbeck or television screen. Thus the rhythm of the cutting has to work for the big screen, not the little one. I think this is why movies are often so disappointing on video.

Something that increasingly becomes clear to the editing team, as the weeks of the cut spin past, is that some actors need all the help the editor can give them. It becomes funny, dreary and then painful to watch them over and over. Sometimes you feel angry with the actors for not being good enough and putting you through such tedium. Such pain is rewarded, however, with interest, by the joy of watching inspired acting. Holly Hunter and Anna Paquin are so good I never tire of watching their performances. Sam Neill is so strong as Stewart, I can't help wondering whether audiences might come to hate him. Some people will be unable to separate character from actor.

The magic of the performances gets stronger as the editor and director cut and polish. The editor doesn't merely tinker with the film, setting this and that to rights. An editor can almost rewrite a film, if necessary. Even in a film with a fairly definite plot line, scenes can be rearranged, dropped, added to or otherwise doctored. Few people understand just how much artistic freedom is possible. There are stories of directors in the Hollywood studio system who shot their films in such a way that the editors had no choice but to cut it in the way the director wanted. Remember, however, that this tactic worked only because both director and editor were working within an understood Hollywood pattern of storytelling in film.

The fine cut of the film is drawing to a close. We all have mixed feelings about this. Jane has been depressed. From now on she loses her real intimacy with the film; from now on other people mostly take over and do what they have to do. The sound editors will do their work, Michael Nyman will compose the rest of the music and it does seem as if the film moves beyond her grasp. Last Monday we met Lee

Smith, the sound designer, and had a screening for him and the other sound people: the dialogue editors, the FX editors, the ADR editors and Gethin Creagh, the sound mixer. Over three or four hours in the freezing Crystal Palace theatre Veronika had to mix the several soundtracks we're already using down onto one soundtrack, while Heidi and I relaxed under the gum trees in the sun. But we froze in the Roxy during the screening again.

The sound men and women love the film. And they've brought a whole new energy into our world; they've intruded into our insularity and opened us up again. Although they work downstairs and we don't see that much of them, they are frequently up and down the stairs and always have something interesting to tell us. They say that one of the actors mouths a line silently before delivering it. This was confusing at first to the sound editors as they juggled dialogue and worked out where to lay the tracks. This is such a subtle habit no audience will ever see it and in all the months of picture editing none of us had noticed it.

THE FINE CUT—MONTH FOUR

Everyone's thoughts are moving ahead. Jan and Jane are thinking about the recording of the music in Munich. The dramatic fall of the British pound means that it would be cheaper to record the music in England but the musicians and facilities are already booked. Jan and Jane discuss entering the film into the Cannes Film Festival. Last minute agonies over the title are thrashed out. Jane has thought of many titles but finally settles on *The Piano*. We thought *The Black Keys* was a contender for a while, but *The Piano* sums it all up.

Our last screenings of *The Piano* are exhilarating. The fine cut is more or less complete. There are technical rough points to smooth out. The soundtrack is yet to be mixed and half the music is missing. Some dialogue has to be rerecorded. The film itself needs to be colour graded in the striking of the release prints, so that the colour tones within each scene are harmonious. Audiences care much less than technicians about technical perfection. In fact, film technicians work mainly for the approval of their peers. A sound editor is judged by other sound editors; a cinematographer by other cinematographers.

On my last day, we have a small champagne party. We finally get to drink the bottle that Jan gave us. Jane has promised to take the cutting crew out to dinner, just the four of us. She does. And we have a wonderful night. Jane gives each of us gifts, including a still from the film, of Flora and Ada on the beach. We sit in Jane's flat before we go out to dinner, leafing through stills. They are so beautiful we covet them all.

CODA—WINTER, 1993

The Piano is given its premiere screening at the Greater Union Cinemas, in Pitt Street, Sydney. This film has nothing to do with the technicians who worked on it any more. I don't feel that I belong at the premiere screening, not with all the well-known faces. What are *they* doing here? What possible involvement can this writer or that famous actor have with this film? None of them could feel as impatient as I do to see the finished version of it. I am almost sick with excitement to finally hear and see everything that's been done to it since last I saw the film. Since then it's travelled the world and won the Palme d'Or at Cannes. There isn't an empty seat in the theatre.

All the way through I am as moved, horrified and thrilled as the rest of the audience, though I've seen the film many times. Or that's what I thought. Of course, like that first time at the Roxy theatre, this is a film I've never seen before.

Jane receives a standing ovation at the end from one of the film's toughest audiences—other film makers and the hardened first-nighters. It's funny entering the Bayswater Brasserie for the party afterwards. Photographers are waiting outside. All the lights flash for David Malouf who enters just ahead of us and then of course the photographers turn away when we come along. We're with Veronika. (Later, Veronika is one of the eight Academy Award nominees for her work on *The Piano*. She is the first Australian editor to be so honoured.) I am speaking to Gethin Creagh, probably the best sound mixer in the Southern Hemisphere. He is elated, almost giddy. More than any director he's worked with, he tells me, Jane knows what she wants. Everyone is so *happy*. And later, as we leave the party that night, the image that stays with me, the image from the film that has always haunted me, is the slow-motion snowfall of Flora's white petticoats as she cartwheels in the blue garden. Some people say the film's happy ending diminishes its wildness, but for me those slow-turning cartwheels arcing through and over the glorious music, that's what we reached, what we achieved, the essence of pure, disciplined, creative joy.

Where
the Mine Was

JOHN DALE

I t grew dark early that afternoon. He was at the back of the house stacking firewood and saw the huge black clouds muscling in over the town and out along the crooked sealed road to where the mine was. He worked harder, piling armfuls of logs hard up against the back wall and squashing the termites dropping onto the concrete path. From the edge of the bush two black currawongs eyed him suspiciously. He went inside and washed his hands in the kitchen sink as rain began to spit at the windows.

The stew pot was bubbling on the stove. He lifted the lid and stirred the thick bits of sweet potato and kangaroo meat around with a long wooden spoon. 'Dinner's ready!' he called to her. She came through. She was wearing her bluey and her faded work jeans, clutching her green helmet in one hand.

'How is she?' he asked.

'Fine, Ray. Sleeping like a baby.'

'Good.' He ladled her dinner into a deep bowl and broke out some bread. They talked of what was happening at the mine while she ate. Two more days to go before he was due back on shift. A Valiant rumbled past the house and pulled up at the end of the street. AC/DC was already pouring from the open doorway opposite and half a dozen four-wheel drives and utes were parked there with their wheels up on the footpath.

Ray took a Boags Draught from the fridge and went over to the window. The curtains were wide open. Men from B shift were drinking out on the front lawn of that new primary teacher's house.

'You filled my thermos, honey?' she asked.

Ray nodded. 'In your crib bag.' He breathed on the windowpane and rubbed it clear with his sleeve. The rain was coming down hard now and he watched the men from B shift scatter like starlings, back onto her porch. Lights flicked on in all the front windows. Even Bon Scott's voice was getting drowned out now by the rain. 'I wonder if she knows what she's doing,' he said. 'Inviting those bastards over.'

Tanita squatted down beside the open fire and attacked the log with a big iron poker. Sparks leapt onto her bluey and she brushed them off. 'Well, she's over twenty-one...They wouldn't've sent her up here otherwise.' She glanced at him as she stood up, winding a strand of that wiry black hair of hers between her fingers.

'How come they gave her a house in the married quarters then? That's what I can't figure. You remember how long we had to wait for a place?'

He dragged the curtains roughly across the window. 'Tomorrow I'd like us to take a run up the coast if this weather breaks. Get some steaks, some decent coffee in. I get sick of that shit they sell up the store.'

Tanita picked up her green lid and her pack of twenty-fives. She swung the crib bag over her shoulder.

'It's pissing down out there,' Ray said quickly. 'You want me to ring in sick for you? You could stay home tonight.' He paused. 'We could do it up on the couch the old way...'

She took her orange raincoat off the hook beside the front door and shook it out. 'You know what C shift are like. It ain't worth the hassle. They got this thing at the moment 'bout the women drivers taking sickies and having babies.'

She was a big strong woman with deep brown eyes and thick lips meant for kissing. Ray put his hands on her shoulders. 'Maybe I'll wait up for you,' he smiled. He followed her out to the carport and watched her pull on a pair of the company's yellow gumboots. 'Take care near the crusher...it's going to be as slippery as hell on that road.'

'You know me, Ray. I'm a cautious woman.'

She slid into the Falcon and fed it some pedal. Water shot out from under the tyres as she backed down the drive. The headlights arced across the roofs of the mine workers' houses and then she was gone.

For a while Ray stayed out on the doorstep. He sucked on the end of his cigarette and watched the rain angle across the drive. A couple of B shift mill-rats were arm wrestling on the hood of a Landcruiser across the street. Ray flicked his butt onto the lawn and went back inside. He stuck his feet up on the round coffee table and trolled the dial on the set. *Escape from Alcatraz* was on, but he'd seen that when he was about five. Was there a station anywhere in the world that showed decent television on Saturday night? Not out here there wasn't. He kicked the off button and sat there in front of the fire, listening to the rain sweep across the roof and staring into the flames.

The phone shook him awake. He sat up like a setter in the chair, blinked and then he rushed down the hall. 'Ray,' a male voice said into his ear. 'That you, Raymond?' He could hear bottles clinking and rowdy voices in the background. Janis Joplin was singing 'I Need a Man to Love'.

'Come over and have a drink, Ray.'

'Who is this? That you, Henderson?'

'There's someone here who wants to talk to you, Raymond.'

'Why don't you bastards grow up,' he said.

The voice laughed. 'What's the matter? Your wife's out on the trucks...Come and have a drink, you cunt.'

Ray jammed the phone down and stood there in the dark, his fingers resting on the receiver. What had she said, the bitch! His heart was fisting against his rib cage. He waited for the anger to pass and then he tiptoed down the hall, to the second bedroom. He poked his head in around the door. A nightlight glowed dimly from the far corner of the room where a dark-skinned girl of fourteen was sleeping. One of her arms was dangling over the side of the pine bed, and two of the fingers on her other hand were pressed against her mouth. Ray listened to her wheezing sound. Christ it was stuffy in here! Her nightie had pulled down over her shoulder. Ray stared.

He tried to think of the car. Of the rust in the rear panels that needed to be cut out. He tried to think of anything other than the sight of his stepdaughter lying there. But he saw himself throwing off his clothes, taking two long strides towards the bed. He stood in the doorway imagining it all, waiting for the current to pass. He knew that it would. It had done before, if you just gave it time.

The girl stirred under the doona. 'Daddy,' she called in a sleepy voice.

It still sounded weird when she called him that. He swallowed hard, shifting his weight in the doorway. 'Yeah, hon, Ray's here. Your chest sounds bad. Want me to get your inhaler or anything?'

'Can you bring me some water. Please.'

He went out to the kitchen and came back with a glass full. Held it up to her lips, let her drink from it like a little bird. He touched her kinked black hair with his fingers. She looked so much like her mother sometimes.

'Thanks, Ray.' Smiling up at him with open eyes.

'Sleep well, Chrissie, okay?'

Her asthma had grown worse since they'd moved up here to the west coast. He shut the door behind him, went down the hall and through the kitchen. He opened the back door and stepped out into the rain. Let it run down his hair and into his face, let it stain his pants. Standing there in the darkness, cooling down. Sometimes he was sure that Chrissie knew. Ten days ago, she'd called him from the bedroom. 'Ray, come here, Ray!' And she was wearing a short, tight skirt he'd never seen before, and fishnets.

'What do you think,' she'd said, turning in a circle. 'Do you like it?' And she'd just stood there.

He shook the water off his hair like a dog and stepped back onto the porch. He bent down and picked up an armful of firewood. Something hairy brushed against the back of his hand and ran up his arm. Ray shuddered as the tarantula leapt from his shoulder into the doorway and crawled laboriously across the kitchen floor. A big one, a female. He followed the spider inside and dropped the logs down onto the hearth in the living room. Christ, he needed a drink! Having a drink right now was his main priority. In the kitchen he yanked the fridge door open and checked the racks. Nothing. They were right out of bullets. The tarantula eyed him, from above the stove now, as if he was the intruder. And maybe he was. Maybe they all were out here. In five years' time this whole town would just be bush again; that was a condition of the mining lease. He lit a cigarette and stood in front of the fire, his lungs kicking. Rain was clattering on the roof and gurgling down the drainpipe. He ran his hand through his damp hair, stuck the screen up against the fire, took his sheepskin-lined coat off the rack beside the front door and left the house.

Music was playing across the road, people were laughing and the front door to her place was wide open. For half a second he toyed with the idea of crossing the road, going straight in and telling her she was crazy. There was a saying in this town that B shift would rather fight than fuck. And trouble here was just too easy to get into and too hard to climb out of. Drawing his head down into his warm fleecy collar, Ray walked up to the only hotel in town instead. Some of the older miners were knocking balls round the worn pool tables and nursing their small beers. They nodded at him and he returned their enthusiasm. He wondered if there was anything more lonely than a public bar on a Saturday night. He ordered a slab of Boags Bitter and two packs of Camels unfiltered. Irene, the bargranny, slapped the box down on the counter like it was no weight at all.

'Tanita working tonight, love?' She rang up the total in the till and turned back to the TV. *Escape from Alcatraz* was on. But he'd seen that when he was about five. Irene was going deaf and she had the sound turned up so loud that he could hear Clint all the way out into the car park.

Ray walked along the side of the main road in the pissing rain, past the blackwoods and the Tassie blue gums. Way off, in the distance, between two hills, he could see the lights from the mine burning yellow. Twenty-four hours a day, 365 days a year those lights burned, while men, women and machines blasted, trucked and crushed the ore, then fed it down the pipe to the giant Japanese freighters waiting offshore. Sometimes, when you were out walking, you could feel the earth trembling under your feet.

At home he got out the bread knife, sliced the carton into four and stacked the door of the fridge with cold ones. He popped a can and sat in the dark, listening to the cars coming and going across the street. Amara Nicholls, that was her. The first time he'd laid eyes on her was at the Asian cooking night that some of the Filipino wives had put on at the school. Ten dollars a head—all the spring rolls, chicken and fried rice you could eat. Most of the married men had gone along. She'd told him a joke that night about single men. 'Bears with furniture' is what she'd called them. And she'd laughed and he'd looked into her mouth.

In the whole town there were maybe twenty single women compared to three hundred bears with not too much furniture. And it was odd how so many of the single women gravitated towards the married guys. As if they preferred their men already house trained. That night they talked about the mine and Windermere—a suburb down in Hobart they both knew well. He'd hardly even noticed her lip then. It was funny how that had never bothered him.

REPUBLICA

Trouble comes in a lot of different shapes and sizes and some men can go a whole lifetime without knowing why they attract so much of it. But Ray knew. Ever since he'd turned thirteen and a half. He reached a hand up behind his head and felt for the underwear drying on the back of the armchair. Casually he picked up a pair of Tanita's black panties and held the soft lacy cotton to his cheek, smelling the warmth from the fire. These were new; he'd never seen these on her before. His eyes scanned the label. Tens. Tanita didn't wear tens, she wore sixteens. Ray threw the panties onto the vinyl sofa and stood up quickly. He drained his beer and went out to the fridge.

Across the street he could hear the twang of a steel guitar and the pounding of drums. He wrenched the door open, plucked four cans from the box and tucked them under his arm.

Out in the carport, he told himself he wouldn't stay long. Go over there, show his face for five minutes, find out what was happening. He went down the drive and crossed the road, the rain running down his forehead and off his busted nose. A miner in a blue and white checked jacket on the front lawn was holding onto the trunk of a tree, the steam rising from between his legs. Ray stopped at the gate, glanced at the line of mud-streaked cars jammed in her driveway and at the big shiny Harley he'd never seen before. He took a swig of Boags and went uneasily up the steps and in through the door.

An old, black voice on the stereo was growling to a loud bluesy beat. *You done me wrong...*Men were leaning against the cement-sheet walls drinking in bunches of fours and fives. Ray threaded his way between them, holding his can out in front of him so it wouldn't spill. The air was thick and blue with cigarette smoke. A pair of young miners lay face down on the floorboards, but most of B shift were standing in a tight circle, drinking, scratching and staring at something happening in the centre of the room. Ray elbowed his way through the checked jackets and peered over a broad set of shoulders at seven women dancing cheek to cheek with their partners while thirty or more single men looked on in silence. Barefoot and slender, Amara Nicholls had her arms around the neck of a large red-haired man wearing a cut-off Levis jacket and a dirty bandanna tied around his forehead. Her eyes were half shut and her mouth was open just a little. She rolled her head softly from side to side and clicked her fingers to the beat. Ray watched as she took a big fat joint, its end glistening, from the red-haired biker and sucked the smoke deep into her lungs. The sweet smell of dope drifted over. He lifted his can to his lips.

He edged nearer the window, wishing now he'd stayed at home. Empty bottles and overflowing ashtrays were littering the food table. The cheese platter and the bowls of chilli chips had all been pawed through, and a cigarette filter was poking up out of what was left of the onion dip. Ray stood there. He stared at Amara. She was swaying her hips to the music and most of the miners' eyes in that room were fixed on the tight backside of her jeans.

'Ray!' she yelled suddenly. 'Raymond!'

Heads turned as she broke free of the red-haired biker's grasp and weaved through the ring of drunken miners towards him. She pressed her mouth up against his cheek. He could feel the ridge of scar there on her top lip.

'I didn't think you were coming,' she said. She slipped a small, warm hand inside his sheepskin jacket. 'I've missed you, Ray.'

'We gotta talk. Can we go somewhere?' He could sense the miners on either side of him tuning in to their conversation. 'The bears,' he whispered. 'How come you invited all the bears?'

She laughed and grabbed his elbow. 'Come on,' she said. 'I need to take a piss.'

From across the room the red-haired biker watched them, thumbs hooked under the big chrome buckle on his belt. He was wearing black riding boots. Ray had a bad feeling about tonight.

But he followed Amara down the hallway, stopped outside the bathroom door. Someone inside coughed and flushed and then a drunken young mill-rat staggered out doing up his zip.

Inside the bathroom Amara closed the door and flicked the catch. Hair clips, tubes of gel and different coloured fish-shaped soap lined the edge of the plastic bath. She looked at him, one eyebrow raised.

'Henderson rung me,' Ray said. The rain was still beating on the iron roof and a bass guitar vibrated noisily through the thin walls. He watched her unzip her 501s and peel them down as far as her knees. 'I think he's twigged.'

'So?' She squatted on the seat. 'It's finished, Ray. All over. That was your decision.'

'But the whole town's going to find out now,' he said. 'They'll be talking about us in the crib room.'

Amara tore off a strip of toilet paper, folded it in her fingers and wiped herself. She dropped the paper into the bowl. 'You know, when I first came to this town all I used to drink was a glass of wine with a meal sometimes. Now it's a bottle every night.'

She stood up. 'Three more months and I'm out of here.'

Ray was staring as she hitched up her jeans. He said, 'I want you, Amara, I want you bad.'

She was tucking herself back in. 'What about your wife, Ray? What about all that stuff you said?'

She took a step towards him and hooked her arms around his neck. Up close like this, she smelled of dope and gin, and something much sweeter.

'So kiss me, Raymond.'

He pressed his mouth tight up against hers, felt her tongue. Her zipper was open and he slipped a pair of fingers inside, worked them down under the elastic.

A fist rapped on the bathroom door. 'Hey,' a voice yelled. 'There's people busting for a leak out here!'

Amara drew his hand out slowly. Her eyes were big and green. She turned and flushed the toilet.

'We just going to walk out there together?'

'There's always the window, Ray, if you're so freaked.'

Above the showerhead, a small, rusted louvre window looked down onto the backyard. No way could he fit through there. He grabbed a face cloth off the rail, ran it under the cold tap. 'Okay,' he said. 'You first.'

Amara slipped the catch. A big-gutted miner clutching a bottle of stout by the neck was standing outside the door, shifting his weight from boot to boot. He took a hand-rolled cigarette out of the corner of his mouth and stared at the face cloth Ray had pressed over one eye.

Stepping past him, Ray said, 'I think you got most of it out.' He followed Amara down the hall, head tipped back.

In the kitchen she laughed. 'You're a bastard, Ray. I think that's why I like you.'

Ray tossed the wet face towel onto the sink. John Lee Hooker was tapping his foot slowly out there to the boogie, and a group of older miners were huddled in the corner talking about future plans. Ray looked out through a cracked glass pane at the rain coming down in sheets. He could smell her still on his hand.

Amara waved an arm in the air. 'Ray, there's someone I want you to meet.'

The red-haired biker with the dirty bandanna was cutting a path through the miners towards them. Ray felt the muscles in his gut tighten.

'Ray this is Eddy. Eddy...Ray.'

Ray came up with his hand fast. If the biker refused it, he could turn then and walk away. But Eddy took it, gripped it hard. Deep acne scars peppered the man's skin.

'You a miner?'

'Ray's a shovel operator,' Amara said. 'He loads up the big trucks.'

'What, them fifty tonners?'

'Yeah.' Ray nodded. 'You looking for work?'

'Eddy works with me, Ray,' Amara said. 'He started last week.'

Ray blinked. 'You're a primary teacher?'

'We've had some problems at school. Eddy's been fantastic with the grade fives.'

'Never let the little monkeys get the drop on you,' Eddy winked. 'Wanna beer?'

Ray refocused on Eddy now, getting a totally different picture of the guy.

'No, I'll get em.' He went over to the fridge and worked two stubbies out of someone else's pack. A voice behind him said, 'Well, well, if it ain't the A shift ladies man.'

Ray turned. A heavily built miner with a thick, black moustache sprouting from under his nose was staring at him.

'Listen, I wanna word with you, Henderson.'

Henderson grinned, displaying his two missing front teeth. 'Mate, I'm all ears.'

'You're all bullshit,' Ray said. 'Don't you go ringing my house again at night. I've got a sick daughter there...'

'Better watch that kid, mate. She's gonna break a few hearts in this town. I seen her walking up the street the other day in this tight little skirt...'

'Shut your mouth,' Ray said.

Henderson whistled, leaned his shoulders back. 'Mate, looks like I struck a nerve.'

'What are you saying?'

'Saying nothing, Raymond. You're doing all the talking.'

Ray slammed two stubbies down on the sink. Glass cracked and beer dribbled down his wrist. The kitchen went quiet. Ray's heart was hammering in his chest and he felt the hairs on the back of his neck. 'I want you to apologise,' he said. The moment the words left his lips he knew they sounded ridiculous, but he was boxed in now.

Henderson grinned at his two offsiders. The B shift pit boss never went anywhere alone. The older miners in the corner were holding their cans still, cigarettes burning quietly off the edge of their lips. Ray could sense them.

'Mate,' Henderson said, 'mate, all I'm doing is filling you in.'

Ray saw the smirk on his face. He grabbed him by his bluey and shoved him hard backwards. A female voice was calling out for them to break it up. Henderson got to his feet, but he wasn't smiling now. A black lick of hair dangled over his eyes. He charged at Ray, head tucked low like a ram. Ray sidestepped and smacked an elbow in Henderson's face. It was crazy, a thirty-nine-year-old man like this, but down deep, Ray wanted to hurt him bad. They tumbled out the back door into the rain. Miners crowded around, eager for some excitement. Ray could smell the tobacco on Henderson's coat. His fist struck bone and he swore, and Henderson came at him again, driving Ray off the path into the mud. Miners were cheering as they slipped around and Ray landed hard with his knees in Henderson's right kidney. He rolled him over like a big winded sheep and fixed both his hands around his throat. Amara pushed her way through the miners. 'Stop it, Ray! Stop it!' And Henderson's tongue was flapping out the corner of his mouth when a siren pierced the rain.

Ray stopped squeezing, lifted his hands in the air. Miners turned their heads towards the faint lights of the mine and everyone quit talking. The siren wailed and wailed off in the distance.

Ray climbed up off of Henderson who lay there clutching at his windpipe with his thick, muddied fingers. Ray wiped the blood off his nose. His heart was still speeding and he stood for a moment in the backyard, listening to the siren. His boots squelched with water as he began to walk.

'Better get out there fast,' an old miner muttered. Men and women were already heading for their cars. Ray grabbed Amara's arm. 'I need a lift quick.'

'Ray,' she said, 'oh my God, Raymond.' She was pulling at her lip.

'What is it?' Eddy said, 'what's going on?'

'That your Hog out front?'

Eddy nodded.

'I'll tell you on the way,' Ray said. 'Let's go.'

In the kitchen Eddy snatched his keys off the pineboard cabinet. Miners were starting up their utes and four-wheel drives out in the street. Lights came on in all the houses, and men and women opened their doors and stood out under the carports in pyjamas and robes looking through the rain towards the mine. The siren kept wailing. Ray jumped onto the pillion seat of the customised Softail as Eddy started it first kick. They shot off down the drive and out into the street before most of the cars had even got their lights on. Down past the tailings dam they flew, Eddy crouching low over the tank and Ray leaning the wrong way into corners, down past the single men's quarters where the lights burned and men were rushing half-dressed out of their cabins, Ray holding onto Eddy's thick belt, his eyes shut tight in the rain, murmuring under his breath over and over the same words: don't let it be her *please, please not her!* Whatever he had done wrong it didn't deserve to come back on Tanita.

'They got a fire out there?' Eddy yelled over his shoulder.

'That's the emergency siren,' Ray shouted back into the rain. 'They only sound it when there's been an accident...My wife's down there now.'

'You're not with Amara, Ray?'

'No,' Ray said, 'I'm not.'

He felt Eddy nod.

The Harley gripped gravel as they climbed towards the yellow lights of the mine, the siren growing louder and louder the closer they got. He clung to Eddy's waist so tightly now that Eddy had to yell for him to ease off. All around them tall dark eucalypts and sassafras were dripping with rain. Ferns, moss and lichen covered the dense rainforest floor and the hills on either side were shrouded in mist. They swept around a sharp bend and there at the end of the road, lit up in the rain, was the mine.

Eddy whistled. 'That is some fucking hole you got here!'

The top had been sheared off a mountain and millions of tonnes of rock scooped out from inside. A wire fence ringed the approach to an enormous open-cut mine that stretched back across the landscape for miles. Steep gravelled roads led down deep into the bowels of the earth. Cranes were standing guard over huge piles of crushed ore as fine as dust.

White hats and State Emergency Service Volunteers were conferring outside the mill beside two fire trucks and a Landcruiser Sahara with its motor running. Ray jumped off the Harley before Eddy had even stopped and ran over to the main gate where a huge yellow sign said:

WELCOME TO SOUTHERN MINES

DAYS SINCE LAST ACCIDENT: 85

OUR BEST PREVIOUS RECORD: 87

MINING OPERATIONS:

SAFETY IS PART OF EVERYBODY'S JOB

Ray burst into the guard's box, water dripping off his hair. 'Who is it, Phil?'

The old security guard puffed anxiously on a cigarette, his face webbed with wrinkles. 'A CAT's flipped over near Crusher Gully.'

Ray just stood there. 'Not Tanita's?'

'All I know, Ray, is we got one truck gone over and a driver trapped down there.'

'Call them up!'

'Can't do that, Raymond. You know the procedure. Radio's only to be used now by emergency crews.'

'I'm going down the pit then,' Ray said.

'You're not rostered on. Mr King's out there. He won't let you through.'

'What's he going to do, Phil, shoot me?' Ray slipped out of the guard's box and under the boom gate. The noise from the siren was so loud now it set his teeth on edge. He made his way quickly across the yard towards the fire trucks. The SES volunteers and white hats seemed to be waiting on some signal. The mine boss was talking rapidly into a cellular phone. When he spotted Ray, he stared at him through his bottle-thick glasses and barked at one of the engineers, 'Get that man a helmet!'

Someone slipped Ray a white hat and he stuck it on as the boom gate kicked up and the town's only ambulance tore in straight past them. Everyone jumped onto the fire trucks then and the mine boss and five white hats piled into the Toyota Turbo. Sirens screaming, they tailed the ambulance down the steep gravelled incline towards Crusher Gully, Ray gripping the shiny handrail of the truck and praying under his breath that it wasn't her. Not now. Not when everything was coming good. An SES volunteer squeezed Ray's arm, but didn't say a word. None of the men were talking and Ray was too busy trying to stop the worst thoughts from creeping into his mind, like water under a door.

Coming out of the mist he saw them, moving slowly across the floor of the mine like enormous four-legged beasts, a convoy of graders, dozers and big yellow trucks. Towers of emergency lights lit up the pit and the granite-hard core of the mountain was exposed now to the rain and the noise of sirens and the whirr of heavy machinery.

Two of the dozers, a grader and the break-down truck carefully winched something up from the edge of Crusher Gully. Even from this distance, Ray could make out the shattered windscreen and the caved-in cabin of a fifty-tonne CAT. Slowly, the truck was being dragged up by its front axle over the edge of the dump and Ray felt a stab of happiness. The number painted on the side wasn't hers! It wasn't her bloody truck!

He bit down hard on his lip to stop himself crying out with joy. The ambulance pulled up ahead and the SES volunteers jumped off the fire trucks, uncoiling hoses and passing down welding gear. Ray stared at the skid marks dug into the gravel right on the very edge of Crusher Gully where the driver had locked the anchors on. His eyes shifted to the other miners standing out in the rain with bowed heads and he felt something dark slip past them, like a thin quick shadow across a wall.

Shivering with cold, Ray climbed down off the fire truck and pushed his way through the white hats and the men and women of C shift, looking for her amongst all the grey overalls and blue coats and green lids. She was at the edge of the line of parked yellow trucks, and she spotted him first. She ran towards him and threw her strong arms around his neck, and he lifted her off the ground and held his big black woman in the air for a second. Her skin and coat smelled of the damp earth and he bounced her up and down, gabbling into her right ear, 'Christ, Jesus fucking Christ, Tanita!'

'I saw it, Ray.' She shook her head and blinked rapidly. 'I saw him go over...'

He lowered her back onto the ground.

'Gary Peard.' The words rushed out of her. 'It's Gary Peard...He was backing up with a full load on and then his wheels just clipped the edge. He went over so fast, like something had a hold of his truck...'

Her big brown eyes looked straight at him.

In all the time they had lived together he had never once seen her cry. He worked a hand up inside the buttons of her bluey, under her woollen shirt and touched her stomach with his fingers. 'You all right?'

Nodding, she sniffed and wiped her nose on the back of her hand.

'I thought it was you, hon,' he whispered. 'I thought I'd lost you.'

The siren quit wailing then. And except for the shuddering from the engines of two large CATS, a heavy silence descended over the pit. The mine boss took off his glasses and rubbed at the bridge of his nose. Miners were standing in a tight circle around the smashed-in truck and Ray and Tanita pressed forward, peering over the shoulders of the men and women from C shift.

They'd cut Gary Peard out of his cabin and had already lowered him onto a stretcher. His crushed helmet lay in front of the giant black wheel of the truck and the town's only doctor, wearing a clean white shirt with the sleeves rolled up to his elbows, was kneeling in the mud doing something careful with his fingers to the top of Gary Peard's head. Then the doctor pulled away and Ray saw.

Tanita was digging her nails into Ray's palm and Ray stared as Gary Peard was lifted into the air and slid neatly into the back of the ambulance. The driver didn't even bother with the siren. Silently, the ambulance climbed the hill, its red light blinking through the mist. For a while Ray stood there with his arms tight around his wife and the light, silvery rain streaking the sky. As they walked back to her truck, men and women from C shift came up and touched Tanita's coat or brushed their rough hands against her wrist. Truckies, dozer drivers and engineers—everyone began to reach out a hand or press the tips of their fingers against a workmate's coat. Even the mine boss whose hair was sticking out the sides was going around gripping men and women by the elbow and the miners were nodding at each other in a curt sort of way as if they'd just come on shift, but no one said a word.

Tanita climbed up into the cabin of her big, yellow rig and Ray squeezed in beside her, perched on the edge of the heater. Steam hissed from the legs of his trousers. His boots were caked in mud. She started the engine. One by one, the big trucks rolled out and when the convoy had reached the top of the road, Ray turned and glanced back down at the open-cut mine, at the bands of iron ore buried so deep in the heart of that mountain they had to be blasted out with explosives. The emergency lights had been switched off and the rain was falling softly on Crusher Gully, falling across the main pit too, and the abandoned craters and steep gravelled roads, falling from one end of that huge, black mine right out to the dark, misted hills in the distance. And Ray wondered who would have to tell old Mrs Peard it was her son.

Outside the concentrating mill the trucks pulled up in a row and cut their engines and the mill-rats came out. They took off their red helmets and walked directly for the gates. Men, women and children, some still wearing pyjama pants and dressing gowns under their orange striped raincoats, had their faces pressed up against the wire fence waiting. The car park was packed with families from all four shifts, and shopkeepers from the town were handing out pies and foam cups of coffee. A young sandy-haired woman was crying at the gate, her fingers entwined in the wire mesh. Ray knew there would be no work at the mine tomorrow. He scanned the faces at the fence and caught Amara and Eddy watching him as he walked through the crowd with his arm wrapped around Tanita's shoulders.

'You drive,' his wife said.

'I want to tell you something, hon...'

'Just get me home, Ray, please.' She threw him the keys, and he opened the door to the ute and adjusted the seat back. She slid in beside him, unbuttoned her bluey and the top stud on her jeans and sat with her legs wide apart, sweat beading the corners of her lips.

'You all right, Neet?'

She was hanging onto the doorstrap, but she didn't answer. Just waved at him to get going. Her chest was wheezing, like she had one of her old attacks coming on, and she wound down the window and gulped in the air. Wet, black trees hissed past on either side, the road cutting through the forest like a part in a man's hair, Ray driving fast now, changing gears quickly, glancing at his wife out of the corner of his eye and thinking how strong this woman was. He took a hand off the wheel, reached up under Tanita's shirt and laid it gently over her sweating belly. Held his hand there as they drove home through the rainforest, sure that he could feel the tiny heart beating.

At Last
I've Found You

for Susan Hampton

PHILIP MEAD

Those polaroids really capture the psychogeography of Lygon Street!
Busy heads, cool cats looking for a kitty, flip-phones among the plates,
the vaguely troubled clouds descending like hairstyles. That's our
      microclimate!
There's Susie bending over her coffee, a small pot of Roman mud,

wondering how the interview could have gone better, the bitches.
And Joe, staring out of frame, the shadow of days trellised across his
      face.
What will he get her for a present? Got it, silk pyjamas and a Mistral
      fan.
He looks like the geomancer, she's the self-fashioned one.

What does it mean being lovers so long. What's in your heart, for
      example?
Are these the meanings haphazardly composed for us, just waiting to
      be read,
the door of the café a strong receding central darkness?
Like some early modern painting, a family arranged around an
      unremarked

and sombre doorway. But it turns out we've been tromped,
like one of those TV ads where the scene is suddenly freeze-framed
and you alone are moving through a streetscape on hold,
poking your finger into someone's ice cream, borrowing a pair of
      sunglasses.

It's actually what it sounds like to be mad. And it occurs to you that
people love you conditionally, though that's not the photographic
      evidence.
What it means is never static, the hand-held style, kids in your arms.
The weather is the other thing, carrying on with its time-lapse
      narrative.

Round the corner at the movie house the doors are wide open
and it looks like everyone is dead in their seats,
except for the person in the front row getting up to leave.
The final scene seems to be two lovers dead in a car, kissing.

The camera pulls back from their tender mouths,
a street of cars piled up behind them, and then further back,
beginning to spin, a whole city quarter impossibly blocked.
As you come up the aisle, the credits roll gently across your face like
    flames.

Our Old House

for Katerina Patrou

ARTHUR SPYROU

It's always easier to
make up the game and
fill in genre as you go
along. So chick-pea coffee
for young adults   .
pine nuts for explorers
tiny hands clashing rocks
again from a beginning
at the corner of a day.
Our shadows were less
black but sharper we
could see them then.
So when the little
devils called us down,
well yes we broke a
window smoked some
loose-grass joints but
never overestimated
our sins. Today the same
seagull floating in the
same sky is stillness
frozen in a snapshot.
The colours seep away
to white and grey the
blisters eventually
on sundials
are sure signs of life.

Terra Australis

ARTHUR SPYROU

We see our roots in the red
sand choked with iron, our
legs splitting amethyst and
quartz where we walk.
Wearing white manes and
cliff tops, eyebrows and
twisted trees on crags. We
dip a sponge in the vinegar
of the sea and drink and
are made glad. Vinegar
runs from our side like
scorn like pride and we
are made glad. The night
around is light with the
trophies of silent yesterdays
the barking of mute dogs
the mantle of rat ke rani
and gardenia. The quiet
waters were amongst
the first midwives
and sometimes when
a parrot's cage casts
a shadow like a spider
we put the dream half-
eaten in its wrapper
and take another. This
is a land with toffee-
apple trees and all who
eat have pierced hands
and make love in cinemas
to an advanced age.

I'm Going

DULA NGURRUWUTTHUN

I'm going to tell you the story of long ago when I used to move around from place to place. I used to sleep with only poor things to cover me, paperbark or a mat, and nothing to rest my head on.

We used to travel, myself and my two fathers, Merarra and Djimbalal and their wives. Merarra had two Galpu wives and a few Marrakulu wives, and the other had wives from Marrangu, Wawilak and Djambarrpuyngu clans.

I was born at a place called Yirrkamarra, near Alyangula. It is an island. My two fathers used to work with turtles, preparing their shells and selling them for tobacco, blankets, axes and knives at Yathikpa. I grew up and became a man, and my two fathers took me through the bush and taught me the law.

In those days, when I was still a child really, I grew to understand what was happening, how the Yolngu would kill Japanese and Whites. The Djapu and Balamumu, Wonggu's sons, killed a Japanese, and my wife's grandfather Dhakiyarr speared a policeman, and also my two fathers speared a white man in exactly the same way.

After that they all went to Darwin. They caught Merarra and Dhakiyarr first, at Batalumba Bay, and then the others were caught at Bal, and they took them to prison in Darwin, leaving Wonggu behind at Bal. They were inside for I don't know how many years, over at Darwin, then Wonggu's sons came out, and went straight back to find Wonggu. And those two, Merarra and Dhakiyarr, they left them behind back in Darwin.

As for Merarra, he disappeared from Darwin, and followed Barrani and Wanumuruk and Larrikin and Gunbiyala. They went through Katherine and kept on until they arrived at Roper, and on until Bickerton Island, and around this way through the Laynha area. All of us others had been living at Gunda, waiting for them. We had been sitting and waiting... until we saw smoke rising from the Wangurrarrikpa, which is near Baniyala. We saw that smoke, so we crossed over by canoe, me, a child. Djimbalal and my mother's mother's brother named Gadurrak. Paddle, paddle, paddle...until we met, actually still in deep water, and looked and recognised them.

'Isn' that Merarra's elbow paddling that canoe? That looks like Merarra's elbow!' Like that, and we were so happy and excited, because he had left us such a long time before.

Yes, we all paddled back to Gunda, and sat there for a short while, talking together and telling our stories. After that, we went up to Baykurrtji, and stayed there, and then up to Gulwittji (Gangan) and stayed there...and when our water dried up at Gulwittji, then we shifted to Galawurrwurr.

Some enemies followed us, and there, the place was bad for Merarra. My father was killed at Galawurrwurr. And we returned to the coast and went eating turtles along Groote, wherever there were open areas, and reefs for catching turtles. I grew until I became big, in the care of Djimbalal, and he continued to teach me the skills of turtle hunting. We would work...then take them to Groote Island, to a small place called Yathikpa and sell them to a white man. He would give us back tobacco, blankets, axes, knives and clothes. We lived at Groote for quite a long time, staying near Wonggu and Gonhiri's father. I continued spearing turtles along this side of Groote, along our Laynha side.

Then we went up to Gangan, and it was there that a sickness came to us, and all our mothers were close to death, and my two brothers Mipila and Dhanawutjpi and my sister named Dhakarra, and many other people who were living there. We left that place Gangan. Then my father and I and my cousin named Gunung went to Elcho Island. And we lived there for quite a while, until Sheppy said to Djimbalal, 'Hey, do you know the work of crocodile hunting?'

And he said back to him, 'Yes I know, because I used to spear crocodiles over at Luthunba.'

So Sheppy gave my Dad the crocodile rope. First, my dad would paint his forehead with white clay, then straight away he would move silently through the water and spear them. He would then sell them to Sheppy.

The place we lived at was called Marapuy, belonging to those Djambarrpuyngu people, and also Milminydjarrk which is near Lake Evela and Burwani and Butjunguru on the other side of Dhanbala. That's where we lived and where we speared the crocodiles. We were living at Galiwin'ku, and Sheppy would fly out to get the crocodile skins. Those Yolngu would sell them, and get money, one pound and two pounds. Yes, and we would buy shovel-nosed spear blades, blankets and axes with that money. We lived there for quite a while, until Sheppy asked us, 'Hey, do you know how to make an airstrip? Because you have been bringing those crocs across on your shoulders for a long time now.' It's true, we made an airstrip at Warrarwurr, and it was from there that we could send the crocodile skins to Sheppy now. He would fly out from Galiwin'ku.

We were living very close to a sacred ceremonial ground at Warrarwurr, and that was where I learned to go into the ngarra ceremony. It was my first time. I saw the style of my father, calling out the names, how it was that he would call out the totems and the dreaming sites of all the different clans and families.

After the ngarra ceremony we cleared out, and all the Yolngu went bitter and they speared each other and then scattered.

And all they could do was go back to their own places, and we went back there to Elcho and had Christmas at Elcho. And again Sheppy asked us, 'Do you want more airstrip work? We'll chop these trees and clear the area around Galiwin'ku and make an airstrip.' Like that. And we answered yes, and worked. We worked until the area was cleared. We started at the end of the rain, and finished during the hot weather before the next wet season. After that we went back to Raymanggirr, land belonging to the Marrangu people, and in the same way made an airstrip, chopping only with an axe, and with our hands, clearing away the trees to make an open space.

The work was finished, when Yolngu came looking for us. They were Gumuk, my mother's mother's brother, Gunbiyala, Walirra's father, and Bandaka, Luwani's father. All the way from Groote they came, crossing over by canoe to Gunda, and leaving the canoe there, and walking across, looking for us. They had come straight through the bush, and found us. When they finally met up with us, we all went back to Raymanggirr, and stayed there again, until a canoe arrived containing Wonggu. We were so happy. 'Yes, yes. Wonggu has arrived here from a completely different place!' Like that.

Yes, so we stayed there for quite a while, until the plane landed at Raymanggirr, after which we went straight to Baykurrtji and stayed right there, year after year, and then back to Raymanggirr in order to get cigarettes and clothes. After that we went straight back across to Umbakumba, and Luwani's father and I brought a letter back this way to Yirrkala. And it was by canoe we came. We paddled the canoe here and came out at Gunda, and we walked at Dhunuputjpi, and passed through Wayawu, and after Maywundji, up through the bush and down to Biranybirany, and we saw the footprints. So we followed them until we got to Dhurrthiri and there we saw the fresh footprints belonging to my fathers, whose names were Yotjing and Ngakaya.

Okay, so we tracked these two sets of footprints. We went out searching, and we cut across the Mulularra, and saw all their things where they had been sitting together in the shade. Those Yolngu were out collecting wild plums, and goodness me, that husband and wife had caught ever so many barramundi. We walked towards them, and the womenfolk saw us from where they were gathering lily roots and called out, 'Come on! Come on! All the way from Umbakumba, from Baway, all the way from Baway, Come on!...' Like that.

After that we went to Yirrkala, and stayed there a long time until Nalwarri was born, my first-born child, in the time of the mission. When the white people were living and working here.

And in those years, maybe 1956 or 1957, until Nalwarri grew up, I used to work with the peanuts. I used to plant that food we call peanuts. Alongside Munhalal, my wife. And we stayed there at Yirrkala for a long time, and two of my children grew up. And my father died at Numbulwar. For that we went back. We finished off my father's funeral rites, and then we came back here. Although we came back here by canoe. We came all the way until we reached Yirrkala, and we stayed here now a long time.

1. Bundjulung Totem

RUBY LANGFORD GINIBI

I heard my totem bird call out, kitchee! kitchee! kitchee! kee,
tellin me this meant to be, you were born to tell these stories.
Whiteman didn't believe that bird talkem to me,
he tellem me good news and bad,
he warn when trouble tell of death,
I always heard his call!
For him messenger bird of my Bundjulung people! that bird, kitchee!
    kitchee! kitchee! kee!
willy wagtail that bird be!

2. Tribal Doctor–
Magic Man

RUBY LANGFORD GINIBI

Magic man of a time long long ago,
your stories about the bush animals, *bunihny*, *burbi*, *binging*,
we sat in wonder listening, warming our toes at the fire bucket
you had inside your hessian bag shack, with its old tin roof.
Me and me little *titis* depended on you to watch us while dad worked.
I remember ashes damper, and corned beef cooked over the open fire
in a big boiler, bunya nuts cooked in the ashes too, swans eggs, and
    turtle eggs and cobra.
You taught us which berries to eat, geebung and lilipili and wild
    cherries,
 ya dug for yams with ya tommy axe and killed goannas and snakes and
    roasted them,
you taught me which bird called up the rain,
how to tell when a storm was comin up, also to tell if it was gonna
    hail.
Clever magic man, I even saw you heal pain,
and in my memory you'll always remain.

3. The Gubberments

RUBY LANGFORD GINIBI

When whitemen bin cummon alonga this way,
Aboriginal people had no place left ta stay.
Gone was his tucker, emu and roo run from the fences the whiteman
   he knew,
that's what is gubberment tellem ta do.
Want no blackfella runnin around free, puttem all on mission,
that's where they all should be,
givem white manager he tellum what ta do;
gotta stay on mission ground, neber wander all ober town,
I gib you all rations ta lubra, and kids, ya gotta work for tucker ya git;
missionary come he teacher us lidgin,
ya gotta be good ta go ta heben;
they allas tellin us what ta do! like we got nothin ta thinkum with too.
Then they takem away our kids, sayin they'll be back one day,
our mother and father have nuthin ta say,
trooper and mission truck, him bin takem away,
and we neber seen em for many a day,
some kids they bin never come ome again!
Whay whiteman cause so much pain??
to all our black mothers, please explain!

4. Mary's Song Cycle

RUBY LANGFORD GINIBI

Mary said!
Where are all my people gone?
where are all my children gone?
where are all our family clans gone?
where is our tribal heritage gone?
where has all the old people's rules gone?
where are all our tribal laws gone?
where are all our traditions gone?
where are all our corroborees gone?
where are all our warriors gone?
Torn apart! and split asunder!
lost in the whiteman's world
of power! greed! and gain!

Then in the nineteen hundreds and nineties
the warriors came back!

then the corroborees came back!
then the tribal laws came back!
and all the old people's rules came back!
then our heritage came back! and the traditions came back!
and all our family clans came back!
then all the children came back!
then all my people came back! back!

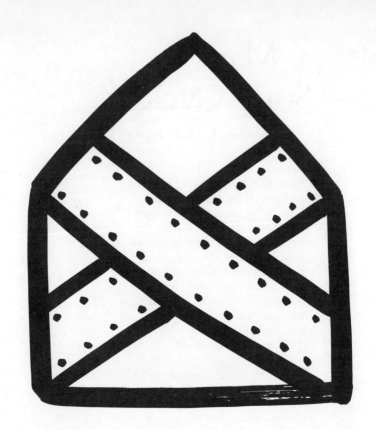

The Tempest
of Clemenza

GLENDA ADAMS

LUDLOW, VERMONT—AUGUST

We had emerged from three days of unrelenting rain. For the moment the sun was shining, and I was again sitting on the open porch. Before me on the rickety table that served as my desk rested the mysterious manuscript, several hundred pages, which had lain hidden in the carton of books I brought home yesterday from The Haunted Mansion Bookshop in Cuttingsville as a surprise for my daughter Clemenza.

During the rain, Clemenza was delighted to forego vigorous exercise and lay reading in front of the fire that we kept going day and night, and I transferred my work to the table in the kitchen, pushing aside the breakfast clutter of soggy shredded wheat, butter with toast crumbs in it, half-eaten boiled egg, and the scented candle. Clemenza liked to light the candle for breakfast, to add atmosphere, and although I found a scented candle so early in the day too great an assault on the senses, I happily indulged her enthusiasms, which are now precious to me. Although the wind that came with the rains whistled through the gaps and the knot holes in the walls, causing the candle flame to flicker and the flames in the open fire to rear up and I saw that our cottage could easily burn down, I kept my fear to myself.

Now, after three days huddling indoors, Clemenza, with an inner tube girdling her waist, capered back and forth on the dock, her pale, thin arms and legs that usually seemed so insubstantial giving her movements momentarily the frisky and optimistic gambol of a new lamb. As I watched, she plunged into the water of Lake Rescue and began to swim and kick in a more robust and spirited way than usual.

But on the other side of the lake, beyond the green mountains, clouds assembling there promised new downpours.

When the storm clouds first arrived three days ago, they were arranged in a column reaching high into the heavens and suggesting that a nuclear explosion had taken place in the vicinity of Bennington. As the clouds approached, the column broadening to form a wall, they started serving raindrops like tennis balls, acing them across the lake through the screen on the porch and onto the oilcloth that covers the rough planks of my desk.

Clemenza and I were driven inside, onto the little square of green rug that defined the living room in this tiny cottage—rustic was the term used in *The New York Times* ad—a two-storey wooden structure, unfinished on the inside.

When the rains began, we took up our defensive positions, crouching before the fire, our wet clothes strung out around us to dry. At Clemenza's request, we passed the time telling stories of life and love and of times and places far away and discussing certain topics of interest to her, such as the need for rules for fire safety, water safety and, it seemed to her, rules for everything in life, as if being alive and breathing were a messy business to be endured, rather than a daily celebration. She was also concerned with the difference between love, romance and infatuation and returned often to the character of Juliet in *Romeo and Juliet*. Shakespeare's decision to make her so young was of special concern to Clemenza, who was approaching Juliet's age and wondered if there was any chance her life would take similar romantic and tragic turns before she died.

On the subject of fire safety, I instructed her that the fire in our living room must never be left untended and the firescreen must always be used.

'Fire scream?' Clemenza asked, wide-eyed, then added, when I opened my mouth to correct her, 'just joking'.

During the year, we lived in an apartment in New York City and had never had to deal with fires and firescreens. Since she was born, Clemenza's life was sheltered and shaped by central heating at home and abroad in the museums and theatres, at school and in the indoor swimming pool where she exercised daily. Her life was so different from mine as a child, on another continent, in another hemisphere, where I spent my days outdoors, camping and bushwalking and surfing. The fires I remembered started spontaneously in the bush, jumping from treetop to treetop, leaping roads and rivers.

The fire Clemenza and I encountered together was at a performance of *The Tales of Hoffmann* by the New York City Opera. In the last scene, which took place back in the tavern, Hoffmann and his fellow students were inebriated after Hoffmann's prolonged storytelling. The tavern keeper carried onstage a bowl of flaming brew— the flames were real. Hoffmann and the students dipped their mugs into the hot wine while they sang. When Hoffmann fell down onto the straw matting in his final drunken faint, his outflung arm knocked the flaming bowl off the table onto the straw matting, which caught fire. This was in the State Theater at Lincoln Center and the incident provided the starting point for our heated discussions here in Ludlow, in front of the fire, while we waited for the rain to cease. As I saw it, the flames from the bowl set the matting on fire, and a row of low flames spread neatly and rapidly across the stage. There was a moment's pause, the audience drew in its breath, ready to rush out through the exits. The singers of the chorus seemed to hesitate as they clutched their mugs. Then, by some unanimous, tacit agreement, they began to stamp on the flames, like Flamenco dancers executing systematic, controlled little steps and simultaneously continued to sing the final tavern chorus. The fire was extinguished and the opera brought to its close.

According to Clemenza, it did not happen that way at all. Hoffmann was alone on the stage. He did indeed knock over the flaming bowl, but the flames did not catch onto the matting. Nothing caught on fire. The opera proceeded to its conclusion.

'No one was hurt, no one was in danger, no damage was done,' she cried. 'Everyone went home and lived happily ever after.'

The day before the rains came was Clemenza's twelfth birthday. A friend, Gilda, drove over from her house in New Hampshire with her daughter Evelyn, who was two years younger than Clemenza. Our plan was to go picnicking and walking in the nearby National Park, nothing too strenuous. But despite our intention to give Clemenza a bit of fun, the day never got past bickerings and the settling of trivial issues, and both Clemenza and I returned to our cottage exhausted.

Gilda arrived promptly at ten. I carried the picnic basket down to the car, calling to Clemenza, who followed me down. I noticed she was wearing a miniskirt that sparkled with sequins and a pair of high-heeled gold sandals that she had found in a thrift shop, which elongated further her thin legs. Her red hat was crammed over her short spiky hair. She still felt the visit to the hairdresser to even up her hair was a mistake, although to me she looked adorable, very French, and she continued to swathe her head in scarves, caps and hats when we went out.

'Is it wise for her to wear those shoes?' Gilda asked me quietly, meaning well. 'Will she be able to manage?'

The question irritated me. Evelyn was standing neatly by the car, appropriately clad in an ironed T-shirt, shorts, white athletic socks and old sneakers. But I had vowed to allow Clemenza to have her way in everything.

Sensing that we were discussing her, Clemenza looked over to me.

'I'm wearing this, no matter what,' she said. 'You know I won't be doing any hiking.'

Gilda looked concerned. 'What if she falls and breaks an ankle?'

Clemenza started shrieking. I was startled. I had never seen her react this way. Then I saw that she was pointing at the body of a baby squirrel lying smashed and bloody on the dock.

'It must have fallen from the roof,' Clemenza said and started crying as she bent over the dead animal.

Evelyn ran over to take a close look.

Gilda stood thinking for a moment, then said, 'I've got a shovel in the trunk.'

'Couldn't we just leave it here?' I asked, hoping it might somehow be gone by the time we got back.

Clemenza and Evelyn piled into the back of Gilda's station wagon and pressed against the windows, watching to see what we mothers would do.

Gilda shook her head. 'I don't mind burying it.' She took the shovel to a patch of earth a little way off the path and dug a hole. Then she picked up the body of the squirrel on the shovel, as easily as picking up a fried egg on a spatula, dumped it in the little grave and covered it over. 'Let's hope all the dogs in the neighbourhood don't come here to dig,' she said.

Gilda sighed. She took some old newspaper out of the trunk of her car and wiped down the shovel. 'Not the pleasantest thing to do first thing in the morning.'

'I don't think I could have done that,' I said.

'Someone has to do it,' said Gilda, sighing again. 'Lucky it didn't get inside your house. I've had to crawl under beds and sofas trying to get squirrels out. And they love to bite.' She looked at her watch. 'We've lost half an hour.'

While Gilda spread her map of Vermont on the hood of the station wagon, I tossed Clemenza's sneakers into the back, then leant back against the warm metal of the door, closing my eyes and letting the sun shine on my face.

It took an hour to get to the gates of the reserve. At the toll gate we paid two dollars to enter and park. We pulled into the parking lot, but before we could open our doors a large red 1950s sedan with New York licence plates pulled in beside us, screeching to a stop, knocking over a metal trash can that stood beside the entry gate.

The can clattered as it rolled across the parking area and lodged noisily against the bumper of our car. Gilda poked her head out of the window.

'Be careful,' she yelled at the red car, which was disgorging its load of seven or eight vigorous teenagers with brightly coloured, cropped hair and rings in their noses. 'This isn't Great Adventure. This isn't the Dodgems.'

I tried to get her to stop. Those teenagers were not a pretty bunch. 'Just let it pass,' I said.

'You're not in Jungle Habitat now,' Gilda persisted.

A tall young man with a red beard, the driver of the red car, gave Gilda the finger as he walked toward us. Gilda drew in her head. We all sat silent, scarcely breathing. The young man stood in front of the car for a moment, then gave the trash can a kick, sending it across the parking area into the bushes. Then he and his group moved off.

Acting as if nothing had happened, Gilda got out of the car and sat down on an overturned plant pot to study the sketch map of the reserve that we had received when we paid the toll.

'There are three picnic areas,' she said. 'The first one is too close to the toll booth and the incoming traffic. The second one has been reserved by some group from Albany for the day—no doubt those New York teenagers belong there. The third one is all that's left. It looks as if it's beside a bubbling brook. And there are hiking trails of varying degrees of strenuousness and difficulty.'

Clemenza stood in front of the wooden sign on which the rules of the reserve were posted. 'The park closes at dusk,' she said.

'When's dusk?' Evelyn asked.

'It's the end of the day, when the sun sinks and disappears and it gets dark,' said Clemenza. 'It's the death of the day.'

'We have hours and hours before then,' said Evelyn.

'But we have to leave at three,' said Gilda. 'Evelyn has her piano practice and her holiday homework. We got a late start.'

'I'm sorry,' I said. 'It was the dead squirrel.'

'No, I'm sorry,' said Gilda, apologetic. 'It's just that I've been on the road since nine o'clock, and we're only just beginning our day in the open air.'

'Everybody's sorry,' said Evelyn. 'Everybody's always sorry about something.'

'Make sure all fires are extinguished,' said Clemenza, reading. 'All dogs must be leashed.'

We walked along the path to the third picnic area, Clemenza teetering adroitly in her gold sandals, and deposited our things around a table and barbecue that were free. Although there were several groups already spread out on the grass, there was no sign of the rowdy group from the red car.

After lunch we began our walk, following the path that led into the forest. Evelyn and Clemenza trailed behind us, Clemenza having quietly exchanged her sandals for her sneakers. Gilda and Evelyn both wore their cameras slung around their necks.

A young couple came running out of the forest, laughing, out of breath.

Gilda asked them where the path led.

'It's wonderful in there,' the girl gasped. 'Not like this picnic area.' She swept her arms around. 'So many people.'

'Once you're in there, you won't see a soul,' the young man said.

'Is it a difficult walk?' I asked, thinking of Clemenza and her interest in young love. 'How far does it go?'

'You could stay in there for days,' said the girl. 'There are paths that go everywhere. It's a bit spooky, really. The path marked in red takes six hours, and the yellow one two hours.'

'We don't even have time for the yellow path.' Gilda looked at me. 'But it would be too much, anyway, wouldn't it?'

The young man put his arm around the girl. I could see that Clemenza was observing them both closely. 'It's great in there. Once you get to the bridge over the creek you'll see the fork in the path.'

They walked off, the girl wrinkling her nose at the picnicking hordes before her.

'Watch out for the mud!' Gilda called to Evelyn, nimbly sidestepping the patch of mud that stretched across the path. 'Well, we at least have time to walk a little way and enjoy that.'

Evelyn decided to photograph the mud and stopped beside the patch, pointing her polaroid camera straight down at her feet and pressing the button.

'Hold it still,' called Gilda.

The print came rolling out of the camera. Evelyn waved it in the air, waiting for the image to appear.

'You didn't hold still,' said Gilda.

The picture was a square of blurred brown, with two bluish blobs representing the toes of Evelyn's sneakers.

'It could have been quite artsy,' said Gilda, 'if she had held still.'

We jumped over the mud and continued along the path, which forked in front of us, one fork ascending the hill, the other descending toward the river. There was no bridge and no colour coding visible.

'Up or down?' Gilda called to the children.

'Up,' they said.

'Let's go down,' said Gilda. 'Let's try to find the river and that bridge.'

We took the downhill fork. Rivulets, little tributaries of the main creek, coursed down the hillside, crossing the path frequently and creating a track of almost continuous mud. Last month, too, there had been a lot of rain.

To avoid the mud we left the path and walked above it, using rocks as stepping stones. Above us loomed a huge rock outcrop, a miniature cliff.

'Let's climb it,' Clemenza yelled with sudden energy.

The children raced up the hill into the brush toward the cliff.

'Is Clemenza all right?' Gilda asked me. Then she called, 'Come back, Evelyn. You'll get lost. Our aim is to find the bridge.'

'Let them climb,' I urged Gilda. I realised that spending the day with Clemenza and me was making Gilda terribly uneasy. I placed my hand on her arm. 'We're not really going anywhere. It's good for them both.'

Gilda looked at her watch. 'There's still Clemenza's birthday cake and afternoon tea. I don't want to get caught in Sunday-night traffic on the way back.'

I smiled, envisioning Sunday-night traffic in Vermont and New Hampshire. Oh Gilda, Gilda, life is too precious for us to stocktake the hours like that. We must somehow learn to seize the day.

We sat on a rock, while the children tried to scale the outcrop behind them.

'There's a cave,' shrieked Clemenza. 'We can hide and stay here forever.'

'Evelyn,' called Gilda without turning around. Watching them climb made her more anxious than ever. 'Be quick! We want to get to the bridge.'

I sighed. 'Do you think we'll be like that young couple ever again? Or is there nothing left for us?'

Gilda gave a little snort. 'All that has passed for us.'

'They were so full of hope,' I said, again thinking of Clemenza.

There was an urgent yell behind us. We both leapt to our feet. I thought it would be Clemenza needing help, but it was Evelyn standing on a ledge some way above us who was in difficulty.

'She's stuck,' said Clemenza.

'Evelyn, get down!' Gilda commanded.

'I can't get down,' Evelyn squealed.

'Of course you can,' said Gilda. 'Just go back the same way you got there.'

Evelyn was pressed against the cliff. Her cheek rested against the rock. Her arms were stretched out, fingers wide, as if she were trying to glue herself there.

Clemenza climbed up to a wider part of the ledge, level with Evelyn. I was impressed with her agility and vigour and resisted cautioning her and calling her back.

'Clemenza shouldn't take such risks,' said Gilda. 'Evelyn can get down perfectly well on her own.'

'Just come back this way,' Clemenza said quietly to Evelyn. 'Move your left foot toward me. Slide it. That's right. Now slide your other foot along.'

Inch by inch Evelyn made her way back to Clemenza, who took her hand, eased her off the ledge, and led her back down to the waiting mothers.

Gilda shook her head at Evelyn. 'Just stay with us now.'

'The bridge, the bridge,' Clemenza called. 'Come on.'

The two girls raced off down the path.

'Not too fast,' called Gilda after them, and to me she said, 'Don't you think you ought to curb Clemenza a little, have her go more carefully, more slowly?'

I shook my head. 'That wouldn't do any good.'

Clemenza and Evelyn in their headlong rush encountered another stretch of mud.

'More filthy slush and slime,' Clemenza called, easily avoiding it by hopping from rock to rock, stone to stone. But Evelyn ran straight into the mud and stuck there, up to her ankles.

'Save me from the quicksand and certain death,' she called laughing to Clemenza, who came back and took her arms, hauling her out of the mud, the two of them laughing wildly.

'My sneaker's gone,' said Evelyn.

Gilda and I were now beside the mud patch. Evelyn was hopping around on one foot, the other, in its muddy sock, she held above the ground. The missing sneaker lay submerged in the mud.

'Lucky they are her old ones,' said Gilda. 'I told her not to wear them. The velcro fastenings had worn out and they're no good. But she wore them just the same. She must have known this would happen.'

Clemenza broke off a long stick from a dead branch and began fishing for the sneaker, flicking little bits of mud into the air each time the stick failed to snag the sneaker.

'You can leave it there,' said Gilda. 'They'll have to be thrown out now, anyway.'

'The rules said we have to leave the reserve as we found it,' said Clemenza, 'like ashes to ashes, dust to dust.' She stepped carefully on the stones and was now close enough to the sneaker to reach into the mud and haul it out. She waved it around triumphantly, the mud flying. The drops of mud spattered Evelyn's face and T-shirt. Evelyn pressed her fingers against her eyes.

'Don't rub your eyes,' said Gilda. 'You'll lose your contacts.'

Clemenza was swinging the sneaker above her head.

'That'll do,' I said, trying to restore order and make everything peaceful among us.

Clemenza threw the sneaker at Evelyn. 'Here it is, catch.'

Evelyn ducked. 'I don't want it.'

'I'll take it,' said Gilda. She picked the thing up by one end of its muddy lace, and as she stood there, hesitating about what to do with it, I had the idea that she would try to bury it.

Clemenza was dancing around on the stones, prancing this way and that. Evelyn was walking through the mud with a sneaker on one foot and only her sock on the other.

'Evelyn,' I said, 'would you mind taking a picture of Clemenza? It'll be a birthday picture.' I was extremely lax about taking photos and didn't even own a camera. Only belatedly I realised how few pictures I had of Clemenza.

Clemenza obligingly balanced herself on a rock. 'For my mother to keep forever, to remember me by, her darling daughter at twelve.'

Evelyn levelled her camera.

'Step back,' called Gilda, 'and hold it steady. It's very dark in here and that means the shutter will stay open longer.'

We stood back. 'I never remember to take photos of Clemenza,' I said, suddenly grief-stricken. 'I have hardly any beyond the baby pictures.'

Evelyn's polaroid started buzzing and the photograph slid out. 'I think I moved,' she said, waving the print around.

When the image became clear, Gilda examined it and pronounced, 'You moved.'

'Maybe Clemenza moved,' said Evelyn.

'That's possible,' said Gilda, looking at Clemenza weaving about on top of the stones and pebbles. 'Try again. Clemenza, stay still.'

Evelyn threw the blurred photograph into the mud and stepped on it.

'Stand still,' I called to Clemenza.

Evelyn pressed the button.

'I think you moved,' said Gilda.

'This'll do,' I said. 'It's just a record.'

Off we went to find the bridge, sometimes stepping in mud and sometimes hopping to one side of the path to avoid the messier patches.

Clemenza pointed at the yellow spots painted on the trunks of the trees.

'The yellow path,' she said, skipping along. 'We're following the yellow road after all.'

The path led us along the river bank with Gilda looking at her watch often and shaking her head. Oh Gilda, I felt like saying. Oh Gilda, Gilda.

We could hear the sound of drums, bongo drums, in the distance.

'Now who would bring bongo drums into the forest?' Gilda muttered.

'These days you have to be dead before you find a bit of peace and quiet?' She looked quickly at me. 'Sorry, that was trite.'

'It must be that picnic group,' I said, 'the ones in the red car.' What people said, their blunders and their discomfort, no longer bothered me. I could only gaze at Clemenza.

Gilda now carried Evelyn's second sneaker. Evelyn rushed ahead in her socks with Clemenza to a fallen tree which lay across the river, sloping down to the opposite bank. They stepped gingerly on the trunk, testing to see if it would hold them and stay steady.

'This is the bridge to heaven,' Clemenza called out.

'Do you think it's safe?' asked Gilda. 'They could fall in.' She raised her voice. 'Be careful.'

'Remember how we were at that age? How we would just go off for the day and balance on rocks and climb trees? My mother didn't see me from dawn till dusk. She had no idea what we got up to.'

'Be careful!' Gilda called again. 'I suppose they're okay.'

Clemenza was halfway across, sitting down and sliding herself along, her legs up in front of her, her arms resting on the tree trunk behind her, all angles, like a grasshopper. Evelyn was preparing to follow.

'If you could have known what it would be like, life, with a child and without a husband or a partner, would you have done it?' I asked Gilda.

'Done what, had a child or left my husband?'

'Either. Both.'

'I would have stayed with my husband,' Gilda said.

'Seriously? With a man who told you you were ugly and who hit you?'

Gilda nodded. 'I think so.'

'I did the best I could. I was in love, but what did I know?' I said. 'I remember I was always eager for the end of the week when it hadn't even begun, wishing my whole life away. The good thing from it all is Clemenza.' Clemenza had reached the other side of the river, heaven as she called it. 'But it's hard,' I went on. 'Now, I don't want even the day to end. I dread the dusk.'

'I probably wouldn't have had a child, either,' said Gilda, 'since having a child cuts you off from other people. But I don't really mean it, because Evelyn is Evelyn and of course she's wonderful.'

Evelyn was wobbling on the log, halfway across the river.

'Maybe she'll fall,' said Gilda.

'Evelyn'll be okay,' I said.

'I suppose if she fell she could swim her way out, drift on with the current and then get hold of a rock, unless she knocked her head on a rock and went under and drowned.'

'Evelyn'll be fine,' I said. 'Look.'

Evelyn had indeed made it to the other side and was hauled onto the far bank by Clemenza. They began to dance on the bank to the beat of the distant bongo drums. Then Clemenza, all of a sudden, sat down to catch her breath.

Gilda called to them both. 'Come on back.'

'I'm going to stay here forever,' Clemenza gasped. She sat for a few moments, then got up and went to the tree trunk. In the same insect position, she edged her way along the log, but more slowly than before. I could see she was tired and the journey along the log was now slightly uphill to the bank where we waited.

'Going back is hard,' Clemenza said over her shoulder to Evelyn, panting.

Evelyn sat at the far end of the log. 'I can't do it.'

Suddenly I was aware of voices and music behind me and saw the group of teenagers led by the young man with the red beard approaching, carrying a cassette player. Three or four barefooted children were now with them, running ahead, past us to the log bridge. They stood watching Clemenza and Evelyn inch along.

'We want a go,' they cried.

I was suddenly afraid. I got up and walked casually to the bank. 'Hush,' I said to these new children, quietly so that the others in their group would not hear and take offence. 'Let them get back first, then you can try it.'

The red-bearded man and his friends came to a halt behind Gilda and me. Surely they could see that things were a little tense, with

Clemenza concentrating in order to get back to the right side of the river and Evelyn marooned on the wrong side.

'I didn't think it was a good idea for them to cross in the first place,' said Gilda. Her displeasure, or was it simply her growing discomfort, seemed to put her in a fighting mood. More loudly she said, 'With all this forest to roam in, here are a dozen of us all standing shoulder to shoulder in one spot.'

'Mum, I can't do it,' Evelyn called. 'Come and get me.'

'You got over,' said Gilda, 'you can get back.'

'She's stuck,' cried the red-bearded man, citing the obvious.

'Listen,' said Gilda, losing her temper. 'She'd do much better if there wasn't an audience just standing around staring.' She waved her arms around. 'There's a whole forest here.'

'It's a free country,' was the man's predictable reply. 'This is a public reserve. And we're the public.'

The children with this group were leaping about, crying out, 'Hurry up, hurry up,' to Clemenza and Evelyn on the log.

Clemenza paused midway across, out over the water. Evelyn had not left the other bank. 'I can't do it,' Evelyn wailed.

The man with the red beard pushed the children from his group aside and stepped on the log. He walked carefully along the log to Clemenza, balancing delicately. He held out his hand to her, and as if in a dream Clemenza took it. She rose from her awkward position and allowed herself to be led back to the bank. The man then crossed the log again, almost flitting across. He held his hand out to Evelyn, and she too took it, rose, and was led back to safety.

'Thank you,' said Gilda, embarrassed at the man's kindness. Then after a brief pause, she said, 'Come on, we have to be getting home. Quickly.' She surveyed Evelyn in her wet and muddy socks. 'You might as well throw the socks away, too. I don't want to have to deal with them when we get back.'

Evelyn peeled off her socks and threw them in the river. The man with the red beard and the group we had at first been so frightened of moved off.

That evening, the rains came and continued for three days, clearing only this morning.

From my desk on the porch I looked over to the mountain to see if the clouds were returning, as they surely would, bringing new downpours. But in this brief respite of brilliant sunshine, all the vacationers, having been confined like us in their cottages around the lake, had taken to the outdoors. On the dock below were two deckchairs that Clemenza had dragged out from under the house, ready for us to sit together and for me to continue telling the stories. Meanwhile she was wallowing and shouting in her inner tube, exactly the way children were supposed to on a summer vacation in the country. Just beyond her, a speedboat was passing, hauling a water skier, coming closer than the one hundred feet allowed by law, and every time it passed I stood up and called out urgently, 'Watch out for the passing speedboat.' I still remembered several nasty accidents on the Hawkesbury River when I was young involving water skiers who had fallen and, having ducked under the water to replace their skis and reappeared on the surface just as a boat was passing over, were decapitated.

I even ran down onto the dock, shouting, 'Be careful!' and repeating, 'Don't go beyond that buoy.' But Clemenza, by now immune to the admonition and practical advice that she met at every turn, shrieked with pleasure as the speedboat passed and sent a wake that lifted her inner tube so that her feet no longer touched the lake bottom.

'I'm pretending I'm shipwrecked,' she called to me, 'and I'll live the rest of my life on an island in a little house, safe from all the dangers and diseases of the world.'

A boy in a canoe and a family of five in a rowboat—a mother, a father, three children, all tied properly into lifejackets—were rocked by the same wake, squealing as the swell lifted then dropped their boat.

Several sunfish were out on the lake, too; and a windsurfer; and strange but true, a man was flying in the air, attached to a red balloon, which was being towed by yet another speedboat.

I heard a buzzing sound, like a saw or an electric lawn mower, and traced it to a group of Vermonters standing on their dock on the other side of the cove pointing. I turned my head and saw they were pointing at a radio-controlled model airplane wheeling and diving above the water. Their dog plunged into the lake and swam wildly after the airplane, barking and grunting, trying to keep up with its dips and changes in direction.

On the dock to my right, a man stood fishing.

The speedboat with the skier passed again. 'Watch out for the boat,' I called.

This time Clemenza shouted back. 'It's miles away.'

I was about to shout, 'Appearances are deceptive,' but checked myself. What did it matter?

On the third day of rain, yesterday, I went to The Haunted Mansion Bookshop in Cuttingsville, a twenty-minute drive from our cottage. Clemenza, who was still fatigued from the picnic and possibly also affected by the damp, did not feel up to coming and stayed home. The bookshop was a two-storeyed white clapboard house with porches and turrets set back from the road. In every room, upstairs and down, and on every porch, books were stacked on shelves to the ceiling and spilled out of boxes and tubs on the floor.

When I walked in, manoeuvring around the tubs on the entry

porch, the proprietor looked up from his papers briefly, then back, and then he lifted his head again to look at me.

'You've come back for more?' he said.

Noting my puzzlement, he asked, 'Weren't you here this morning?'

'Last week,' I said.

This was a special sale day. For twenty dollars a customer could buy a sealed carton of books—a kind of pot luck—and this was what I did, anticipating Clemenza's delight when I brought her the unopened box and her excitement unpacking it.

I paid by cheque. The proprietor was dubious, but relented and accepted it after I was able to provide a local address and phone number.

With the rain still drumming on the roof and walls, Clemenza and I ate our supper on our knees before the fire. She had chosen to save the opening of the surprise carton of books until we had eaten, savouring the anticipation. As we ate, the electricity failed completely. To Clemenza's delight, we had to light candles, the scented candle included.

That was last night. I took Clemenza's tray and mine to the kitchen, then watched Clemenza kneel beside the cardboard carton. I offered her scissors to cut the tape sealing the box and neatly she cut the top flaps free, then took out the books one by one, holding up each one and reciting the title, waiting for my response.

'*Melmoth the Wanderer*, by Maturin,' she announced.

'A gruesome, gothic tale within a tale within a tale, concerning death and love gone awry,' I said.

'*Robinson Crusoe*, by Daniel Defoe,' said Clemenza.

'He was shipwrecked and lived on his island for decades before being brought back to civilisation,' I said.

'*Castaway's Baedeker to the South Seas*.' Clemenza handed the book to me. It was a manual prepared in 1942 for naval aviators in the Pacific during the war, who ran a greater risk than anyone in the navy of becoming a 'castaway' on one of the islands of the 'South Seas' (quotation marks theirs, not mine).

'"The greatest of all obstacles for an individual to overcome is psychological—fear of the unknown,"' I read out.

I handed Clemenza the manual. 'You can take this with you on your island.'

Clemenza turned back to the box. 'I'm not afraid,' she murmured and held up the next book. '*The Sheik*.'

'That's a real tale of adventure and romance,' I said.

'*Saturn over Water*, by JB Priestley,' Clemenza announced.

I shrugged to indicate I knew nothing of this book. She read out the jacket copy. '"A novel of entertainment in the classic tradition. It begins with enquiries about a missing husband and ends with the discovery of a fantastic world conspiracy. It starts in Cambridge and finishes in the mountains of Queensland, Australia, arriving there by way of New York, the desert coast of Peru and the volcanic country of southern Chile.'"

'The *Complete Works of Shakespeare*.' Clemenza turned immediately to *Romeo and Juliet*. 'Whoever owned this has written all over it.'

I could see that the margins and text were marked in ink as Clemenza read out some of the comments: 'The characters of Romeo and Juliet change in a short space of time. In the beginning they are youthful, immature and in the end, older, mature.'

I took the volume from her and saw it had belonged to someone called Robert A Russell, who seemed to have read every play. Beside 'All the world's a stage, and all the men and women merely players,' he had written 'absolutely' and underlined 'merely'. Another note read: 'Average Elizabethan had lust for life, carpe diem philosophy, typical renaissance attitude.'

And for *The Tempest*: 'whole action completed by dusk.'

'My guess is Mr Russell used this book when he was in college,' I said.

Clemenza reached into the box. 'I won't be going to college.'

The volume of Shakespeare I was holding slipped from my hands to the floor, falling open at *Henry IV Part I*. 'A man's play,' Mr Russell had penned, 'The women are of no importance, but Lady Percy well handled, really human.'

Jammed at the bottom of the carton was a box of seventy-eight records. It was *The Magic Flute*, too heavy and awkward for Clemenza to lift.

She took up *The Sheik* and read aloud the first page:

'"Are you coming in to watch the dancing, Lady Conway?"'

'"I most definitely am not. I thoroughly disapprove of the expedition of which this dance is the inauguration. I consider that even by contemplating such a tour alone into the desert with no chaperon or attendant of her own sex, with only native camel drivers and servants, Diana Mayo is behaving with a recklessness and impropriety that is calculated to cast a slur not only on her own reputation, but also on the prestige of her country. I blush to think of it. We English cannot be too careful of our behavior abroad. No opportunity is slight enough for our continental neighbors to cast stones, and this opportunity is very far from being slight. It is the maddest piece of unprincipled folly I have ever heard of."'

Clemenza and I both burst into laughter. When she was able to speak again, Clemenza continued: '"And drawing her wrap around her with a little shudder, Lady Conway stalked majestically across the wide verandah of the Biskra Hotel."'

Clemenza looked up. 'What exactly is a wrap?'

'In my day,' I said, glad to have the opportunity to use that expression, 'in the 1950s, ladies and girls had wraps, in case there was a sudden change in the weather. Stoles, we called them.'

I saw that Clemenza was tired after the excitement. Willingly she went to bed while I continued to browse among the new books. Suddenly I heard a knock, or rather a banging, at the door. When I opened it, the candle I carried was immediately extinguished by the wind. The rain slanted into the kitchen. At first, I could see no one, so black was the night, so deafening the rain. Then I made out a shape—I couldn't tell if it was a man or a woman—in a black waterproof poncho. As my eyes grew accustomed to the dark, I saw that the water was cascading from the figure as if it were a fountain. Although the hood was up and pulled well forward over the stranger's forehead, the rain, which was blowing horizontally off the lake, had drenched the pale face peering out at me.

The dripping figure stepped into the cottage without my having invited it, and I closed the door. The only light came from the fire. I took the poncho, folding it in on itself to contain the raindrops and placing it on the counter next to the sink. I then saw that the visitor was a woman, about my own age, extremely distressed. Then, as I continued to stare at her, a most uncanny sensation overcame me. With growing alarm I saw that this wet stranger had the same brown hair as me, the same pale skin. In fact, she looked like me in every respect. I looked away from her, finding the presence of what I feared was my double unbearable. And I remembered with a shudder that such an encounter with a double heralds death.

The woman appeared not to notice the resemblance between us or my terror. She apologised rapidly for turning up without warning, but she had an urgent request. Without exchanging any small talk about the appalling weather or revealing her identity, she told me she had found my name and the address at The Haunted Mansion Bookshop. Earlier that day she had taken several boxes of books to sell—this was the way the place acquired much of its stock—but inadvertently a diary of hers, a manuscript, was caught up with the books. She was now trying to track down everyone who had bought boxes of books to see if her manuscript was in it.

When she caught sight of our carton and the books stacked beside it, she knelt down and searched among them, scattering them across the rug. She peered into the carton, lifted out the heavy box that contained *The Magic Flute* and upended the carton, shaking it as if the manuscript might miraculously fall out, even though it was obvious the carton was completely empty.

Then she stood up and left, grabbing her poncho and throwing it on as she flew out the door. I heard her car start up and the wheels spinning in the mud.

I had said nothing the whole time. I simply remained standing, in my apprehension avoiding eye contact with her, while she rummaged around and muttered. 'The past,' I think I heard her say. 'It's gone.'

I stood in the middle of the rug for some time after she left, stunned at the eerie encounter. I began to persuade myself that there had in fact been no visitor, that I had seen an apparition. Even when I remembered that the proprietor of the bookshop had greeted me as if he had seen me that same morning, I still was not persuaded. The past, I nevertheless found myself repeating, the past is never gone. It's the future that is in danger of disappearing.

Finally, I moved and began once more to stack the books neatly, just as Clemenza had left them. When I picked up *The Magic Flute*, the box seemed too light for records. I opened it, and there, instead of a dozen seventy-eight records, was a stack of yellowed pages, partly handwritten, partly typed. *Nineteen Fifty-Six: Sydney, Australia* was the title. This clearly was the missing manuscript. Again, I felt that shiver of alarm, because Sydney was the very place I had spent my childhood.

I ran to the door, but the woman in the black poncho had disappeared.

The Fat Lady

BEV ROBERTS

We all know it's not over
until she sings—
whatever *it* is
and why *fat*
and why not the fat *man*—
but let's not be squeamish
or ideological
about our symbols.

On TV I saw them in Washington,
a whole choir of them
singing outside the White House
on election eve,
an unmistakable message
for Mr George Bush.
I didn't catch the words
but they don't matter—
let's not be too literal
about our symbols.

I thought of the great future
for fat ladies,
solo, duet or choir.
'What's that, dear?'
asks the wife of the man of power,
waking to the sound of singing
on the lawn.
Peering through blinds they see
in large and lumpish silhouette,
like malevolent shrubs
in the moonlit garden,
the singers of doom.

Cheaper than bombs,
more accessible than guns,
and above all subtle,
the fat ladies who can carry a tune
could be the end of violence
as we know it.

We'd run from them, though,
seeing them walking up the street,
shove fingers in our ears
if their mouths began to move
on the faintest hint of a song.
This is unimaginable power:
just being there,
being fat
and threatening to sing.

holidays

DOROTHY HEWETT

Our father rises gasping from the sea
our mother overarms in her bathing cap
shivering in his one-piece woollen bathers
he makes a run for it
while we with castles dressed
in fan-shaped shells
win the Temperance Competition
and sign the pledge.

Out beyond us lies the Southern Ocean
Bald Head and Dunder Rock the granite islands
history like a postcard shrilling gulls
steamers with painted funnels sliding
over the edge of the world.

Goose pimpled huddled wrapped in towels
he suffers under the Danger Board
his shadow falling black
on sand dunes whipping up for rain
the undertow dragging us out
on waterways we struggle
past cuttlefish and dumpers mother screaming
to some oblivion we cannot fathom.

Inheritance

DOROTHY HEWETT

I have travelled a long way from my origins
is there anything left of the child
with the wheaten hair who listened for owls
loved poetry and winter fires remembered
the strange moment in the dark fields
when the pet lambs grown into ewes and weathers
trotted along the fence lines bleating to be let in?

You can never go back only onwards
into the world leaving behind
all the loved things the grandfather
flying on his winged nag through the frosty paddocks
the handsome father haloed in sparks
roasting spuds in the ashes of the playroom fire.

Where do you go from there concealed in darkness
glowing with the heat in the grass the hawk in the wood
the plovers spinning of spring in front of the plough —

to the old woman watching for her bulbs to come up
the irises lining the patch the white cockatoos
in a flurry of wings a visitation of angels.

Elegy

i.m. Martin Johnston

JOHN FORBES

...into the Country of Unconcern
WH AUDEN

Yes, that's where you've gone I
guess, along with Bob & Buckmaster
& Dransfield—if you include our
elders who died before their time,
Campbell, Buckley, MacAuley, Gilbert,
Webb—it's quite a list. & now that
each drink helps turn my liver
into dreck, I want to ask you this—
are we poets supposed to connect
to some tradition of pointless
Australian death, joining those
blokes whose ships' boats off Gaba
Tepe suddenly filled with blood? Or
the vestigial bodies the Japs lined
Three Pagoda Pass with? I think of
that print you had of backblocks
shearers dancing like rough Graces
breaking down the cheque, or
the crim in a Kevin Mackie poem
singing 'Tie Me Kangaroo Down Sport'
beneath the warders' boots & fists
& I suppose there's something noble
about this—but mate I tell you, come
the next anniversary of your death
it won't be doctors' orders stopping me
from having a drink to your memory.

love poem

JOHN FORBES

warm, articulate
& watch this space
an over-bright party stares
at the new moon
suffusing an overcast Roman sky
     (slowly my defences
collapse like air bags
after a smash—the driver
was all right but his
Pajero was trashed)
the temperature goes up & down
we think we've invented
a new way of moving around the world
simply by breathing
& we have, we have.

Ode to Karl Marx

for Rob Hitchcock

JOHN FORBES

Old father of the horrible bride whose
wedding cake has finally collapsed, you

spoke the truth that doesn't set us free—
it's like a lover made of words no one's

learnt to operate. So the machine it once
connected to just accelerates & each new

rap dance video's a perfect image of this,
bodies going faster and faster but dancing

on the spot. At the moment tho' this set-up
works for me, being paid to sit & write &

smoke, thumbing through Adorno like *New Idea*
on a cold working day in Ballarat, where

adult unemployment is 22% & all your grand
schemata of intricate cause & effect

work out like this: take a muscle car &
wire its accelerator to the floor, take out

the brakes, the gears the steering wheel
& let it rip. The dumbest tattooed hoon

in Ug boots—mortal diamond hanging round
the Mall—knows what happens next. It's fun

unless you're strapped inside the car. I'm
not but the dummies we use for testing are.

Senescence

JOHANNA DYKGRAAF

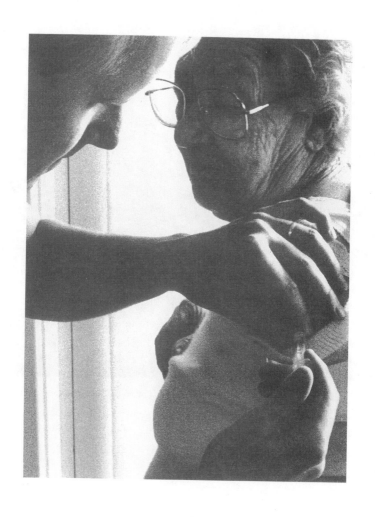

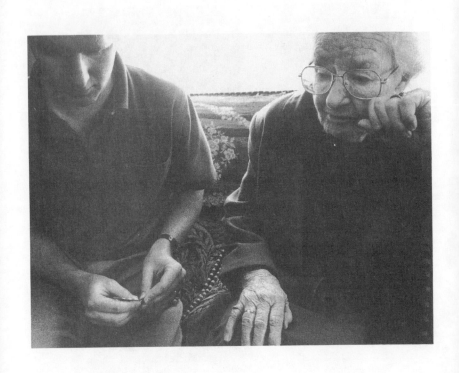

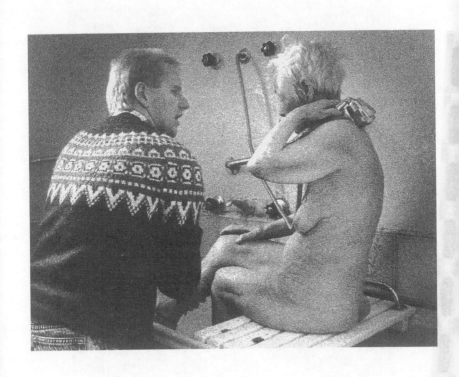

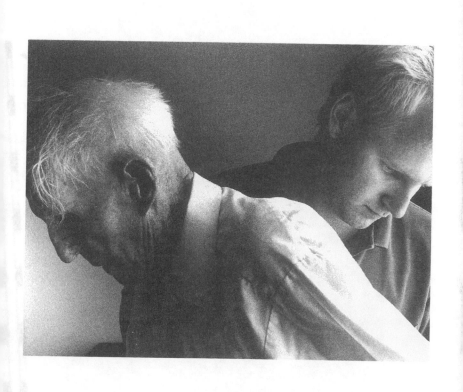

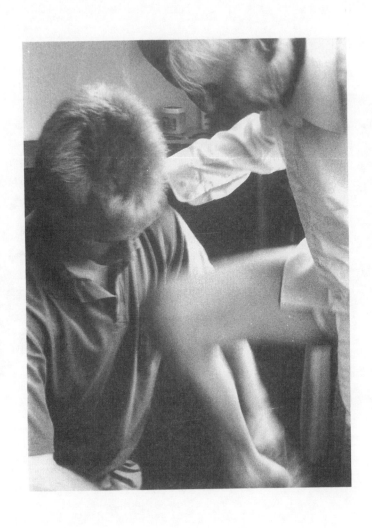

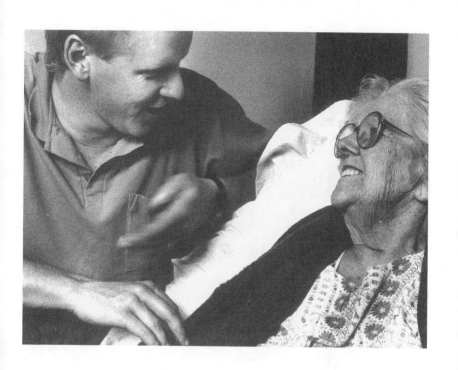

Abstract Happiness

PAMELA BROWN

I

50s values return
   the vinyl bunting fades,
      sunset's
   a bankable moment
         & a man becomes tearful
under an aerial photo
   of the city   he loved.
Indoor fingertips singed—
      stuck to a frosty tin
         of low alcohol beer.
      The wide din
of the take-off
   takes over   & you feel
   like a decoy
      a clay duck
         a tin rabbit.

            O eastern summer
time   icy-pole paper
      blows in on a southerly—
               wind-sick
      & suffering
         shocking dreams:
pinned flat
      by a bus,
   hairy-faced women
cowering
      in ancient fear
         of the chloroform
                  murderer,
   the second bombing,
      a theme park crisis,
         the carnival-tour-de-lex.

Recondite
   & difficult
      you supplicate
   via failure—

it's only a tiny part
of the plan—
refusing to be shoved
into virtue
by ambitious hooligans
waving their dividends
like paper flags.
Ultimately developing
museum-allergy   (you've
never liked the way a white-straw hat
says 'english department'
or 'film producer')
you go for a walk—
Europe & Asia
are over your head,
in fact
from here   everywhere
except Antarctica
is elsewhere,
even in your home town
you'll need a map.

II

This is the quid—
nowadays you never watch
TV
you simply record programmes
& shelve the tapes

The abstract happiness
of ignoring
soaps game shows docos
(those medical close-ups—
scopic probes
enter the body
at the groin   to trace
the way to the heart—
rendering passé a fascination
with the revelations
of the cut—
those beautiful golden
gelatinous globules
of fatty tissue)

Living on air—
  february follows february.

III

A feverish bee   alights
  on your Salem cigarette
& regards   the bubbles
    in the lemonade.
So   how can you
    concentrate on
  the New Formalists
with the case-moths   a-chomping
        through the ground covers?

Where's the pesticide?

Someone arrives with a book
  full of doozies—
(I've had a bookful of this!)

That Freddy Sauser
  & that...that ...
      Willhelm Kostrowitsky!
  no connection with
        New Formalism at all
& BOTH
  patriotic zealots!

Now   now   (bordering on
    critical)—settle down!

Get Densey Cline!
  Quick!   Spray
    that wasp!
& don't take the drooping balsam
        personally—

A volcano erupts   & you're caught
    pottering
      in the car port.

Precious

REBEKAH SANDELL

I t was very bright, this scene before her eyes: the clear sky, the arid plateau, the old house crashing down the side of the subsiding cliff in a cloud of dust.

Georgia had always found it easier to work things out with pictures and with processes than with words, and when this image had come to mind—a scene from an old movie—she had fastened on it, sharpening the focus, bringing in colour, investigating the process of disintegration in slow, elaborate detail.

She was twenty-three years old and thinking about her life.

Once things start to slide, they go down, right down, over the edge in one great sudden shift, and down, into the chasm. There might have been something to warn you. Some little crack, some plaster flaking off a wall, something seemingly trivial which you noticed and dismissed, while all the while, in the earth itself, great boulders were shifting, giving way. Then everything goes down and you see what kind of fool you have been. The kind who builds on the edge of cliffs.

Around her the night was unusually dark. New moon. No moon. No light and no lights. By starlight she could sometimes make out the shoulder of the hills on the horizon, blacker even than the sky. But it was a Tuesday night, so there had been virtually no traffic since she had turned off the main interstate highway. The road she was on led only to old towns, gold towns, dead towns crumbling away under their expansive verandahs beside the twisted peppercorns that turned lurid green in her headlights as she cannoned through, not bothering to switch down from high beam. Little townships, all closed up by 10 pm.

She was humming snippets of Spanish-sounding song. On the radio last night, on one of the obscure, unpopular stations, she had picked up a program of old Mexican and South American folk songs. There were songs in which tragedy followed tragedy, and husbands kept arriving home to find their wives in the arms of their best friends. There were knives and there was blood, and prisoners went unrepentant to the firing squad. *If I was born again, I would kill them again…I will follow their footsteps into eternity.* She had trusted Margie almost completely. And Heather. She was in the mood to sing along.

Stretched along the back seat of the car was a large canvas sausage bag, a seaman's bag she had got from a disposal store. It was stuffed full of neatly folded clothes. Small gas bottles, drills, and a selection of equipment that looked as if it might belong to a particularly brutal dentist were piled together in two plastic crates, stowed behind the front seats.

Partially hidden by the sailor's bag, and firmly tucked into the back seat, there was an old and battered fishing-tackle box. Its appearance was deliberately deceptive. The shelves of the little compartments meant for hooks and flies and sinkers were padded with cottonwool.

Little packets of precious and semi-precious stones nestled there instead. Under these shelves there was a substantial quantity of gold sheet and wire, and some silver.

Georgia had all the things she felt she needed, and she was quite prepared to admit to herself that she was running away. It wasn't as if it were the first time. Her good fortune was that she had somewhere ready to run to. She cursed herself, though, for having forgotten to ring and let Mr Sutherland know she was coming.

Jim, as her mother called him, was an old and close friend of the family—of her grandfather and father originally—generally known to the world as James Sutherland, sculptor, a dignified old pillar of Australian Art, at the base of whose pedestal laurels continued to accumulate quietly, unsought and apparently unheeded. Georgia had worked it out that when her father had died, leaving Marion, her mother, with three small daughters, Mr Sutherland must have taken it upon himself, as some sort of duty, to keep an eye on them. In any case, he had always been around.

It was Jim who had noticed Georgia's own abilities and comforted her mother with his assurances. When she had finished her training, he had offered her a section of his studio in the country, given her the keys to his house, and encouraged her to consider both her own, to use whenever she wanted to get away from the city and get on with the work. And she had done so, many times.

But in a sly way she had used them for other purposes too. When she wanted to escape there was always a perfect excuse to hand—she was going up to the studio to work. So she could keep her pain to herself. A bitter, defensive pride refused to ever let her mother or her sisters see. For them, she was always all right, impassive and unchanged.

She cursed herself again. It was not that she had forgotten to ring, she had just not bothered—or, more truthfully still, she had not been able to muster enough strength to address her host with pretense. Now she was going to come barrelling in, in the middle of the night, unheralded and at least faintly distraught, and he would be bound to notice that something was up. The old man was not deaf and no fool. She knew he must have overheard at least some of the impassioned telephone calls she had not been able to prevent herself from making when she had done this before, in the past. Georgia sighed and comforted herself with the thought that at least this time there would be no more calls.

When the sign announcing Shay Creek appeared, she put her foot down. The almost non-existent town was situated at the end of a low, undulating plateau. Just beyond it, the land dipped slightly and flattened. In Georgia's imagination, an invisible line ran through Shay Creek, a border. Once she had crossed it, she was no longer leaving

Melbourne, but approaching the studio. She kept accelerating all the way up to, and through the town, only easing off as she reached the shallow descent on the other side.

Fuck Margie. Fuck Heather. If they turned up at the pub on Friday night, they wouldn't have her for an audience. Not that she wouldn't like to corner Heather in the corridor behind the bar and bang her head against the wall. It could be done. And she had justice on her side. But she had always stayed well away from that sort of thing. She just didn't like it.

Still, she mused, they might piss themselves waiting for her to show up. And make, at least, a scene.

Temporarily consoled, she chose to turn her mind to her work.

In the tackle box she had packed a clutch of quince-yellow ambers, bright and clear, and another of blood-red garnets, some faceted, others *en cabuchon*, round and smooth like the amber. There was a cabuchon diamond, too, an antique, not quite pure, slightly cloudy. Light seemed to slip through its surface and move through its depths in a rainbow arc, just as a sliver of white light shifts through the mist of a moonstone. It was her prize, and she had pages of designs for setting it but she was loath to do so. Setting it signalled selling it, letting it go, and it was too mysterious, too important for that. It was precious. Whether she let go or not, things were always going away, but in this case she had no intention of even beginning to loosen her grip.

She had other things to work on anyway, pages of designs for the amber and the garnets and the gold. Firebirds.

The palm at the end of the mind, she began to recite to herself,
Beyond the last thought...

'Guess what?' Celia had shrieked with delight, bounding into the family room where Andrea was lounging with her friends. Celia was her younger sister, thirteen at the time, and Andrea the elder, then about seventeen. They must have all turned to look.

'Georgia's in her bedroom, reading *poetry*!'

'How do you know she's reading?' Andrea had drawled, loud enough for her voice to carry down the hall. 'I mean, how do you know she's reading and not just looking at the pictures?' A chorus of amusement. Andrea showing off to her friends.

'Because,' Celia had piped, not to be outdone, 'there aren't any. She's reading a real book. You can see her lips move.' Laughter yet again.

A gold-feathered bird
Sings in the palm, without human meaning,
Without human feeling, a foreign song.

Georgia had to slam on the brakes to stop herself shooting straight off the road and into a paddock. The road was about to take a sudden sharp left turn across a railway line. On the other side of the line there was a hard right, after the left. The car squealed and squealed again.

When she had straightened out, her lights picked up the sign beside the road. 'Hempleden', it said. 'Population 1000.' She pulled over suddenly onto the shoulder of the road and stopped. It was the worst time to want to cry. Without realising it, she had reached her destination.

'Shit,' Georgia moaned to herself, 'oh, shit.' She rested her forehead on the steering wheel, her body swaying slightly in the faint rhythm of distress. She remained like that for several minutes, taking slow, deep breaths. When she was certain there would be no tears, she sat up, sighed, ran her fingers through the closely mown field of her hair and switched on the ignition again. The car pulled back onto the road and crept into the township.

Once she had pulled up outside the old house, Georgia realised that the effort she had made to compose herself had been in vain. It wouldn't have mattered if she had arrived howling. The garage was empty and the house was in darkness. It didn't feel like a relief, though. She hadn't anticipated more solitude, more darkness.

She leant over to the glovebox, took out a flashlight, and climbed out of the car. Outside, her breath startled her by forming a long, thick plume.

She put the flashlight on the bonnet and then went back to retrieve the canvas bag and the tackle box. With the canvas bag over her shoulder, the box in one hand, and the torch and keys in the other, she let herself in a side gate and set off toward the back of the house.

The palm stands on the edge of space, she continued doggedly,
The wind moves slowly in its branches.
The bird's fire-fangled feathers dangle down.

The poem was titled *Of Mere Being*, and Celia was right, Georgia concluded. She had never been sure that she understood it. She just liked the sound of the words.

Jim Sutherland considered it one of the blessings of his life that he was entirely free of arthritis. Even so, on these cold inland mornings, he was stiff. He put his mug on the ledge beside the door and grasped the huge key hanging limply in the lock. At the sound of the click, Georgia, who was squatting on the bricks of the little paved courtyard outside, in a patch of weak morning light, leapt to her feet, spilling her own coffee as she did so.

Jim was stooping as he came through the doorway and out into the light, but it was the smallness of the old door, not age, that made him bend.

'Good morning, Georgia! I saw your car when I arrived home last night, and you weren't in the kitchen just now, so I thought you might be out here. Enjoying the sun, for what it's worth.'

'Mr Sutherland.' Georgia was smiling. 'I'm sorry I didn't ring.'

She paused. No excuses.

'I hope you don't mind.'

She looked down, partly in apology, and partly to study the flood of coffee draining over the edge of her immaculately polished riding boot. She hated mess, things spoiled.

The old man chuckled and waved his hand dismissively as he came around behind her and into the sun, straightening himself as he went.

'Glad of the company,' he wheezed, and began searching in his pockets for a packet of cigarettes. He had once told Georgia that he had been trying to give them up since World War I. It was a detail that rose in her mind whenever she saw him smoke.

'Got an exhibition coming up?'

'Aaaah.' She sounded vague. 'Yeah...But not until October. I've already got a lot done. There's just some stuff I want to do. Concentrate on.'

She paused.

'I was thinking of staying for a couple of months, if that's all right.'

She turned her face to look at him.

Georgia was pale at the best of times, with very fine white skin. But now she looked even paler, unevenly pale. Unhealthily transparent. And the skin under her eyes was blue-tinged and slightly swollen. Jim smiled gently.

'My dear, you're very welcome for as long as you want.'

He was deliberately holding her gaze.

'You know that,' he added, 'I hope.'

When she turned away he began to chat lightly about the family.

It bothered Jim that Georgia had turned up again like this. She was, in fact, as welcome as he had led her to believe. What bothered him was a sense of his own powerlessness, of being bound and gagged by discretion. He had no idea what he could say without, perhaps, seeming to poke his nose in where it was none of his business, or just giving offence.

Georgia couldn't have known it, he didn't think—he was sure Marion wouldn't have told her—but he had been, so to speak, on her side all along. It was a fault of Marion's generation, he considered, that they seemed to think they could, and ought to, fix everything. When Georgia was seventeen, Marion had insisted on sending her to a psychiatrist, searching around among her colleagues and contacts— Marion was a doctor—for someone appropriate. It was hardly necessary, he had tried to reason with her. The girl wasn't mad.

As he had explained at some length, a friend of his had married a woman who had turned out to be a lesbian. In 1920, divorce would have ruined them both. One or the other would have had to agree to be the guilty party in an adultery case, furnishing evidence for the other to present in court. Instead they had each had a girlfriend—and taken care to see that they were treated decently, too.

The four of them used to go about together, to the theatre, and on picnics, and boating. You used to see them around, Jack and his harem. Oh, for years.

What he had been trying to get across to Marion was that things—situations, people—had to be dealt with as they were. Not *fixed*, to suit yourself. But Marion had stared back at him fiercely, as if he were suddenly devoid of all sense.

'You wouldn't say that,' she had erupted, 'if it was your daughter. Making herself look like a freak. Celia is embarrassed to be seen with her!'

He had wanted to say to her, very calmly, that he too had known Georgia since she was born. But it was pointless to seem to be laying claim, competing. And for what? Closeness? Ownership? Marion was her mother.

'I expect Celia will survive,' was all he had finally chewed out. Tartly.

The sun had risen now over the roof of the house. The courtyard was flooded with its chill light, which was pouring into the studio windows. When Georgia came back out of the kitchen, their refilled mugs in her hand, Jim rose from his perch on the studio step.

'Since you're going to work here, you'll be pleased to know I've rigged up some gas heaters. They make the devil of a noise, but it's much more pleasant.' He chuckled.

'I bought them for myself in anticipation of my eighty-second birthday.'

His chuckle became a whistling laugh.

'Did you know I was interviewed for the National Arts Archive, or whatever they call themselves?'

Georgia looked up.

'Yeah? Mum didn't say anything.'

'Oh, they were up here a couple of times with all their cameras and equipment. Cords and things everywhere. They were so nice to me, so patient. Every time I coughed—I had a cold at the time—you could see them all frown.'

He sniffed and cleared his throat.

'I had the impression they were worried I was actually going to expire before they had finished.'

Georgia laughed but looked away. It was not the thought of mortality that frightened her so much as change and loss. In any case, on occasions she herself had come in to find him resting on his couch after a day's work and a couple of pre-dinner sherries, and had tiptoed over to see that he was still breathing. His profile, in repose, reminded her exactly of a photograph she had once seen of an unwrapped mummy of one of the pharaohs, remarkable for its state of preservation. The same aquiline nose and eyes bulging under the lids in the sunken sockets—packing in the case of the mummy, she supposed—and the same few wisps of white hair below the crown. Except that Mr Sutherland, still alive, was a sort of orangey-red colour, purpling at the points, and unguents had not so far smoothed his slight scaliness. He was an extraordinarily vigorous man for his age, she reflected, and very charming, but he looked every one of his years, and then some.

'So I thought, right, that's it.' Jim was continuing on with his tale. 'A revered ancient with one foot in the grave deserves some comfort.'

Still looking away, Georgia chuckled too.

'So you're a Priceless Living National Treasure?'

'Something like that, apparently.' He looked down at her. 'And I can't say I really enjoyed it.' He was shifting from side to side as he spoke, in a characteristic hula, yanking the belt of his trousers back over his skinny hips.

'Now you know what you've got to look forward to,' he added.

Georgia snorted.

'Hardly! The Benvenuto Cellini de notre jour!'

'Well, you're going about it the right way.'

The young woman was laughing out loud, wryly and softly, but laughing all the same. It suddenly struck Jim that his moment was to hand.

'When I was a young man—which you probably can't imagine, but I was—I used to get myself worked up about things, you know.'

Jim noticed his voice taking on a somewhat British tone. It tended to happen in thorny situations, the fruit of his early training. It was a dead give-away, but there was nothing he could do except go on. He turned to look Georgia in the face.

'Used to get myself into a terrible mess. Well, it felt like it. I used to think the world was caving in. You do something, say something...you can't take some things back. Or she does,' he added quickly, seeing Georgia's face begin to sour. He managed to hold her gaze.

'There's nothing you can do sometimes. To fix things. You just have to accept it. But I always used to get back to my work. It's something of your own. Hang on to it.'

He dropped his gaze and began fishing in his pocket for his keys.

Georgia had been staring at him flatly throughout this speech. Her formlessly dark blue eyes, like baby eyes, were ideal for the purpose. Perhaps he had said too much. Or looked it. He glanced at her face again as he raised his eyes, turning toward the studio door. He was relieved to see a weak smile.

'I suppose you're right,' she agreed, her voice suddenly hoarse. 'Yeah.'

He could hear her swallowing hard.

Jim opened the studio door and gestured her in.

Georgia began by dusting down, then wiping, her workbench. She turned out and wiped all her drawers and dusted the few tools she always left there. Then she went out to the car and began bringing things in, the crates from behind the seats first.

'I'll have to go back to Melbourne and pick up a few more things eventually,' she remarked. 'I wasn't sure if it was all right to stay.'

But Mr Sutherland hadn't heard. He was busy tidying and cleaning the rest of the studio, as if they were going to start work together.

Georgia wriggled and sighed. She was starting to relax, and as the tension went out of her she felt tired and aching, battered almost, and softening at the edges. She kept finding herself close to tears, though not, for a change, tears of rage. Just tears. Of some sort.

When she was finished here she might go for a walk around the town, then have some lunch, and lie down and sleep in the afternoon. Afternoon naps were not the sort of thing Georgia normally allowed herself, but today she found herself feeling kind.

She studied her workbench with satisfaction, then turned her attention to what she considered her section of the floor.

Mr Sutherland had charge of a broom, and was reaching under a bench with it. Hunched like that he looked very stiff and old. Studying him, after having been removed for a short while from total absorption in her own affairs, Georgia suddenly realised where he must have been last night.

For some years he had been carrying on an affair with Magda, a plump and lively widow, originally from the city, who lived in the area and owned and ran a small business in the town. Everyone who knew him—or rather, her—knew this, but since it was a reality that Jim never even publicly hinted at, it was never alluded to in his presence. As a matter of honour, Georgia presumed, he was taking care not to compromise Magda's good name.

Georgia had overheard Magda talking in the kitchen with a friend at one of the boozy local parties she had very occasionally attended. When Georgia had realised what the conversation was about, she had paused in the hall to listen.

'But aren't you afraid...?' the friend had enquired.

'What? We take the usual...' Magda had retorted. She was inclined to be sharpish.

'OOOh!' Magda had burst in on herself. 'OOOh! I see what *you* mean!' They had both begun hooting with laughter. 'No, no, no!' Magda had gone on. 'Not at all. He's such an old-fashioned gentleman. If he was going to have a heart attack, he'd excuse himself and go and die in the hall.'

Georgia had tiptoed away.

Staring at the floor she began to snort in a combination of amusement, horror and dismay. Jim heard her this time and looked up.

'Something funny?' He sounded hopeful.

'No,' she answered vaguely, dryly. 'Just something I remembered.' He went back to sweeping the floor.

Georgia could not help but think of Magda, and what must be her particular knowledge: how he would feel and taste. But since her mind seemed only to be able to skate unsteadily around the idea of the older woman and her disturbing awarenesses, Georgia decided to turn her attention back to the task at hand. She looked at her floor again, and at the old man's bent back.

'You haven't got another broom, have you?'

It was the obvious way to go on.

Wantoks

MARY-LOUISE O'CALLAGHAN

Perhaps that was the problem. After ten years 'on the road', I was beginning to catch planes like buses. But it was hard to convince even myself that appearing at the departure gate of Port Moresby's Jackson Airport with ticket, passport, but no PNG cash for the 10-kina departure tax, was the act of a seasoned traveller.

Early Sunday morning and already Jackson Airport was the familiar steamy morass of bodies and fumes. Too hot and too miserable to stand still, with a complete absence of grace, I relinquished my place in the immigration queue. After three weeks on Bougainville, I was ready to go home. I had half an hour before the flight to beg, borrow or steal that 10 kina, and looking around, I could discern neither opportunity nor inspiration rushing my way.

Then, a bobbing head of black curly hair, ducking and diving through the crowd of monotone black curly heads, suddenly turned into Tiki. Now here was a man who could beg, borrow or steal standing on his head. And why would he do it for me? Because he was my wantok. Within minutes Tiki had everything under control. He was cashless, as I expected, at 7 am on a Sunday morning, but also as I expected, this was no deterrent.

'Wait here, I'll get it,' he said, and he headed for a door marked 'Restricted. Authorised Personnel Only'. Judging from the uniforms going in and out it appeared to be the pilots' staff room and offices.

Smiling now, and confident, I watched for Tiki's re-emergence. Five minutes fled. No sign. Was my wantok going to let me down? I wondered whether my judgment had been wrong, whether I had embarrassed him into disappearing, with an impossible request. There was now twenty minutes before the flight.

'M–L!' And a triumphant finger tapped me on the shoulder. Tiki, grinning, thrust a 10-kina note straight at me. And I grinned back. No, of course my wantok would never let me down. 'I got it from one of the pilots. He's a wantok of my wife's brother-in-law...'

We shook hands, both very pleased with our lightning transaction. Neither of us spoke about repayment. I owed him some. He owed me some. That's how it is with wantoks.

I ran for the plane.

Rough but effective, flexible but reciprocal, the wantok system in Papua New Guinea's modern cash economy is a curious mix of pragmatism and moral obligation. As elsewhere in the South Pacific, this informal but peculiarly effective safety net, known affectionately, although sometimes disparagingly, as the 'wantok system', pre-empts many of the social problems which are faced by most other developing (and even developed) nations. The term refers to the social obligation one has to look after one's relatives or wantoks. Pronounced 'won-tock', the term is pidgin for 'one-talk', and in Papua New Guinea, where more than 700 separate languages still exist, the term is used to denote people who share the same language group, but more specifically, those who have some blood or marriage ties, no matter how distant. A kind of compulsory, customary tickle-across effect. Those who have the means look after those who have the needs.

It is also a perfect metaphor for Australia's relationship with Papua New Guinea.

Prior to independence we were the Big Brother—unashamedly so. Although the 'Fuzzy Wuzzy Angels' who led our wounded diggers along the Kokoda Trail, and the Coastwatchers and the native scouts of World War Two, are certainly not the gesture of some naïve junior sibling, they are probably some of the earliest recorded incidences of wantokly behaviour from the Papua New Guinea side towards Australia. Ever since Papua New Guinea's ascension to statehood in 1975 we've all been searching for a better metaphor to describe the close and binding relationship we still share with Papua New Guinea. 'Father-to-a-rapidly-maturing-son' was tried a few years ago. Although the creation of the then Papua New Guinea Prime Minister, Mr Rabbie Namaliu, its paternalistic overtones soon saw it discarded. (Funny that geo-realpolitik never seems to draw on matriarchal images. Perhaps because, even at their best, such relationships rarely get close to being a nurturing process.)

'Partners' has been a more recent favourite but, as the officials and politicians in both countries currently dealing with the hands-on mechanics of the relationship know, this is more reflective of an ideal than any reality.

No, in the world scheme of things, what Australia and Papua New Guinea really are are wantoks. And to understand the massive aid programme which so dominates Australia's bilateral relations with its former colony, we need look no further than the wantok system. Australia and Papua New Guinea share a common history and heritage; more significantly, we share a common future and, not the least, we share mutual strategic interests. Australia's annual aid of more than $300 million to Papua New Guinea is an act born both out of the angst and obligations of our colonial past, and the rather more straightforward fear of having a complete basket case on our back doorstep sometime in the future.

To an outsider, brought up in the modern Western tradition that the individual's freedom is paramount, the wantok system can seem an intolerable one-way drain of a wage-earner's hard-earned cash; nearly twenty years after independence Australia has cumulatively provided close to $6 billion in direct budgetary support to successive Papua New Guinea governments. The large-scale untied aid was designed to keep Australia's involvement in Papua New Guinea's internal affairs to a minimum.

In reality, the wantok system is an adaptation of the traditional, local and regular redistribution of wealth which took place in the days when communities held their wealth in the form of perishable goods and edible animals. The flow of benefits is by no means one way. Although a considerable burden on some individuals, especially wage-earners in Papua New Guinea's urban centres who can find themselves supporting ten or even twenty close and not-so-close wantoks—all of whom will happily doss down on a small living-room floor at night— the wantok system is the sole reason 'street people' are still unheard of in Papua New Guinea, and beggars are only rarely sighted on the streets of Port Moresby where the per capita income is just about 4 per cent of that of the United States. Ultimately, the modern wantok system is one based on merit and mutuality (despite all the talk of the Big Man and traditions of hierarchy in Melanesia). The assistance requested, and any eventually given, is essentially determined by the capacity of the individual to provide the cash or the skills required. So a young wantok fresh from the village whose school fees are paid by an elder brother, cousin-sister, or even uncle, will often return the investment with care and consideration for that person and their family, but later, when he or she has made good.

Wantoks can be called on to keep intruders at bay—a geographic buffer to Indonesia, Papua New Guinea's strategic importance to Australia has been acknowledged and defended in the past, and is now most directly reciprocated through Australia's Defence Co-operation Programme with Papua New Guinea. Wantoks can be counted on to change your tyre when it's flat, and they provide decent food when you are sick. They will help you to the market when you have goods to sell. And when the customers are scant and the sun is going down, they'll buy your woven basket or the last of your fish—Australian business now has more than $1.6 billion invested in Papua New Guinea which, in return, each year provides a market worth $1 billion for our exported goods and services.

Because the non-wage earners within the wantok system will often try to pay back in kind—through services such as child minding or other labour—the wantok system absorbs almost the entire burden of providing social welfare services that would otherwise fall to the state, or, in the case of a developing nation such as Papua New Guinea, just not happen at all. Not only that, but the services provided out of moral obligation frequently also come with true affection and concern. There is a human face. For all their love of the salacious, Papua New Guinea's newspapers never carry a story of an elderly Papua New Guinean's body being found days or weeks after death. Everyone has wantoks in Papua New Guinea; no one dies alone.

Unlike the traditional forms of power, the wantok system is not gender based. If your aunty, sister or even your niece can help you, then chances are they will. Indeed, when it comes to the crunch for school fees or cash for a doctor's visit, the independent working women in many Papua New Guinea families are a far more reliable bet. As most are not tempted to drink away their weekly wage, they usually have a little salted away for emergencies. A lot of these women work to support their wantoks, but while they are at work their wantoks are watching the children, cleaning the house, gardening and cooking.

Frequently it is not even the individual you have helped, but someone else enmeshed in your own network of wantoks that will have the skill or commodity you need when your turn comes around and you look to your wantoks for help.

Australia's constructive and essentially positive relationship with Papua New Guinea since independence is an important benchmark in our relations with the South Pacific island states. It has done much to maintain and enhance our standing as a pillar in the regional establishment. Now, as we push forward, north to new markets and new kinds of relations in Asia, a mature and harmonious relationship with our former colony is vital to our credibility. Literally straddling the South Pacific's border with Asia, Papua New Guinea, as it too 'looks north', is uniquely placed to help us establish our credentials as a potentially genuine partner of the sometimes prickly Asian states.

Of course some wantoks are more sensitive than others. While some will stay for weeks on end and barely contribute anything more to the household than an extra mouth to feed, others go home, gather up their own form of wealth—food—and ship it down to you. Finding six freshly caught and cooked crayfish on the back doorstep is one of the best things about having wantoks. At its best, the wantok system is not about dependency but reciprocity. And Australia is only just coming to terms with the reciprocal nature of its relationship with Papua New Guinea. The most detailed acknowledgment that there are mutual benefits as well as responsibilities in the relationship is to be found in the Joint Declaration of Principles signed by the Prime Ministers of the two countries in 1987. This sets out mutual commitments on trade, security and consultation between the two states. A little less than two years ago, a new Development Co-operation (aid) treaty was signed. This provides for a staggered but rapid reduction in direct budget support to a point where, in the year 2000, it will be replaced altogether with aid which is tied to specific projects and sectors.

Although it's been negotiated with the Papua New Guinea government—it's been agreed to by them, and signed by them as well—this ultimate shift to tied aid has for the most part of the past year been strenuously fought against by the Papua New Guinea cabinet who see a guaranteed and ready source of revenue for the ever-growing and already competing demands on expenditure slipping away. Papua New Guinea's Deputy Prime Minister, Sir Julius Chan, who as Finance Minister signed the treaty, later claimed that the switch to more tied or targetted aid could distort Papua New Guinea's own priorities and called for the whole agreement to be cancelled. Australia has essentially responded by stressing its desire for Papua New Guinea to set its own priorities under the new arrangements. In February 1994, Papua New Guinea's current Prime Minister, Paias Wingti, used a trip to Australia to meet Canberra halfway. He set priorities for targetted aid; he named education, infrastructure and Bougainville, where a battle for secession has been waged since 1988. Assisted under Australia's Defence Co-operation Programme with training, funds and equipment, Papua New Guinea Defence Force troops have been engaged against the secessionists since 1989. Allegations of human rights abuses abound and there has been mounting domestic pressure in Australia over the accountability, effectiveness and even morality of Australia's aid programme, especially this Defence Co-operation. Although not initially so, the move to tied aid is now directly linked to this dilemma.

To come to the assistance of a wantok is not simply a social obligation, it is a moral one, and to accede to or refuse any request ultimately involves a moral judgment. Plenty of Papua New Guineans will talk disparagingly about their wantoks to anyone who isn't one of them and the simple reality is that you don't always 'like' your wantoks or find the wantok system an easy burden. You don't always agree with what a wantok is doing and you don't automatically say yes to every request. Sometimes you don't say anything at all. You don't have to. That's how it is with wantoks.

Mother with Broom

From some archival footage found in the year 2044 AD

JS HARRY

On bare (of tree or house)
bleached winter-white grass,
in some post-
Chernobyl-like landscape,
a young mad woman
with a post-natal belly
dances nude
in great slow circles
to an audience of one: a dead child:
whom she is carefully avoiding
touching with her eyes.
She is hopelessly miming
fuck with a broom,
scraping its wood
hard
up and down
in her crotch. The child, who is not
the one the woman
has recently lost
from her belly,
is trailing her limbs pliant and lax
towards the earth
she will soon be a part of, over the edges of
the cart on which
unseen ones
have borne her to here. Wisps of fine
childlike hair
curl
around her face in a coronal. She has married death.
In her play clothes.
She is maybe six.
The mother
with a sweet
distant childlike smile
of a mind in a private place
continues her slow

bland yet
becoming more urgent
fuck with the broom. Does she
relive
the dumb
moment of this child's
death's
conception? Or foretell the next?

Fifty years ago,
an invisible technical crew
set their equipment running
(hoping, perhaps, by chance,
to catch some tell-tale
fragment of the unknown
human's
gutteral or visceral utterance?
Catching, instead, themselves),
the tips
of their boots and some legs
left unedited—in the left-hand corner
—for the 'truth value', as are
their voices—
'Shoot her!' the cameramen scream.
She is authentic human
reaction to disaster.
They have
not come for her
but they
are happy to have found her.

Outside the time in which
she was filmed with the broom
yet temporal as the film
upon which she is caught
and with which
she is contemporaneous
the mother continues
implacably trying to fuck.

Excavation

Pella, Jordan
LUKE DAVIES

A la fin tu es las de ce monde ancien...
<small>APOLLINAIRE, 'ZONE'</small>

*And all the world is biscuit-shaped
it's up to me to feed my face...*
<small>XTC, 'SENSES WORKING OVERTIME'</small>

From Jordan I am drawn
down the funnel of the Rift,
backwards through prehistory
to a hot rush of galaxies.

I feel a beginning tremor
at the destruction horizon
of Pella. I wind up fearing
the Heat Death of the Universe,

jetlagged at this confluence
of continents, believing
and beliefs. High on
Jabal Sartaba fossils throw

themselves at my feet
saying, 'Trilobite. Arthropod.'
My head pounds in response
to the earth's tectonic squeeze.

Storms circle the valley,
trapped for days. Then suddenly
they clear, and on Tel Husn,
watching the sun skirt the sky

as the earth curves away,
the wind screams through
my head. At eye level
hundreds of birds

ride on turbulent currents
of light through the cliffs.
On Tel Husn men as old
as time cart dirt

around a closed sphere.
'In the end you are tired
of that world of antiquity'—
because of home, the beach.

Because the beach is there.
Because the beach is always
and forever only ever
of itself; and because

it's always 6.00 pm, long
daylight saving days,
at the end of a hot one,
hours of light to go.

and through the gnats and dust,
in tachyonic vertigo, all
is superluminal, hyperlight,
each atom a mind waiting

to recognise itself, all
the world a wave function
waiting to be popped.
Above my head a swoosh

of wind brings consciousness
of waterfalls: I look up
to a flock of birds
effortless on jetstreams

of pure momentum
over my right shoulder,
swooping to the river
far below. Gliding,

and all the world aglow.
'In the end you are tired
of that world of antiquity.'

At sunset the sun
leaves a pulse and a print
on my eye, trembling
utterly liquid
on the black rim of earth.

The sun itself always
a print of what it was
seven immense minutes ago
across a cold arc

through space. Bearings
Bearings. I think of Bondi
in two directions
over two horizons

War Museum

YANG LIAN

Forever   fire is fire   a rose is a rose
Death only embarrasses your body
The carved glass on stone faces   like an eyeball
Slowly emerges   explodes
Suddenly collapses
Nobody can remedy the pain of detonation afterwards

The half cut-off tower stands upside down
Records turn moonlight every night   into earpiercing
The sound of a bell waves its hands impatiently to drive the
     drunkard away
Blood   like grass can be numb as well
Let deaf mutes sit on the ground soaking up the cheap perfume

Broken walls run madly outside candlelight

When stone heads fall down and break   the scenery is also upset
Baby   from an exploded stomach   cries loud like spring
Pipe organs have inherited a smoky throat
Heaven has never yet had a mother

The muscle of this face is always twisted
Doves don't look like white bullet shells
like dice thrown one by one into a golden wheel
Darknight is the pocket you empty out every day

You walk down one step each time you admit loss

Being locked in another cement basement
Exhibiting a piece of art that makes the self disappear
There children use their innocent pupils   keep shooting
The destruction of the city handed over to another pair of small
     hands
Just a piece of toy   let you play again
Playing in the deep body where fire and rose shift
fire and rose forget each other
The tower is too high   you can only die alone

TRANSLATED BY HEATHER S J STELIGA WITH SHI-ZHENG CHEN

Game of Lies

YANG LIAN

When we lie the tiger's stripe cleaves the dark night
When the road is betrayed by light
lies replace pedestrians

We are walking   but an ant breaking into forbidden dreams
has to understand   finger
Each time the moon falls down   the fatal weight
and tiny foolish throats cry

No   nobody ever lies to himself
Only words play with themselves
Play sleep   we dream of the ocean
Play ocean   we float to another island
Landing there   we are hungry
So we raise or kill parrots and monkeys
Again   become violent stones

But we don't say   When we don't speak
two hands become crocodiles biting each other's tails in dead water

We thought the words we lied to ourselves   were just
really   the end of time in every line of poetry
were keeping a face in a long broken mirror
A long earlobe
is hanging on a boy's rolling iron hoop

The eternal sun has always rolled into the sharp hill of a dark night

When words fall down   the mute are born
The crazy silence in the mute's heart
is the silence in the tiger's heart when it pounces on a lamb
A body being flayed   cannot even make a paper sound
We are always mute
Therefore lies play us like toys

TRANSLATED BY HEATHER S J STELIGA WITH SHI-ZHENG CHEN

fiction: a sentence

JOANNE BURNS

probably the best thing
about the approximately
chubby
pale and slightly
balding
thirtysomethingish merchant
banker who's wandered
out of the water looking
like a baby in a nappy
ad to slip on
a t-shirt listing
the names of the best
mexican beaches in
a paragraph
(does he own one) is that
he's phoneless on the
sand and about to
read something
by conrad
that's joseph not
black

people like that

JOANNE BURNS

people like that: who pause in the middle of the road
to check out the facades of investment properties up for auction
at the widest angle possible without getting hit
by a car, or falling backwards into a gutter: dressed
in clothes so stiff they look like they've never been
worn before there's such a big gap between the heart
and the lapel: people like that holding snazzy
prospecti like fig leaves in front of themselves

people like that
who try to buy up all the buildings
overlooking their latest mansion, they don't
like the company of strangers, and demand
bus stops be removed from opposite their front
gates the drivers belong to unions and
might stir up their chauffeurs

people like that who wear
designer facemasks to avoid sharing
germs
in public who demand the installation
of strictly new padded
toilet seats when they arrive at
their hotel suites

people like that: who finance private sanatoriums
and hospices where celebrity bankrupts feeling
poorly can go into
remission

MIGRANTS LOVE CONCRETE.

CONTRIBUTORS

Glenda Adams is an award-winning writer whose credits include the Miles Franklin Award, the Age Fiction Award and the National Book Council's Banjo Award for Fiction. Her most recently published book is the novel *Longleg*. This extract is the first chapter of her forthcoming novel, *The Tempest of Clemenza*.

Ian Anderson was born in Tasmania in 1965. He has lived in Victoria for the past twenty odd years. He graduated in medicine from the University of Melbourne in 1989. He is now the Medical Director of the Victorian Aboriginal Health Service. A writer in the areas of health and social sciences, amongst others, he is also currently pursuing post-graduate studies in sociology and anthropology at Latrobe University. In 1993 he was one of the ABC's Boyer Lecturers.

David Band was born in Glasgow in 1959. His work has appeared in a wide variety of magazines throughout the world, as well as on record sleeves and book jackets. His paintings are exhibited at Australian Galleries, Melbourne, at Rex Irwin, Sydney, and at Rebecca Hossack, London. His latest exhibition, 'Stories of Me', was based on the work of Paul Kelly.

Anamaria Beligan is a film maker, writer and linguist. Born and educated in Bucharest, she graduated from the Film Academy there in 1981. One year later, she fled Ceacescu's regime and settled in Australia in 1983, after a year's stint in a German refugee camp. *A Few More Minutes with Monica Vitti* is one of a number of short fictions from a collection of the same name which she is currently completing. She is also working on a novel.

Pamela Brown lives in Sydney. Since 1971 she has published eleven books of poetry and prose, including two volumes of selected poems. Her most recent collection, *This World/This Place*, was published in March 1994.

joanne burns is a Sydney writer. Her most recent book is *on a clear day*, published in 1992.

Brian Castro was born in Hong Kong in 1950 and was transported to boarding school in Australia in 1961. He is the author of five novels, including *Birds ' of Passage* (which was the joint-winner of the Australian/Vogels Award for 1982), *Pomeroy*, *Double-Wolf* (which was awarded both the Victorian Premier's Vance Palmer Award for Fiction in 1992 and the Victorian Premier's Award for Innovative Writing) and *After China* (which was awarded the Victorian Premier's Vance Palmer Award for Fiction in 1993). His latest novel, *Drift*, has recently been published. This monologue was commissioned by the Sydney Festival and Carnivalé and was performed in January this year.

Claire Corbett was born in Vancouver in 1964 and moved to Australia in 1973. She has worked as an assistant editor on a number of feature films and has also worked as a freelance writer. She is currently working on her novel, *Between the Flags*.

John Dale was born in Sydney and has worked in a wide variety of jobs. His novel, *Dark Angel*, will be published in early 1995.

Luke Davies was born in Sydney in 1962. He has worked as a cellarman, roofer, bartender, journalist and teacher. His first volume of poetry, *Four Plots for Magnets*, was published in 1982. A new collection of poems, *Absolute Event Horizon*, was recently published.

Johanna Dykgraaf is a Dutch-Australian who was born in Sydney and grew up in Canberra. She has been photographing professionally since 1987 and has freelanced in Australia and overseas since 1992. *Senescence* is from a series of photographs that looks at the work of the community nurse in our society.

Ruby Langford Ginibi was born at the Box Ridge Mission on the north coast of New South Wales, in Coraki, in 1934. At the age of fifteen she moved to Sydney where she qualified as a clothing machinist. She has a family of nine children whom she raised mostly by herself. She worked for years around Coonabarabran at fencing, burning off, tree lopping and ringbarking and pegging kangaroo skins and, at other times, she lived in the Koori areas of Sydney where she worked in clothing factories. She is the grandmother of twenty children. Ruby's autobiography, *Don't Take Your Love to Town*, which was first published in 1988, has been reprinted many times. Her book of stories, *Real Deadly*, was published in 1992, and a biography of her people, *My Bundjalung People*, will soon be available. She is currently working on a book based on the life of her son, Nobby.

Geoff Goodfellow often writes about work and workers. His highly successful collection of poems, *No Ticket, No Start: Poetry from the building sites,* was published in 1990 and has since been reprinted many times. He is currently working with the Metalworkers' Union, recording the lives of workers and performing readings on the factory floor.

John Forbes's latest publication was *New & Selected Poems*, published in 1992. His work is discussed in Meaghan Morris's *Economics & Ecstacy*.

Tony Haritos was born in Darwin in 1956, where he lives with his partner and their daughter. He was educated there as well as in Adelaide and Perth. He also lived in Melbourne for some time but he reckoned it was too cold. He works as a journalist with the Northern Land Council. 'Rope' is a series of extracts from his novel in progress.

JS Harry lives in Sydney. Her latest book was *A Dandelion for Van Gogh*. Her fourth poetry collection, *The Life on Water and the Life Beneath*, will be published soon.

Dorothy Hewett lives in the Blue Mountains. Her latest publications are a novel, *The Toucher* and *Peninsula*, a collection of poetry.

Nicholas Jose is an Australian writer who grew up in Broken Hill, Traralgon, Perth and Adelaide. A Mandarin speaker, he was Cultural Counsellor at the Australian Embassy in Beijing from 1987 to 1990. He has published three novels and two collections of short stories. His recent work includes his translation (with Sue Trevaskes) of Sang Ye's travel book, *The Finish Line*. Nicholas Jose's new novel, *The Rose Crossing*, will be published this year.

Amanda Lohrey is the author of the critically acclaimed novels, *The Morality of Gentlemen* and *The Reading Group*. She has been lecturing in creative writing at the University of Technology, Sydney, and is completing her next novel, *Camille's Bread*. She is a member of The Nation Group.

Angela Lynkushka was born in 1947. In 1985 she established the Young Women's Photographic Collective in Melbourne. She began working at her own photography in 1976, after the birth of her second child. Her life in working-class Brunswick generated much of this material. Her photography has been exhibited in a number of venues, including the Australian Centre for Contemporary Art in Melbourne and the Australian National Gallery in Canberra. Her latest collection, a series of studies of Australian choreographers, is titled 'Dance Genius' and was exhibited at Southgate as part of the Melbourne International Festival and also in the Queen Victoria Building as part of the Sydney Festival.

Peter Lyssiotis lives in Melbourne. His photographs and photomontages have been exhibited in a wide variety of venues and have appeared on book covers and in publications all over the world. His own publications include *Journey of a Wise Electron*, *Three Cheers for Civilisation*, *The Harbour*

Breathes (with Anna Couani), *Absence* (with Antigone Kefala) and most recently, *C.D.s and Other Things* (with Gyorgy Scrinis). He is also publisher of the small press, Masterthief Enterprises. His photo-essay, '...From the Secret Life of Statues', will be featured in the next issue of *RePublica*.

Philip Mead was born in Brisbane in 1953. His most recent collection of poetry was *This River is in the South*, published by UQP. In 1991 he coedited, with John Tranter, the *Penguin Book of Modern Australian Poetry*. He is currently Lockie Lecturer in Australian Writing at the University of Melbourne.

Jacqueline Mitelman was born in Inverness, Scotland. She has been freelancing as a photographer since 1977. Her publications include *Faces of Australia*, a compilation of over 120 portraits, which was published in 1988. Her folio and exhibition history are extremely varied, featuring studies of young people, writers, performers, landscapes, streetscapes, refuges and sheltered workshops. She has recently been creating photographic studies of various musicians and singers, in performance and 'at home', for Mushroom Records.

Mudrooroo was born in Narrogin, Western Australia, in 1938. He is a prolific writer of poetry, prose and criticism. *Wildcat Falling*, his first novel, published in 1965, is still in print. Other works such as *Master of the Ghost Dreaming*, *Wildcat Screaming* and his most recent novel, *The Kwinkan*, are also extremely popular. Mudrooroo has been very active in Aboriginal cultural affairs—he has been a member of the Aboriginal Arts Unit of the Australia Council, he cofounded (with Jack Davis) the Aboriginal Writers, Oral Literature and Dramatists' Association, and he has been responsible for piloting Aboriginal literature courses at Murdoch University, the University of Queensland, the University of the Northern Territory and Bond University. He is, at present, working on a novel set in India where he lived for seven years, three of them as a Buddhist monk. This song was first presented last year at the Warana Writers' Festival in Brisbane.

Dula Ngurruwutthun is an elder of the Munyuku clan, Bulang 'skin' group, and is a widely acknowledged ceremonial leader, or dalkarramirri, of the Yirritja moiety. His Homeland Centre is at Rurrangala, near Blue Mud Bay in north-east Arnhem Land. Dula still travels a lot in east Arnhem Land, mainly in his role as dalkarramirri. He tells a story here about his early life as he travelled around the region (the Japanese and Europeans were speared at what is now also known as Caledon Bay) in the 1930s. Later he worked for 'Baba Sheppy' (or the Rev Mr Shepherdson, as he was also known) on Elcho Island, spearing crocodiles to be sold, and clearing airstrips.

Mary-Louise O'Callaghan finds herself blessed with two lots of wantoks: five living generations of Irish Catholics in Australia and an ever-expanding clan on the islands of Mungiki and Mungava in the Solomon Islands. South Pacific correspondent for *The Sydney Morning Herald* and *The Age* for the past seven years, the best thing she has produced is her daughter, Erin Mary King Tehakatahinga O'Callaghan Tuhanuku.

Archie Roach ranks among Australia's greatest contemporary music artists. His first recording, *Charcoal Lane*, was acclaimed by critics and audiences all over the world. The album won Aria Awards for Best Debut Album and Best Indigenous Album, the Mo Award for Best Folk Artist and a Human Rights Award for the song, 'Took the Children Away'. His release in 1993, *Jamu Dreaming*, has been receiving an equal amount of acclaim. *You Have the Power*, a collection of Archie's lyrics, was published recently.

Bev Roberts is a Victorian poet whose work has appeared in many literary magazines and anthologies. Her most recent book is *The Exorcism Trip*, published in 1991.

Edward W Said is Parr Professor of English at Columbia University in New York. He is a prolific writer on a wide range of topics including literature, music, cultural criticism and Palestinian issues. He has authored such titles as *Orientalism*, *The Question of Palestine*, *After the Last Sky: Palestinian Lives and Musical Elaborations* and, most recently, the landmark *Culture & Imperialism*.

Rebekah Sandell lives and works in Melbourne. This story is from her forthcoming collection of linked stories, *Little Butterfly*.

Adam Shoemaker teaches in Australian Studies at the Queensland University of Technology in Brisbane. He is one of the editors of *Paperbark*, the first national anthology of Black Australian writing. His most recent book, published last year, is *Mudrooroo*, the first critical study of the leading Aboriginal writer.

Glenda Sluga lectures in modern European history. Her parents emigrated from Yugoslavia to Australia in 1956. She has published articles on ethnicity, gender and nationalism in Triestine historiography over the past two years, writing mainly on the war and ethnic relations in the former Yugoslavia. She is also currently reviewing for *The Sydney Morning Herald* and *The Independent*.

Arthur Spyrou is a student at the University of Sydney. His translations of Yannis Ritsos' *Monochords* will be published soon.

Deb Westbury lives on the South Coast of New South Wales, near Wollongong. Her first collection of poems, *Mouth to Mouth*, was published in 1990. *Our Houses are Full of Smoke*, her second collection, was published this year. She is currently a writer-in-community based in Western Sydney.

Banumbir Wongar was born Streten Bozic in modern-day Serbia and came to Australia in 1960. He has spent an extensive period of time living in the Northern Territory, where he came to use his present name. His works, including novels, short stories, poetry and non-fiction, have always told of the contact between Aboriginal and European Australians and, as a writer, Wongar is as influenced by European and Aboriginal oral traditions as he is by European literary ones. He is perhaps best known for his 'nuclear trilogy' of novels, *Walg*, *Karan* and *Gabo Djara*, which have been translated into a number of languages. His most recent book was *Last Pack of Dingoes*. Wongar's novel, *Raki*, from which this extract has been taken, will be published later this year.

Yang Lian was born in Switzerland in 1955. When he came to Australia in 1988 at the invitation of Carnivalé Writers Week in Sydney, he was well known in the People's Republic of China as a poet and a dissident. He now lives in New Zealand and elsewhere in the world at large. Lian's recent collections of poetry, *Masks and Crocodiles* and *The Dead in Exile* (translated into English by Mabel Lee at the University of Sydney) are available through Wild Peony Publishers in Sydney.

Galarrwuy Yunupingu is an elder of the Gumatj language group near the mining town of Nhulunbuy/Gove in north-east Arnhem Land. He is the four times Chairman of the Northern Land Council, an Aboriginal land council formed in 1976, which is responsible for the northern half of the Northern Territory. He received his political baptism as a twenty-three year old when he served as a court interpreter for his father in the Yolngu's (the Aboriginal people of the region) battle against the federal government and the Swiss company Nabalco. This court case was regarded as the first Native Title case, one which went against the Yolngu.